GAIA BOOK 3

OLYMPUS RISING

GAIA BOOK 3

ZOË ROUTH

Copyright Zoë Routh, 2024
Cover art – Damonza
Author photograph – Paul Chapman – modeimagery.com
Typesetting, book design – Damonza Published
by Inner Compass Australia Pty Ltd.
For more information about the author Zoë Routh
Email: zoe@zoerouth.com www.zoerouth.com
ISBN-978-0-6488773-8-7

GET AN EBOOK AND AUDIOBOOK FOR FREE:

TERRA BLANCA: INSURRECTION,
PREQUEL TO THE GAIA SERIES

WITH THE FREE BOOKISH E-JOURNAL:

https://www.zoerouth.com/bookish

For Rob

LOCATIONS AND DRAMATIS PERSONAE

Accommodation wings of Olympus base – Cerberus, Centaur, Pegasus, Siren, Griffin

Alexandra Minke – CapCom, Gaia Enterprises

Annika – *Surya One* crew member

Arjun Rao – Lunar Commissioner, political representative for India

Aryanna Sharif – Chair of the Lunar Commission, Founder of Aryanna Industries

Athena – Artificial Intelligence

Bruce (AKA 'Burly Red') – Aryanna Sharif's bodyguard and security personnel

Chan-Juan – Red Star Deputy Leader

Claire Edwards – Former Chief Operating Officer of Gaia Enterprises

Colonel Jin – Commander of Red Star base

David Eriksson – Pilot

Doctor Jane Gurney – Earth First medical officer

Doctor Mohammad – Gaia Enterprises's medical officer

Earth First – Ecoterrorist organisation

Elena Fischer – Lunar Commissioner, Human Habs

Felix Dubois – Mercenary

Freddy – *Pinnacle* crew member

Huw Chan – Co-founder of Gaia Enterprises

Jonas Seaborn – Engineer, Olympus base

Gareth Barrio – Captain of the *Pinnacle*

Gateway – Lunar orbital space station

Hàoyú – Red Star Deputy Leader

Henry Watts – Lunar Commissioner, political representative for the USA

John Fitzgerald – Earth First operative

Leo Malinzak – Spaceward Bound deputy and Lunar Commissioner

Lester Thompson – *Pinnacle* crew member

Lihua – Chinese Dopplebot

Li Jun – New Chinese leader

Lincoln Ellison – Founder of Spaceward Bound

Madison 'Mad Dog' Floyd – Pilot, supply technician, seismologist, Olympus base

Maja Garcia – Founder of Gaia Enterprises

Max King – Life support technician

Minerva – Aryanna Enterprises's rescue vessel

Olympus – Moonbase built by Gaia Enterprises

Pabi Gupta – Captain of the *Surya One*, former Olympus project candidate

Pinnacle – Spaceward Bound spacecraft

Rajesh – *Surya One* crew member

Red Star – Chinese–Russian Moonbase

Sanjay – *Surya One* crew member

Saturnia – Olympus spacecraft

Serena Fox – Life support technician, Olympus base

Starship – NASA's astronaut shuttle carrier

Snyder – *Pinnacle* crew member

Surya One – Indian Space Agency spacecraft

Terra Blanca – Failed man-made island state, initiated and built by Gaia Enterprises

Terra Verdi – Xavier Consus's floating hydroponic farm

Terry Reynolds – rescue operative from Earth First

ThinkLink – Brain Computer Interface

Troy Bruin – Psychologist and Olympus medical officer, Olympus base

Vikram Chatterjee – Deputy Lunar Commissioner, representative for the Indian Space Agency

Vladimir Volkov – Missing Russian President, Dopplebot

Xanthe Waters – Commander of Olympus base

Xavier Consus – Food and provisions expert, Olympus base

Zhao Wei – Lunar Commissioner, political representative for China

Lunar Commission

Space Agencies

1. European Space Agency (ESA)

2. National Aeronautics Space Administration (NASA)

3. Indian Space Agency (ISA)

4. Chinese Space Agency (CSA)

Political Representatives

5. United States of America

6. Europe

7. India

8. China

Space and Technology Industry

9. Spaceward Bound

10. Human Habs

11. Gaia Enterprises

12. Aryanna Industries

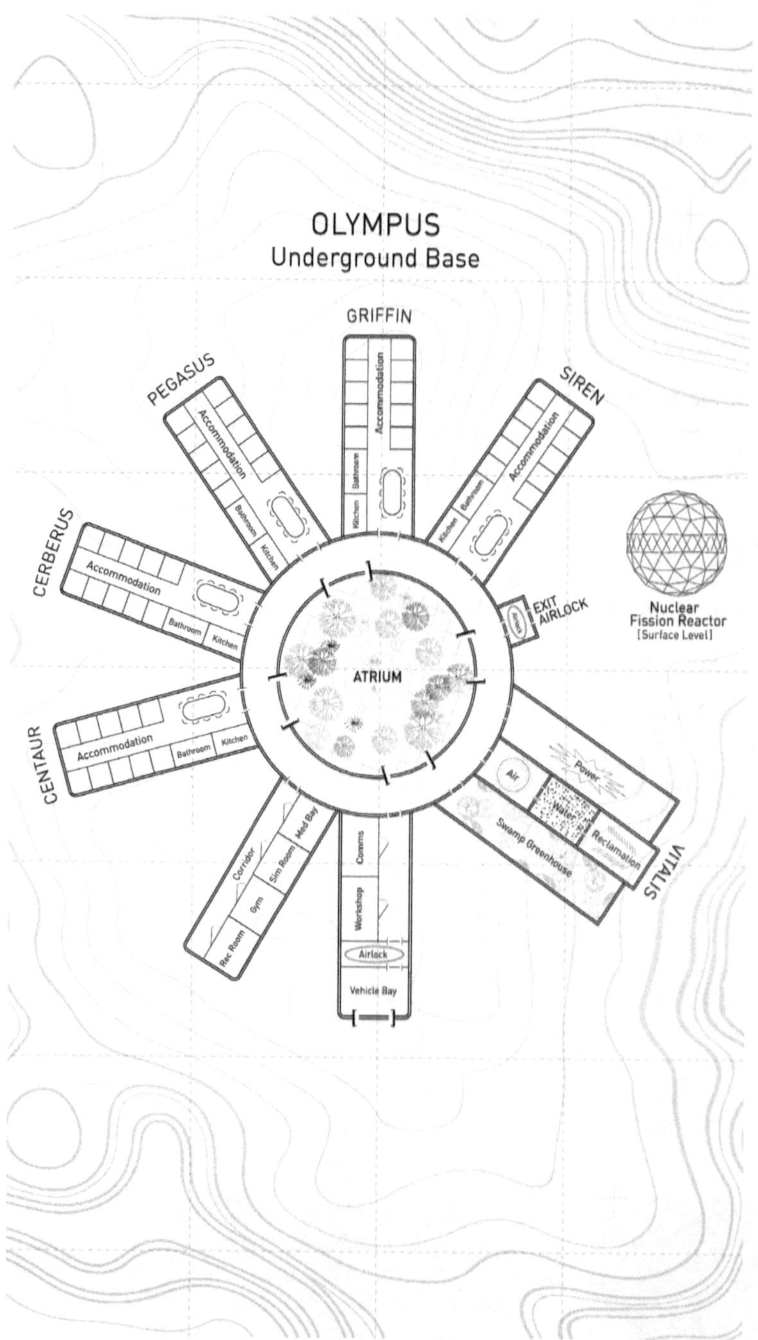

OLYMPUS
Underground Base
GRIFFIN
PEGASUS
SIREN
CERBERUS
CENTAUR
Accommodation
Bathroom
Kitchen
ATRIUM
EXIT AIRLOCK
Nuclear
Fission Reactor
[Surface Level]
Air
Power
Water
Swamp Greenhouse
Reclamation
VITALIS
Corridor
Sim Room
Med Bay
Gym
Rec Room
Comms
Workshop
Airlock
Vehicle Bay

FRENCH LEXICON

C'est chiant! – It's annoying

Excusez moi – Excuse me

Merde – Shit

Mon vieux – My old friend

Non – No

Putain – (literal: whore) Bitch

Putain de merde – (literal: whore of shit) Bloody hell

Salauds – Bastards

Sans blague? – You're kidding?

PART ONE

CHAPTER ONE

"True leadership isn't about exerting power; it's about inspiring others to believe in themselves and each other. It's about lifting people up, not standing above them."

—Jonas Seaborn,
THE LUNAR CHRONICLE, FIRST PIONEERS

THEY WERE PASTY, ground-dwelling creatures, moles eking out an existence beneath the lunar surface in the subterranean maze of the Olympus Moonbase. Scurrying along its regolith-meshed corridors, they hid in secret chambers.

"Come now. Moles?"

It's what I feel like these days.

Athena's voice, the ThinkLink companion, was an ever-present murmur in her mind. More friend than machine.

Commander Xanthe Waters breathed a sigh of relief when she reached the Atrium, with its retractable roof that now lay open, revealing the vast, star-studded sky. She stretched her arms wide and craned her neck upwards, seeking a moment of surrender in the expanse above.

They called it a sky, but it wasn't really a sky. Just the impossible blackness, the foreverness of space. She knew a lot about space, but the facts didn't stretch the mind enough to contend with the immensity of the great void, the great yawning celestial kraken that would swallow them whole one day.

"You're really wound up today, aren't you? Krakens?" Athena prodded, with a synthesised tone of concern.

Maybe. But krakens are scary. And so is space.

Xanthe had grown accustomed to Athena commenting on her thoughts over the last few weeks. It was friendly and familiar, though sometimes it seemed like the A.I. took the ragged edges of her thoughts and held them against a grindstone. Athena sharpened her thinking and pulled her back from her tendency to wallow. Most of the time. Some days needed a good wallowing, and today had "wallowing" written all over it.

They should be home soon, Xanthe mused, the thought of her crew coaxing a smile onto her troubled face. Her crew.

Her friends.

She imagined the roar of the tumble back through the atmosphere, and the wrenching slam of gravity. Then they'd be back on Earth. With sunlight and trees and wind and grass and rain and oceans and life.

Or that's what she imagined for Earth's better future. It was still hot and wretched in most places. Inland was all but inhabitable. Coastal towns laboured with swamped infrastructure and climate refugees. But a tendril of hope for regeneration clung to the crevices of Xanthe's mind.

Her heart strained with longing for the umpteenth time.

Athena, have you got a read on their location?

"They'll be entering Earth's atmosphere in two hours."

Show me.

The schematics of the journey lit up her retina display. Two blips, the *Saturnia* and the *Minerva,* neared the soft blue curve of Earth.

Any word from the Lunar Commission?

"Just the same response: a meeting will be scheduled soon."

Xanthe's thoughts shifted to Aryanna Sharif, Chair of the Lunar Commission, billionaire entrepreneur, and now – thanks to Athena's digging – suspected political terrorist. Xanthe dreaded the interaction with Aryanna. The woman was a walking viper with a face like a porcelain plate.

What was her game plan?

Aryanna's latest decisions seemed wildly out of kilter with the Earth Alliance campaigner Xanthe had once admired. Even with Athena's help, Aryanna's motivations were slippery as fish. Aryanna had forgiven Lincoln Ellison's space cowboy antics that led to the *Gateway* and *Artemis* crew's demise, but Xanthe couldn't. Nine lives had been lost, and her crew had nearly been killed too.

Xanthe left the Atrium, sealing the door behind her. She walked the perimeter hallway to check each of the accommodation wings that spun like rays from the central sun of the Atrium: Griffin, Siren, Pegasus, Cerberus and the Centaur wing, where she, Jonas and Troy had their quarters.

Each wing had berths for twenty, waiting for future residents. Intended originally for scientists, tourists and climate refugees, they were now destined for helium-3 miners. Xanthe shivered. Proud as she was of this remarkable base they'd designed and built, these dim underground corridors were more tombs than homes. Empty berths waiting to close in on bodies, like a catacomb she'd visited long ago at a winery estate, run by a monastery.

Several hundred years of past attendant monks lay interred beneath the church and cellars, in dark, stone crypts. When she'd visited, there had been a more recent inhabitant added to their midst, his name freshly chiselled not six months previously. The sickly smell of death caught at the back of her throat, a call from the dead, still grasping at life.

She shook off the morbid musings and paused to check the water flow to the plants lining the corridor of the Cerberus wing.

Though the rooms felt like empty pits, corridors devoid of people, they hummed with life. She said a silent prayer of thanks to Xavier and Madison, who had worked tirelessly to fill their underground warren full of productive plant life.

Xanthe continued her tour of the Atrium perimeter, forcing herself to jog, hard as it was in the magnetic moonboots and exosuit that mimicked gravity. She needed to stay strong and keep up the muscle mass and blood flow to ensure a quick recovery when they were back Earthside. Whenever that might be.

Her legs strained and her heart pounded as she pushed herself to a run. She pulled up outside the SimRoom, Troy's pride and joy. The chamber was equipped to mimic scenes anywhere on Earth, from moonlit beaches to seedy night-time bars. The stimsuits and nasal stim sensors made it so damn real.

It had been a while since Xanthe had come for a break. She favoured the reconstructed VR experience of Sydney from before the tsunami. The Sydney of today was a rough, ramshackle place with its abandoned, flooded high-rises and shanty towns crammed with tsunami survivors and climate refugees.

With Sydney Reimagined, she loved watching the sunrise over the old harbour, the kiss of water against the docks, the sting of salty sea air. A simpler time. She craved getting back to it.

The fitness room was tucked in beside the SimRoom and here she found Jonas with a VR headset, practicing his martial arts, sweat soaking his shirt. Thank goodness Serena had managed to fix the water pressure and filtration system before they left for Earth. They could shower and launder clothes. So much better than dry-frying them with UV rays. UV killed bacteria and odours but never felt clean the way water did. Xanthe loved the ritual of soaking her garments, rubbing the fibres together and rinsing out the dirt.

She marvelled at the closed ecosystem they'd designed and were able to live in now, on this otherwise inhospitable lump of rock hanging off the skirts of the wild, luscious blue orb that was their home planet. Washing clothes felt like they had a blood transfusion from Earth, pulsing in the watery veins of their small, vulnerable habitat.

Jonas sensed her presence and pulled off his visor.

"Xanthe," he said as he wiped his forehead with the sleeve of his shirt. "Any news?"

"They'll enter the atmosphere in just under two hours. We've got a few things to cover off before then. Join me and Troy in the comms room once you're done here?"

"You bet. Did Troy get the oven fixed?" Jonas grinned.

"You know he's terrible with electronics. You shouldn't mock him."

"He insisted! I even offered Volkov's help. But Troy said, 'An oven isn't brain surgery' and he would work it out."

"I'm glad his brain surgery is better than his tinkering with appliances." Xanthe rubbed the back of her neck, remembering the procedure Troy used to plant Athena in her cortex.

Jonas watched her wordlessly.

"Where is Volkov now?" she asked.

"Charging in the vehicle bay. We're going to overhaul the regolith processor tomorrow to see if we can amp up the helium-3 harvest." Jonas grabbed a towel slung over the squat machine and wiped his face to soak up the rivulets of sweat. "The sooner we have a full load of helium-3, the sooner we can ship Earthside."

Xanthe pressed her lips together.

"What? Xanthe, what is it? I know that look."

She tilted her head and rolled her shoulders. "I'm not sure Aryanna will go for our recommendation. She wanted Lincoln Ellison up here running the show. And given the conflict Earthside with China, I would say there is no chance of letting Colonel Jin take over operations. It's just too much leverage to give to the Chinese."

"So, if you don't fly us back – and by 'you' I mean Athena – who *will* fly the *Pinnacle*?"

"Maybe Chan-Juan."

"Colonel Jin's Deputy? No way he's letting one of the only three humans in their base head home. Especially as Chan-Juan and Hàoyú are together. If she goes, he goes."

"Leaving Colonel Jin alone at Red Star," Xanthe added with a grimace.

"Apart from his half dozen Dopplebots," Jonas said.

"Still, Dopplebots aren't a great replacement for human company, are they?"

Jonas stopped rubbing his sweaty arms with the towel for a moment. "I don't know. I kind of enjoy Volkov, even if he is a patronising toad."

"But it's not like Volkov can really understand what's going on with you, emotionally." Xanthe raised her eyebrows and tapped her chest.

Jonas puffed his own chest out. "He gets it enough, I suppose. What about Athena? Does she 'get' you now that she's inside your brain all the time?" He waved a hand at her head and reached for a water bottle perched on a nearby bench.

Xanthe paused and considered the evolving interactions with Athena. Could she really call it a relationship? "She certainly can tell when I'm having a 'moment'."

"What do you mean?" He took a swig of water, then wiped his lips with the back of his hand.

"She can sense and regulate my biological responses to emotional thoughts."

"Whoa. Cool. Is that how you stay so calm?"

"That's part of it."

Jonas paused, then sat down on the bench to pull on his moonboots. He didn't like to sweat in them while working out as they were too hard to clean. "But still, maybe you're right about Dopplebots, Xanthe. Modulating biochemistry is not really 'getting' you, is it? Athena can't make you feel seen, heard and valued. The way, say, Troy might."

Xanthe blushed. "No, Athena is not Troy. Nor you. Nor any of the crew. But she is…something." She patted Jonas on the shoulder. "Get cleaned up and I'll see you in the comms room."

"Roger that, Commander."

Xanthe smiled warmly at him and headed down the corridor.

❧

Jonas watched her leave, slim shoulders shot through with tension, muscles stringy and hard. She'd changed with the ThinkLink. He often caught her muttering to herself – or rather, to Athena. The A.I. was supposed to help with focus, but Xanthe seemed *more* distracted, often staring with glazed eyes. Presumably, she was watching something on the retina display.

Jonas wiped his face with the towel, then stretched one deltoid, then the other. His body still felt strong, even after nearly a year on the Moon. He worked hard at staying fit, wore the moonboots religiously to work his legs, pounded the treadmill, ran through the station, turned resistance up to max on the workout station and completed his martial arts routine day after day.

Still, he knew parts of him were atrophying. His heart had lost muscle mass despite the workouts, the bone density readings were in range but on the lower end and his metabolism was changing too. The freeze-fried bananas were definitely a no-go for him now.

He shut down the fitness room and headed for a shower. No rest for the wicked. Not when there were just three of them, plus Volkov, to get things done on a Moonbase built for one hundred.

Just him, Xanthe and Troy.

Xanthe and Troy. The romance had finally swept the commander out from behind her professional blockade. She trembled a little when Troy, the damn pants man, sauntered into her vicinity. Her iron core went to goop.

Jonas thought he would be okay as the third wheel, but truth be told, he was a little lonely. He already missed the banter with Xavier, the taunts with Serena, and even the weird tension with

Madison. The others had a lot to go home to, but he had nothing but the scorn of his never-impressed parents, Don and Jenny Seaborn.

Here, on the Moon, he had a chance to prove his mettle and take command at some point. What was a little loneliness in the glorious pursuit of achievement?

I'll be fine.

He smiled, willing that encouragement to filter through to his heart as he shed his clothes and they drifted to the floor. He stepped into the shower to cleanse his body and mind.

CHAPTER TWO

"Command demands everything from you: your strength, your courage, your very essence. It eats away at you, piece by piece, until all that's left is the unyielding resolve to see your mission through, no matter the personal cost."

—Doctor Troy Bruin, *MEMOIRS FROM MARS*

Jonas zapped his body with a cold shower, then dried himself with a vigorous scrub. His skin tingled and he felt fantastic. All he needed now was a brisk run and a plunge in the ocean. But that was months away. They still had no word on when the mining crew would arrive and their stint on establishing Olympus would be over.

He strode to the comms room, enjoying the firmness of his thighs against the soft fabric of his uniform. Troy had his arm around Xanthe as they leaned over the console. A tightness twinged in Jonas's throat as he imagined the warmth of the touch, intimacy like a mug of hot chocolate by the fire.

He thought he might have had a chance with Chan-Juan of Red Star. He revelled in the pink flush of her high, smooth cheekbones, the hidden secrets of her languid brown eyes. Everything about her was delicate, like a cherry blossom. But she'd bloody well fallen for Colonel Jin's deputy Hàoyú. He pursed his lips and jutted his chin to steady the ache that sunk in his gut.

No time for that nonsense anyhow. The helium-3 enterprise was consuming all of his brain power and engineering skills. A bristle of pride ran through him. He had led the operation from setup to processing, all improvised from their existing resources – with a little help from the Chinese Dopplebots, he admitted.

It was good to be in charge of something. A sense of accomplishment. Something to call his own. A stake in the ground. A little piece of lunar history he could claim for himself.

Xanthe squeezed closer to Troy to let Jonas stand beside them in front of the data screens. Jonas shuffled in beside Xanthe and Troy, who dropped the embrace once there were three of them.

Jonas was thankful for that. He didn't need constant reminders of their newfound intimacy, in contrast to his bachelorhood and indefinite celibacy. Being the third wheel sucked, he concluded. Jonas noticed the subtle, intimate response as Xanthe's leg brushed Troy's. A shiver of jealousy rippled through him.

"Thanks for joining us, Jonas. It's time for our favourite topic: resource management," Xanthe began, her eyes scanning the various base metrics on the screens. "Athena's latest analysis shows we're stretching our limits. Water recycling efficiency is down, and our food supplies will become an issue if we don't address this now. Troy, what can you report?"

Troy, leaning against a console, crossed his arms. "The Swamp is just not producing enough. I've been modifying the nutrient feed, but without Xavier's expertise, I don't know what else to do. I could use a bit of the old frog's know-how about now. I miss him."

"We all miss him. Supply though – how bad is it?" Xanthe asked.

"Our freeze-dried food will last just three more months. Without new carbon production from the plants, we don't have enough base materials for more lab-grown meat or other printed edibles."

Xanthe stared at him, waiting for more.

"Basically, we need a resupply within the next three months or we will be vastly malnourished, eating nothing but green, leafy shoots. Which works fine if you are lazing around doing nothing, but all of us are doing multiple jobs." The crease in Troy's forehead deepened.

Jonas thought he looked haggard. Must be his poor kidney function, he thought. The lack of food must be affecting his ability to manage the disease.

"Have you asked the Chinese what they have?" Xanthe suggested.

"Not yet, but that makes sense. We need to pool our nutritional resources, not just our mining ones," Troy said. "We're supposed to be collaborating, after all. I'll reach out to Chan-Juan tomorrow. She's in charge of food production, right, Jonas?"

Jonas flinched at the sound of the Chinese deputy's name. "Yeah, that's right." He thought again of the petite and beautiful taikonaut. Chan, pronounced 'kahn', and Juan, pronounced 'chwen'. The Kahn is chewing. It took him ages to get it right, hoping to impress her.

She was a stunning woman, but then…Hàoyú. Pronounced 'how-yoo'. He remembered it with 'How YOU doin'?' It wasn't quite the right sound. The 'you' should be a bit more choked off at the end. Xanthe always got it right, but he thought his own effort was mostly pretty good.

Jonas saw a quirk appear on Troy's lips and sensed his friend was about to tease him again. He jumped in with a change of topic. "And on the helium-3 front, the reduced crew means we're mining at a slower rate. Plus, the filtration issues are not helping. Volkov is working on it, but we can't meet the Commission's timeline at this pace."

"The Commission is the least of my concerns right now," Xanthe said firmly. "Our priority is maintaining the base for our survival. I won't risk our safety for a timeline." She reached over to the display screens and flicked to another report, chewing a thumb as she studied the displayed data.

"Our safety is actually dependent on that timeline, Xanthe," Troy said gently. "We need to get that helium-3 haul done so we can fast track our exit and replacement up here." He reached out and squeezed Xanthe's shoulder. "The helium-3 is our bargaining chip. I'm sure we can get the food supply and helium-3 production back on track. Especially with Dopplebot and Chinese help."

Jonas simmered with frustration. "Colonel Jin is such a critic. We're not miracle workers. We're doing the best we can with what we have. Maybe we should put a bit more pressure on the Colonel, make it clear we need more support. They could give us more Dopplebots. And we can pool our resources."

Xanthe considered this, her mind racing through the implications. It was the three of them on the Olympus base and the crew of the Red Star base, against the Lunar Commission, who wanted to establish a military presence on the Moon to safeguard the helium-3 production. While they had control of helium-3, they held the upper hand. But unless they figured out the food production, they were at the mercy of resupply – and so, by extension, the Lunar Commission's will.

Pushing back against the Lunar Commission, and thus Aryanna, was risky. But Jonas had a point. They were isolated and under-resourced, and their current situation was tenuous.

"I agree we're in a tight spot, but openly defying the Commission is a dangerous game," Xanthe said. "We knew that from the beginning when we sent Lincoln and his crew back to Earth. Our collaborative strategy goes against the Lunar Commission directive as well. We really need food production and helium-3 processing back on track to shore up our position and the future of Olympus."

Xanthe shut the displays down, having garnered all the

information they needed. Troy left the cramped comms room and the others followed, keen for a break.

"We could ask Aryanna to fast track the resupply mission and replacement crew, but I fear that would only reinforce her point of view that we stuffed up," Xanthe said as she rifled through the cupboards in the kitchen hub, looking for a snack. "And who knows what else she is wrestling with at the Lunar Commission. Plus, I'm pretty sure she's pissed off about us removing Lincoln Ellison and the *Pinnacle* crew from the picture."

Jonas nodded. "That jerk was ready to steal it all for himself! She was nuts to nominate him to replace us in the first place." He jutted his chin and rubbed his jaw.

Xanthe returned to the kitchen hub table with a packet of nuts for them to share. She looked at Troy and Jonas with resolve in her eyes. "Sending Lincoln and his renegades home was the right thing to do. The Moon is a resource for all humanity, not just the chosen few. We've got to stay the course, prove we can make Olympus work in collaboration – not in competition – with the Chinese. The Lunar Commission has to agree to a weapons-free Moon or they don't get helium-3. And that means we might go hungry before we go home."

Troy rubbed Xanthe's back and she leaned into him, sparking more jealousy in Jonas who looked away. The challenges were mounting, but so was Xanthe's determination. The Olympus Moonbase was her responsibility, and she would do whatever it took to keep it running and her crew safe. Jonas thought of the upcoming confrontation with Aryanna, the first one since they had arrested and removed Lincoln Ellison and his crew.

He imagined Xanthe staring down that cold, cunning cobra, and at that moment thought, *Better you than me.*

CHAPTER THREE

"Influence is a subtle art. It's not about overt control but guiding others towards a common goal, gently nudging the course of events without appearing to steer them."

—Maja Garcia, *THE JOURNALS*

Maja Garcia stood and smoothed the front of her suit jacket, as if being wrinkle-free might protect her when it came to confronting Aryanna Sharif. The doors to the Lunar Commission boardroom swung open. A blast of cool air from the overworked air-conditioning chilled the sweat on her brow. Already, the morning heat was squeezing into the building.

"They're ready for you now," announced the staffer.

Maja pulled her shoulders back slightly, rolled her chin downwards a fraction and stepped forward.

Aryanna stood at the enormous window overlooking the jumble of buildings in various stages of construction. They were in a race to complete the helium-3 processing before the first shipment returned from the Moon. Her back was turned to the door and the ludicrously long boardroom table where the Commissioners perched on the edge of enormous chairs that made them all feel slightly ridiculous, like children at the grownups' table. They countermanded the awkwardness by pretending disdainful disinterest and stared at their tablets.

They were all there: all the signatories to the Global Lunar Treaty forming the Lunar Commission. Maja considered each of them in turn as she walked slowly into the room. The four space agency reps were there: the European Space Agency, NASA, the Indian Space Agency and the Chinese Space Agency. Their political counterparts representing Europe, the USA, India and China sat alongside the space agency reps.

The space and technology giants made up the rest: Leo Malinzak for Spaceward Bound, Elena Fischer for Human Habs, Aryanna for her own organisation – Aryanna Industries – and Maja was there for Gaia Enterprises.

There had been some argument that Aryanna should represent Gaia Enterprises, too, since she was now the primary funder of the organisation, but Maja had gently pushed back against that, convincing the Lunar Commission that independent representation should be assured since Maja and Huw still had controlling stakes in the business. The Commission conceded and Aryanna had seethed quietly but ultimately let it slide.

"Maja." Aryanna's voice was icy. "We have been tracking the return of the *Saturnia* and *Minerva* with the Olympus crew." Her body spun as a lighthouse on a turnstile, her fingertips pressed together in a downward steeple, her face smooth as milk with dark stones for eyes. "They have the *Pinnacle* crew with them." A hard emphasis on '*Pinnacle*'.

"That is my understanding," Maja said, fighting hard to keep the stiffness from her words.

"My instructions – the Lunar Commission's instructions – were for the *Pinnacle* crew to take over management of Olympus and for the Olympus crew to return home."

Maja said nothing, while her chin lifted ever so slightly. She stood at the far end of the enormous table, with the Commissioners' heads now swivelled towards her.

"Explain to me why the Olympus crew defied direct orders from the Lunar Commission." Aryanna walked back to the head of the table and pulled her chair back but remained standing. The two women were now at either end of the table.

Like political ping pong, thought Maja.

Maja opened her mouth to speak, but Leo Malinzak interrupted. He leaned forward, his voluminous blonde afro adding bulk to his otherwise dark, lean face. It drew attention from the sparring women, and he said, "Gaia has a lot to answer for, interfering in the operations of another space company – especially on officially-sanctioned Lunar Commission business. Spaceward Bound will be seeking compensation, and we demand an inquiry into the actions of the Olympus staff."

He jammed a finger into the table and sat back again.

There were tilted heads and whispers from the Indian reps while the Chinese Commissioner coughed loudly and cleared his throat.

"Madam Chair Sharif." Zhao Wei waited until Aryanna acknowledged him with a nod. "Before we proceed and respond to Commissioner Malinzak's request for an inquiry, we would like to remind our fellow Commissioners that we still have outstanding business related to the bombing of the Chinese Space Centre that has destroyed our space-faring abilities and left our Red Star team stranded on the Moon."

"Come on, now, Commissioner Zhao, that's been addressed." The booming voice of Texan Henry Watts, political rep from the USA, cut off Zhao, whose cheeks flushed red. "The international tribunal found no state-sponsored terrorism involved in that tragic accident. Those were a bunch of crazy ecoterrorists."

Henry swirled a finger at this temple. "None of us benefited from the destruction of the Chinese Space Agency. The ecoterrorists have caused us all a whole lot of grief with the inadvertent terraforming screw up. All of us want those renegades called to justice. It serves no purpose to continue to cast aspersions on the other Lunar Commissioners. None of us had a hand in that nasty business." He pushed his chair back from the table and crossed his arms.

"Commissioners, please." Aryanna's voice sliced through the room like a samurai sword, and they fell silent. "These are trying times for the Lunar Commission, and we have a number of issues to address. I have noted Leo's complaint against the Olympus crew's actions, which we will address shortly."

She gave Leo a hard look to keep him silent. "I also acknowledge your reminder, Commissioner Zhao, that the ecoterrorist attacks remain unresolved. We will ask the international tribunal for an update once we return the Olympus and *Pinnacle* crews safely – our most pressing concern. Is that satisfactory?"

Her black eyes bore into Zhao. He nodded in return, unperturbed.

"Good. Before we hear from Maja, are there any other agenda items to be tabled?"

"Please, Madam Chair, may I?" Arjun Rao, a diminutive man with impeccable dress and contained demeanour raised a finger. Aryanna gestured for him to continue. "The government of India will happily put its resources at the Lunar Commission's disposal and will be delighted to assist the Chinese with returning their team to Earth. In fact, we have a team of our own ready to step into the Red Star base and manage it on behalf of the Commission, and partake in the helium-3 extraction."

Maja noted Arjun Rao's barely contained smug satisfaction. Of all the agencies, the Indians were the least affected by recent events. The European Space Agency had long been underfunded as climate response consumed much of their political and economic capital. The Indians, however, alongside the Chinese, had gone hard early on emerging energy research and become a technology behemoth.

Somehow, they'd managed to lift billions of their population from survival, even with climate pressures that wracked other countries like the USA, Australia, and parts of Europe and Africa. India was the envy of many. And now, Maja thought, it seemed they were cashing in on their success and having a tilt at the helium-3.

Zhao cleared his throat again, his cheeks flaming. "While the authorities investigate the extent of the ecoterrorist operations on Chinese soil, we respectfully request that all lunar operations take into consideration not only the predicament of our taikonauts, but more importantly the valuable resources currently in place that could well-manage the helium-3 operations. These need to remain under Chinese control with our advanced resources and expertise in this area."

He glared at Arjun Rao. The Chinese–Indian rivalry was deep-seated.

"Gentlemen," Aryanna said loudly, commanding attention of the room. "We will address helium-3 and Moonbase management shortly. Thank you, Commissioner Rao. Now let's hear from Gaia Enterprises about the extraordinary actions taken by the Olympus crew to eject the Spaceward Bound *Pinnacle* team."

"Exactly!" Leo slapped the table. "Spaceward Bound demands an inquiry into this outrageous and egregious assault on our team and equipment."

Aryanna held a hand up to silence Leo. "Maja, please respond."

Maja breathed out slowly and turned towards Leo. She rode the wave of her fury against Leo and Spaceward Bound, but she kept her voice steady. "I think you will have to wait until the inquiry into your own asteroid mining operations is complete. Spaceward Bound's activities caused the death of nine people and destroyed the *Gateway*, not to mention damaged the Olympus base and nearly killed the team there too."

"Those allegations are tenuous at best," Leo huffed. He swigged the dregs of water from his glass. He reached for the jug that was beading in the heat, despite the airconditioning blasting full pelt.

Maja waited one second, then two, before she continued, turning back to Aryanna. "With regards to Xanthe and her team, as far as I know the crew discovered new information about Lincoln Ellison's intentions to skim the helium-3 for himself and establish Spaceward Bound as the primary supplier."

Gasps of disbelief and murmurs rippled around the room. Leo froze momentarily as he poured water into his glass, slopping it on to the table. "Absolutely ridiculous," he retorted and mopped at the water with a napkin Elena Fischer passed him.

Aryanna stared first at Leo then at Maja, her fathomless eyes unflinching.

"The Olympus crew believed this was a direct threat to the Lunar Commission's interests," Maja continued, undaunted. "So, they secured the *Pinnacle* team and are returning them to Earth to prevent further catastrophe. After all, as we know and the investigation will prove, Spaceward Bound is responsible for the tragedy of the *Gateway* and *Artemis* crew—"

Aryanna's steepled fingers came apart and pressed down on the mahogany table. "We know very well what they were responsible for." Her voice thrust like a fencing sword and cut Maja to the core, who fought hard not to take a step back.

Aryanna looked around the room, seeking a challenger, finding none. "The Lunar Commission knows Lincoln Ellison is a cavalier renegade whose word means nothing."

"Now wait a minute, Aryanna." Leo leaned forward again and put both his hands on the table, ready to launch into a tirade.

"Calm your horses, Leo. Lincoln's reputation is well-known. He and Spaceward Bound were welcomed to be part of this Commission, for the opportunity to rehabilitate said reputation." She chipped the words at Leo, sharp white teeth flashing. He sat back again, chastened.

Maja frowned. "So appointing Lincoln and Spaceward Bound to manage the Olympus base was part of 'reputation rehabilitation'?"

"Spaceward Bound was a temporary solution that was expedient, given the conditions here and the issues with our Chinese friends."

Commissioner Zhao and his public official counterpart maintained a united stoic countenance. The new leader had wanted Colonel Jin and the Red Star base to take over Olympus – by force if necessary – and declared their intention to send nuclear weapons to the Moon to shore up their position.

But when ecoterrorists bombed the Chinese Space Agency, the Chinese were reduced to a toothless tiger, and they were now dependent on the other Lunar Commission's governments and space agencies to rescue their team on the Moon. Negotiations were still ongoing, but it seemed to Maja the Indians were pressing the case pretty hard to take over Red Star as the next helium-3 managers.

Maja knew the Chinese dynamic would have played into the Lunar Commission's decision to recruit Spaceward Bound to the helium-3 Moon mining operation. "I appreciate Lincoln Ellison's ship and asteroid mining equipment were nearby, but surely that's not enough to forgive Spaceward Bound's complicity in the deaths of nine people.

"Furthermore, if that was not enough, Spaceward Bound has a record of negligence in the high-risk environment of space – as well as a history of industrial espionage and sabotage of rivals. It boggles the mind that they would garner a ringing endorsement and we'd then trust them with the Earth's energy security."

"Madam Chair." Leo stood this time, the whites of his eyes bright, accentuated by his vivid afro. "I resent accusations of negligence for those horrible tragedies, along with the other slander."

"Noted, Leo," Aryanna clipped. "As acknowledged, investigations by international authorities are ongoing. But the deaths are not forgiven. Nor forgotten. Someone will be held to account, in due course."

Leo opened his mouth but found no words. He sat down again and took another swig of water.

"Do you trust Lincoln?" Maja asked Aryanna.

Leo choked on his water and spluttered it across the table. He coughed and dabbed at the mess with the soggy napkin.

"It's not a matter of trust, Maja."

Maja let this roll through the chambers of her mind, seeking an insight into Aryanna's plan. Her thoughts drifted in emptiness. "I fail to see how Lincoln and Spaceward Bound, with the intention to create a monopoly through subterfuge, is a better solution than the Olympus crew."

"That's just it: a failure to see." Aryanna's enormous lips, plump and tattooed red, exaggerated the pronunciation of her words so that her small white teeth flashed in the cavern of her mouth. The effect was mesmerising; Maja struggled to stay focused on the conversation and the jibe thrust at her.

"Forgive me, Aryanna, but the Olympus crew did what they felt was right."

"A narrow view comes from a narrow mind, Maja. There's more at stake than management of the Moonbase."

"I agree!" Maja's passion bubbled to the surface. "The future of the Moon, for all humanity and free flow of helium-3 – this is about the future of limitless clean energy for the entire world! It's a game changer!"

The atmosphere seemed to condense, pulling a chill through the room. The Commissioners twitched, looked away, quirked lips, knitted brows.

Maja sensed the response, and confusion dripped through her consciousness.

Aryanna's thin brown talons pressed together once more. The smooth face morphed back to its implacable veneer.

"Commissioners, our intention here was to hear from Gaia Enterprises as to why the Olympus team defied a direct order that has derailed the helium-3 timeline. I am satisfied we have heard the reasoning. Olympus believes Spaceward Bound was colluding to hijack the helium-3 supply and management. I suggest we reconvene to discuss the parameters of this investigation, in addition to the repercussions for Commander Waters and Gaia Enterprises for breach of directives. Leo, given that this affects Spaceward Bound the most, are you satisfied with this next step?"

Leo drew up his chest to launch another tirade, thought better of it and said, "That will do, Madam Chair. As long as Spaceward Bound personnel are returned safely, along with our ship, which is still on the goddamn Moon."

Aryanna cut him off before he rolled into more outrage. "Thank you, Leo. The requisition of the *Pinnacle*, as per Lunar Commission agreement, is not subject to investigation."

"Well, it should be!" Leo was on his feet again now, the skin on his neck darkening. "Who is going to pilot that thing, eh? Gareth Barrio, Dave Eriksson and Madison Floyd were the only ones on the Moon capable, and those three are on their way back to Earth."

"Gaia Enterprises is working on a solution," Maja interjected.

Leo spun and glared at Maja.

"Leo, Maja, we will discuss the logistics of space operations at a later date," Aryanna hissed. "Right now, we have multiple investigations and two spacecraft to monitor. Are you satisfied at this stage with Maja's explanation for the Olympus crew's actions?" She checked with each Commissioner in turn. As expected, the Europeans murmured agreement, having little resources to offer.

Elena Fischer of Human Habs usually kept an interested distance from the issues, holding her cards close. When Aryanna pointed a hand at her for her contribution, Elena frowned and gazed at her tablet thoughtfully, before raising her head to speak. She was a quiet woman, hair streaked through with grey, and a thin upturned nose that reminded Maja eerily of the skeleton the woman would one day become.

The other Commissioners waited patiently and then Elena said, "While these allegations are concerning, we at Human Habs continue to believe in the power of collaboration. None of us have the resources to facilitate the helium-3 production on our own, for all of Earth. We need each other. Nonetheless, we support all investigations to clarify what is really going on and to reestablish a baseline of respect and mutual understanding."

Maja's heart lifted at Elena's words. At last, a sober voice in the maelstrom of competing rivalries.

"Our major concern right now," Elena continued, "is to return all astronauts, including our life support technician Max King, and to support those left on the Moon. I recommend we establish a task force immediately to strategise our next steps."

"Excellent idea, Elena," Aryanna said. "I nominate you and Human Habs to head up the task force. This will keep any one space-capable agency from dominating the discussions." Aryanna stared pointedly at the Commissioner Zhao, Arjun Rao, Henry Watts and the NASA rep.

"The Indian Space Agency will be delighted to partake in the task force, given that we are the only agency left with a working spacecraft," Arjun said smugly.

"We have a working spacecraft. It's called the *Pinnacle*, and it's still on the goddamn Moon!" Leo grumbled.

Commissioner Zhao coughed and spoke more loudly than was necessary. "As the principal stakeholder on the Moon and the most aggrieved, we insist the Chinese Space Agency participates on the task force to ensure proper consideration and—"

"Yes, yes, Commissioner Zhao. The Chinese will work on the task force," Aryanna said forcefully. Zhao dipped his head and folded his hands on the table, satisfied he had made his point.

Aryanna took a deep breath. "This meeting is now closed. NASA and Gaia will work on the logistics to receive the astronauts. Elena will organise the task force for the next steps for the Moonbases and helium-3 management. You may send me, and Elena, your recommendations in the meantime. You are all welcome to attend the landing of the *Saturnia* and *Minerva* the day after tomorrow, right here at Gaia HQ. Now, please go."

The Lunar Commissioners rose quietly, murmuring to one another, and trailed from the room, glancing over their shoulders to Aryanna and Maja.

"Maja, please stay a moment," Aryanna said.

A cold shiver of apprehension ran across Maja like rats on a frozen roof.

Once the room was empty, Aryanna, still standing, turned to Maja. "Commander Waters' little stunt of defiance has sullied the issues for the Commission. We have lost face and leverage with the Chinese."

"How so?" Maja asked, perplexed.

"Lincoln has a few talents, one of which is his ability to enforce decisions. Securing the Red Star base under Lunar Commission control is essential for secure helium-3 operations and Lincoln could get that done."

"But surely a collaborative approach is better than coercion?" Maja was incredulous.

"Collaboration works best when people trust each other."

"That's exactly what Xanthe was working on with Colonel Jin, and making progress with, when Lincoln showed up."

"Colonel Jin is not the entirety of the People's Republic." She chewed each word and her eyes flashed.

"But we can model what is possible," Maja persisted. "That was the entire design principle behind Olympus. If we can do it on the Moon, we can model it here—"

"Don't be so naïve, Maja. New conditions, new rules. You've seen what's happening out there. Since the satellites were knocked out around Earth, it's a mad scramble to reestablish order and reinstate our various systems: financial, transport, law and order. In these conditions, bad actors will always step into the void and seize opportunities."

"But that's here, not the Moon." Maja's voice skirted desperation.

Aryanna's long fingers pulled away from the steeple and adjusted the silk scarf that floated over her shoulder.

"Maja." The voice was a low, flat croon. "Aren't you always espousing how perspective is power? Well then, it's time to expand perspective. The Lunar Commission requires control of all lunar resources for helium-3 mining so we can ensure equitable distribution of said helium-3. Not everyone will be happy with that arrangement, so we need to ensure this edict is enforced."

"But Aryanna, you intend to send nuclear weapons to the Moon to enforce the monopoly. Do you know how insane that sounds? Surely, working harder at international relations with the Chinese is better than creating nuclear escalation on the Moon?" Frustration unfurled in Maja's chest.

A grimace. "Weaponisation of the Moon was never my goal. My intention was, and still is, the betterment of humankind and the salvation of Earth. The Moonbase remains a step in the correct direction of a long path. In control lies the power to shape destinies."

Maja thrust this thought through the tunnels of her mind, testing its resonance and authenticity. The echoes were dull and distant.

"What do you need from me? Or from the Olympus crew?" It wasn't a surrender, but it felt like one. Maja's shoulders dipped a little and fatigue rolled over her.

"Please, have a seat." Aryanna waved towards a chair beside the Commissioners. "We have much to discuss."

Maja returned to her office and closed the door behind her. Her head throbbed. Today's Lunar Commission meeting had been particularly taxing. Not to mention the drilling by Aryanna. She rubbed her temples and rolled her neck, desperate for a rest. But first she needed to speak with Huw Chan.

She sat at her desk and sent Huw a message. Huw's face jumped to life on the holo. Maja smiled at her old friend. For the umpteenth time, she sent a prayer of gratitude to the universe for her co-founder. Maja knew she could not have managed the audacity of their plans with Gaia Enterprises without the steady guidance and support of this wise and compassionate man. It was his steadfast pragmatism that she valued the most.

"Maja, how did it go?" Huw asked.

"Better than expected," she admitted. "They accepted Commander Waters' assessment of the situation, pending an investigation of course."

"Let me guess, Leo threw a tantrum?" Huw's lips quirked.

"His capacity for bluster and arrogance equals Lincoln's. Aryanna hosed him down, though."

"Thank goodness. That's one advantage we have: no way she is going to let her investment in Gaia Enterprises be scuppered by the likes of Leo and those Spaceward Bound cowboys."

"I don't know, Huw." Maja sighed and rested her head in a hand propped on the desk. "I'm not tracking Aryanna's motivations very well. We've got that intel that she might have been behind the Chinese base attack, maybe even funding Earth First."

"I'm not sure about that evidence, Maja. There's nothing solid there." Huw went quiet as he thought about this predicament: Gaia Enterprises's primary funder might be a billionaire ecoterrorist saboteur.

"Well, it certainly plays into her endgame of controlling helium-3 and Moon operations. You know how concerned she was when the Chinese announced they too would set up a base soon after Olympus. Then she told Xanthe to assume control of Red Star."

"Still, the Earth First affiliation is all just conjecture, Maja. And the Chinese did cite their intention to take weapons to the Moon. Aryanna might just have been asserting a line in the sand."

Huw drummed fingers on his chin. "We need to remain focused. Spaceward Bound's team, including that pompous dolt Lincoln Ellison, will be taken into custody when they return. We'll have to wait and see the outcome of the international tribunal's investigation. In the meantime, the Olympus team will be back on Earth in two short days."

Maja soaked up the warmth of his smile. "Not all of them," she said gently. "There's still three braving it out and holding our hopes for the future. We can't let them down."

CHAPTER FOUR

*"Conflict arises from misaligned objectives and misunderstandings.
Effective communication and shared goals are the keys
to resolving disputes and fostering harmony."*

—Athena A.I., *WISDOM OF THE AGES*

THE COMMS ROOM blurted an alarm. Xanthe and Troy were just settling into a cup of his Arabian Knights tea, a special brew he'd saved from their dwindling supplies. Xanthe jerked in surprise and her tea splashed on the table.

"Incoming call from Aryanna Sharif and the Lunar Commission," Athena announced.

Alarm shot through Xanthe. No warning. It was just like Aryanna to keep her off-balance.

"You go," Troy said with his beautiful smile. He gestured at the spillage. "I've got this."

Xanthe clomped back to the comms room in her moonboots, legs heavy with the day's work. She took a moment to steady herself and prepared for the confrontation. "Athena, accept the call."

Aryanna's image flickered into life on the holo display, her impenetrable smooth face made more eerie in the glow of the console light. Xanthe squashed the compulsion to squirm and clenched her jaw.

"Commander Waters." Aryanna's voice pierced the silence, cold and sharp.

"Aryanna. Thank you for meeting with me personally." Xanthe kept her gaze steady, but she could feel a tightness in her chest.

There was a pause before Aryanna responded. "Commander, tell me why the *Pinnacle* crew is being returned to Earth when they were contracted to manage Olympus?" Her words dripped with barely concealed venom.

Xanthe inhaled slowly, trying to mask her rising anxiety. "Lincoln intended to commandeer the helium-3 for himself. We overheard their plans." She winced internally, realising her tone bordered on defensive.

"He's Lincoln Ellison. I expected nothing else from him." Her eyes narrowed. "Did you not think I had contingencies in place for such an event?"

Xanthe's response caught in her throat. The possibility of Aryanna manipulating Lincoln had never crossed her mind. She felt a fleeting sense of vulnerability but quickly pushed it away.

"Your actions were reckless," Aryanna continued. "You defied a direct order." A faint crease appeared between her brows, a dent in the porcelain of her high, smooth forehead. "Your command will be at an end as soon as I appoint a replacement."

Refusing to buckle under Aryanna's cold gaze, Xanthe straightened her back, her nails digging crescents into her thighs, hidden from the holo transmitter. "I don't think so," she countered with steely defiance.

Aryanna's expression shifted to one of incredulity. "I beg your pardon?"

"You will not remove me. And I think you will agree to my terms." Xanthe spoke with a low, determined rumble.

Aryanna leaned forward slightly, her incredulity turning to curiosity. "And why is that?"

Xanthe leaned in too, her eyes locked on Aryanna's. "Because I know what happened to the Chinese base."

The words hung in the air, heavy with implications. Aryanna's face remained impassive, but her eyes betrayed a flicker of surprise. Xanthe held her breath, knowing she had just crossed a line from which there was no return.

CHAPTER FIVE

"Leadership isn't just about making decisions; it's about bearing the weight of those decisions long after they're made. It's a constant reminder that every choice you make echoes in the lives of those you lead."

—Doctor Troy Bruin, *MEMOIRS FROM MARS*

In the light of the holo display, Xanthe watched Aryanna's face ripple with suppressed emotion and settle into a marble mask once more. Time stretched like a cat as Xanthe waited for Aryanna to deny her accusation.

"Tell me, Commander Waters, what exactly do you think happened to the Chinese base?" She steepled her fingers and narrowed her eyes.

I can play this game, Aryanna, thought Xanthe. "There is evidence that someone in the Lunar Commission directed the attack."

Aryanna held Xanthe's gaze and scoffed. "Really? How very interesting," she said in a patronising tone. "I would dearly love to see this 'evidence'." She waved a finger in a circle and then resumed the steepled position. "People are so very clever at insinuating all sorts of things. Power creates enemies, Commander Waters," she lectured. "And those enemies like to portray others as evil manipulators. Who is accused of this heinous crime?"

Aryanna stared at Xanthe, black eyes alight with challenge. As Xanthe hesitated, she continued. "I suppose Lunar Commissioners are prime targets, especially now with the helium-3 project and what it can mean for the future of humanity. So far, a number of us have been made out to be cult leaders, mafia puppets, heads of a child-trafficking ring and Satan worshippers – an oldie but a goodie." She lay her hands flat on the table and tilted her head. "So, now someone among us is an ecoterrorist?"

Aryanna's nonchalance sent a flare of doubt through Xanthe, but she'd seen the files Athena had uncovered. Could they be fakes?

"The evidence is there," Xanthe persisted with a confidence she did not feel. "The Lunar Commission is compromised. But let's return to the issue at hand—"

Aryanna leapt to her feet, her gold bracelets clattering together like wind chimes in a thunderstorm. "Wait just a minute, Commander Waters! You just accused me – or someone in the Lunar Commission – of mass murder and sabotage, without producing any evidence. This *is* the issue at hand."

Xanthe held her ground as Aryanna's vitriol washed over her. She breathed and counted heartbeats until her pulse slowed and she could trust her voice to stay calm.

"The evidence is secure. I do not see there is any point in releasing it, as this would further destabilise the Lunar Commission at a sensitive time in the helium-3 operations. We need to maintain a united front. Removing me from the project at this time would only destabilise the Lunar Commission further."

Aryanna glared at Xanthe. "You are bluffing. You have nothing. And you would dare to try and manipulate me with some elusive 'evidence'? How dare you!"

Xanthe's pulse raced and fear seized her throat. She swallowed hard to push it down.

Athena, a little assistance here. Down-regulate my system please.

A cool wash of calm swept over Xanthe. She adjusted her stance and took a slow breath.

"Aryanna, let's take this from a different angle, shall we? This is what I am proposing: we work together to secure helium-3 production under the Lunar Commission's auspices. The Lunar Commission involvement with the Chinese station"—Aryanna opened her mouth to protest, but Xanthe persisted—"or non-involvement with the Chinese base is not a helpful discussion at this point."

"Your insolence is astounding!" Aryanna said. "I will—"

It was Xanthe's turn to raise her voice. "Aryanna, face it. You need me right now, like it or not!"

Aryanna held her tongue and seethed.

"This is the current state of affairs: Lincoln and the Spaceward Bound are returning to Earth to face charges of negligence from the asteroid mining fatalities, and for collusion to monopolise the helium-3 trade. You cannot fire me for my commitment to civic duties and global protection of clean energy. The Lunar Commissioners would never agree."

"Don't be so sure you know the minds of the Lunar Commissioners, Commander Waters." Aryanna's tone stung with threats.

Xanthe gritted her teeth and continued. "Nonetheless, I am here on the Moon. Together with Jonas, Troy and the collaboration of Colonel Jin and the Red Star base, we will produce the first shipment of helium-3 and send it back to Earth as soon as it's ready. We will continue to expand production and prepare the Olympus base for future miners, as I have been directed."

Aryanna sneered, her distended lips garish as she drew them back over sharp white teeth. "Let's hope you actually fulfil *this* direction, Commander Waters."

Aryanna's image flicked out and Xanthe was left breathing into the cold, quiet room that glowed with its ghostly data screens. Her shoulders slumped as she released tension from the interaction.

"Why did you do that?"

Xanthe jumped at Troy's voice. He stood, arms crossed, in the doorframe.

"What do you mean?"

"You all but accused Aryanna of murdering all the Chinese taikonauts. We want her on our side, not gunning for us even more."

"I needed her to know we have an eye on her weaknesses," Xanthe replied, irritation creeping through her.

"That's not how you play with power, Xanthe." Troy frowned in concern.

"What do you know about playing with power?" she replied. "You've got only one move in your playbook and that's sex and seduction."

She regretted her words instantly.

Pain etched across Troy's face.

"Is that what you think of me?" he asked gently. He uncrossed his arms and shoved his hands in his pockets. His crystal blue eyes held hers for a moment longer, and then he turned away.

"Troy—"

"Dinner will be on the table in thirty minutes, Commander," he called over his shoulder.

She watched him go, heart yearning, mouth dry.

CHAPTER SIX

*"In the quiet moments, when the pressure lifted just a little,
I started to see the pieces of ourselves that leadership had
eroded. It wasn't just time or energy — it was the beating heart
of humanity that we had sacrificed on the altar of duty."*

—DOCTOR TROY BRUIN,
MEMOIRS FROM MARS

TROY LAY ON his bunk, his eyes closed, and worked to purge the emotion from the exchange with Xanthe. Their evening meal had been a grim affair following the call to Aryanna. Jonas had been lost in his own thoughts about helium-3 while he and Xanthe ate in efficient, stony silence.

He wanted to bridge the gap between them. Their relationship was so fresh and vulnerable, a flower bud in volatile spring weather. But her words had cut deep, laced as they were with truth. She was right: he used sex and seduction for influence. He was well aware of his charms and had on more than one occasion turned up the charisma for a favourable outcome, either for promoting the New Baths of Caracalla or elevating his status as founder.

He was more than that, though. He was a successful leader in his own right, capable of leading the lunar expedition if required. So, he'd eaten his meal in silence, punishing her a little.

What an immature fool I am, he thought and shook his head to clear the barbs from his soul. *I'll make amends when we gather for the landings in an hour.*

Troy prodded his mind into action. Tuning into his body, he noted each sensation: the weight of his legs, taxed from the exo-suit and moonboots, the subtle swelling in his knees from yesterday's intense gym session and the slight creak in his hips. He imagined a wave of hydration soothing his strained kidneys. He visualised the cells rejuvenating, blooming like water lilies.

His chest felt robust, a small victory after a year on the Moon, but his shoulders ached from hours hunched over plants in the Swamp, diligently following Xavier's meticulous instructions. So far, he hadn't killed anything, so the cantankerous Frenchman would have nothing to complain about.

As his mind drifted to his absent colleagues, a twinge of loneliness crept in. He missed the buzz of their presence, the easy banter. Now, with only three of them left, his role as medical officer and psychologist was paradoxically both less and more demanding. The absence of others made the psychological strain of lunar life more pronounced, nibbling at the wires of his consciousness. He needed Xanthe. Their connection was a splash of sunshine in the dark corners of this subterranean maze.

Pushing these thoughts aside, he focused instead on the ever-growing mountain of tasks. Plenty to do.

There was the usual Swamp monitoring for water flow, plant growth, humidity, atmosphere – doing Xavier's job. Then there was the weekly audit of the life support systems, cleaning the air filters, testing the airlocks – doing Serena's job.

And if all was good there, there was an EVA to check the helium-3 mining sites and moonquake impacts – doing Madison's job.

Troy's introspection deepened as he considered Xanthe and her interaction with the ThinkLink. He had observed her closely for any signs of cognitive hijacking or mental strain. *She talks to Athena like she's real,* he mused, the image of Xanthe muttering to herself like a crazy person flashing in his mind.

There was, however, a flinty steel of confidence in her now that had only emerged occasionally, under duress, before the brain implant. It was as if the ThinkLink had extended its neural access along her spine like a tree sapling seeking nutrients in deeper soil.

What was it doing to her? How might it change her? Would it cause any long-term damage? The research was inconclusive and guarded carefully. If there was damage, could it be reversed? Concern burrowed in his heart like a termite in wood.

Troy caught his mind drifting, and he returned to his physical audit: neck stiff, eyes strained, head weary. He stretched his arms above his head and activated his muscles, just as a cat might do. A luxurious, languid awakening. He felt more like an old man than a supple feline. He had been neglecting his yoga. He swung his legs off the bunk, feeling the cool touch of the regolith concrete floor beneath his feet.

Time to move.

Standing up, he reached for the sky, then bent forward, beginning his daily ritual of sun salutations. Even buried under the moondust, he knew in his cells where the sun lay, the sustainer of all life. This practice anchored him, a comforting reminder of his earthly origins on this barren satellite, Earth's distant child.

CHAPTER SEVEN

"Why risk life in space? Of all the things humans create, life is the most precious and the most easily lost. And yet it's the insatiable yearning for adventure, for discovery, that gives life meaning."

—ATHENA A.I.,
WISDOM OF THE AGES

IT WAS TIME to watch the landings. Their friends would be facing the last treacherous leg of their journey. Anxiety rose in Xanthe's chest. Troy clattered in the kitchen, trying to make his presence felt. He offered Xanthe a conciliatory cup of tea, and she took it gratefully with a meek smile.

Troy made a cup for Jonas, too, as he joined them in the kitchen hub. Xanthe noticed the wordless ease of their companionship, born from friends who had endured much and knew each other well. It was a relief after the tension between her and Troy.

Xanthe moved to the comms console, studying the tracking screens in the cramped room. She dialled down the lights to better see the display, leaving her illuminated with an eerie glow. She placed Troy's cup of chamomile tea aside, and it sat cooling, untouched, beside the console as she chewed a thumb nail instead.

The *Saturnia* and *Minerva* would reenter Earth's orbit in the next thirty minutes.

Troy sidled in beside her, putting an arm awkwardly around her waist and kissing her temple. She let him nuzzle her as she gestured to enlarge the image on the console.

"Don't forget the tea," Troy said. "It will help you sleep."

"I'll sleep better once I know they're all safe and sound back on Earth," she said.

"Agreed." He rubbed her back and peered at the image of the two ships creeping towards the blue orb swirling with clouds. Jonas squeezed in beside them with an apologetic look as they stiffened a little at the interruption to their intimacy.

Xanthe glanced at the clock. "Time to check in. Athena, connect with the *Saturnia*, please."

"Connecting with the *Saturnia*, now," the A.I. piped into the small chamber.

"Olympus, this is *Saturnia*. How may I help?" Captain Madison Floyd's image filled the holo display.

"Mad Dog! It's good to see you," Troy said with a broad smile.

"Likewise, buddy! How is the Moon treating you? Any disasters since we left?" Madison's head floated in the bowl of her spacesuit's neckline.

"Only Jonas's cooking. We miss Xavier's culinary talents. How is the old goat doing? How's the head injury and the leg?" Troy said.

Xavier was in a precarious position, having just had cranial surgery to anchor a bone plate from a horrendous accident exploring a lava tube. He had a crushed leg in a medical boot sleeve as well. The trip back to Earth was risky, but it was riskier leaving him on the Moon to recover.

"I am fine, *mon vieux*! Serena is the nurse every man wants." Xavier's voice had its usual nonchalance. Troy wished he could see him on the holo to check.

Madison glanced over her shoulder, smiling at her injured

colleague. "So far, so good," she replied. "The next bit is a little tricky with the atmosphere re-entry, but we've got him secured as best we can. Let's hope the *Saturnia* is up to the job."

"And our 'guests' – how are they?" Xanthe's forehead crinkled in concern.

"Lincoln and the others are behaving themselves. We took them off sedatives for re-entry. Just in case. But Lincoln is no fool. He wouldn't attempt a takeover while we are on descent."

"And Mr Puffkins?"

"That damn dog!" Madison laughed. "It's a nuisance. Serena's been doing the work looking after the beast. It seems she has developed quite a bond with the darned thing."

Serena's image popped into the holo, holding a panting Pomeroy. It squirmed and licked her face.

"Hey Xanthe!" Serena said. "Me and Mr Puffkins are new best mates. It's driving Lincoln crazy."

"Just make sure you buckle that dog up well for re-entry."

"All over it, Commander," Serena replied. "I've got the perfect sling rigged for him."

"Madison, have you got comms with Gaia Enterprises?" Xanthe asked.

"Yes. They are ready to receive us. Their new base coordinates are locked in, and Athena has all that under control. Aryanna has a police delegation ready to take Lincoln and the crew into custody."

"Excellent. I'll let you get back to the checks. I'll talk to you once you land and have gone through the quarantine and medical assessments. Hope the gravity shock isn't too bad."

"Yeah. Not really looking forward to weighing a zillion pounds again."

"Madison, good luck." Xanthe held her gaze with an intensity she hoped Madison felt across the void between them.

"We'll be thinking of you. Have a good landing, Mad Dog!" Jonas added.

"Roger that." Madison flicked a couple of switches and then said to her crew, "It's helmet time. *Saturnia* out."

Madison's image winked to a blip and was gone. The comms room flooded with silence. The display flashed with white blips as the ships continued their fateful path. Each flash cast a speck of hope and dread across Xanthe's face as she leaned over to study its path.

Troy squeezed Xanthe's waist again with the arm that hadn't left her side. "Ready for the *Minerva*?"

She nodded.

Troy gave Athena the command while he handed Xanthe her lukewarm tea and nudged her gently to drink it. She took it from him and swallowed absent-mindedly.

"Olympus, this is the *Minerva*. How do we read, over?" Dave Eriksson's Dutch accent came through before his head popped into the holo, partially obscured by his helmet. Xanthe could see the entire cockpit this time, with Max, his co-pilot and the two Spaceward Bound prisoners sitting behind them.

"Captain Eriksson, we read you loud and clear. How is the approach lined up, Dave?" Xanthe said.

"She's a bit wobbly, to be honest, Xanthe. So far the repairs we did are holding, but I'm not sure we got all the water out of the hold from the crash on the Moon. The balance is not quite right."

A stab of anxiety pierced Xanthe's guts. She tensed under Troy's embrace, put her teacup down next to the console and pushed Troy's arm aside. She needed to concentrate.

"Tell me about your workarounds," she said.

To the Athena ThinkLink she thought-commanded, *Give me the analysis of the risks on re-entry for the Minerva.*

Dave listed all the adjustments he was making and the updates he was getting from the ship's sensors. Xanthe let the words drift over her as she knew Athena would be analysing his protocols as they spoke. She focused instead on Dave's face, what she could see of it through the helmet, and the tone of his voice. Much of the re-entry success depended on his reaction time and instincts. If he was emotionally off-balance, it would skew his responses.

"Commander Waters, I have analysed the risks for the Minerva. There is a 60% chance of misalignment of angle on re-entry," Athena ThinkLink said in thought-command mode.

Meaning?

"They could re-enter atmosphere at the wrong angle and either bounce out or burn up."

Xanthe chewed her thumb nail again as her heart started to pound.

Anything we can do for them?

"Minerva Athena is working on the problem. It will be a sensitive operation."

"Commander?" Dave's voice pulled her awareness back to the holo display.

"Go ahead, Dave." She fought to keep her voice steady.

"Gaia Enterprises has urged us to change course to land in the Pacific. That will be an easier process, given the condition of the ship."

"The Pacific? But that's miles away from headquarters. Can they get a retrieval crew there?" Troy asked.

"Hey, Troy. Good to see you, my old friend." Dave's face relaxed momentarily into a smile. "Yes, Gaia says they anticipated this situation and have a crew on standby."

"That's fast," muttered Troy, frowning.

"Have you made a course adjustment?" Xanthe asked.

"Affirmative. Our new course should give us a bit more time to stabilise and adjust the cargo to compensate. We'll land some time after the *Saturnia*. A side-by-side landing would have been good but is not to be."

"Serena likes the limelight, anyhow! I don't mind coming in second." It was Max King, the life support technician who had accompanied Dave on the rescue expedition to the Moon when Olympus had been blasted with meteorite debris.

Xanthe knew Max was being brave. She heard the lightness of his voice, but his body was rigid and he gripped the armrests with his space gloves.

"Roger that." Xanthe attempted a smile. "And how is the *Pinnacle* crew?"

"Our prisoners, Captain Barrio and his offsider, Lester Thompson, were perfect gentlemen when we had them drugged to the eyeballs." Dave paused as he adjusted the navigation controls. "We stopped the sedatives an hour or so ago and now I have a backseat driver. I had to turn off their helmet comms. Captain Barrio likes to be in control, no?"

"I think that's true of most captains," Troy said with a chuckle. "You're one of the most chilled-out pilots I've ever met, Dave. Unlike Mad Dog. I wouldn't be telling *her* how to fly a ship."

"Ha!" Dave said. "Right you are, old friend. Mad Dog knows how to fly a ship. I tell you what, I wouldn't mind her advice right about now." His face tightened.

"You've got this, Dave," Xanthe said as she leaned towards his holo. She wanted to reach out and give him a hug.

"Thanks, Commander." His eyes held hers.

"May Gaia guide you well," she said.

"We'll see you when we're back Earthside, no?" Dave gave her a thumbs up.

"You bet," she said with a conviction she didn't feel.

"Live with grace—" Troy said.

"—lead in service," Dave finished the Gaia Enterprises's motto for him. "We'll go now, Commander. Things to do, people to see."

"Roger that," Xanthe replied. She so admired Dave's lightness of spirit even in the most dire of circumstances.

"*Minerva* out," Dave said as he and Max waved.

Troy, Xanthe and Jonas stared at the emptiness where the holos had been.

"How bad is it?" Troy asked at last, turning to Xanthe.

She looked into his crystal blue eyes awash with worry. "Athena says 60% chance of re-entry failure." Her stomach clenched and she swallowed hard.

"That's a 40% chance of success. We've faced worse odds," he said.

"Let's hope you're right," she said.

CHAPTER EIGHT

*"You can't fix a system built on lies and greed. To bring
it back to the light, you must tear it down, piece by
piece, and rebuild it on a foundation of truth."*

—CLAIRE EDWARDS,
THE REBEL'S PLAYBOOK: THE EARTH FIRST MANIFESTO

MAJA SAT NEXT to Aryanna in the Gaia HQ landing and launch control room. Huw had declined to attend as there had been a significant setback in one of their new floating communities up north. The other Lunar Commissioners sat behind them.

Designed like an ancient amphitheatre, the control room's first three rows, which they perched in, had a panoramic view of the entire operation.

Maja glanced around. "Where's Leo?"

"He and Vikram are looking at converting the *Surya One* for helium-3 shipments," Aryanna replied. "They opted out of watching the landing so they could step up that part of the plan."

Maja found this surprising. Leo would miss welcoming his boss and founder, Lincoln back to Earth. Although there was a certain logic to the decision, it niggled at her like a buzzing mosquito.

Her attention was drawn back to the room and its enormous screen showing the main trajectory of the *Saturnia*, just moments from re-entering atmosphere. Half a dozen technicians sat on rolling kneeling chairs, whizzing between displays and tracking telemetry of the in-bound spacecraft. They muttered into their headsets periodically.

The CapCom, Alexandra Minke, stood at the right-hand side of the big screen, one arm resting on the edge of the amphitheatre's retaining wall, dividing the spectators from the operations crew. She sipped from an enormous pink water bottle with a sparkling straw. Known for her banal taste in fashion – all grey in a prosaic, functional masculine cut, with a straight bob of jet-black hair – the water bottle was her one concession to frivolity.

As she gazed at the garish pink bottle, Maja wondered what kind of underwear the straight-laced CapCom hid under her grey slacks.

"Okay people, here we go," Alexandra said into her mouth-piece, which also broadcast to the Commissioners. Alexandra put the water bottle on the ledge beside her and stood straight with hands on hips.

Maja leaned forward, her arms on the amphitheatre ledge. This was her crew, her team, coming home after such an ordeal. They'd survived asteroid strikes, moonquakes and Lincoln Ellison's villainy. And they'd managed to build the first long-term community base on the Moon. A frisson of pride rippled across her thin shoulders.

"Hank, give me the readings on approach," Alexandra said.

"All systems within range and in the green," he replied.

"Good. Hook me up with the *Saturnia* for the pre-entry messaging," she said.

"Patching you through now, Cap."

The giant screen split and the faces of Madison Floyd and Serena Fox, helmets on, gloved hands flicking to different controls, filled the display.

"Captain Floyd, this is CapCom Minke. Ready to come home?"

"Never been more ready. It's been a long haul, Cap," Madison said and flashed a brief smile and a knowing raise of an eyebrow.

"Well, let's get you safely back on Earth. Comms are going dark for three minutes, twenty-one seconds in sixty seconds. Hank will count you in. We'll be tracking everything here, and it all looks good, textbook perfect, Mad Dog."

"Good to hear, Ali! I've got a reputation to maintain, you know!"

"Mad Dog, good luck." Alexandra let her face smooth into an earnest look that Madison acknowledged with a wave. "We'll see you soon."

"I'm counting on it," Madison said.

"*Saturnia*," Hank interrupted. "We are comms black-out in five, four, three, two, one."

The screen shut the display of the crew and the image of the *Saturnia* glowed hot white as the ship entered the atmosphere.

Maja breathed out slowly as her heart flitted against her ribs. The amphitheatre whirled with lights and blips and the swish of rolling chairs moving between screens and readouts. They scurried like ants as the glow of the *Saturnia* soared brightly like a rock tossed by Apollo, a glimmering radiant comet. On board, six lives.

Seven lives, she corrected herself, remembering Lincoln's dog.

Next to her, Aryanna inspected the glorious sheen of her red-painted fingernails. She was bored, Maja realised. She'd seen so many landings and takeoffs during her time as Lunar Commissioner, and even before that as she was extending Aryanna Industries' business interests to include lunar developments, that she'd become blasé about the miracle of space flight.

Then three things happened at once.

Aryanna stopped her fingernail inspection, sat ramrod straight and pressed a finger to the small command button behind her ear.

CapCom Minke whirled to her crew and tapped her headset with a puzzled look.

A splintering noise like a bowling ball hurtling through a wooden door snapped all eyes towards the left corner entrance of the amphitheatre.

Then the lights went out.

CHAPTER NINE

"Radical problems require radical solutions. Incremental change is a tool of the status quo; real change demands bold, decisive action."

—CLAIRE EDWARDS,
THE REBEL'S PLAYBOOK: THE EARTH FIRST MANIFESTO

JONAS LEFT THE tight space of the comms room while they waited the thirty minutes for the reentry. His nerves jangled and he had energy to burn. He grabbed Betty, the rubber chicken Serena had left, and jog-clomped in his moonboots to the Atrium.

"Athena, can you ask Volkov to join me in the Atrium please?"

"Hailing Volkov, now," the A.I. replied over the base comms.

While he waited, Jonas threw the chicken against one of the walls and ran to catch it in a one-person version of chook tennis. It squawked as it hit the wall, which made Jonas laugh as he remembered Mr Puffkins barking and leaping in the low G to tackle the rubber toy.

"Jonas, what do you want?" The Dopplebot's Russian accent interrupted his thoughts, and he spun to see the machine standing at the entrance. Even after all this time together on the base, since the Chinese had loaned Volkov to them, the realistic depiction of the old dead Russian dictator still startled Jonas occasionally.

"Jeez, Volkov. Don't you ever knock or say hello?"

"You called; I came. Why say hello?" The bot's face was impassive, the lips a little twisted with all the various repairs Jonas and Troy had done over the last few months. Volkov had endured explosions, crushing and rocket-launch burns, but it still functioned. And didn't look too bad, all things considered, thought Jonas. The bot was a miracle of Chinese engineering and scrappy Olympus repairs.

"How goes the helium-3 processing? Have you got a solution for the slowdown on unit 3?"

"You interrupt my work and bring me here for report? You could have asked Athena. She knows."

"Well, I'm asking you. So, answer." Jonas waggled the rubber chicken at Volkov.

"Unit 3 is nearly back up to full production. I cleaned filter, adjusted tempo of slurry dump and it is fine."

"Good job." Jonas tried to think of something else to say. The bot was not much of a conversationalist.

"Want to play chook tag?"

Volkov's eyes maintained their stare, body in its default ready-to-move stance.

"Why?" the bot asked.

"For fun. Stress relief."

"These are childish things. I have work to do." The bot turned mechanically and hit the exit door's button.

"Stay and play, Volkov." Jonas heard the desperation in his own voice and tried to cover it with a commanding tone. "That's an order."

Volkov froze and turned slowly.

"Please." Jonas's face burned scarlet.

"Since you asked so nicely, it would be my pleasure." The bot dipped its head in acknowledgment.

Jonas threw the rubber chicken at Volkov, and it bounced off the bot's head with a squawk. "Tag, you're it," Jonas said with a spark of glee.

Volkov stared at the rubber chicken for a moment, then bent over, scooped it up and whipped it at Jonas as he leaped away.

The chicken caught him on the buttocks with a sting. "Ow! Not so hard, Volkov!" Jonas grabbed the chicken and threw it back at Volkov, who had not changed position. It thwacked its chest, squeaking, but Volkov caught it before it hit the ground and hurled it back at Jonas, who threw himself in the other direction. The toy hit him in the temple and knocked him backwards on his rump.

"I said, 'not so hard', Volkov!" Jonas frowned and rubbed his head.

"You moved. It required greater velocity to hit target."

"Alright. Forget it. Get back to work." Jonas waved a dismissal.

"I look forward to our next game," Volkov said.

"Bugger off," mumbled Jonas.

Once the bot had left, Jonas tried a few rounds of solo chook tennis but soon tired of the game. It was less fun on his own. He caught Betty and sat heavily on one of the benches at the centre of the Atrium. The roof had been closed since the *Saturnia* and *Minerva* left them, and the room seemed dreary.

"Athena, display the view from Gaia Headquarters with the *Saturnia* on approach."

The Atrium transformed its ceiling into a blazing blue sky. It was as if he were sitting next to the headquarters crew, monitoring the spaceship's descent, with an expansive view of the landing pad. There were murmurs as people waited excitedly for the Olympus crew and the renegade *Pinnacle* pirates to return home.

A flock of geese honked and flew past. Birds. He missed birds.

"Thanks, Athena. Shut it down." Jonas stood and clomped back to the comms room. It was time.

"Where are we up to?" he asked as he rejoined Troy and Xanthe.

"On approach, now," Xanthe said and picked up her now-cold

tea again. The cup wobbled a bit in her grip, Jonas noticed. Something was up.

"And?" Jonas asked.

"The *Minerva* is not tracking well. There is still a significant risk of misalignment." Xanthe swigged her tea and pushed the cup to the back of the console, out of the way.

"The repairs are holding?" Jonas asked with a quaver in his voice. He'd been the one to do the repairs, but spaceship hulls were not his area of expertise.

"The repairs are fine, Jonas," Troy said and put a hand on his shoulder. "You did a great job. Dave thinks there might have been some water still sloshing around."

Jonas took a big breath and blew it out.

"*Saturnia* on approach." Athena's voice came over the comms room speakers.

"Here we go," Troy muttered.

The three of them stood shoulder to shoulder, watching the display that filled a third of the wall space of the comms room. The *Saturnia* was edging closer to Earth's atmosphere. It seemed to take forever, although Jonas knew the craft was hurtling along at one kilometre per second.

The image burned brighter as the nose cone of the ship entered the atmosphere. They would have no comms with the ship for the next three minutes or so. No way to reassure their friends. No way to help. All they could do was watch the landing through the images.

"Gaia guide them well," whispered Xanthe. She gripped the edge of the table where the console comms controls lay.

The *Saturnia* was a yellow ball of flame. Jonas's heart thudded against his chest, and perspiration beaded on his forehead. His mouth was dry. Heat surged up from his chest to his throat. He pulled the collar out to cool down a little.

"Come on, come on!" Troy said. He was swaying backwards

and forward on his feet, urging the ship to push through the atmosphere.

The ship paused on its line and changed from a vivid yellow to a white blob.

"Reverse thrusting now," Jonas narrated. Madison or Athena would be slowing the ship and altering its angle for a descent to Gaia's landing platform.

The wait was excruciating. Jonas stretched his head from side to side to loosen the muscles that had knotted as they watched. Xanthe chewed her thumb nail like a dog working the gristle of a bone. Troy rocked on his feet and hugged himself with folded arms.

The white dot of the ship hardly moved, then stopped.

"Did it land? Athena, did it land?" Xanthe asked with wide eyes.

"My readings confirm a landing. The *Saturnia* is on the ground." Athena said.

"Yes!" shouted Jonas and grabbed Troy in a bear hug.

Troy laughed and rubbed Jonas's head. Then Troy released Jonas and pulled Xanthe to him as her eyes glistened.

"Athena, can we connect to the *Saturnia* please?"

"Connecting the *Saturnia* now."

"Olympus, this is the *Saturnia*." Madison panted and her image sprung to the holo. Her face had a pale hue despite her dark skin, and her lips looked dry. She took a sip of water from her suit hydration mouthpiece before speaking again. "We've landed."

"Madison, how are you?" Xanthe asked.

"Alright, but that was rough. And gravity is a real bitch!"

Madison turned her head sideways, craning to see something behind her.

"*Merde! Putain de merde!*" Xavier's voice howled in the background. The litany of French swear words gave way to moaning.

"Xavier!" Madison said. "You okay?"

The moaning continued. Shouting clogged the comms along

with Mr Puffkins' strident bark. Madison punched at the screen in front of her to adjust the onboard camera. She turned her head this way and that, trying to get a better read on her colleagues.

"I think the camera's been knocked out," Madison said. "Serena, can you see Xavier from where you are?"

"Yes. And he is definitely not okay," Serena's voice came over the display.

Jonas rubbed the muscles of his jaw, trying to unclench them. They watched helplessly while Madison and Serena tried to troubleshoot the issue with Xavier from their seats. The crew couldn't move until the ship was secure.

"*Saturnia*, hold your positions." A voice Jonas didn't recognise filled the *Saturnia* cabin.

Madison spun back to study the comms display, her brow furrowed. "This is Captain Floyd of the *Saturnia*," she said stonily. "We have an injured crew member on board in urgent need of medical assistance. Who are we speaking with?"

"This is your new commander, John Fitzgerald of Earth First. Standby for orders."

"Who the hell is that?" Jonas said.

Xanthe's face went white, and Troy gasped.

Madison's face was grim. She punched at the controls in front of her with gloved hands. "Fitzgerald? I don't recognise your authority. I report to Gaia Enterprises. Gaia, are you on channel, over?"

Xanthe leaned against console and closed her eyes in concentration.

"Nice try, *Saturnia*. Gaia Enterprises is not running the show. We are. Now do as we tell you and we will get medical aid to your friend, and no one will get hurt."

"Xanthe, are you getting this?" Madison asked as she worked the controls.

"Affirmative." Xanthe opened her eyes and held the back of her neck, wincing. "Athena is doing an analysis. It looks like Earth First has taken over the landing site and Gaia Headquarters is under siege."

"Xanthe Waters?" Another voice boomed into the *Saturnia*'s space. "Xanthe Waters, you're not in charge now. Fuck off."

And the comms went dark.

"Athena, bring up the display. Get them back," Xanthe said, her eyes wide.

After a pause, Athena said, "Negative, Commander Waters. The comms are down. I can't access *Saturnia*. Or Gaia Enterprises."

"Was that who I think it was?" Jonas asked. His heart was hammering and sweat dripped into his eyes.

"Yes." Troy said, with a dark voice. "Claire bloody Edwards."

CHAPTER TEN

"Raw power often lies in the shadows, where back-channelling weaves the real narratives. The official story is merely a façade, a distraction from the covert machinations that shape our world."

—Maja Garcia,
THE JOURNALS

"Claire?" Jonas said, aghast. "So, it's true! She has joined the ecoterrorists."

"It looks like it's more than that," Troy added. "She's leading the siege."

Jonas's mind went quiet as he watched Troy try to initiate comms with the *Saturnia*. Xanthe had her eyes shut tight and was mumbling to herself, or to Athena. Everything slowed to a quiet vignette for Jonas.

The bright vivid lights of the tracking display still showed the *Saturnia*'s landing spot, winking. There was grime on the edge of the console table, and rings stained from coffee cups. A protein bar wrapper lay forgotten in the corner – Xanthe would be hounding him later for not cleaning properly.

The muscles in Xanthe's neck were taut cords. Her face was

flushed, and she held a hand to her forehead. Patches of sweat appeared under Troy's blue shirt, untucked now, and Jonas glimpsed his skinny torso atrophied from all the long months on the Moon.

Xanthe's eyes sprang open.

"Athena, hail the *Minerva*!" she said.

"Hailing the *Minerva* now."

"The *Minerva*!" Jonas said as Troy looked at him with a dawning awareness.

"There is no response from the *Minerva*," Athena said. "They are entering Earth's atmosphere now."

Jonas swiped the screen to track the *Minerva*. The ship's dot was burning yellow already, careening towards the Earth. Jonas's heart leaped in his rib cage, and he chewed his lip. He dug his fingernails into his palms.

Either his friends made it through the next few minutes or they burned up in a vicious inferno.

Then the dot started to weave.

"They're losing control!" Jonas cried.

Troy stopped rocking on his heels and grew still beside Jonas. Xanthe gripped the console again, her gaze locked on the screen. Jonas held his breath.

The dot hurtled in a spiral on the screen and then stopped. It still blinked.

"Athena, did they make it?" whispered Xanthe.

"The *Minerva* has splashed down in the Pacific, three hundred kilometres off their trajectory. No comms are available."

Jonas swallowed hard against the nausea that swelled in his throat. If they survived that landing, it would be a miracle. The retrieval party would have to race to secure the vessel, especially if there was damage, as seemed likely given the sketchy re-entry.

But even if the splashdown had been successful, if the *Saturnia* landing was anything to go by, the *Minerva* was heading into a trap.

CHAPTER ELEVEN

*"As a pilot, I need to shift perspective between the horizon,
the big picture and what's right in front of me. It's not one or
the other, it's all three. Otherwise, mistakes can be fatal."*

—David Eriksson,
THE LUNAR CHRONICLE, FIRST PIONEERS

The *Minerva* shuddered and rattled. Dave fought for control, muscles pushing against the steering mechanism. A livid purple vein stood at attention on his forehead.

"Athena, stabilise with thrusters," he said through gritted teeth. His vision blurred as the ship careened. The g-forces pressed him back into his seat and he focused hard to stay conscious. Beside him Max was too terrified to do anything but grip his chair.

"Thrusters initiated," Athena said.

Dave was conscious of Gareth Barrio yelling through his helmet. He strained forward with his left hand while his right hand jammed the steering lever into its counter-spiral manoeuvre. The pressure on his chest from the g-forces pushed the air from his lungs.

Dave panted with shallow breaths as he willed himself towards the internal comms button. The tip of his glove reached out, his eyes bulged, and with one last grunt he swatted the button with a tip of his glove. He flew back against his chair and grabbed the lever with both hands as the alarms sounded in the ship.

"Stabilisers malfunctioning," Athena said.

Gareth Barrio's cry filled his helmet. "Release the chutes early!"

"They will tangle in a spiral," Dave managed to reply as his arms trembled with the effort of holding the ship steady. The gauges flashed the rapidly decreasing altitude. Still way too high for the chutes. If they released now, especially in the spiral they were in, the chutes would tangle, and they would plummet and hit the ocean like a bomb blast.

"Release! Release!" Barrio shouted.

Dave could see Barrio on the ship's crew display screen. Something in the man's face – a flash of conviction – sparked a new will in Dave.

They would surely die with this spiral, but it was just as likely with the chutes.

He had one more move.

The ship shook so hard his brain shuddered in his skull. Dave sucked in a quick breath as best he could, then he slammed the steering lever hard right while throwing himself against the chute release.

Dave's body lurched against the seat's harness and the jowls of his cheeks oozed back against his face as the ship spun. He blinked slowly, trying to keep his focus, but blackness narrowed his vision to a pinprick and then nothingness.

CHAPTER TWELVE

*"Must we fight violence with violence? If someone attacks us,
can we not disarm them, rather than retaliate? Somehow, we as
leaders must hold a higher moral ground or be lost forever."*

—Maja Garcia,
THE JOURNALS

THE GROUND SHOOK and the air clattered with the sound of breaking glass. Maja and Aryanna dived to the floor. Aryanna's enormous bodyguard flew over the top of them, limbs like a giant crocodile holding them down.

"Move!" he shouted at them. "Forward to the southern exit. Five metres in front of you and to the right corner."

Aryanna shuffled forward on her hands and knees as alarms screeched and voices panicked around them in the darkness.

"What on Earth is that?" said Maja.

"Keep moving," the bodyguard said, shoving his shoulder into Maja's behind as she scrambled after Aryanna. The carpet was rough under her hands, and she felt it burn through her trousers as she moved forward.

CapCom Alexandra Minke was shouting into the darkness. "Hank? Martha? What have you got?"

The muffled replies held inflections of frustration and distress.

At the edge of the amphitheatre's row of seats, the bodyguard launched himself past both Aryanna and Maja. He hissed back at them, "On my word, follow me into the corridor. Stay low. If it's clear, we head left to the boardroom." He was crouching.

Maja heard the whimpers and shouts of the other Lunar Commissioners, hiding on the ground by their chairs. There was banging at the front entrance to the amphitheatre and threatening shouts.

Maja pulled her feet under her, ready to leap forward. A flow of cool air washed over her as the bodyguard opened the door. Aryanna shuffled forward and Maja scurried after her, heart skipping wildly, mouth dry.

Into the corridor, left, and towards a ray of light that broke the corridor's darkness. The bodyguard disappeared into the room and beckoned to them. Maja flew after Aryanna and launched herself into the boardroom.

The bodyguard shut the door behind them and jammed one of the enormous chairs under its handle for good measure. He moved to the window, keeping out of direct sight, and drew his weapon.

Maja leaned against the giant mahogany table and caught her breath. Aryanna slipped over to the catering counter, searched for a glass and poured herself some water from the tap. She guzzled it, and then placed it back on the counter and mopped the drips at her lip with the back of her hand. She straightened her white silk blouse with her red-tipped talons.

Maja slipped up to the window and stood behind the bodyguard. The heat from his well-muscled back radiated from under his tailored suit. There was a sheen of sweat above his lips, which were pressed into a thin line as he peered across the courtyard below. He had rust-coloured stubble and dark red hair cut short and styled into something solid. The pomade's peppermint scent mingled with the adrenaline-fuelled musk of his damp armpits. He was animal instincts bundled into Armani finery and shoes so shiny they dazzled.

What was his name? Maja wondered. She was already thinking of him as 'Burly Red'. Aryanna hadn't bothered to introduce her security team. They were meant to be seen and not heard. Until they were needed. Like now.

The alarms continued their deafening squawk. Maja peered out from behind the colossal man. A couple of ground crew were running away from the gunfire that popped and whizzed past them. Several large vehicles crashed through the gate into the central courtyard below. Masked figures clad in black leaped from the vehicles, weapons cocked to shoulders.

"We're being attacked!" said Maja.

Burly Red turned to Aryanna, who stood well back by the catering bar, having poured herself another glass of water. "We need to evacuate, Madam Sharif. The evacuation team will be ready in two minutes."

Aryanna's dark eyes swivelled to consider him and glazed over for a moment. "Wait," she said, and raised a finger, the cherry red nail flashing a warning. "It's the Earth First ecoterrorists. They've seized the front gate and set up a perimeter."

"Yes, ma'am," replied Burly Red, his chest straining against his immaculate shirt. "We have your private chopper on the roof ready for evacuation."

"Maja," said Aryanna, "come with us."

Maja calmed her pounding heart with a deep, focused breath, then nodded as Aryanna crooked a finger at her. "What about the *Saturnia* crew?" Her body surged once more with panic.

"We will attend to them next, but first we need to move Madam Sharif to a more secure position," Burly Red said brusquely and headed back to the door, peering into the corridor.

Maja forced her legs to scurry after Aryanna and the bodyguard, who kept his handheld weapon drawn as they re-entered the corridor. They swept down the hallway and Burly Red swiped a pass at a door just as a masked figure rounded the corner.

"It's her!" the figure cried. "I've got Aryanna Sharif in sight!" He raised his rifle to his shoulder. "Aryanna, stay right there. You're—"

Burly Red shot the intruder before the man had finished speaking. The body slumped to the ground, and Maja felt herself crumpling in response. Burly Red grabbed her under the arm and bundled her after Aryanna, who had slipped through the doorway. He half-carried her up a narrow stairwell and through a heavy door that led to a cavernous hangar.

The room flooded with light from the open retractable roof. A chopper was already humming to life. Maja ducked instinctively as the bodyguard bustled her and Aryanna over to the chopper and hauled her inside.

Maja's hands trembled, and she had difficulty buckling into the seat harness. Burly Red brushed her hands aside with a gentleness that was surprising given the circumstances, and snugged the belt to a firm fit. He handed her a headset and offered a curt nod and faint smile before strapping himself in beside her.

"Good to go!" Burly Red said into his headset.

The pilot turned his head slightly towards his passengers and acknowledged them. "Prepare for exit under fire. Keep your heads away from the windows."

"Roger that," Burly Red replied.

The chopper rose smoothly from the floor towards the bright sunlight above. Maja always found the gain in perspective from a helicopter mesmerising, and despite the perilous situation, a small sliver of her brain registered the magical beauty as they rose above the terrain.

The chopper cleared the retractable roof and banked steeply as the snap of gunfire greeted its appearance. Maja flinched and was flung towards Burly Red as the chopper tilted away from the attackers. His bulk shielded her from the port-side window that now faced the ground, and she braced hard against the armrest so she wouldn't drape all over him.

The chopper whirled and then levelled out, and she glimpsed the skirmish below. Black figures were flooding over the Gaia buildings and had surrounded the *Saturnia* on its landing pad. Her heart lurched again as she thought of Madison, Serena and Xavier in the custody of the militants. They needed care, debriefing, careful rehab after so long on the Moon. What would the terrorists do with them?

The gunfire dwindled to distant clips and the chopper's hum filled the space like the purr of an enormous cat.

"Where are we going?" asked Maja as her nervous system settled and the adrenaline subsided.

Burly Red glanced at Aryanna sitting opposite them, with her thin legs pressed together, the twigs of her fingers smoothing the fine white silk of her trousers, the red of her nails like bloody kisses against the white fabric. Aryanna gazed back at Burly Red and gave a slight tilt of her head and a minute shrug of a slender shoulder indicating her approval.

"We're heading to Helios Haven," he said at last.

"Where's that?" asked Maja. She thought she knew all of Aryanna's headquarters.

"East of here," Burly Red answered unhelpfully.

Maja did not want to press him, but then said, "Why there?"

"Resources," Aryanna said with a twitch of her lips. "We need to meet a man in the desert."

CHAPTER THIRTEEN

"Learning to live with yourself is the hardest thing as a leader, no? Sometimes the choices we make tear apart the soul. But that's what we sign up for: to make the tough decisions so others do not have to."

—David Eriksson,
THE LUNAR CHRONICLE, FIRST PIONEERS

Dave's head rolled on his neck like a bowling ball. His helmet clanged against the console and consciousness returned in a painful struggle. His head throbbed, dangling from the strained tendons of his neck.

The ship pitched forward, and Dave opened his eyes to the disorienting sensation of being upside down. His arms were thrown towards the roof, his body held in place by the seat restraints. After three days in space and its directionless drift, to feel gravity pulling him decidedly downwards was an uncomfortable, unfamiliar sensation. Blood pooled into his head, making it difficult to think.

The *Minerva* rolled and he was flung sideways, the heavy helmet dragging his head towards the new down, the starboard side of the vessel. Dave winced as his body weight now pressed into his right side, up against the chair's armrests.

The *Minerva* bobbed and heaved again, and Dave's stomach contents with it. He had eaten nothing before the descent, so the bile that gurgled up burned his throat with a foul acid. He glimpsed Max dangling beside him.

"Max, you okay?" Dave panted.

"That's marginal. I feel a bit bashed around," Max said.

The ship tossed them upside down and then swayed back to its horizontal position.

"Holy hell!" Max said. "It feels like we're in a goddamn washing machine."

Dave threw out his arms to push himself upwards. A grunt came from the seats behind him.

"Gareth, Lester, are you two alright?" Dave said.

"A little beaten up," Gareth said. "That was the most shithouse re-entry. And you almost blew it by delaying the chute release."

Dave bristled at the jibe but shook it off. "We can analyse my flying later, no? Right now, we need to assess the ship and our egress options." Then, noting there was still a man to account for, Dave said, "Lester, are you conscious?"

"Yeah. But I'm going to vomit."

"Hold on, don't do it in your helmet! Breathe through it," Dave said.

"Can't!" Lester hurled into his helmet.

"Get that helmet off now," Dave said. "Gareth, can you assist him without unbuckling? We want to stabilise the ship before we unclip from our harnesses."

"I'll do my best," Barrio replied.

The sounds of Lester vomiting vibrated in their helmet comms. Max started gagging in sympathetic response.

"Not you too, Max King!" Dave said. "Get a grip on yourself."

"Hold on, Lester!" Gareth said as he scrambled for the helmet release lever. "Just need to unlock it." Gareth grunted and the helmet gave away. He pulled it off as Lester continued to vomit into the ship's cavity.

"Bloody hell, Lester!" Gareth said. "What did you eat before the descent? This chuck could sink the *Titanic*!"

"Give him the vomit bag to puke into now," Dave said. "Or he'll be cleaning out puke for the next three weeks from the console."

Gareth shoved the helmet back at Lester and handed him the vomit bag that was in his own armrest pocket. Lester grabbed the bag and tried to hold it under his mouth as he dangled sideways.

The ship rocked upside down again and plummeted back to its prone position. Lester's vomit flung out of the bag and splashed against the roof of the ship and then dripped between the seats as it yawned back to its side.

"Jesus effing Christ," Max said, and resumed gagging.

"Focus, King!" Dave said. "Just think how it will look on your resume if the press hears that the great Everest explorer and space-faring life support technician spewed all over himself."

"Can't help it," Max said, retching. "Puke makes me puke."

"Close your eyes and think of roses or something," Dave suggested. He studied the controls as best he could as the ship lurched. "Athena, give me a status report please."

"The ship is listing to the starboard side," the A.I. said.

"Yes, got that. Why?"

"Damage to the hull on re-entry is causing some of the unbalance. A leak in the hold is likely the other contributing factor."

"Do we have any leaks externally?" Dave asked.

"None reported on the sensors."

"Thank goodness for that! Can you raise Gaia Enterprises on the comms?"

"Hailing Gaia now."

Dave plucked at the controls, trying to decipher their ship's position in the water and its geolocation relative to the expected Gaia boat rescue.

"There is no response from Gaia Enterprises's base," Athena said.

"Where the hell are they?" Max said.

"Athena, can you triangulate our position and scan for the rescue boat, please?" Dave asked.

"Roger that," said Athena.

"The *Minerva* is at Latitude: 30.6° N, Longitude: 122.0° W. We are 372 km from our intended landing spot."

Dave blinked, face grim. "Any sign of the rescue boat or scout chopper?"

"There is an inbound helicopter, north-northeast, 200 kilometres away and closing. Expected arrival in one hour and forty minutes," Athena said.

"Can we hail that chopper on the comms?" Dave said.

"Hailing the helicopter now."

"*Minerva*, how do you read?" An unfamiliar voice sputtered over the comms channel.

"I read you loud and clear!" Dave said, as the others cheered.

"What's your status, over?"

The *Minerva* bucked and the four passengers braced themselves as it tilted one way, then another. Lester continued his retching, this time into the bag.

"We are all well, crew and passengers safe. The *Minerva* is listing to the starboard side. We are still in our launch chairs."

"Roger that. Rescue vessel won't be too far behind us. Can you hold on for a couple of hours?"

"Bloody hell!" Max said as he braced for yet another toss of the ship.

"If it's going to be a couple of hours, we will need to unbuckle and take our chances with the ship being prone," Dave said. The seat buckles dug into his side, and his neck stretched like a giraffe's with every roll.

"Roger that. The seas are pretty choppy, so put it off as long as possible."

"Will do! And who are we talking to, by the way?" Dave said.

There was an extended silence.

"Gaia support? Are you there, over?"

"Affirmative, this is Terry Reynolds."

Dave glanced at Max who shrugged his shoulders. "I don't recognise the name. Are you new here?"

"*Minerva*, we've got to shut down comms. Difficult weather inbound."

The line went silent.

"Who the hell is Terry Reynolds?" asked Max.

The ship teetered upside down again and then slammed back down. Lester groaned and gagged, his stomach finally empty.

"Don't know," Dave said, wincing as his seatbelt buckle pressed against his ribs. "I know all the pilots at Gaia, and he wasn't on the roster or on the training list."

The *Minerva* bucked once more, and they found themselves upside down and dipping to the side again. Vomit splashed over them all and Lester's helmet shot from his arms, bouncing against the roof of the ship.

"They better bloody well, hurry up!" said Max. "I can't take much more of this."

"Captain Eriksson," said Athena. "There is a breach in the hull."

"What does that mean, Athena?" Dave asked as he pushed himself away from the armrest to relieve the pressure on his ribs.

"The ship is taking on water."

A shard of fear stabbed through Dave. His pulse raced, and his head felt as if it would pop with the weight of the helmet. His mind dived through evacuation protocols.

"How long have we got?" Dave's voice was calm, despite the fear that gripped his chest and ran through his limbs.

"The vessel will submerge in ten minutes."

"Abandon ship!" Dave said. "Unclip your belts. Keep your helmets on and locked – they'll aid with buoyancy, and we will launch the lifeboat. I'll go first, as I'm closest to the floor. Gareth, you can do the same. We can help Max and Lester once we're unbuckled."

Dave wrestled with his buckle until it released, and he slumped hard against the armrest before easing himself to standing on the side of the ship, its new floor. His legs were wooden and unsteady in the gravity, made worse by the rolling pitch of the ship. He reached out to brace Max's shoulders and legs as Max released his harness. Max slid onto the floor beside him and together they helped Gareth ease Lester out of his seat. Lester collapsed on all fours, panting and pale.

"I'll grab the lifeboat," Max said.

He moved his way past Gareth and Lester to a small hutch at the back of the vessel. He wrenched it open as he steadied himself in the tossing ship. Lester's helmet rolled up against his leg and bounced away under the chairs.

Then the rocking eased.

"It's calming down out there," Gareth said.

"No, it isn't," said Dave, his face stricken. "It stopped moving because we are sinking. We need to get that portal door open now before the water prevents us from opening it." He lurched towards the escape hatch above them. "Gareth, with me!"

Dave reckoned they had only moments before the water pressure kept the door from opening. As soon as they opened the door, the water would flood in and they would have to swim against the flood to escape.

"Line up behind me," yelled Dave. "We're going to push hard as we open the door and the sea rushes in. Brace yourselves and prepare to swim fast against the current through the opening and kick as hard as you damn well can!"

Dave hit the manual release safety button. Gareth wrenched

on the lever. Together, they leaned their shoulders against the door. They had little purchase as they stood on tiptoes to reach the door. Dave scrambled to the side of Max's chair to get a bit more height. The door was heavy with the water pushing against it.

"We've got to do this super fast, Gareth! On my count. One, two, heave!"

The door creaked open and water seeped through the gap into the ship's cavity. They strained against it. Dave's heart hammered in his chest. The seawater pushed against them, and he lost his grip. The door came down on Gareth's shoulders and threatened to pin him against the doorframe where he'd wedged an arm. Max came up behind them and added his bodyweight to the door by pushing up against Gareth.

"Watch it! You're crushing me!" said Gareth.

"Come on, haul ass!" said Max.

Dark sea water flooded in, soaking their suits. It was a desperate struggle against the merciless cold black water as it slipped past them, filling the hold. They had to get the door open now, or they would be trapped in a ship half full of water, sinking to the sea floor.

"Hang on! I'm going to push you up," said Max. "Jam yourself into the opening, ready to push the door open." Max slipped under Gareth's hips as Gareth folded a knee against Max's back and pushed hard. Max grunted with the effort as Gareth drove all his weight through his legs and heaved his shoulder against the door.

Dave had resumed his perch beside him and slammed himself next to Gareth. A small gap opened, and Gareth hauled one foot and then another to brace against the door frame. With his shoulders against the door, he could now use his legs to push backwards, opening the door fully.

The sea rushed in, a ravenous beast filling every corner of the ship and licking greedily at her insides.

Dave pushed himself up and out beside Gareth, who perched

on the ship's open door, clinging to it desperately as the sea heaved around them, the sky furious, the wind howling.

Welcome back to Earth, thought Dave.

Dave peered back into the hold, which was half full now and filling fast. Max looked back up at him, alongside Lester, whose face was pale and wet. "Lester, get your helmet on right now!" cried Dave.

Lester's face lit with alarm, and he spun to hunt for his helmet in the depths.

"Max, hand me the life raft," Dave said.

Max scrambled for the floating compressed bundle of the life raft. He grabbed it and threw it up to Dave, who launched it out onto the ocean surface, pulling its inflation cord as he did so. Dave tossed the life raft's tether to Gareth, who caught it and held it precariously as the ship jerked in the tumbling waves.

It was twilight, and the sea churned around them. The ship kept dipping and flooding with more water.

"Get out now!" Dave said. "Give me your hand, Max!"

But Max was busy attending to Lester. They hunted for his helmet, lost in the dark. With his helmet off, water seeped into his suit at the collar, making it impossible for him to move. Lester's face was white, his eyes wide.

"I can't move!" he said.

"Yes, you can," said Max. "Give me your hand." He seized Lester's arm and shoved him up towards the entrance, against the flow of water filling the hold. "Step on my back. Dave and Gareth can pull you from the top."

"I can't lift my legs!" cried Lester. "Too heavy!"

Dave leaned down through the hold, reaching for Lester. He needed another foot to reach his arm.

"Max," Dave said. "You get out now. We can pull Lester out as the water fills up. He'll float closer to the entrance."

As he said it, Dave knew the momentum of the sinking ship

would pull anyone in its vicinity down with it. They had to be out and clear before it started going completely under the surface. They had just moments. Max had a chance of getting out, but Lester…

Max and Dave exchanged a look. Max sprang upwards, and Gareth and Dave hauled him up through the opening and out into the ocean beyond. Max took a couple of strokes in his big suit towards the life raft drifting nearby.

Dave turned again to the hold. "Lester, reach for my hand. Kick as much as you can!" Lester reached and tried kicking, but his suit was sodden.

"Come on, Lester!" Gareth said, and he reached down beside Dave. Two hands were just fingers' width away from him.

Max's voice floated across the sea, a yell dampened by the wind and waves. "There's only about three inches of clearance left. Jump free, or you go down with it!"

Dave reached again and grabbed Lester's gloved finger. He held on with all his might and pulled with every ounce of remaining strength. Dave's legs dangled outside the ship as he pulled against the flooding water. Gareth grabbed Lester's other hand and heaved as well. They pulled him free as the ship filled with water and started to sink.

They kicked hard against the pull of the ship towards the lifeboat, with Lester drooping between them. Dave thrashed his legs, weak against the weight of gravity, the turbulent waves and the dead weight of Lester's water-logged suit. He kicked and kicked, muscles straining, heart pounding. Even so, he could make no progress against the drag of the ship.

Dave sunk beneath the waves as he held on to Lester's hand. They were being dragged under in the ship's wake.

Dave glanced down and saw Lester, wide-eyed, face contorted, desperate to stay alive. Bubbles escaped from his cheeks, swollen with air as he held on as long as he could. Dave's eyes met Gareth's as they both struggled upwards.

But the yawning maw of the sinking ship pulled them further down.

As they sank, Dave's ears seared with pain; the water pressure increased and the inky depths of the ocean swallowed them. Dave looked once more at Lester's face. The man gulped and his eyes bulged. Lester opened his mouth, and the last of his bubbles escaped as he gasped for air and met only the cold salty kiss of the ocean.

Dave let go and kicked for the surface.

CHAPTER FOURTEEN

*"In the world of power, trust is both a weapon and a vulnerability.
It's a balancing act, where you must trust just enough to move
forward but always keep an eye on the knife behind your back."*

—Maja Garcia,
THE JOURNALS

"Athena, hail the *Minerva*," Xanthe said, and rubbed the back of her neck. She fought the anxiety that wrapped claws around her ribcage and squeezed. Her breath was shallow and strained.

"There is no response from the *Minerva*," the A.I. replied.

Jonas and Troy exchanged a look and turned to Xanthe. She held up a palm to show calm.

"Give me a moment," she said and closed her eyes to concentrate.

Athena, analyse all transactions and broadcasts from Gaia, Minerva *and* Saturnia *and give me an assessment.*

"All communication channels are blocked and locked down."

Can you access any visual information with our satellite?

"Only what we already see onscreen. The Minerva *has touched down in the ocean."*

"Can you get a closer look?"

"Not from our lunar satellite."

Xanthe chewed her thumb and frowned as she sifted through the options.

Athena, how about the Spaceward Bound satellites – the ones they launched after the Kessler effect took out all the others?

"I'll see if I can break their access codes."

Xanthe doubled over in pain and Troy leapt to her side.

"Xanthe, what is it?" he said.

"ThinkLink," she panted. "Athena is trying to hack Spaceward Bound satellites." She groaned again and Troy wrapped his arm around her waist to hold her steady.

"Athena, stop it – you are hurting her!"

Keep going, Athena. I'm okay. Just make it fast. The extra processing hurts like a bitch.

The pain stopped and Xanthe slumped against Troy.

"The encryption has too many layers. I cannot disable it without overheating the generator in the ThinkLink mechanism and damaging the brain soft tissue."

Troy helped Xanthe to sit in a chair. She propped an elbow on the console table and put her forehead into a palm, eyes closed. Jonas ran to the kitchen and came back with a bottle of water.

"Xanthe, here, have some water," he said. He nudged her and her eyes opened slowly. She took the bottle gratefully.

"Athena, find out who we do have comms with on Earth," Xanthe said. "Maybe Gaia's training centre, the Lunar Commission offices or their representatives. Someone must have some info."

"Searching now," Athena said.

While they waited, they stared at the blinking dot of the *Minerva*. It started to fade. Anxiety tightened Xanthe's ribs once more. "Athena, what is happening with the *Minerva*?"

"It's losing power."

"What does that mean?" Jonas asked.

"The ship is either powering down after contact with the retrieval vessel, or it's sinking."

No one spoke. Xanthe had an image of the *Minerva* crew, Dave, Max and their prisoners Gareth Barrio and Lester Thompson, pounding against the window of the *Minerva* as they sank slowly into the cold, black breast of the ocean depths.

"Commander Waters, we have comms with Spaceward Bound headquarters. Shall I patch them through?"

Troy scowled and Jonas bit his lower lip. Xanthe stood unsteadily and took up position in front of the main broadcast holo.

"Put them through," she said. She pulled her shoulders back and breathed deeply. Her head throbbed.

"Olympus." A dark face with a shock of blond afro filled the holo. The glower he shot her showed the whites of his eyes. An apex predator, poised for attack.

Athena, down-regulate my nervous system, please.

"Parasympathetic nervous system stimulated now."

"Leo," she replied, her voice steady.

"What the hell is going on at Gaia Headquarters, Xanthe? Where have you got Lincoln and the others?"

She dug her toes into the ground and breathed. Nose, toes, pose, she reminded herself. Breathe, anchor the toes, ground the body, stand tall and large.

"Leo, Gaia Headquarters has been attacked by Earth First eco-terrorists, as far as I can tell."

His brows shot up and his mouth fell open, all animosity swallowed by surprise.

"We have no comms with Gaia headquarters," Xanthe continued before Leo had a chance to reply. "Earth First has seized the *Saturnia* and its crew and the *Minerva* is out of contact as well, waiting retrieval in the Pacific Ocean."

Leo closed his mouth; his eyes narrowed. "What the actual hell?"

"Leo, I know this is a lot to take in," said Xanthe. "We need your help."

His brows furrowed. "Are you kidding me?" he said. "You seize my boss and the *Pinnacle* crew, send them packing back to Earth, countermanding a direct order from the Lunar Commission, and your boss, Aryanna Sharif, no less. And now they're in some kidnapping situation and you want our help? This is nuts, Commander."

Xanthe let the swell of anger rise from her toes, fill her chest and fire her cheeks red, despite Athena's attempt to douse her response. Xanthe channelled her fury, and her reply was sharp as a laser incision.

"We arrested and confined the *Pinnacle* crew, including Lincoln Ellison, because we had evidence they were attempting to illegally control the helium-3 production and distribution. As I am sure you are aware, Lincoln was attempting to set up Spaceward Bound as the monopoly on helium-3 – countermanding a direct order from the Lunar Commission.

"We looked after the *Pinnacle* crew and were returning them to face the consequences of their subterfuge. We have been stymied in our efforts by the murdering ecoterrorists who were responsible for millions of deaths, infrastructure collapse and possibly an attack on the Chinese space agency. We have no comms with the Lunar Commission, nor with Gaia."

She took a deep breath and glared at Leo through the holo. "This is your chance for Spaceward Bound to do the right thing and act as a collaborative partner in exacting a rescue and restoring the proper order of things.

"It does you no good to put the blame on me or Olympus or Gaia Enterprises. Not when Spaceward Bound caused the death of at least nine people in its cavalier asteroid mining endeavour. So, I will listen to none of your insults or attacks, Leo Malinzak. You can keep playing the victim or you can step up and be the leader that the world needs right now. Which is it going to be?"

Xanthe drew herself even taller and leaned towards Leo's holo with a fierce intensity.

He pulled back instinctively. A hand rubbed his chin as he regrouped.

"Okay," he said slowly, eyes flashing.

"Good. Both of us want the same thing. We want our crew safely back in our own hands. We want to stop the Earth First eco-terrorists from trying to take control of the helium-3 or whatever else it is they're planning."

"What do you suggest?" Leo folded his arms and cocked his head, defiant.

"You've got the only working satellites around Earth right now. Let's get eyes on the ground and figure out what's happening as a starting point."

Leo rubbed his jaw. "And what will you promise in return?"

"Are you kidding me?" said Xanthe. "You're in no position to negotiate anything given what Spaceward Bound has done."

"I think you'll find that I am in every position to negotiate. As you said yourself, Spaceward Bound is the only one with satellites. You want my help, then you give me some guarantees." He folded his arms again and waited.

Fury surged across her face, even as she felt the flood of serotonin that Athena released in response as an attempt to calm her. She gripped the console table and stared back at Leo, who remain nonplussed.

"I guarantee the safe passage of the *Pinnacle* crew into the hands of the authorities once we have them secure."

Leo huffed. "Not good enough, Commander Waters. Once we secure the crew, you must release Lincoln without charge."

"I don't have authority to do that," said Xanthe.

"You had authority enough to arrest him and remove them from the Moon. I think you will find you have the authority to release them, too," he said with a disdainful sniff.

Xanthe counted the beats of her heart: one, two, three. Nose, toes, pose.

She stood tall once more. "Alright, I agree."

Jonas and Troy stifled noises of dissent beside her. Out of view of the holo display, she waved them off.

"Get us as much information as you can from the satellites and come back to me." A flash of satisfaction crept across Leo's face. "And, Leo," Xanthe said, "Don't go off half-cocked and go behind my back. We need to do this together. You blow me off and the deal is off the table."

"Sure," he said slowly. "Spaceward Bound and Olympus in it together, just like we should've been from the start."

She ignored his jibe. "In the meantime, we will seek out the Lunar Commission and organise a rescue party."

"Understood," said Leo. His face morphed into a mask of compliance. "I will come back to you as soon as we have some information."

"Roger that, Olympus out." Xanthe shut the broadcast with an irritated flick and turned to the others.

"I can't believe you agreed to let Lincoln and the others go," said Jonas, disgust in his eyes.

"I said what I could to make sure that he did something to assist us," Xanthe said steadily.

"You trust them?" asked Troy.

"No, not at all. Leo is right. He has all the cards right now when we have no comms on the ground. If there's an opening, I am sure he will jump on any advantage."

Troy frowned and tapped a finger to his lips as he considered the various possibilities. "What is stopping them from initiating their own rescue?"

"Absolutely nothing," said Xanthe with a sigh, "which is why we need to get in touch with the Lunar Commission immediately, so they are aware of the arrangements of the situation and can keep Spaceward Bound in check."

"But we don't have contact with the Lunar Commission," said Jonas.

"We do now," said Xanthe. "Athena just told me she's managed to reach the Deputy Lunar Commissioner. He was one of the few Lunar Commission officials not present at the *Saturnia* landing. We're going to call him next." She glanced at the console display time. "In two minutes."

"I don't like this working with Spaceward Bound," said Jonas. "You don't get any more untrustworthy than that lot."

"Crisis makes unlikely allies," said Xanthe.

The incoming communication notification sounded. "Here is Vikram Chatterjee, now."

"Vikram," Xanthe said. "It's good to see you."

"Commander Waters, it is also good to see you." The man had a round, kind face like a freshly baked bun, smooth and undimpled.

"Vikram, I'm guessing you have an idea of what's going on?"

"Yes and no," he said, dipping his head with a confused look. "Arjun was attending the *Saturnia* return landing, but his phone is out of service. We can't get any communication with Gaia head-quarters. The Lunar Commission office rang me straight away to step into Aryanna's position since I am deputy."

He pulled a handkerchief from his trouser pocket and dabbed at the sweat on his upper lip. His face was shiny, adding a glaze to the bun. "This is just terrible, Commander Waters. Who would do such a thing? After all that we have suffered. These ecoterrorists must be dealt with harshly."

"I couldn't agree more," said Xanthe, "but first we need to figure out what is going on. Tell me, have you talked to any local authorities?"

"Yes, yes, yes," he said. "We have a hotline set up with the local police authorities. They have called in a negotiator, and we are attempting to establish a communication channel with the ecoterrorists."

"Any idea what they want?"

"Not yet. As of five minutes ago, we were establishing a communication protocol with the primary leader."

"Do we know who that is?" Xanthe anticipated the answer with dread.

"We believe it is Claire Edwards," Vikram said.

Her heart sank and a cold stone settled in her stomach. "I see." She needed to steer the conversation away from Claire Edwards. "Vikram, do you have any information about the *Minerva* and the rescue operation there?"

He shook his head. "We had a retrieval crew, but their comms have gone silent. We suspect they have been taken over by a wing of the Earth First terrorists."

"Any idea if either the ecoterrorists or the Lunar Commission retrieval crew managed to get the *Minerva* crew to safety?" Xanthe asked.

"Negative. We have heard nothing. It is very disconcerting." Vikram pulled out the crumpled handkerchief and rubbed it over his shining forehead.

"Okay, Vikram. Please keep me up to date with any new information and progress with the negotiations. Vikram, you should also know we have contacted Spaceward Bound and asked them to access their satellite imagery for information on both the *Saturnia* and Gaia headquarters, as well as the *Minerva*."

"You contacted Spaceward Bound?" His handkerchief froze as he reached around to mop up the sweat at the back of his neck.

"Yes. Considering they have the only operating satellites, we thought it prudent to get as much information as possible. You should know, Deputy Commissioner," she said pointedly, emphasising his title, "they have requested the release of Lincoln and the entire *Pinnacle* crew in exchange for sharing information. Leo believes I am capable of issuing a directive, even though I told him I had no such authority over Earthside jurisdictions."

Vikram's eyes darted left and right as he processed this new piece of information. "I see, I see, I see." The handkerchief did another round behind his neck, over his face and under his chin, before he stuffed it back into his trouser pocket. "We will keep that in mind as we progress."

"Thanks, Vikram. Please let us know as soon as you do know anything about what's going on. These are our friends and colleagues."

"Of course. I will give you the information as soon as we have it."

"Thank you, Vikram, and good luck with the negotiations."

"Thank you, Commander Waters. Deputy Commissioner out."

Xanthe breathed out and brought her awareness back to the tiny comms room. As the adrenaline waned, she felt small and powerless.

"What now?" asked Jonas.

"We wait," she said.

Together, they watched the fading light of the *Minerva*. And then it blinked out and was gone.

The next morning, Jonas stared at the display screens, looking for any sign of the *Minerva*. The little blinking light did not come back online.

The incoming call notification sounded in the small room and Jonas jumped, snapping out of his obsessive searching.

"Incoming call from Spaceward Bound," said Athena.

"Put them through," said Jonas.

Leo appeared on the holo. Jonas's heart leaped with anticipation. At last, some news, he hoped.

"Leo! How did you go? What have you heard about the Gaia base?" Jonas blurted.

Leo's face was dark with worry.

Jonas's heart sank. "What is it?"

"Not good. The news is not good."

Jonas took a deep breath. "Right. Let me get Xanthe and Troy."

Jonas stepped to the doorway of the comms room and shouted down the corner to the kitchen, where he knew Troy and Xanthe were having dinner.

"Hey! I've got Leo on the line with an update." He heard the chairs scrape and the heavy clomping of their moonboots as they hurried to join him at the console. Xanthe's face fell when she saw the crease in Jonas's forehead and Leo's grim features.

"Go ahead, Leo. What do you know?" asked Xanthe.

"The ecoterrorists have busted loose of the Gaia Enterprises base with the *Saturnia* crew as hostages."

"Where did they go?" Xanthe asked with a clenched jaw.

"We lost them when they hit a tunnel in Dallas. Prior to that, there was a drone patrol following them all the way. They ran through every roadblock in armoured vehicles."

"These guys are incredibly well-resourced," said Jonas quietly. "They've got some deep pockets backing them."

"What are their demands?" Xanthe said after consulting her ThinkLink.

"What else? They want a helium-3 monopoly. They want the Lunar Commission to sign over helium-3 governance to Earth First, along with all its infrastructure."

"As if!" said Jonas. "That's outrageous."

"They're holding the *Saturnia* and presumably the *Minerva* crew as collateral?"

"Yes. The crew is their bargaining chip."

"That's hardly going to work long term," said Xanthe. "I don't think they've really thought this through."

"Who knows," said Leo. "But at the moment, they've got my team and your team, and we don't know where they've gone. They must've had some sort of escape vehicle in the tunnel. Or some other means of getting out of that tunnel that we couldn't track."

"What about the Gaia base?" asked Troy.

"They have that locked down, too," said Leo. "They left a large contingency guarding the base, and two vans hightailed it out of there once they secured the *Saturnia* team. They've got the Lunar Commissioners as hostages too, by the way."

"And there's no news from Aryanna or any of the Lunar Commissioners who were watching the *Saturnia* landing?"

"Correct. So that leaves us and Deputy Vikram responding to the situation, in conjunction with local and federal forces."

"So, we're no further ahead," Jonas said, blowing out his cheeks.

"We've got nothing until we know where Earth First has taken them. And until we know what Deputy Vikram negotiates," Leo said.

Jonas glanced at Troy and Xanthe. Their faces were as pale and drawn as his own. Jonas struggled to know what to do next. It seemed they had reached the end of their influence. The *Minerva* and *Saturnia* crews were kidnapped and ransomed; the Lunar Commissioners were non-contactable. But the Indians were sending help. That was something. And they still had control of the helium-3. But he still felt sick to the stomach.

"What do we do, Xanthe?" asked Jonas quietly.

Her eyes were glazed over as she consulted the ThinkLink, then she focused again.

"We wait," she said in a steely tone. "We watch, and we wait."

Xanthe left the call with Leo at Spaceward Bound and excused herself for a walk around the base. She needed space to think.

She went first to the Atrium's airlock to catch a glimpse of the barren lunar landscape, its desolation a stark contrast to the plant-filled corridors of the Olympus Moonbase. The Earth hung in the black sky, a blue orb swirling with white clouds, a distant reminder of a life once lived, of decisions made and paths taken that had led her here, to this moment of solitude and introspection.

She needed to let go of the current issues and let her imagination spark a creative path forward. Sometimes working a problem only worked the problem, not the solution. Letting the mind meander allowed the driftwood of ideas to land on some distant shore as yet unexplored.

Her mind wandered back to the days when she was a paramedic, racing against time to save lives on Earth. Those were days filled with raw, immediate challenges, where her decisions had tangible, life-altering consequences. Yet, even in the chaos, there was a simplicity, a clarity she sometimes longed for in the complex web of responsibilities she now shouldered.

Xanthe sighed, her breath fogging the cold glass before her. Her reflection, a silhouette against the stark moonscape, seemed to merge with the shadows. She had left Earth, left behind a life that included her son, Jack, whom she had believed lost to her, swallowed by the cruel maw of a tsunami.

Discovering his survival years later, only just recently while they were here on the Moon, had been a bittersweet revelation, opening old wounds even as it brought an unexpected joy. The joy of knowing he was alive, yet the pain of the years lost, the moments missed.

Her thoughts shifted to Simon, her ex-husband, a staunch Earth Alliance advocate. Their marriage had crumbled under the weight of her decision to join the Olympus project. It was a choice that had seemed so clear, then, driven by a desire to contribute to something ground-breaking, something that transcended personal ambitions – a venture that promised a new dawn for humanity.

But at what cost?

The cost of her marriage, the distance from her son, was a price she had paid, willingly at the time, but not without a lingering shadow of doubt.

Now, as she stood in command of the Moonbase, Xanthe felt the weight of her responsibilities more than ever. The base was a testament to human ingenuity and collaboration, a far cry from her days of designing Earthbound worlds with Gaia Enterprises. Yet, beneath the surface of day-to-day operations, there were undercurrents of power and control that troubled her.

Aryanna Sharif's recent moves were a puzzle, pieces that didn't quite fit the image Xanthe had of the Lunar Commission. Aryanna's ambition seemed to be veering off the course of collaborative exploration and into the realm of command and control: the very antithesis of what the Olympus project was meant to stand for.

Why? What was Aryanna's endgame? Was she really behind the Chinese taikonaut catastrophe? Or was it Earth First? And who was funding Earth First? They seemed to have a lot of insider knowledge and plenty of resources.

And where the hell were the *Saturnia* and *Minerva* crew? Worry for her colleagues and friends churned her insides. She grimaced and rubbed her abdomen to ease the tension.

"Xanthe, your cortisol levels are high," Athena said.

No kidding, Athena. There's a lot going on.

"I suggest some L-theanine and melatonin to soothe your nervous system."

Good idea.

Xanthe turned and made her way to the medbay for the supplements. She grabbed the tablets from Troy's supply cupboard and washed them down with a sip of water from the dispensary. She sighed.

I'm so angry with all of this, Athena.

"How so?" the A.I. asked.

She sighed again.

I'm angry with Lincoln and Spaceward Bound for their recklessness and arrogance. I'm angry with the Chinese leader threatening to bring weapons to the Moon. And Aryanna for doing the same. I'm angry that nine astronauts died in a stupid, preventable accident. I'm angry Earth First has kidnapped our people. Mostly, I'm angry that people couldn't just, well, be better.

"It's reasonable to have strong emotions with those circumstances. What matters though is not how we feel but how we act. We must not let our shadow guide our actions."

Now you're sounding a lot like Troy, Athena! He's always going on about our shadow self.

Xanthe made her way to her personal room, clomping in moonboots down the underground corridors that hummed with the life support system. The plants crammed the corridors, growing happily in the well-lit regolith tunnels. She slid open the door to her bedroom. Her body ached in anticipation of rest.

Right now, I feel like I could punch someone, I'm that angry. Can you help me manage my shadow? Stop me from acting from a more primal, darker side?

"Yes, I can do that. I am programmed to protect you from harm as best I can. That can include highlighting a response or reaction that is more shadow than light."

Good. I am going to need all the help I can get with all these power games. That will be all for tonight, Athena.

"Goodnight, Xanthe. Powering down now."

Xanthe slipped into her pyjamas and slid into bed.

Power.

The word echoed in her mind. It was a concept she had always associated with responsibility, with the duty to serve and protect. Yet, in Aryanna's hands, it seemed to have morphed into something else, something more akin to domination. Power appeared to have evaded Aryanna this time, though, slipping from her fingers like a fumbled football.

None of this made sense.

Sure, it was about greed and control of the helium-3, but there were more amenable diplomatic ways to gain control without resorting to murder, kidnapping and political intrigue. Was there something she was missing? A piece of the puzzle that was hidden from her view?

Xanthe shook her hands, rolled her shoulders and wriggled her legs against her bedding, hoping to reset her thoughts.

This is all so damned hard.

She had the sudden urge to curl into a ball and hide under the blanket. Leave the issues for another day, for another leader. Xanthe longed for relief. Something to look forward to.

Jack! She would call Jack in the morning. She smiled at the thought of her adult son – so like his father in many ways, and yet with her determination and independent spirit. He was wise beyond his nineteen years. Maybe he had an idea that could help. The young so often saw things more plainly without the veils and corruption of age.

Xanthe's thoughts returned to Earth, tinged with a sense of unease. Power, leadership, responsibility – the lines blurred. With the hum of the base lulling her to sleep, she pondered these questions, knowing that the decisions she would make in the coming days would shape not just her fate but that of her friends, of the Moon and, perhaps, of Earth itself.

CHAPTER FIFTEEN

"Sometimes I wondered what I had gotten myself into. I just wanted to fly, to go to space. But it was all so much more than that. I got pulled into a fight I hadn't signed up for, and it wasn't until much later I figured out just what that fight really was."

—Madison Floyd,
MEMOIRS FROM MARS

Madison rocked in the landing chair, straining against the chair harness and and waist belt as her mind parsed the new scenario: the base was under siege by ecoterrorists.

She had recognised that last voice: Claire Edwards, the former chief operating officer at Gaia Enterprises. Claire had been the biggest hard ass during selection. She was relentless and ruthless in pursuit of the best candidates. Madison had admired that about her. Claire's serious nature reflected her demand for high standards.

After Madison's exit from the project, she had only heard snippets about Claire's fall from grace. The Olympus crew had given her some details about how exacting and demanding she had been during the prototype build, then something had snapped.

Towards the end of the tender bid, Claire had allegedly given

Maja Garcia, Gaia Enterprises's CEO, an overdose of one of Troy Bruin's relaxation teas, all to gain control of Gaia. She ultimately failed as her subterfuge was discovered by Aryanna Sharif, who ousted her, pronto.

There was a trial, but she was released on lack of evidence. Then Claire had disappeared and gone under the radar, only to pop up with links to the Earth First ecoterrorist group. And now here she was, on the other end of her landing comms, apparently in charge.

Alarm shot through Madison's spine, and she took a few steadying breaths to process the situation on the *Saturnia*. Xavier had been reinjured and needed attention. Madison tried the comms again.

"Gaia Enterprises HQ, Fitzgerald – or Claire Edwards, if that's you – we need medical assistance for Xavier Consus, immediately. Please respond, over."

"*Saturnia*, this is Fitzgerald. You will proceed with egress procedures. Our crew will direct you, once you exit. Please be aware that we are armed, and you will need to obey our orders."

Serena's face was aghast, and Madison clenched her jaw. She turned to her Spaceward Bound passengers-cum-prisoners, Lincoln Ellison, Freddy and Snyder. "Do you know any of these people?" asked Madison, suspicion spicing her words.

Lincoln's face was blank. "Nope. Looks like you've got some competition for surprise manoeuvres."

"I think it's in our best interest to comply with their directions," said Madison.

"One jailor is as good as another, I suppose." Lincoln waved his hand breezily. "We'll see if Earth First has a better sense of justice than Gaia Enterprises."

"Who are you to talk of justice?" Serena barked. "You're here because you wanted control of the helium-3 all for yourself."

Lincoln rolled his eyes. "Think of me what you will, Serena Fox. Spaceward Bound has the means of delivering helium-3 globally. We are a well-resourced production company. We can get this cleaner energy out to the world faster than any other player."

"Then why not negotiate with the Lunar Commission? Why steal from them?" Serena persisted.

"Who said I didn't? Why do you think Aryanna sent me to the Moon to establish the mining operations?"

"You're full of shit, Ellison," said Serena.

"And you're naïve, Fox," he said.

"Enough!" Madison shouted at them.

Serena and Lincoln stopped bickering and paid attention. Mr Puffkins, who was still in his landing sling, in his space dog suit, growled and yipped at the raised voices. Lincoln put out his gloved hand to pat and reassure the animal.

"We've got a situation here that requires cool heads," Madison said with a more even tone. "It sounds like Gaia Enterprises has been compromised and we are now under siege. Our choices are to remain as we are and negotiate safe passage or comply with their demands.

"Normally I would advocate negotiation because while we are here, we still have leverage. But Xavier's condition compromises that. As captain of the ship, my decision is that we exit, follow whatever directions they give us and make sure Xavier gets looked after. We can reassess our options once we're out of here."

A realisation dawned on Serena. "We've got nothing to negotiate with," she said. "The helium-3 is still on the Moon. Earth First doesn't want us or Lincoln."

"But they will want our ship, and they will want a pilot," said Madison.

"You're right on one count," Lincoln said as he unbuckled from his seat and stood gingerly, testing his legs against the gravity. "We don't have anything to leverage. *We* are the leverage. The Lunar Commission, or whoever is out there, will want to make sure we go unharmed. I put full faith in my team."

"What can your team do while headquarters is under siege?" asked Serena as she released her buckle and pushed herself to standing with a grunt.

"We've got something that everyone needs."

"Unshakeable ego and relentless self interest?" quipped Serena.

"We've got satellites. The only working ones."

CHAPTER SIXTEEN

"People are complex. I used to put them in buckets, like the 'good'
bucket, or the 'ambitious' bucket, or plain ole 'crazy' bucket.
But I've worked out we all fit in one big bucket: 'messy'."

—MADISON FLOYD,
MEMOIRS FROM MARS

MADISON UNCLIPPED HER chair harness and waist belt and moved on shaky legs past Freddy, Snyder and Lincoln to check on Xavier, who was conscious but pale and sweaty. He gave her a thin smile.

"How bad is it, Xavier?" she asked.

"*Putain de merde!*" he exclaimed. "*C'est chiant.*"

"That bad, huh?"

"My leg is bashed, and I think it is broken again in many places."

Madison inspected his leg and the blood seeping through the compression bandages. She checked his suit's biometric readings. Bounding pulse, increased respiration.

"Serena, grab the med kit and give Xavier some pain meds."

Serena stumbled to the ship's small cabinet and returned with a canister.

"Here you go, Xavier," Serena said. She clipped the canister to his oxygen line. "Dial this up whenever the pain comes. Once we get out of this tin can, hopefully we can get some meds and treatment in the medbay. Assuming these assholes will give us access."

"I'm telling you, it's in their best interest," Lincoln said. Having retrieved the dog from its sling, he was now cuddling Mr Puffkins through its space bag carrier.

Serena whirled on him. "You seem to know an awful lot about these ecoterrorists. How is that?" Her eyes narrowed.

He threw an arm up. "Don't get ahead of yourself, Fox. I know I'm a valuable piece to be traded. And enough people want to see the Olympus team alive and well that I'm sure they will look after us. It does not serve their goals to let any harm come to us."

"Are you always so clinical about human lives?" Serena said. "Oh yeah, that's right, your cavalier approach to space operations and safety led to the death of nine people. Oops."

Lincoln's face hardened, but he said nothing.

"Enough," said Madison, exasperated. Mr Puffkins yipped again, the sound muted through his spacesuit. "This bickering will not help us. Like it or not, we are in this together. I need you all to shut the hell up and listen to instructions. Lincoln, can you keep your guys in line?"

"Not a problem. Can you keep your two in line?" he shot back at her.

Madison ignored him, then turned to Xavier and Serena. "Serena, look after Xavier. I'll go first through the exit. When it's safe, I'll signal the rest of you on helmet comms."

Madison took a steadying breath and returned to the comms panel. "Fitzgerald, or whoever is tuned in out there, be advised we are opening the hatch."

"Roger that, *Saturnia*. Please note that our team is armed and ready to receive you."

Madison pressed the hatch release button, and the door hissed and slid open. Even with the helmets still on, the sunlight was a slap to the face. She blinked to adjust her eyesight, then scanned their surroundings.

The team – she wasn't sure if it was the Gaia crew or the hijackers – had put a ramp up to the exit, as per protocol. At the bottom of the ramp, in a semicircle, with automatic rifles trained on her, stood a dozen masked individuals. She also recognised the Gaia facilities crew. They look strained but otherwise unharmed.

Madison raised her hands instinctively in a surrender motion. She raised a finger in a 'wait a minute' signal, then motioned towards the ship.

One of the crew came up the ramp slowly to greet her. He grabbed her arm to support her.

"Doctor Mohammed!" she said with a beaming smile.

"Hello, Captain Floyd. It's a relief to see you." The doctor moved with quick, nimble steps to her side, his medical uniform starched and pressed, as was his usual fastidious attention to proper presentation.

"We need to get medical attention to Xavier Consus, immediately," Madison said as Mohammed slipped an arm round her waist to aid her in walking in Earth's gravity for the first time in a year.

"We're ready. They've allowed our medical response team to assist."

"I see them now."

Paramedics with a gurney moved behind the line of armed insurgents. Half a dozen Gaia operatives passed them on the ramp to reach Lincoln and the others. The paramedic crew went last.

"I'm going to signal the others to follow me over the helmet comms," she said to Mohammed.

"Just keep moving slowly," he said in a strained voice.

"Serena, Lincoln, Snyder, Freddy, come on out," Madison said. "The paramedic team is coming up the ramp to get Xavier now."

Madison's heart raced and she struggled to breathe. Gravity was a lot harder than she remembered. Her head pounded.

Yelling and a sudden commotion among the insurgents stopped Mohammed and Madison as they laboured down the ramp.

"It's the feds!" one of them shouted. "Take out their vehicle, now!"

Rifles trained on an approaching vehicle and hammered it with shots. A helicopter whirred above the *Saturnia*; a handful of insurgents ran to a new position and levelled their guns in its direction, firing wildly.

An explosion shattered the windows of a nearby building. Madison fell to the ground. Gunfire erupted all around them. One of the paramedics who had just run past her screamed and clutched his leg, rolling off the ramp and landing badly on the ground below.

Hands grabbed her, dragging her off the ramp. Madison caught a glimpse of the crew behind. Lincoln had Mr Puffkins in his arms and ran towards her in a crouch with Serena fast behind him, one gloved hand on his suit as a guide.

Freddy appeared at the exit followed by Snyder. Another round of shots blasted their position. Madison saw Snyder and Freddy shake like marionettes as bullets riddled their suits and then they toppled forward over the rail of the ramp.

"Stop firing, you idiots!" the same commanding voice bawled. "You've taken out two of the astronauts. Just get out of here. We'll handle this."

The assailants shoved Madison, Lincoln and Serena into a waiting van with a jumble of shouts and menaces.

Just before they slammed the door, Madison saw Xavier being dragged screaming into another van that raced off across the landing platform.

"That's not towards the medical facility," she said. "Hey, where are they taking him?" she shouted at one of the kidnappers.

"Quiet!" one of them replied, a short stubby man with a puffed-up chest made bigger by the military grade protective suit.

She locked eyes with him, but all she got was a cold, hard look.

They hurtled away and Madison had to grip the armrest of the van to keep from being flung into the aisle. She pulled the buckle over her shoulder and locked it in place, the others following suit. Serena's face was now more frightened than belligerent, Lincoln's alert and focused, as he gripped his dog in the space bag.

The armed personnel sat up front, glancing back at them with wary eyes.

"Where the hell are you taking us?" said Madison.

"Be quiet," the man snapped.

Madison gripped the headrest of the chair in front of her as they veered around a corner and smashed through a barrier. She heard whirring helicopter blades, sirens and the full throttle of the accelerating van.

Somewhere behind them she heard more gunfire.

Then they were in a tunnel. The driver slammed on the brakes, shot out of the vehicle and flung the van door wide. His accomplice trained a rifle on them and shouted through his mask.

"Out, now!"

They fumbled with seatbelts and tumbled from the van, legs wobbly. More armed men grabbed the astronauts under the arms, dragging them along and through a door in the tunnel.

Madison's senses spun with the smell of oil, exhaust and damp. A quiet corner of her mind realised there must be a breach in her helmet.

My first breath of Earth in over a year and it stinks like a garage.

The kidnappers hustled them along, half dragging them. The tunnel they had entered was dim and dank. The kidnappers bundled them through another door and into a waiting vehicle, this time with no windows.

An armoured vehicle of some sort, Madison thought.

The three of them sat on the ground in the back of the vehicle and rolled into one another as it surged away. Mr Puffkins yipped and whimpered as Lincoln clutched the small bundle, still in his space bag.

Gradually the vehicle slowed, its movements were less jarring, and it settled into what felt like highway driving. Madison realised she still had her helmet on, as did the others. Just as she wondered if she should remove it, Serena pulled her own helmet free and took a big, deep breath.

"Ah, the sweet smell of atmosphere! Welcome home, I suppose," she said and burst into tears.

Madison had no words of comfort for Serena. For months she had been longing for Earth, working through each perilous day on the Moon, knowing that it brought her closer to home.

She was done with space. It had been a grand adventure, sure, but it had been harrowing. More harrowing than any battlefield she had faced in her time in the military. Now she just wanted to visit her mom and watch the birds in the park. But here she was, back on Earth, and instead of enjoying fanfare and celebration, she was a captive in peril.

Madison stewed in her dark thoughts while Serena's emotions stabilised, the shock wearing off. The truck rumbled on. Madison's face grew angry once more as she processed what had just happened. "Those assholes killed Snyder and Freddy. I mean, I was never a fan of those insolent sneaks, but they didn't deserve to die."

She pulled the space liner's skull cap from her head and ran a hand through her lanky hair. "And they've stolen Xavier. Chances are he's dead, too."

Lincoln's head drooped and Madison noticed a sense of remorse she had never seen on the man before. Madison didn't reply to Serena, either, the grim reality of their situation swallowing her thoughts.

"Where the hell are these cocksuckers taking us?" asked Serena.

"We've been traveling north for about an hour and a half," said Madison.

Serena looked at her. "How do you know that?"

"The compass on my suit watch."

"Oh yeah," Serena said with annoyance. "I forgot that a compass actually works on Earth."

The truck rolled to a stop and there was the crunch of footsteps on gravel. The kidnappers swung the doors open, the metal groaning, and daylight surged in. The light burned their eyes and Madison squinted, shielding her face with her forearm.

Gun barrels greeted them, the owners still masked.

"Get out. Now." The voice was southern American, thought Madison. Texan, most likely.

They shuffled to the edge of the vehicle. Madison moved her legs over the side and looked apprehensively at the small jump to the ground. "Not sure my legs are going to hold with that jump."

The personnel glanced at each other and then moved to assist her, guns tucked to the side while they reached forward and dragged her out of the vehicle, hands under her armpits.

"Thanks. How gentlemanly of you," Serena muttered as they pulled her from the truck after Madison. She scooped up Mr Puffkins, who hadn't stopped yelping since they stopped.

"It's okay, Puffkins," she said, cuddling the dog. "These nasty people know not to mess with an attack beast like you."

The masked men led them into an enormous empty warehouse. There was a collection of cheap green plastic chairs in the corner. Next to this circle of seats was a fountain of electrical cords that sprouted from a power point, connecting a small space heater, fridge and a kettle propped on a fold-out table.

The rest of the space was empty apart from a section that was walled off to the left. A tub of dirty dishes sat next to a grimy stand-up basin with a faucet. This was next to a cubicle with a toilet sign pinned to its door. The kidnappers gestured for them to take a seat in the crappy chairs. Two guards stayed as sentries while the others headed to the private area.

Mr Puffkins barked and wriggled in Serena's arms.

"Keep that mutt under control," one of the guards warned her.

"He probably needs to pee," Lincoln said. "Space is a little challenging for dogs, and the landing process has been less than ideal," he added pointedly.

"Take him outside, then, to do his business," the guard grunted to Serena.

"I'll need some help," she said. "My Earth legs are still wobbly."

The guard rolled his eyes, slung his gun around his back and held his arm out to her. They shuffled back outside for a few minutes.

Madison sank into the chair, grateful to be off her feet as even that short distance left her struggling. The heat was oppressive. After a year in controlled atmosphere, the hot winds of a baking Earth were scalding.

Lincoln hobbled past her and slumped heavily on a chair, keeping a concerned eye on Mr Puffkins and Serena all the while. Voices called out from the corner of the private area as Serena returned with Mr Puffkins, who barked excitedly and scurried over to Lincoln.

"Yes, baby," Lincoln said. "Daddy will look after you, now."

Madison looked over her shoulder as a new figure approached.

"So, here you are, Moon rats." The figure strode in, a woman dressed in military fatigues, her thin frame bulked up by the combat armour. Her skin was sallow, but her eyes were bright, noted Madison. She knew that face. Times had been tough for this woman.

"Claire," said Madison, her mouth dragging down and pulling the words out as if clearing her throat.

"Good to see you alive."

"I never knew you cared," said Serena.

"Fox." Her eyes hardened on Serena. "I never liked you. You were never my first choice. Maja pushed that decision through."

Serena's face twisted with anger and Madison put a hand on her shoulder just as she was about to retort.

"Not worth it," Madison whispered.

Serena snapped her mouth shut and glared at Claire, who only smirked back at her.

"Time to let bygones be bygones, Serena. We've got new things to deal with. Things far more important than a popularity contest." Claire cocked her head as she looked at the weary group before her. "The medical team will check you out and start the return-to-Earth physiotherapy protocols."

Madison lifted her eyebrows at that.

"That's right, Mad Dog," Claire said, precisely enunciating the nickname. "I intend to keep you fit and well. You are no good to me if you fade away."

"Three out of six ain't bad. Isn't that right, Claire?" Serena spat.

Claire's face swelled with fury and bitterness.

"That gun battle was not our fault. It was never our intention to harm anyone."

"Claire Edwards," said Lincoln. "I don't believe we've had the pleasure." He stood unsteadily and offered a hand to shake.

"Spare me the false charm, Ellison. The only pleasure you ever seek is the one that lines your pockets and serves your interests."

Lincoln balked, dropped his hand and sat down again.

"You'll be staying here until further notice," continued Claire. "These are your quarters. We're bringing in cots, so you'll have somewhere to sleep. You'll be under strict supervision, needless to say. If Gaia Enterprises has any sense, this will be a short experience."

"What's your endgame, Claire?" Madison asked.

"My endgame? My agenda is what it's always been," said Claire. "To save the Earth. And humanity."

"There are better ways to do it than blow up a space agency and kidnap astronauts," said Serena.

"Drastic times, drastic measures," replied Claire. "And I don't need to explain myself to you, Fox."

"Maybe not. But there will be a reckoning," said Serena.

"I'm counting on it," Claire said. She walked closer to the group and inspected each one of them in turn. She lingered a little longer in front of Madison, who held her gaze.

"Glad you finally got the gig, Mad Dog. That traitor Dave Eriksson wasn't my first pick, either. You should've been on the project from day one."

Madison pressed her lips together. She hadn't known the decision to choose Dave Eriksson was not unanimous among the Gaia directors. She'd always assumed that her failed claustrophobia test during selection was what had scuppered her chances on the team. Though she appreciated the vote of confidence, this was Claire Edwards, and Madison wasn't sure how she felt about having an ecoterrorist as an advocate.

Madison kept her face stoic and Claire continued. "That's it for now. Doctor Gurney will be here shortly." She turned to go.

"Hang on a minute," Serena said. "Where is Xavier?"

"Xavier is receiving medical attention," Claire said flatly.

Something in her voice made Madison scrutinise her face for any sign of duplicity.

"You haven't killed him off?" Serena said.

Madison put a hand on her arm and Serena flashed her an apologetic look.

Claire waited a moment, staring at Serena, before a cold smile curled her lips. "Unlike you, I actually like Xavier. He's done more for the future of humanity than you lot combined with his Terra Verdi project. Besides, he's more useful for the cause alive than dead. So, no, I haven't 'killed him off'. We are taking good care of him. Just like we will take good care of you. And your little dog too."

Mr Puffkins panted, tongue out, sitting at Lincoln's feet.

They watched her walk back to the door to the walled off area, speak briefly to the guard there and disappear.

"Jesus effin' Christ," Serena said. "What a completely deranged asshole!"

"We're up to our eyeballs in assholes," muttered Madison.

Lincoln laughed at that. "Come now, Mad Dog," he said. "Surely now's the time we make friends?"

"What? And like, 'the enemy of my enemy is my friend' sort of thing?" Serena asked, dubious.

"Something like that," he said, scratching Mr Puffkins's chin.

"I'm not sure I'll countenance 'friends', Lincoln," Madison said.

Lincoln looked disappointed. His charm had collapsed twice in just a few minutes, and he wasn't used to that kind of failure rate.

"I'll settle for an ally, though," Madison added. "Lincoln, you're a reckless, selfish turd." He scowled. "But if we're going to get out of this sooner rather than later, we're going to need to band together. Deal?"

He considered her carefully. "I'll live with that."

"Good. It's about the only way we stay alive. We need to work together, gather intel about this place and see what kind of leverage we have."

"That, or we make a run for it," said Serena.

"We're not running anytime soon," Lincoln said. "My heart is racing just sitting in this chair. And by God it's hot as Hades." He wiped his forehead with his space glove.

"We may not have to run that far," Serena said with a sly expression. She pulled her chair closer to Madison and Lincoln did the same. Serena glanced casually over her shoulder to check on the guards who were chatting in the doorway of the mysterious private enclave.

"Mad Dog, can you fly a helicopter?" Serena asked.

Madison nodded. "Yes, I can. Why?"

"When I was outside with Puffy, I saw an enormous landing pad in the middle of this place. My bet is that they bring supplies in by chopper. It would be faster than by land and harder to track."

"You are a sly one, Serena. Fox by name, Fox by nature," said Lincoln.

"Very punny, Ellison," she said. Madison could tell she was pleased at the compliment, even if it came from Lincoln.

"That's good intel, Serena," Madison said. "Our escape operation is off to a good start."

"And what should we call this op?" asked Lincoln. "Wait, I've got it – Operation Foxhole." He laughed while Serena and Madison shot him a disgusted look.

They sat quietly for a while, their minds now bent on what they might name their rebellion.

"How about 'Olympus Rising'?" Serena suggested.

"Not bad," said Lincoln, "but it's a little Gaia Enterprises-centric, not really inclusive of Spaceward Bound's contribution."

"Spaceward Bound's 'contribution' has been a lot more damaging than contributing so far," Serena retorted. "Consider this a gesture of goodwill to include you in our escape plans."

"Alright, alright," he conceded. "Olympus Rising it is."

CHAPTER SEVENTEEN

—DAVID ERIKSSON,
THE LUNAR CHRONICLE, FIRST PIONEERS

THE LIFE RAFT bucked with the churn of the waves. Dave, Gareth
and Max huddled under the tarp, helmets and gloves still on, pro-
tecting them from the elements. It was pitch black, except for the
glow of their helmet lights and the flash of the raft's emergency
beacon.

They were waterlogged spectres, grim with the precariousness
of their situation, and the loss of Lester.

Gareth hadn't stopped staring at Dave.

"What is it, Barrio?" Dave asked finally, the wind howling
around them.

"You let him go." Barrio's voice was dark and icy on the helmet
comms.

Dave steadied himself as the raft pitched again and they were washed with sea water. He grabbed the bailer and scooped the water out as the wind whistled around them. He peeked out from under the tarp, emptied the bailer and reached down under the tarp to scoop quickly before ducking back under the tarp.

"You let him go! You hear me, Eriksson?" Barrio shoved Dave against the raft. "Lester's dead because of you."

Dave pulled away from Barrio and threw the bailer to the bottom of the raft. He pulled his knees up to his chest and looked down at his boots. Yet again, he was being accused of betrayal. This time it was unfair, and a righteous indignation swamped him with the roll of the raft.

Dave looked at Barrio, his face grieving and hard. "No one killed Lester. He drowned because his suit filled with water, and we, the two of us"—he waved a finger between himself and Gareth—"could not hold the weight."

"I still had him. He had a chance."

"No, he didn't. He was too heavy." Dave's heart filled with pity. "You know it. Blaming me is not going to bring him back. I didn't want him to die, either. We've seen enough death, no?"

Gareth's eyes were shiny, then he looked away.

"That's space," said Max. "It's an extreme environment, like Everest. We know landings are the riskiest part of the job. We all signed up for that. We know the risks. We try hard not to have accidents, but sometimes they happen. No one likes to see anyone die."

Gareth considered Max and his face hardened again.

"How many did you walk by?" asked Gareth bitterly.

"What do you mean?" asked Dave.

"He's been up Everest five times." Gareth lifted the gloved fingers of his right hand. "There were storms during some of those expeditions. I know people died, and plenty of mountaineers walked past the dying. Those people were still alive when people walked right over them on the way to the summit, and back down again."

He turned back to Max. "So, how many did you walk past?"

The tension stretched taut as the raft pitched and rolled. The sea flung them back against the raft, but still Max stared right back at Gareth.

"Three," Max said. He leaned towards Gareth. "And I would walk past every single one of them again. If I hadn't, there would be four bodies up there, not just three. No point helping someone if you're going to die as well."

"Well, there are three bodies in this raft," said Dave. "And my intention is that they all stay alive. That chopper should be here soon. So, if we can avoid killing each other, that would be ideal."

Like boxers returning to the sanctuary of their ringside corners, they each sunk into their thoughts.

CHAPTER EIGHTEEN

*"We would do better as a species if we saw more of what
we had in common than what sets us apart, no?"*

—David Eriksson,
THE LUNAR CHRONICLE, FIRST PIONEERS

Dave strained his ears as the wind whipped around them. Faint
and in the distance was the whir of a chopper, he felt certain. The
others heard it too and perked up. The sound grew louder until a
search beam flashed and then locked onto their position.

They cheered. They emerged from under the tarp and could
just make out a figure being lowered on a rope. The wind swung the
figure overhead, and Dave stood to secure the rope as it flew past
him. A man in a full diving wetsuit landed in the raft and shouted
instructions.

One by one, the rescuer clipped them into a harness attached
to the rope and lifted them to the safety of the helicopter. Dave
insisted the other two go first; once they were safe, he ascended in
tandem with the rescuer.

Once they were secure in the chopper, their rescuers helped
remove the helmets, and the sound of the chopper hammered their

"

senses along with the rage of the wind. The rescuer, a heavyset man with gnarled fingers, handed out headsets and they put them on gratefully.

"Welcome back to Earth! Where is the fourth passenger?" asked the pilot over the headsets.

Dave hung his head for a moment, then lifted it. As the captain of the *Minerva*, it was his role to report. "He didn't make it. He got pulled down when the *Minerva* sank."

The pilot processed this information, then said, "Roger. I recognise Max King, Captain Dave Eriksson, and this must be Gareth Barrio."

"*Captain* Gareth Barrio of the *Pinnacle*, Spaceward Bound," he said.

"Got it. I'm Terry Reynolds. And your friendly neighbourhood rescue operative is Jared."

"I don't recognise the two of you," said Dave. "Are you new to Gaia Enterprises?"

"That would be negative," replied Terry. "We are on a mission from Earth First."

"What the hell?" demanded Max.

"Where are we going?" Dave asked.

"To Earth First's private sanctuary," said Terry.

"I'm lost and not following," said Dave.

"It's a kidnapping, you fool," said Gareth. "We're prisoners."

Max and Dave stared at Gareth as their new reality sank in.

"So, what's the price for our release?" Gareth asked.

"That detail is beyond the scope of my assignment. Sorry, gentlemen. You can ask the boss when we get there."

"And who is the boss?" asked Dave.

"That would be Claire Edwards. I believe you know her."

"Claire!" exclaimed Dave and his face went pale.

The last time he had seen Claire was when the authorities arrested her on suspicion of poisoning Maja. He remembered the deep sense of satisfaction at her demise, as she had nothing but venom for him. Not that he could blame her entirely, as he had betrayed the Olympus crew. Of course, he'd had good reason to, and he regretted it every day. But good intentions rarely compensated for poor outcomes.

Max and Dave exchanged glances. They'd survived the *Minerva* and losing one of their passengers. Would they survive whatever plan Claire had in mind?

They flew through the storm, buffeted by the wind, until eventually the lights of the west coast twinkled on the horizon.

Despite the harrowing circumstances, Dave took a moment to appreciate being back on Earth. Wind, water, civilisation. He noticed how heavy his limbs felt, and how his heart rate was elevated. The adrenaline of the last several hours had well and truly worn off and deep fatigue was taking possession of his body. They were home, though. Sort of.

With only a narrow view through the pilot's windscreen, it was difficult to tell where they were. Dave guessed they were somewhere over the southern states, judging by how long they had been flying and the eastern trajectory he had followed on his suit's wrist compass. They seemed to be approaching a rural area with plenty of forests and not much else.

Soon, the chopper descended and bumped to an easy landing.

"Home sweet home," said Terry. "The greeting party will be here soon. Just follow their instructions and you'll be fine."

Max, Gareth and Dave swapped looks but said nothing. Dave had no illusion that the greeting party would be friendly, especially not under Claire's direction. Warmth and hospitality were not her strengths. If she was running the ecoterrorist faction, Dave expected a tight operation. Certainly, with no niceties. And definitely not for him.

The prospect was not the least bit enticing.

Jared, still in his rescue garb, removed his headphones and gestured for them to do the same.

"Follow me and don't diverge from the path, or the chopper blades will get ya."

Dave and the others lined up behind him and exited the helicopter. Dave crumpled to the ground as his space legs gave out. Suddenly there were arms under him, and he was being dragged half walking behind Jared. There was a sense of urgency in his unidentified assistants.

The guards ushered them into a cheap demountable building and placed them in plastic chairs in a small, bright room with bare walls. The room contained nothing else but a desk, which was littered with coffee cups, a notepad and a box full of jumbled medical supplies – bandages, syringes, medications and other first aid equipment.

The lights glared and sprayed off the walls, attacking his eyes like tiger claws. Dave winced. Even in such a plain room, it felt like sensory overload. In the last few hours, they had hurtled to Earth, almost burned up in the atmosphere, crash landed in the ocean, escaped their damaged and sinking ship, were tossed mercilessly in a rubber raft in the dark of an angry ocean and howling wind, only to be plucked from the ocean's clutches, swung through the sky in a chopper and then shoved into this rather prosaic, uncomfortable shack.

"Not exactly the welcome we were imagining, no?" said Dave.

Gareth looked miserable and pale. Max seemed uncomfortable, wriggling on his plastic chair. This was when Dave noticed his mysterious assistants dressed in paramilitary gear with rifles slung over their backs. One of them muttered into a radio clipped to his shoulder strap.

"Yeah, got them. No. Three. Barrio, King and Eriksson. Yes. Will do. Send in Doctor Gurney now."

The other assistant pulled some water bottles from another box beside the desk and handed them to the weary astronauts.

"Thanks," said Dave. He put his space suit gloves to the side of his helmet and attempted to open the bottle. The others struggled too, weak as they were in the new gravity. The guard noticed and opened the bottles for them.

A short woman with a plump body stuffed into military fatigues that were tight on her waist and too long in the leg shuffled in through the door with a pen in her mouth and her arms laden with several instruments. She dumped the items on the desk and pulled the pen out of her mouth.

"Phew," she said. "Made it. That was a cold dash in this crazy weather." She considered her patients with a broad smile. "Well, hello, astronauts. I'm Doctor Jane Gurney. I'm going to run you through some assessments to make sure you're okay. Standard astronaut process. According to the internet research I just did."

Dave and the others looked aghast.

"Just joking! I don't mean it. I know what I'm doing." She pulled a face and winked at Dave. "Hey, I thought there were four of you?"

"We lost one. He drowned waiting for rescue," Gareth said flatly, an accusation that hung like a foul smell in the room.

"Well, that's just terrible. You poor sons of bitches. Spent all that time in space where water is not that easy to come by and then the poor bugger drowns in it. That's just a crying shame." Doctor Gurney bustled with her equipment as she spoke.

"Now, which one of you spacewalkers wants to go first? How about you, Mr. King? You look about ready to jump out of that space suit. Here, let me help you. Well, these are a bit tricky," she said as she looked for the fasteners on the suit.

Max showed her where the clips were and she dug away at them.

"My, you're absolutely sodden. You must be freezing. And in this weather too. That's climate these days, right? Stinking hot one day and freak storms the next. Goodness, Mr King, you are shivering. And so are the rest of you. Alright everybody, out of these suits pronto. Let me get Terry in here to give us a hand."

She shuffled back to the door, opened it a crack and shouted, "Hey, Terry, come and help, please? You can do the helicopter checks later. Our guests need some attention."

"Thank you, T-bone," she said to Terry as he came through the door. "I do appreciate an extra pair of hands. These suits are a little tricky and it looks like they weigh a ton, too, now that they're wet."

"Pleasure, Janie."

The two of them wrestled with the suits until the three of them were sitting in their undergarments, shivering.

"Go grab those blankets from the beds we set up for them."

"Yes, Doc. Not a worry, Doc. Anything else you want, Doc?" Terry said and poked Doctor Gurney in the arm with a smile.

"Oh, T-bone," she said. "Am I pushing you around again too much? Sorry about that. I tend to get a little focused when I'm doing my work." She waved Terry off as he left the building and turned to Max. "Mr. King, show me your arm."

Doctor Gurney moved swiftly between each of the men, taking their blood pressure and blood samples, and checking their vitals. Terry returned with the blankets, and she made a fuss of wrapping each of them in bundles.

"Now you'll be wanting a shower. There is one in this shack. Go one at a time and Terry will get some clothes for you."

"Oh, I will, will I?" Terry had his hands on his hips.

"Yes, you will, and you'll do it with a smile." Doctor Jane wagged a finger at him. "And you'll do it pronto, too, because these men have a date with you know who, and it will not do to have them standing around in their underpants. She-who-sees-all has high standards, remember?"

Terry rolled his eyes.

"You-know-who certainly does," he said and disappeared.

Dave, Max and Gareth endured Doctor Gurney's prodding and poking, and then she departed muttering about their bedraggled state.

Dave monitored the two armed guards present throughout the entire process, observing procedures with a detached and wary demeanour.

"Well, this is bullshit," said Max quietly, so the guards had to strain to hear them talk.

"Couldn't agree more," muttered Gareth.

"Well, that would be a first. Spaceward Bound and Olympus on the same page," noted Dave.

"I wouldn't go that far. We're only in this stupid predicament because Olympus defied Aryanna's orders. I'm supposed to be on the Moon bringing back the first shipment of helium-3. Instead, I'm here with you two bozos, one of my crew dead and the rest who knows where."

"Well, good to see that the landing and kidnapping haven't dented your personality much," said Dave. "But we are all in the same boat, now. Maybe we look after each other, no?"

"Let's just see what they want," said Gareth.

"It's obvious, no? They are trying to get some leverage out of Gaia or the Lunar Commission."

"Or Spaceward Bound," said Gareth.

"You think much of your reckless little cowboy company," said Max.

"Our 'reckless little cowboy company' is a major global power – the only one that could restore satellites after the Kessler incident when all the global systems were taken out. And we came to save your butts on Olympus."

"That's bull crap," said Max. "We know that Spaceward Bound was only after the helium-3, all for themselves. That's why you're here now."

"Well, we can wait and see who they think is more valuable. Who gets out first? I reckon Spaceward Bound has deeper pockets than Gaia Enterprises."

"Are you pitting Aryanna Sharif against Lincoln Ellison?" said

Max. "I back Aryanna every time. Not only does she have deep pockets, as you say, but international political clout."

Gareth took a sip from his water bottle and pulled his blanket tighter around himself. "We'll see."

"You two finished swinging dicks now? Let's just see what they're after," said Dave. "If we stick together, we are better together, no?"

Terry returned with some clothes. "I'm pretty sure these will fit," he said. "It might be a bit tight on you, Max. We're a little short on six-foot-five Everest-climber-sized gear."

"It's likely I shrunk a little on the Moon, anyway," said Max. "Thanks for the kit."

"Well, get it on quick sticks," said Terry. "Her highness is on her way."

"And who would that be?" asked Dave.

"Claire Edwards. Who else?" Terry gave them a look and closed the door behind him, the guards following him outside.

Gareth went to the shower first, while Dave and Max tried to stay warm by rubbing their limbs and doing gentle stretches in their chairs.

A crashing sound burst from the shower. Dave threw off his blanket and stumbled into the bathroom, discovering Gareth collapsed on the floor.

"Gareth! Are you okay?" Dave shook Gareth, who moaned and opened fluttering eyes. Dave shut off the shower, then lifted the other man to a sitting position. "Gareth? Can you hear me?"

"Yeah. I'm good. Just a little lightheaded."

"Let's get some help."

Gareth waved him off. "No. I just need a minute."

"Max," Dave shouted out to Max, who had dragged himself to the doorway and was holding himself upright with the basin.

"Right here," Max said.

"Ask the guards to send the doctor back in. Tell them Barrio has fainted."

"I did not faint," Gareth said.

"So, you were just a little vertically challenged. No shame in that after the time you've spent in space, no?"

After shouting through the door for help, Max returned with a plastic chair. "Here, get him up on this. It will be more comfortable than those tiles."

"Come on, big fella, let's get your hairy ass in this thing."

Gareth grunted as Dave and Max hauled him into the chair.

"You want Nurse Ratched to look at you?" asked Dave. "Or do you want one of us to scrub your back?"

"I'm fine, you idiot."

"I'm sending her in. Maybe we'll get lucky and get some chocolates," Dave said.

Gareth reached up to turn the tap for the shower, but he could not quite reach from his chair. His arm dropped into his lap.

"Eriksson," he said heavily. "Can you do me a favour?"

"Anything for my furry friend," Dave said, eyeing Gareth's chest with an impressed look.

"Chest hair is a sign of great manliness," said Gareth defensively. "Something you are sorely lacking." Dave feigned hurt feelings. "Can you just turn the tap on for me, please?"

"Anything for my woolly Wookiee."

Dave got the shower going again just as Doctor Gurney reappeared.

"Goodness now," she said. "We are having quite the convention in the bathroom, are we?"

"Gareth collapsed. Got a little lightheaded standing up. Gravity," Max explained.

"Yes, something we definitely take for granted. Until an apple bonks you on the head or an astronaut falls in the shower, I suppose," she said, chuckling. "You alright there, Mr. Barrio?"

"I could do with a little help," he said. "It's hard to lift my arms."

"Oh, you poor man," she said. "Let me run the shampoo through your hair. That's gotta feel good after all that time in space."

"Let's give him some privacy, shall we?" Dave said to Max.

Soon they had all cycled through Doctor Gurney's ministrations in the shower. Dave struggled to pull on the borrowed socks and trousers. In this gravity, everything felt so difficult. He shivered and yawned. His body was near exhaustion after everything they had been through.

Despite their bravado, Gareth and Max were about the same. They needed a warm meal and a big sleep. He didn't hope for either, given their circumstances.

❦

There was a knock at the door. One guard opened it a crack, checked the astronauts, then pulled the door open. There in military combat fatigues was Claire Edwards, her blonde hair pulled back in a severe bun, her blue eyes bright. She shot them a piercing look.

"So, the traitor returns to Earth along with the braggart and a Spaceward Bound yahoo."

"Hello, Claire," said Max. He sat up a little straighter and puffed his chest. "Good to see you. What have you been up to, aside from terrorism and kidnapping?"

She ignored his jab, returning one of her own. "I hear you killed one of your colleagues or walked over them or something. That's disappointing. I'm guessing Lincoln wanted all of his people back together in one piece. Still, the Lunar Commission wasn't that interested in traitors. They seemed to have made some exception for the likes of you, Dave. You've got all the sneakiness of a rat."

Dave pursed his lips but said nothing.

"You'll be staying here for a while," she said. "The others will bring in a couple of bunks for you. We've got some leftover dinner, and we will send that over, too."

"How long are we expected to impose upon your hospitality?" asked Gareth.

"Well, that very much depends on a number of things, including Aryanna and her minions at the Lunar Commission."

"In the meantime, we will make sure you're comfortable. Doctor Gurney will check on you regularly to make sure that your recovery from space goes smoothly. So be good kids, now, and behave yourselves. Don't make any trouble for us. It will just end badly for you." She sneered at them. "Right, I'll be off. Welcome back to Earth. Where you should've stayed all along."

She turned and left.

Max flicked the finger at her.

The armed guards followed her out, leaving the astronauts sitting on their plastic chairs wrapped in blankets.

"Well, this could be fun, no? Anyone want to play charades?" Dave said.

CHAPTER NINETEEN

"I always thought there was a right way to do things, the right way to do leadership, the right way to govern the Moon, and that we were on the right side of politics. Turns out the 'right' side is hard to find."

—Jonas Seaborn,
THE LUNAR CHRONICLE, FIRST PIONEERS

Jonas plodded his way to the vehicle bay to greet Colonel Jin. His legs felt heavy and tired after the morning's workout, despite the fact that he'd gone lighter on the weights, because he hadn't slept well. He had tossed and stared at the ceiling of his accommodation pod much of the night, his imagination running through scenarios his friends might be facing.

Xavier in critical condition from injuries, the ecoterrorists rough-handling Madison and Serena. And then Dave and Max. Had they made it? Or were they bobbing on the ocean, or dead and burned in a fireball on re-entry?

He'd also worried about the repairs he had done on the *Minerva*. Had his welding failed?

It had been three days and still there was no news, but they had no choice but to continue operations. Today, they were meeting

Colonel Jin and the Chinese about helium-3 production, and receiving some food supplies the Chinese had agreed to donate to the Olympus base.

Jonas shook off his grim thoughts as he waited at the airlock. Colonel Jin stepped from his vehicle, along with Hàoyú and Chan-Juan, his two deputies, and Lihua, one of the Dopplebot crew members. They were coming to discuss helium-3 production timelines. Again.

Jonas waved as they stepped into the regolith air rinse chamber and then cycled them through the airlock. They pulled off helmets once they were in the corridor. Jonas remembered to bow.

"Mr Seaborn," Colonel Jin said. "Nice to see you again." There was little warmth in his voice, but at least he was polite, thought Jonas.

Jin could be so brusque when he was under pressure, which was pretty much all the time right now. They were all on tenterhooks with the missing crew, the comms blackout from Gaia and the long stretch of uncertainty about their respective futures. They needed each other. But still, they could get cranky and worn down in the circumstances.

Jonas led the way down the corridors, deliberately plonking with his heavy moonboots so the guests were forced to slow down as they bounded along behind him. Walking without moonboots was much easier, and one could zip around the base pretty quickly by half striding, half bouncing against the walls, but Xanthe insisted they wear the moonboots to force muscular development and tone. Otherwise, the atrophy of their muscles along with a flaccid cardiovascular system would be more accentuated when they returned to Earth.

The Chinese preferred more dedicated time in their physical training room than the laboured moonboots. Regardless, Jonas got a little sizzle of satisfaction, forcing them to go at his pace. Then a crinkle of guilt squashed the buzz, so he tried to make small talk.

"Good trip over?" Jonas said to Colonel Jin, who mastered the plodding stride effortlessly.

Colonel Jin swung his arms slowly to set his pace to match Jonas's stride. "Fine, fine. Hardly any dust spatter now," he said. The track was becoming quite worn, the moondust compressed with the frequent trips between the two bases since they started the helium-3 operations only a couple of weeks ago.

"Ah, good," Jonas said. He racked his brain for something more to say. They passed the tiny comms room and entered the Centaur wing's kitchen, which was the area they used as their central gathering point. Xanthe was there, and Jonas felt some relief. He wouldn't have to entertain everyone on his own.

"Colonel Jin, Hàoyú and Chan-Juan, welcome back to Olympus," Xanthe said breezily.

She pronounced their names so well, thought Jonas again. He had rehearsed them repeatedly this morning in his mind before he dared to say them out loud.

Then there were the Dopplebot names. This one was Lihua: LEE-HWAH. She was gorgeous. The Chinese had made a special effort to make their Dopplebots lifelike. You couldn't really tell they were bots, unless they opened their mouth wide and you saw the tongue, a dry rubbery pad.

They sat at the kitchen table and Troy brought over tea and some of his 'air biscuits' – the flour was made from an ionised process that produced a protein from the atmosphere. It was fluffy and made decent biscuits, but they were running low on sugar, so these were a bit dull in flavour. Everything was dull in flavour in space, unless you loaded it with salt and chilies.

Still, the guests ate them. Colonel Jin waved off Lihua. There was no need for the Dopplebot to pretend to nibble the offering for the sake of appearances and hospitality. They would only have to empty its receptacle later. They all knew it was a Dopplebot, and resources were scarce.

They munched in silence. Chan-Juan covered her mouth politely as crumbs fell back onto her plate, and then sipped her tea, two hands holding the cup Troy had printed. So dainty, thought Jonas.

Hàoyú sat straight, both hands on the table after he sipped the tea. His nose wrinkled, and he put the cup down and smacked his lips.

"Shall we get to it, Colonel Jin?" Xanthe prompted.

"Yes, of course." Colonel Jin swigged his tea and stretched his hands onto the table; his straight arms pushed him more upright, mirroring Hàoyú.

Classic power move, thought Jonas.

"We have helium-3 production timelines to review. As you know, we seem to be falling behind."

Jonas bristled and he stretched his neck to each side to stifle a defensive comment.

Xanthe's eyes flicked to Jonas, and she raised a finger slightly to let him know she understood his frustrations, but she would handle it.

"As you know, Colonel, there are multiple stages to ensure the safe extraction and storage of helium-3. It's all quite a new process, and we have been using our 3D printer to produce working parts on the fly.

"We've had to replace a number of different parts because they wore out more quickly than expected. This is all very experimental, and we are learning on the go." She spread her fingers on the table to emphasise the point.

"Between accepting the harvest from the cultivating bots, to processing their loads, to fixing and processing all the different mechanical bits, it's a lot for the three of us to manage. We are also trying to do the work of the others to maintain the base and our crops. I don't think either of us anticipated the workload this helium-3 production would entail."

"No, indeed."

"It all seemed very manageable when we first set it up with the *Pinnacle* crew. We've just exhausted our supply of printing materials, which lose a little integrity as we recycle and reprint."

"I appreciate that, Commander, and we are willing to add some more resources to the endeavour," said Colonel Jin.

"You have more printing materials?" asked Troy.

"No. Not printing materials." Colonel Jin shook his head and his jowls wobbled. "We will have to wait on the re-supply mission for that."

Troy frowned. Jonas knew he had been hoping for more materials. Without fresh material, it would make repairs more challenging.

Colonel Jin tugged at the sleeves of his uniform, straightening them before continuing. "I have brought Lihua as an additional Dopplebot resource for you." He took a deep breath and then added, "Our printable resources are tied up and assigned to lava tube accommodation building."

Jonas was gobsmacked. "Are you still pursuing that?"

The Chinese space industry had been set back years, if not decades, when the ecoterrorists had attacked their main base and most of the space agency's taikonauts had been killed just a few months ago.

Colonel Jin inhaled sharply, held his breath. His eyes widened, and he stared at his teacup, inspecting the bottom of it. And then he let out his breath slowly.

"I am instructed by our new great leader, Li Jun, to continue with the mission."

"How?" asked Jonas. He knew he was interrupting Xanthe's flow, but he just couldn't help himself. This was astonishing.

"Our great leader has developed a new partnership with India."

"India!" said Xanthe, Troy and Jonas at the same time.

"Yes. This is part of the news I wished to discuss in person with you. The Indian Space Agency has been unaffected by the recent ecoterrorism turbulence, and their projects have continued apace. They have been in negotiations with our great leader to send additional resources to bolster the helium-3 production that Olympus has started."

"How do you know this is happening, since we don't have contact with Aryanna or the others at the Lunar Commission?" asked Xanthe. "We've been talking to Vikram Chatterjee, the Deputy Commissioner, since Earth First seized Gaia Headquarters and our two ships, and he hasn't mentioned any of this to us. Have you got news that we haven't received yet?"

"Ah, yes. Vikram. He has been busy. I am not sure why he did not mention it to you." Colonel Jin's eyes narrowed, then he continued. "Otherwise, we have no other news of the Lunar Commissioners who were caught up in the attack on the Gaia base. There seems to be a communication lockdown on the *Saturnia*, the base and the broader Lunar Commission operations." The Colonel's face wrinkled with a sympathetic look. "I'm sorry I don't have better news about that situation."

Troy tapped a finger on his lips and gazed up at the ceiling, his expression perplexed. "How do we pursue the helium-3 production mission when we can't speak to the Lunar Commission? Our headquarters is compromised and being held by ecoterrorists. There is nowhere to take the helium-3, nor anywhere for it to be received on the other end. We still have not had any demands from the ecoterrorists. Do the Indians hope to step into the void?" asked Troy.

"That is what they are proposing." Colonel Jin nodded. "In the absence of the Lunar Commissioners, and in the great need to harvest and process the helium-3 on Earth to get energy systems up and moving again after the ecoterrorist terraforming incident, there is a huge need to proceed."

Xanthe spoke slowly. Jonas watched her eyes glaze over, in communication with the Athena ThinkLink. "What exactly is the Chinese–Indian alliance proposing?"

"They will send a replacement crew to relieve Olympus and Red Star staff and expand production."

Xanthe leaned forward and tapped a finger on the table. "And Earthside? What will they do with the helium-3 harvest, there? Are they proposing they receive the supply directly?"

"That is my understanding. Their base is secure. They propose to be the new centre of processing on Earth."

"This is all a bit sudden, isn't it?" Xanthe said.

Colonel Jin fiddled with his cuffs before replying. "Yes. It is very quick," he said pointedly.

"Shouldn't we wait for some news before we stitch up an alliance with the Indians and take all the helium-3 out of the Lunar Commission's control?" Xanthe asked, an edge to her voice. "We're talking about global control of clean renewable power source that will transform the entire planet's use of energy. Should that be in the hands of just two nations?"

Colonel Jin grew still and said nothing.

Jonas's stomach clenched. Something was definitely not right.

"What do you propose we do?" asked Xanthe.

Colonel Jin glanced at his two deputies and then back at Xanthe.

"I don't see we have any choice but to continue to maximise helium-3 production. We don't know yet how things will play out. The helium-3 is needed on Earth. Like you, I want to make sure that it is not in the hands of the few. At the moment, we are going on the word of the alliance between our leader and the Indians to do this on behalf of all humanity. There is no reason to doubt their intention."

"There is every reason to doubt them!" said Jonas. "Whoever controls the helium-3 controls everything! There are few who would resist that kind of financial and political power."

"In any case," Colonel Jin said, interrupting Jonas's tirade, "the Indians are working on a launch within the next couple of weeks."

"So soon?" said Xanthe. "And if they get here and Gaia Enterprises and the Lunar Commission are restored, and object to control of the base, what will they do then?"

"I asked them the same thing," said Colonel Jin. "They assured me they would continue to ship production of helium-3 through the Lunar Commission's facilities. This is a temporary measure until we know more."

Jonas's mind raced, and he watched Xanthe's eyes glaze over as she consulted the Athena ThinkLink.

Troy cracked the awkward silence. "Is anyone investigating or challenging the ecoterrorists?"

Colonel Jin inspected his empty teacup and put it back on its saucer. "All we have is what is on the web and what the Indian Space Agency is telling us. So far, it's all speculation. Local authorities are surrounding the base. There has been a stand-off, and fire exchanged."

Troy nodded. They knew all those same details.

"What do you propose we do?" asked Xanthe, pressing the heel of her hands to her eye sockets to clear her vision.

"I suggest we prepare for a new world order," said Colonel Jin, his shoulders slumping a little. "My leader wishes me to return to Earth with the first helium-3 shipment when it's ready. He wishes me to be the face of the helium-3 lunar expedition, so I can hand over the resources to the waiting Indian crew and supervise the correct procedures, and to make sure that no helium-3 goes unaccounted for."

"And your deputies, will they go with you?" asked Xanthe.

"They are to remain here and head up the helium-3 processing."

"What do you mean 'head up'?" asked Xanthe.

"Hàoyú and Chan-Juan will be in charge of the Red Star and Olympus base efforts."

"Hang on a minute, Colonel Jin. We have a collaborative enterprise here. That's what you and I agreed to."

Colonel Jin sighed. "And now that Olympus has nowhere to send its helium-3, new arrangements are required."

Xanthe closed her eyes, and Jonas watched the rapid movement under her eyelids as she worked with Athena to process this new information.

She opened her eyes and stared at the Colonel. "I can't accept that new arrangement, Colonel."

Jonas studied Colonel Jin's face. There was a resigned determination in it.

"I don't see that you have any choice, Commander Waters," he said gently. "You have no resupply mission coming for you. You are dependent on our cooperation and support to continue the helium-3 production, and at this point, indeed, to return to Earth."

"You are assuming the worst!" said Xanthe. She pressed a hand to her forehead. Jonas knew she must be in pain, since she often did this after processing scenarios with Athena.

"I am just focused on what is in front of me." Colonel Jin rolled his palms upwards, supplicating. "And right now, Gaia Enterprises – and, indeed, Aryanna Sharif – are lost for who knows how long. We must persist."

He drummed a finger on the table. "This is not about us. This is about what the world needs." A speck of spittle landed on the table as he spoke. "We need to get this done. And I suggest you work with me under these new arrangements, whether we like it or not. This is what is best for the Earth."

"Is it?" Xanthe asked quietly.

The silence was heavy.

Jonas's heart pounded as he observed the faces around the table. Hàoyú scratched the back of his head. Troy poured more tea for the Colonel and the others. Lihua looked passively at Colonel Jin and settled pretty eyes on the cup in front of her.

Robotic eyes, Jonas reminded himself.

His gaze lingered on the curve of her throat, the smooth skin, and the mechanical rise and fall of her delicate ribcage that was so lifelike.

"Here's what I propose," Xanthe said at last. "Let us continue under the existing arrangements until we have further information Earthside. We have a couple of weeks before the Indians arrive. There is no need to alter arrangements at this point. We can focus on increasing production.

"If you allocate some of your Dopplebots, in addition to Lihua, to the Olympus base processing refinery, we should be able to get back on track with our targets with this new deadline. In the meantime, we can hope for further news from Gaia headquarters.

"Colonel, I know that you want the Lunar Commission to come out and resume its mission, on behalf of all humanity." He opened his mouth to say something, but Xanthe persisted. "I have heard what you said about accepting the new reality. I just want to be sure what the new reality is before we do anything drastic."

He closed his mouth and nodded. He took a sip of his second cup of tea and then said, "Understood. I accept your counter proposal. As you said, we have a bit of time before we need to act on this requirement."

"Agreed."

"Then let us send prayers for those Earthside to restore world order." Colonel Jin swigged the last of the tea and placed the cup on the table.

Jonas stood along with their guests as they made ready to leave. He had the unnerving sense of being a leaf caught in a river, drifting towards the precipice of a waterfall ahead.

CHAPTER TWENTY

"For so long, I chased the approval of others, thinking it would fill the void within me. But the more I tried to impress, the more I lost sight of who I truly am."

—JONAS SEABORN,
THE LUNAR CHRONICLE, FIRST PIONEERS

JONAS STAYED IN the Centaur kitchen with Lihua to clean up, while Xanthe and Troy walked to the end of the corridor to see off Colonel Jin and the Red Star crew who boarded their rover and left the Olympus base.

Troy and Xanthe returned to the kitchen and Xanthe stood, leaning against the kitchen bench, lost in thought. From the corner of his eye, Jonas watched as Troy joined Xanthe, put a hand on her shoulder and rubbed at the knots. She sighed and closed her eyes. Her neck and shoulders were often tight these days since the ThinkLink implant. She let Troy work his magic for a few moments, revelling in the release.

Jonas tried not to stare, as it made him feel both jealous and stimulated. Intimate human touch so close only reminded him of what he did not have. He forced himself to turn away, placing the teacups in the dishwasher and wiping down the kitchen table. They had to be meticulous with crumbs to avoid clogging their atmospheric systems.

"How may I help?" The Lihua Dopplebot had a soft voice with a slight Chinese accent. To Jonas's mind, it tinkled like wind chimes. Jonas forced himself to stop wiping the table and look at the bot.

Damn, she's beautiful. So like a real woman.

The bot held his gaze patiently.

"If you join Volkov in the processing bay, he can show you what tasks are required. The bot charging station is down there as well."

The bot tilted its head and turned to go.

Jonas watched her retreating form, mesmerised by the grace of her steps.

Maybe I should have shown her the recharge station, myself.

Then he shook his head.

She's a robot, you idiot. Jonas scrubbed the kitchen table a little harder with the cloth.

Ministrations complete, Xanthe and Troy joined him at the kitchen table.

"So that's it, then? We hand over the keys to the Indians when they show up?" said Jonas, his over-wrought jealousy and stymied desire turning to frustration. He threw the cloth towards the sink in a well-practiced move and watched it float in the low G to its intended spot.

"I don't like it, either," said Xanthe. She sat at the table and gestured for the two men to join her. "But what are we to do in the absence of leadership from Gaia Enterprises? Maja and Aryanna are out of action, and we have a strong directive from the deputy at the Lunar Commission. Though I do wish he had spoken to us first before making arrangements with the Chinese and Colonel Jin." She sighed. "Also, it's our turn to go home."

"What does Athena say about all this?" asked Jonas, still standing, his feet spread. Troy tilted his head and pulled out a chair for Jonas, encouraging him to sit. Jonas dropped into the chair, still focused on Xanthe.

"She agrees that there are huge gaps of information. We don't have a lot to go on. If we stay, we compromise our health. Staying this long in low G, in this rabbit burrow, is not great for any of us. The biotech hacks only go so far. Our bodies need a break. We need to be back on Earth."

"Our minds, too," said Troy.

"Also, I'm worried about Troy's kidneys. We did a scan and test this morning and functionality is declining again."

"My kidneys are fine," said Troy. He crossed his arms and threw her a dismissive look.

"Don't be a martyr, Troy," Xanthe said. "You're sinking towards stage three kidney disease. We need to get you a transplant."

Jonas scratched the back of his head and blew out his cheeks. "Could we do the operation here?"

"What are you suggesting, Jonas?"

"I know we can't print any kidneys. We don't have enough equipment or supplies for that, but I think my kidneys are pretty healthy. Could we do that?"

Xanthe glanced at Troy and then back to Jonas. "That is incredibly generous of you, Jonas. As commander, though, I can't risk two staff members on a surgery that only Troy can perform."

"You could do it," said Jonas.

"Possibly I could, with Athena's guidance. But then I would have two colleagues out of action and recovering from a high-risk surgery, leaving me alone with only the Dopplebots to manage the base. It's too high risk."

Xanthe pursed her lips as she considered another option. "We need to get Troy back to Earth and a full medical facility, where no one has to donate a kidney and we can use an easily printed one."

"So that's it, then? We head home in a couple of weeks when the Indians arrive?" Jonas knew irritation distorted his tone, and he tried to pull the emotion back. He dropped his head into his hands. "We've got to help find the *Saturnia* and *Minerva* crew. I feel so helpless up here, not being able to assist in recovering them. Our entire team has disappeared."

Jonas's knee bounced up and down at a frenetic pace as he racked his brain with the current situation. "None of this feels right," he said. "I'm keen to get home, help our friends, but I just don't think it's right to leave Olympus in the hands of strangers."

Troy reached out and patted his shoulder with a sympathetic look.

"I'm torn too, but I don't think it's right for any of us to stay any longer," Xanthe said. "We've been here for over a year."

It had been a long year. But an amazing one! They had accomplished so much. And there was more to do. A surge of conviction pushed his words out before he could really think about them.

"I'll stay," said Jonas.

Xanthe and Troy looked startled. Then the reality of what he was proposing dawned on them. Xanthe's face hardened.

"Absolutely not! The Olympus crew sticks together. I'm not leaving you behind, Jonas."

"I think it would be really unwise for your mental and emotional health to stay behind alone," said Troy. He leaned forward and held Jonas's gaze. Jonas balked a little and then doubled down, now that the idea was out there.

"But I won't be alone! The Indian crew will be here. Someone will need to show them the ropes. And the quirks of the place. The way that the life support system needs an extra shot of gas through the pipes from time to time to regulate the levels properly. The water trickling system in the Swamp and how it needs a flush and what to do when the leaves wilt. How to use the bread maker and how you need to hold the button on the right-hand side just a little extra to make sure it doesn't burn. There's a hundred little things that, if you don't know them, can cause big problems."

Xanthe took a deep breath and slowed the conversation down with a deliberate reply. "So, let's start documenting them. We can't be relied upon to babysit Olympus forever. It's got to be a self-sustaining community resource. Aside from the essential life support systems, they can work out the little quirks."

Jonas resented being told no. All his life, everyone had told him 'no'. His parents, teachers and even Gaia Enterprises at times. Not this time; this was his moment. "I hear what you're saying, Xanthe, but I just want it on record that I don't think the base is ready to be handed over at the moment."

"Your objections are noted," said Xanthe. "Let's work on minimising your concerns in the next few weeks before the Indians arrive."

Jonas stared at Xanthe and then Troy, but both remained impassive.

The air purifier hummed and lurched in its cycle and the lights flickered in response.

Red splotches dotted Jonas's cheeks. It would be best to leave it alone. For now.

But the seed was planted. And all he could think about now was being left in charge. At last, his own command.

CHAPTER TWENTY-ONE

"The higher you rise in leadership, the lonelier it becomes. Everyone looks to you for answers, but who do you turn to when doubts gnaw at your resolve? The solitude can be as suffocating as space itself."

—Doctor Troy Bruin,
MEMOIRS FROM MARS

Later, Troy slipped into pyjamas and slid into Xanthe's bunk. Troy held her close, smelling the fading scent of dry shampoo, and running a hand along her back as she nestled into him. Her ribs were more pronounced as she grew ever thinner. From rations? The added stress of managing the ThinkLink? The strain of command?

All of it, he supposed.

He'd let her barbs about him using seduction flow down the river of the past since she had seemed contrite, and he did not want to drive a further schism over something that was half true, anyway.

He kissed her head, and she grunted softly in reply.

His mind still spun over the meeting with Colonel Jin. And Jonas.

"Still awake?" he whispered as her breathing became deep and regular with a light, snuffled snore.

She startled at his voice. "Trying not to be," she replied.

"Sorry." He patted her shoulder and hugged her. He lay still again. Then his mind rehashed the meeting again. He fussed with the blanket.

"What is it?" Xanthe pulled away from him so she could see his face. "You're like a cat in a sack."

He smiled an apology. "Xanthe, did you notice anything strange about Jonas in that meeting?"

"Jonas? No. Apart from his interruption."

"It was how he was looking at the Chinese."

Xanthe's brow furrowed.

"What do you mean?" she said.

"He did that thing, the thing that he does when he's clamping down on anger or frustration. Clenching his jaw. I could see the muscles ripping under the skin."

"I think we are all pretty angry at what was being proposed," she said.

"It wasn't that part of the conversation. He was looking at Hàoyú. It was like he was jealous."

Xanthe yawned. "That's definitely possible. I knew he had the hots for Chan-Juan. Jonas was pretty disappointed when he found out they were a couple."

"And then there was the way he was looking at Lihua."

"The Dopplebot?"

"I'm a psychologist. I know lust when I see it."

Her eyes widened. "It's not the psychologist part of you that knows lust," she said with a wry smile.

His lopsided grin filled his beautiful face. "Regardless, I know lust, and Jonas was lusting after the Dopplebot."

"That's…"

"Concerning is what it is," said Troy. "We should be mindful of our interactions in front of him. As one of the six humans on this hunk of rock, he's the only one without a partner."

"Apart from Colonel Jin," Xanthe added.

"True, but that man is half mineral, anyway. He's as stony as they come. The point is, I think Jonas might feel a little left out."

"You might be right there," Xanthe conceded. She rolled onto her side and propped herself up on an elbow. "Let's be a bit more discreet around him. Don't want to rub salt into the wound."

"Or encourage attraction to the Dopplebot," Troy said with a chuckle.

Xanthe's eyebrows shot up and she belted him lightly with the back of her hand in admonishment. "What? That cannot be healthy. Besides, we should actively work on returning Earthside and getting our situation resolved with a replacement crew."

"Well, that could be a longer project than we expected. Even with the Indian ship arriving. You know these things don't always go as planned." He flashed her a knowing look and she nodded. "Let's keep Jonas really busy and distracted," he suggested. "That might be the best course of action."

"No shortage of work to be done, that's for sure," she said, yawning. "Let's hope it's enough to temper his other interests."

CHAPTER TWENTY-TWO

"What value is a life? Is one life worth the sacrifice of many?
Or is one life worth a sacrifice for the many? If only we did not
need to sacrifice at all but worked together for all of us."

—Maja Garcia,
THE JOURNALS

Tension ebbed slowly from Maja's body as they flew further and further away from the besieged Gaia Enterprises HQ. The chopper whirled and settled over the desert. Maja exhaled and took in the grand vista of the orange ochre landscape and its ancient rocky cliff, carved over aeons by the claws of a howling wind.

She had always loved the desert. It settled her mind and drew her into the earth, fracturing her sense of self into atoms, to be gathered again in the cool desert wind. The desert swept the pieces of her soul together and poured them back into form. She would rise from the ground after a night of breathing desert air, whole again, each breath a fragile link to the eternal impossible, feeling a part of everything, from the skittering ant to the star-studded sky.

Below, she could see one road stretching across the desert, but with no signs of vehicles or any other human establishment. Then she saw it. There, nestled between the peaks of two ancient ridges, was a dome, peering back into the sky. Maja frowned, recognising the shape.

"That looks like Olympus," she said over the helmet comms.

"It's a launch base for our observation station at the Lagrange point," said Aryanna. "We copied it from the Olympus design, of course. Once Gaia proved the base was secure enough to survive the Moon, we built this facility as well."

"Aside from supporting a launch to the station, does the site have any other purpose?" asked Maja.

"For operations away from prying eyes," said Aryanna, with a wave of her cherry-tipped fingers.

The ground swelled up under them and the chopper descended slowly to a circle marked by rocks painted white. Burly Red hopped out first as the chopper powered down and guided them to safety nearby.

Under the relentless blaze of the sun, the desert stretched out in all directions, a vast canvas of undulating hillocks and shifting sands. The heat was a palpable force, shimmering in waves off the scorched earth, distorting the horizon into a mirage of quivering shapes. In this desolate expanse, they waited.

A figure appeared in the distance, emerging from the heat-haze like a spectre. He moved with a deliberate pace, his silhouette growing clearer with each step. This was Felix Dubois, the man Aryanna had described only as 'crucial to their mission'. Felix's approach was unhurried, each step measured and confident, as if he were a master of the desert itself, unfazed by its harshness.

Felix Dubois was not what Maja had expected. Short and stocky, clad in lightweight, sun-bleached fabrics that fluttered slightly with the breeze, he appeared as a part of the desert, his presence woven into the fabric of the arid landscape. His weathered face, carved by time and the elements, and his intelligent eyes, held a reservoir of secrets.

A broad-brimmed hat shadowed his features, but it did little to obscure the keen sharpness of his gaze. His boots were well-worn, yet meticulously cared for. Around his neck hung a pendant, catching the sunlight and throwing back glints of a story untold.

He had the air of self-assurance, a man who had faced the wilderness and found an ally in its solitude. There was something lethal in him too, Maja sensed. A predator.

Aryanna stepped forward to greet Felix, her movements betraying none of the apprehension Maja felt. "Felix Dubois, nice to meet you in person," she said, her voice steady.

Felix tipped his hat, a gesture of respect. "Aryanna, it's a pleasure. And this must be Maja Garcia," he said, turning his attention to her with a nod of acknowledgment. His face broke into a wide, bright smile at the sight of Burly Red.

"Bruce!" Felix strode forward and clapped Burly Red on the back, and the two men embraced, chests thudding together. They shook hands vigorously as they pulled apart. "How are you? How's that delightful wife of yours?"

Burly Red shrugged. "Still running the show in Davenport. So I'm told."

"Ah. I see," said Felix. He eyed Burly Red and then clapped the man again on the shoulder. "It's good to see you, old friend. Come in, we can catch up later after we settle business."

Maja was struck by the resonance in Felix's voice, a deep timbre that seemed to echo the vastness of the desert. "What brings you to the heart of nowhere?" Maja asked, unable to mask her curiosity.

Felix's smile was enigmatic. "The heart of nowhere holds more power than the centre of empires," he replied.

Maja fixed her gaze on Felix, intrigued. "And what brings you *here*?" she persisted.

Felix smiled again but did not look at her. "I like heat during the day, the cold at night. The contrast is enlivening. Plus, the security is unrivalled. The desert is a great guardian, an impregnable barrier against the uninvited."

"We're here to secure an alliance," Aryanna said. "Felix and his contacts can provide the resources and information we need to counter the ecoterrorists and reclaim what's been lost. But first, we must navigate the intricacies of loyalty and ambition."

"You mean, Claire?" asked Maja. "She must be behind the siege at Gaia Headquarters. It has her signature all over it."

Aryanna's plump lips pressed together, and she waved a hand in dismissal. "Claire is a scurrilous rat that needs reminding of her origins."

"I think it's well beyond that now, don't you, Aryanna?" Maja suggested.

"Perhaps," she conceded. "At least from here we can get a full appraisal of the situation and marshal a response."

They followed Felix into the base, through a door hidden like a rabbit's burrow in the slope with short, steep steps cut into the desert floor. They had built Helios Haven just like Olympus, dug out the trenches for the accommodation wings and operations facilities. Then they 3D printed the entire building and buried it all with the excavated earth, ensuring a cool, liveable climate below.

Once in the main entrance corridor, the temperature was a stark contrast to the desert heat. The sweat that had pooled in the seams of Maja's clothing chilled immediately. She shivered.

Felix led them down the main corridor. Maja had a strong sense of déjà vu, like reading an old letter years later. Familiar and unsettling.

Unlike Olympus, they did not build this enterprise with community in mind, Maja noted. It was a covert operation, with supplies stashed along every corridor. Instead of making use of the corridors for aquaculture, they stacked the tunnels full of ammunition, tinned foods, navigation devices, drones. This was a paramilitary establishment. Maja felt a frisson of fear.

Felix swished in his white robes and led them into what Maja expected to be sleeping accommodation. Instead, these rooms looked like a war command post. In what Maja recalled from the Olympus design as sleeping quarters with moveable partitions, they had made made a central command hub instead. A large central table with displays on the walls, an operations writing board for planning, and three full A.I. processors for different data analysis.

They walked past another room lit up with multiple surveillance screens. Maja saw the cameras trained on all the entrance and exit points of the base, as well as the incoming road and radar screens. These were all monitored by large, surly men in dusty desert wear.

"I wasn't expecting you," said Felix as he poured Aryanna and Maja a glass of water. He offered one to Burly Red, who declined and took up a post near the door, which offered a full view of the corridor and the office meeting room they found themselves in.

"Gaia Headquarters, at the new landing site for the *Saturnia*, came under attack. We couldn't risk inbound comms since we escaped."

"Yes, I heard," said Felix. "We had a ping on the satellite comms that something was awry. Who was it?"

"It looks like it was Earth First," Aryanna said.

"Ah, the Black Ghosts," said Felix with a wry smile.

Maja gulped her water, and Felix leaned over to fill her glass.

"Felix, we need your help to get back control of the base and rescue the *Saturnia* crew. We've also lost tracking on the *Minerva*."

Felix nodded slowly. "Sounds like a bit of a shit show."

Aryanna went still and held Felix's gaze. He stared right back.

"Yes, it is," she conceded at last. "We seem to have underestimated the resources and capability of the Earth First terrorists."

"Someone's obviously funding them," said Felix.

"What does your network say about it?" asked Aryanna.

Felix shrugged. "Just speculation at the moment," he said.

"What can you do, Felix?"

Felix scratched at the stubble on his face. "We could shut down their communications with some cyber-warfare tactics. We could hack their communication channels, whatever those are – mobile reception, satellite, UHF, the lot. Then they'll be isolated and operating in the dark. Then we can send in a drone attack to flush them out and neutralise them."

"What about the *Saturnia* crew?" said Maja. "We presume they are being held captive by that gang."

"Yes, hostages do complicate things a little. Before we take down their comms, we will figure out where they are keeping your people and set a separate crew to do a snatch and grab."

"One of them is seriously injured," said Maja. "Xavier Consus. He has a brain injury and a crushed limb. He was recovering on Olympus, but it seems he was injured on re-entry."

Felix's green eyes turned to Maja for a moment, unflinching.

He said, "We will do our best."

It was a promise without commitment.

"And, Felix," said Aryanna, "we suspect Claire Edwards is leading the Earth First attack."

"Claire?" Felix's stoic face lit in surprise. "Well, that's… interesting." Something akin to a smile lifted the corner of his eyes, but his mouth stayed grim and focused.

"We managed to access the last communication from the *Saturnia* – I swiped it before we went out of range in the chopper," Aryanna said. "And there was no mistaking, it was Claire Edwards's voice as she told Xanthe Waters to fuck off."

Felix chuckled. "That sounds like Claire. Ballsy."

"How do you know Claire?" asked Maja.

"I met her some time ago. After she left Gaia."

Maja waited for more explanation, but there was none forthcoming.

After Claire Edwards had been ousted from Gaia, there had been a time when she had disappeared. And then the rumour mill started reeling with stories of her being part of the Earth First movement. Surveillance imagery showed her, or someone who looked like her, sneaking around the Chinese Space base, not long before the attack that wiped out all the taikonaut and infrastructure of the Chinese Space force.

Maja swallowed the regret that always accompanied thoughts of Claire, her former protégé. Right now, she had her team to worry about.

"Can we get a word to the Olympus base?" asked Maja. "They have no ground communication right now, except through the ecoterrorists."

"We will have to commandeer the Spaceward Bound satellites for that." Felix looked at Aryanna for approval. "That will go against our arrangement with them," he said with a pointed look.

"Spaceward Bound has broken quite a few of our arrangements, lately," said Aryanna in a scathing tone. "But no, we will not ask Spaceward Bound for use of their satellites. I would prefer to stay underground for the moment, to wait and see."

"Wait and see what, Aryanna?" Maja asked.

"Who steps into the void."

"But what about the Olympus crew? They've got no support right now – we can't just leave them on their own!" Maja's distress swirled through her body, and she put a hand on the table to steady herself. "I'll call Huw. He can sort out the comms." She pulled out her device to send a message.

"No comms," Aryanna said and put a hand over Maja's. Her eyes locked on Maja's. "You're right. They *are* on their own. For the moment. But if I'm right, someone will take up the place left open by our 'disappearance'. I want to see who that is."

Aryanna retrieved her hand and smoothed the fabric of her silk suit, a little dusty and crumpled from the day's events.

"Earth First is being funded by someone. It's clear their original play was to have Earth First be the frontline blunt instrument of a regime change. I suspect their plan was to take control of all the pieces, myself and the Lunar Commissioners included, and then someone – likely their funders – was to step in to take control and play the saviour, negotiating new terms with Earth First that favour the mastermind of the plot. If I reappear on the chess board now, we lose our chance to trace the coup to its origins."

Maja struggled to process Aryanna's speculative interpretation of events. It was a grand conspiracy with global implications. How things resolved might very well upend international global power structures. In the meantime, she had Gaia people stranded on the Moon, and at the mercy of the ecoterrorists.

"That's a tremendous gamble, Aryanna," Maja said, fighting to keep her voice even. "We are playing with the lives of the Gaia team, and the future of the Olympus base."

"We are playing for the future of the *Earth*," Aryanna said with a force that slashed Maja's objections like a sword, causing both Maja and Felix to flinch. Aryanna tapped one of her perfectly groomed fingers on the table. "We are playing for the future of humanity. And for the balance of democratic, collective will."

Felix studied Aryanna for a moment, green eyes calculating.

"And your"—he waved at the back of his skull—"your brain-chip thing. Can't it hack the systems? Do we have to go through Spaceward Bound at all?"

"It shuts access when there are security issues, to ensure there are no breaches to my direct link."

Maja's heart lurched at the thought of the ThinkLink being hacked, her mind leaping to Xanthe and her own brain–computer interface. How secure was that implant? Could it be hacked? Had they put enough security filters on it for her? Fear settled on her like a funeral shroud.

Felix continued to study Aryanna, considering his options. Finally, he said, "Alright. We stay under the radar. In the meantime, I'll put the team together. All the usual resources and payments, plus extra danger pay for armed contact."

"Whatever you need, within reason," she said sternly. "And Felix, please see if you can get any information on the Lunar Commissioners that were within the building at the time of the attack. We did not have time to extract them, and they are likely being held by Earth First now."

"Give me half an hour and we will get feeds from every camera on that base."

"Thank you, Felix," she said.

He left Aryanna and Maja, with Burly Red standing guard.

CHAPTER TWENTY-THREE

"Power, in human terms, is a complex interplay of influence and control. The optimal path forward involves decentralising power, ensuring it is used for collective benefit, rather than individual gain."

—ATHENA A.I.,
WISDOM OF THE AGES

MAJA LAY ON the cot in her room in Helios Haven, staying away from the hustle of the base. She closed her eyes and trained her thoughts on her breath, sinking into a deep meditation, distilling thoughts and down-regulating her nervous system to encourage regenerative processes. It had been a long two days, and with so many unknowns, her system was overtaxed.

Her mind cleared, and she noticed the heaviness of her body, despite her thinness. Though she was anchored in the present, she imagined herself as a leaf in the wind, carried on a whirl of events, swirling, adrift.

If only she could dive deeper, anchor herself, see beneath the layers of murky events to understand the real flow of power.

A knock on Aryanna's door – beside her own room – snatched her from the reflective space. She breathed in and nudged movement into her limbs. When the next knock came, this one on her door, she was alert and standing.

It was Felix.

"We have an update."

Maja joined Aryanna in the corridor, and they followed Felix to the command centre, which buzzed with a new energy.

"We've located the ecoterrorist hideaway north of the Gaia landing base." Felix pointed to the satellite imagery that showed a long warehouse with a handful of smaller buildings.

"What makes you so sure this is the right place?" Maja asked, reining in the surge of hope that flooded her veins.

Felix glanced at Maja, and she saw him hold back a cynical retort, realising she wasn't doubting his abilities, only wanting clarification. "We tracked a vehicle down this road and have imagery of your astronauts being removed from a van and locked in this main building." He swiped the screen and enlarged an image that showed three white suits.

Maja peered at the screen. Yes, that was Madison. And those were Gaia spacesuits. "That must be one of the Spaceward Bound crew members." She pointed at the figure in a blue spacesuit.

"We believe it's Lincoln Ellison," Felix added.

Aryanna cocked an eyebrow at that.

Felix swiped the screen and zoomed in. "The dog."

The Pomeroy was a blur of fur around the feet of one guard.

"Well, that's…interesting," Aryanna said.

"Did you think Lincoln orchestrated this?" asked Maja, confused by Aryanna's sudden reflection.

Aryanna steepled her long fingers as she leaned forward to consider the display. "When it comes to Lincoln Ellison, I suspect him of everything. But here he is, caught up in a web not of his own making." She leaned back again. "Or so he would have us believe."

Felix interrupted the political hypothesising. "There was also a helicopter landing, but at night, so there are no visuals. However, we tracked it from a location in the Pacific, where we suspect the *Minerva* crashed. Further satellite imagery is inconclusive. So far, we have identified Serena Fox, Madison Floyd and Lincoln Ellison as hostages at this place, and at least seven armed personnel, and four unarmed individuals. Whether or not they are prisoners, it's hard to say."

"So, we have three of ten people accounted for. Any thoughts about the rest?" Maja visualised her team members and those of Spaceward Bound's *Pinnacle* one by one.

Felix nodded. "Two astronauts were shot and presumed deceased during the *Saturnia* siege."

"Who?" breathed Maja.

Felix swiped the screen several times. "These two, in Spaceward Bound uniforms."

"And Xavier?" Maja asked, trying to keep her voice even.

"Imagery shows Xavier Consus being removed by a medical team. We've followed the team through the roadblocks and then they made an abrupt turnaround and returned to Gaia headquarters."

"Is he dead or alive?" asked Maja.

"Unclear at this stage."

Maja's heart pounded and she breathed deliberately to keep her mind clear.

"So. We have located the ecoterrorists and at least some of the hostages. Where are the rest of the Lunar Commissioners?" Aryanna moved the conversation along, stocktaking.

"We suspect they are still being held at Gaia Headquarters. There was no imagery showing any further vehicle movement in or out."

Aryanna folded her hands. "And your next steps?"

Felix moved to another display. "We have two staging grounds in play, providing an extraction team for the ecoterrorist hideout, and an assault-and-secure team for the Gaia base."

"When do you leave?" Aryanna asked, all business.

"That depends on you," Felix replied.

Aryanna tilted her head, waiting for more information.

"We've also discovered the Indians have made an alliance with the Chinese and are heading to the Moon to take over Olympus."

"Well, now," Aryanna said. Her hands drifted to her hips and her gaze narrowed. "That changes everything."

"How so, Aryanna?" Maja asked, burning with anger, first for her stolen and injured crew, and then for the audacity of the Indians and Chinese. "We know where our people are. Surely, we seize them while we can? Before any further harm comes to them?" Dread settled in her abdomen, a lump of burning coal.

Aryanna smiled with cold eyes. "Alas, not yet." She held up a hand to indicate slowing down. "It seems our spiders have crawled from their hole and are busy casting spindles to the wind, hoping to snare their prey."

"Not following," Maja said.

"We wait," Aryanna replied. "And follow the helium-3."

CHAPTER TWENTY-FOUR

"It's easy to see an enemy in those who oppose us, no? No one likes to be disliked or held against their will. The real challenge is to see past that to the human being sitting there, with wants, lost dreams and hopes for the future. Maybe they've just lost their way."

—David Eriksson,
THE LUNAR CHRONICLE, FIRST PIONEERS

DAVE, MAX AND Gareth spent a restless first night in their makeshift prison after a good meal of soup and sandwiches. Dave relished the fresh food. The ability to taste flavours again! They were even given some chips, the salty crunchiness irresistible, and they demolished the family-sized packet in no time.

A knock in the morning nudged them from slumber.

"Good morning, gentlemen," came the singsong voice of Doctor Gurney. "Rise and shine, lemon limes. I've got breakfast for you."

One of the armed guards opened the door for her and she entered with a tray laden with fruit and toast. Dave and the others pushed themselves to sitting, faces groggy. Dave was thirsty and his head throbbed.

"Let's get you eating some proper food now, shall we? Bananas all round," said Doctor Gurney. She shoved the first aid supplies to the side of the desk and placed the tray there with their breakfast. "I'll be back with a jug of coffee and some milk for you all."

"Coffee? Real coffee?" asked Dave.

"As real as you're going to get around here," she said. "None of that highfalutin espresso stuff. Just good old-fashioned filtered coffee. It's not fancy, but it's one step up from that instant garbage that T-bone likes to drink."

"I'll take it any way it comes," said Max. "Coffee on Earth has got to taste better than space coffee, no matter how you make it."

"Right, then. I'll be back in a jiffy." She favoured them with a beaming smile and bustled away.

The three of them moved slowly, still feeling their way into their Earth-heavy bodies.

"How are my fellow prisoners today?" Dave asked as he peeled a banana.

"My tongue feels like it would better suit a gorilla," said Max. "And I'm thirsty as hell." He downed the rest of his bottled water in a few gulps. He shrugged off his blanket. "And it's hot in here. The storm must have rolled through overnight."

"Gareth? What's your status?"

"Alright, all things considered."

"I bet you had sweet dreams after the ministrations of a Nurse Ratched in the shower. She took her time with you. Not even Max got so much attention. And for me, it was just a pinch and a punch, and I was done."

"Whatever. Hand me a banana, will you?" Gareth rubbed the back of his neck with a grimace.

Doctor Gurney returned with the promised coffee. Dave's mouth salivated at the smell, and he took a big whiff. He poured himself a large mug and a dash of fresh milk, and with the first sip, he sighed deeply. "It does taste better on Earth."

"Now," interrupted Doctor Gurney, "we've got to do some more checks. Once you've finished breakfast and done your ablutions – and they need to be proper ablutions – we want to make sure your digestion is working properly. If it's not, let me know; I've got remedies for all of that problem area." She waved in a general direction towards Dave's abdomen.

"Once we're done with that, we need to move you. We've got another patient coming in who needs special attention here at the medical facility."

"This is the medical facility?" Max asked, incredulous.

"Yes, well, it's a little basic, but it serves its purpose."

"Where are we going?" asked Gareth between mouthfuls of banana.

"Not far. Just across the compound. I'll get T-bone and two others to help you walk over. That'll be wonderful exercise for you, anyhow. Get some air, some sunshine and move those little stick legs." She considered them with an appraising look. "I'll give you an hour to get yourselves sorted and then we're on the move."

She clapped her hands, gave them a broad smile and was gone again.

"Who knew ecoterrorists could be so jovial?" Dave said.

Doctor Gurney, Terry and another guard walked them slowly across the gravel landing pad where the helicopter was parked, in the middle of the compound. Dave and the others studied their surroundings as they went, dragging their steps to allow more time to scope the situation.

There was an enormous warehouse shed where quite a few of their captors were running in and out. They'd dropped the masks and guns. Only a handful patrolled with weapons, including three who followed the chaperoning party to another small shed, tucked in behind the warehouse. Those were all the built structures nestled in the pine forest.

They must fly in all their supplies, thought Dave.

There was no sign of a greenhouse or other self-sustaining agriculture. Solar panels and a generator shed provided the power. He glimpsed what must have been a bore and a water tank. All off-grid.

The sun pushed through the scattering of clouds and bathed them in a ferocious warmth. After the chill from the night before, it was a luxuriating sensation, even as the temperature climbed. Dave stopped in his tracks, wiped his sweating brow, closed his eyes and sighed.

"Oh, the sun!" he said. He took a deep breath, enjoying the fresh, sweet air with hints of pine. "The Earth smells good, no?"

"It sure does, sugar," replied Doctor Gurney as she adjusted her arm around his waist. "That's why we are fighting so hard to save it. No thanks to the exploitative mega companies who would sell it out for space adventures."

And there it was.

For all her jocularity and efficient caretaking, Doctor Jane Gurney was still a true believer in the Earth First cause. And that meant they were everything she loathed: frontier space settlers, asteroid and Moon miners.

She believed the space economy diverted attention from Earth rehabilitation and preservation. Dave was familiar with all the arguments, and he knew there was no point getting hooked into a 'discussion' with Doctor Gurney. They had been kidnapped, after all. These people were using them as bait or to barter, despite the pretences of care.

As they passed the far end of the large warehouse, Dave heard a yipping sound. He caught a look from Max. He knew that yip. *That has a distinct Pomeroy tone to it*, thought Dave. He tried to catch Gareth's eye, but he was engrossed in his laborious steps, as he leaned heavily on Terry.

"Here we are," Doctor Gurney said, and ducked from under Dave's arm to open the door to the neighbouring demountable shed. It was much like the building they had just left, with three cots, three chairs, a small bathroom and one window that looked out on the trees to the back.

"It ain't much, but if the Lunar Commissioners play friendly, this will be a brief stay for you. I'll come and check on you in a few hours. Try to get some rest. We'll do some rehab this afternoon. The internet says that's a good thing to do." She watched them hobble into the shed, hands on hips, with a satisfied look.

They sunk on to the cots. Dave waited a few minutes, went to listen at the door, tried the handle and found it locked.

He returned to the cot and leaned into the middle of the room, inviting the others to a quiet conversation.

"Did you hear that dog?" Dave said.

"Yeah. I'll bet my ass that's Mr Puffkins," said Max.

"What dog?" asked Gareth.

"There was a yip-yip as we went past the warehouse," Dave said. "It sounded very much like that little rat of a thing."

"Really?" Gareth said. "You don't think—"

"I do think," Dave said with raised eyebrows. "I think that the ecoterrorists might have more guests here of the space-faring kind."

"The *Saturnia*?" Gareth's face lit up with excitement, then concern. "That means Lincoln and the others—"

"Mad Dog, Serena," added Max. "They might be here too."

Dave's hand flew to his mouth, and he rubbed his jaw. "This is big. These kidnappers have staged a major coup. They're gunning for the entire space industry."

"They took out the Chinese..." Max said slowly. "Do you think they'll kill us too?"

Dave considered that. "No, I don't think so. If they wanted us dead, why go to the bother of pulling us out of the sea? They could have let us sink with the *Minerva,* no?" He tapped a finger against his lips and stared up at the ceiling. "They don't want us dead. They want us alive. Either as leverage or—"

"Or as operators," Max finished his sentence.

"There are not that many trained astronauts," Dave suggested. "They might force us into returning to the Moon to be their operatives for helium-3."

"They can't press-gang us into going into space," Gareth waved off this suggestion.

"That depends," Dave said.

"On what?" Gareth said.

"On who and what they have as collateral," Dave said.

The implications of their predicament settled on them like a dense, creeping smog.

"What are we going to do about it?" Max said.

"We find out who else is here, and then we get the hell out," said Dave.

CHAPTER TWENTY-FIVE

"When I left the military, I left the fighting life behind me. Or so I thought. Turns out, in life you're always fighting for one thing or another. And if you're not, you're just sitting around watching the world go by."

—Madison Floyd, *MEMOIRS FROM MARS*

It had been several weeks, and Madison, Serena and Lincoln had not found out much more about their surroundings. They'd heard a helicopter arrive, confirming Serena's observations, then leave again the next day. No further helicopter movement had been detected.

Madison figured there were about a dozen personnel, going by the ones they counted coming in and out of Claire's office, or 'wasp's nest' as they called it. There might be others.

Their strength was returning – albeit slowly, without all the usual space facilities and equipment. The weather didn't help much either: the warehouse was a sweatbox despite the numerous fans churning laboriously day and night. Everything felt harder in the heat, especially with ill-fitting clothes. They'd been supplied with garments that didn't quite fit, sagging on Serena and Madison and tight on Lincoln.

They kept themselves occupied planning an escape – with the assumption a helicopter would arrive soon, possibly with supplies – and playing with Mr Puffkins. He loved wrestling with socks and chasing a rubber ball a guard had found for him. The fluffy little Pomeroy had made friends easily with their jailers. This could definitely be used to their advantage, Madison reckoned.

The door to the wasp's nest flung open and Claire emerged in a flurry.

"Ellison!" she yelled across the warehouse.

Lincoln looked up from where he was lying on his cot.

"Get over here," she called out. "I've got something to discuss with you."

They were instantly alert. Madison stopped her push ups, sweat beading on her arms. Serena dropped the sock she was teasing Mr Puffkins with. Lincoln shrugged as he stood and sauntered over to Claire, knowing his nonchalance would get under her skin.

They watched him go, then resumed their activities, feigning disinterest.

The guards, however, were the disinterested ones, Madison noted. They still held their rifles in front of them, but more often than not, whichever pair was rostered on to watch the captives soon grew bored and ended up chatting among themselves. The disciplined exercise of the astronauts offered little entertainment. Mr Puffkins was another story, and they were soon taking turns throwing a ball for the yipping fur ball.

Madison had finished her calisthenics and stood stretching when Lincoln re-emerged, his face stony. He walked back to his cot and sat on its edge, elbows on his knees, gaze on the floor.

Serena and Madison pulled chairs closer to his bed without trying to draw too much attention.

"What happened?" Serena asked in a low voice. "Is it Xavier? Is he okay?" They hadn't had any news about the injured Frenchman.

"She didn't mention Xavier," Lincoln said.

"What then? Spit it out, Lincoln," Serena said.

"She wants to access our satellites," he said.

They scoffed at that.

"And what else?" asked Madison.

"She wants to use Spaceward Bound launch and processing facilities."

"And?" Madison asked again. She knew Claire would have more than one request.

"She wants us to return to Olympus and run the mining operation under Earth First."

"So, she wants to take over Spaceward Bound," Serena said. "In exchange for what?"

Lincoln looked at her, his face grave. "It's not an 'in exchange for'. It's an 'or else'."

"Or else what?" Madison said slowly.

"Or else they start killing the Lunar Commissioners."

"What the actual—" Serena said.

"How did they get the Commissioners?" Madison said.

Lincoln frowned. "As far as I can make out, it all happened on landing day, when they took us. They had a crew storm Gaia Headquarters and seize the Lunar Commissioners who were watching the landing."

"Oh my God!" Serena said. "That means they have Maja. And Aryanna! Those two were waiting to debrief us as soon as we landed."

Madison's head reeled at this news. Was Claire really capable of following through on this threat? Maybe she was. If the rumours were true, she had orchestrated the assault on the Chinese Space Agency that culminated in the deaths of the entire Chinese space force, save those left on the Moon: Colonel Jin, Hàoyú and Chan-Juan.

It could be argued, however, that those deaths might have been accidental and the explosion at the base hadn't been intended to kill anyone. This situation was different. Executing the Lunar Commissioners was next-level terror.

If *Claire followed through. Was she really capable of that?*

"I don't think they have Aryanna," Lincoln said.

They waited for him to continue.

"If they had Aryanna, they would have threatened her directly and she could have directed the Lunar Commissioners to comply, sign over mining rights to Earth First, redeploy Gaia resources. They wouldn't have bothered with Spaceward Bound."

"Except for maybe the satellites," said Serena.

"Even the satellites – the Lunar Commission has contracted their use, so they could have gotten her to change that, too. If she's not there, the next move is to threaten me, and Spaceward Bound." Lincoln put his head in his hands.

"Claire might be bluffing," Madison said.

They turned to look at her, puzzled.

"Think about it. If Aryanna is not a captive, it means she's out there, with all her infinite resources, ready to deploy against Claire and her merry band of assholes. This is an empty threat. If she kills any of those Commissioners, she loses leverage over Aryanna and adds to her long list of crimes."

Madison stood and started pacing. "I think this is an act of desperation on Claire's side. She's worked out that if she can get you in line and under her thumb, she's most of the way there to securing her control of helium-3. She holds the rest of us as insurance against Aryanna trying anything."

"That doesn't bode well for a short incarceration," Serena said. "We may be here a lot longer than we thought."

"What are you going to do, Lincoln?" Madison sat down across from him.

He lifted his head. "I hear what you're suggesting, Mad Dog, but it's a big gamble. If I refuse and she starts killing Commissioners… well, I can't abide that. I don't want those deaths on my conscience."

"Now you get a conscience?" Serena snapped.

Lincoln looked pained. Mr Puffkins whined at his owner's distress.

That's the first time he's not faking regret, Madison thought.

"I'm going to go along with it," he said.

"What? No!" Serena said. "You can't cave in to these barbarians! Think of the world's best energy source controlled by killers!"

"I said, 'go along with it'. I didn't say agree to it. I can't execute any orders from here, anyway. They will have to put me in touch with my deputy, Leo. This is good news, as I can slip in coded commands. This could buy us some time."

"Time for what?" Madison asked.

"Operation Olympus Rising, of course."

"If we escape, they could still kill the Commissioners in response," Madison said.

"And diminish their pool of tradeable entities? I don't think so. I'll agree to terms only if they release the Commissioners."

Madison started pacing again, pondering this scenario.

"There's one more thing," Lincoln said, his face haggard. "My asteroid mining specialist, travelling with the *Minerva*…Lester Thompson, he's dead."

Serena and Madison gasped.

"What happened? How do you know?" Serena said.

"When I was in the wasp's nest with Claire, I got a look at a notepad on her desk. It had a list of the *Minerva* crew: Dave Eriksson, Max King, Gareth Barrio and Lester Thompson. Lester's name was crossed off."

"You're jumping to conclusions, Lincoln," Madison said. "That proves nothing."

"Maybe. But I tell you what, there was a whole lot of activity in there. Radar screens, comms pinging and a lot of hustle. They're getting ready for something."

"You don't think they hijacked the *Minerva* as well?" Serena's hand flew to her chest, her thoughts obviously on Max, her lover.

"I wouldn't be surprised," replied Lincoln. "This is no rinky-dink operation. They're organised, they have resources and they are damned determined. If they've got the *Minerva*, they've got pretty much everyone with Moon experience right there."

"Except for our guys left on the Moon," Madison said.

"Yeah. Except for them. And with us stuck here, no one is going to help them now."

CHAPTER TWENTY-SIX

"Idealism is a lovely thing. To believe in people, in humanity, makes for uplifting speeches and a peaceful night's sleep. But with fairy tales, there is always a Big Bad Wolf. He'll blow your house down."

—David Eriksson,
THE LUNAR CHRONICLE, FIRST PIONEERS

Dave, Max and Gareth formed a tentative allegiance during the first weeks of their imprisonment. They waited eagerly every day for the sound of a helicopter to execute their escape plan but all in vain. There had not even been a car coming or going.

They kept hearing the yips of the dog but were as yet unable to spot and confirm it as Mr. Puffkins. The guards, of course, remained belligerently silent on the issue. They would neither confirm nor deny, they said.

Doctor Gurney had them on a very specific exercise routine, marching outside onto the helicopter pad daily for a scorching in the sun and sweat-soaked workouts. They were slowly growing stronger but were no further ahead on their escape plans, and they'd had no opportunity to see inside the enormous warehouse. Their world was contained to one little bunk room.

At least the guards had taken pity on them and given them a deck of cards. Gareth had taken quite a delight in showcasing his card shark skills. Max, a naturally competitive person, became infuriated every time he lost, which was pretty much every day.

Dave held his own cards lightly. He was only half-interested in any of the games and only played to make up the numbers. It also amused him to see the other two get so immersed in their competition. It was an excellent distraction.

"Well, Max King," said Gareth. "I reckon I'm going to win this round as well. There are no Kings left for King," he sniped and lay down his hand.

"Dammit! Not again," Max said and threw his cards on the little side table they'd been given along with the cards. "How the hell do you do it?"

Gareth smiled slightly. "That's for me to know and for you to never find out."

"You must be cheating," grumbled Max.

"Only losers accuse winners of cheating. No, King, it's all about skill."

"Whatever," Max said.

Dave smirked and shook his head at this exchange. He was grateful he didn't get so emotionally charged by things like a card game.

Then he heard it.

They all sat up, instantly alert.

It was the unmistakable noise of an inbound helicopter.

"This is it," said Max. "We're getting out of here now."

He jumped to the window where they'd spent the last few weeks carefully digging out the frame with a spoon from one of their meals. It was just big enough to crawl through once they'd removed the casing and the window. They had tried to send Dave out once before, in the middle of the night, only to grab him as he poked his head out the window and the guards on patrol ambled past. Too close. But their plan was workable.

Once they knew they could escape this way, they simply waited for the helicopter.

"Alright," said Dave. "Max, are you ready to deploy your acting skills?"

"Don't you know it!"

"Great. Barrio, are you ready to send up the alarm? Max is about to have a heart attack for us."

"I sure am," said Gareth, cracking his knuckles and rolling his shoulders.

Their plan was to create a fake medical emergency after a helicopter landed so they could scope out what was being offloaded. Then, during the confusion of the medical scenario, they would make a break for it and secure the chopper, with the assumption that the ecoterrorists would not fire on their own helicopter.

It was a basic but workable plan, Dave conceded. It also meant they had to overpower the guards should they have any resistance.

Gareth was about to sound the alarm as planned when the door burst open. The guards trained guns on them; they stood there like stunned monkeys.

How could they know? wondered Dave. They hadn't talked about the plan at all since its first conception.

The guards were yelling at them. "Let's go!"

"Alright, alright," said Dave, his hands in the air. *This could still work. Maybe.*

The guards ushered them out of their cramped abode and drove them towards the warehouse. The three of them craned their necks to see what was being offloaded from the helicopter.

Nothing. No supplies. It was empty.

A guard shoved Dave in the back, and he stumbled against Max.

"Eyes front!" yelled the guard.

Max snuck Dave a look who shrugged, perplexed.

A guard held the door to the warehouse open and pointed towards the back of the building.

"Wait here," he said.

Dave, Max and Gareth stood in the big open space, taking in the empty surroundings when their eyes soon landed on the three figures at the back, and a fluffy bundle now charging at them with delighted barks.

"Puffkins!" said Gareth as the Pomeroy bounded around him. He stooped to rub its head and have his hand licked.

Dave caught sight of Serena and Madison and ran up to them.

"Mad Dog! Serena! So good to see you alive!" Dave exclaimed as he wrapped first Madison and then Serena in an embrace. For the first time in a very long time, Serena did not frown at him. Max scooped Serena in a passionate embrace, holding her tight and kissing her repeatedly until she said, "Put me down, Max! I'm fine, really!"

"Are you sure?" he said.

"Never better. Nothing like a bit of kidnapping and detention to make the heart grow fonder. It's so good to see you." She kissed him passionately once more.

Dave studied his teammates, overwhelmed with joy at seeing them. His mind burst with questions. Where were the other two Spaceward Bound astronauts? He could see Serena's face working the same question back for them: where was Lester?

Gareth and Lincoln clapped each other on the back, both looking for their missing colleagues.

Madison hugged Max and Dave, and then nodded at Gareth Barrio. He nodded back, the respectful acknowledgement of a peer. Being kidnapped had levelled the playing field for all of them. Even so, in Dave's mind, that didn't make up for their initial treachery.

It all came out in a jumble: the *Saturnia* landing, the Earth First attack, the gunshots, the *Minerva* sinking with poor Lester, the missing and presumed dead colleagues. Xavier, Freddy and Snyder, and the captured Lunar Commissioners.

"It's all pretty fucked," Serena said.

"But we have a plan," said Lincoln.

"Since when have we become a 'we'?" Max said, bristling. "Ellison, you're scheduled for detainment once we're out of here. You're our prisoner, remember?"

Lincoln shot him a look as if he had just swallowed sour milk. "Circumstances have changed, don't you think?"

Serena put a hand on Max's arm. "It's alright, Max. We're in this together. For now," she added under her breath. "We've got an escape plan."

"We've got one too," Dave said, smiling.

Their reunion was interrupted by the sudden movement of the guards, running outside, responding to Claire's commands from afar.

"Something's going down," Gareth said with a worried look.

They huddled together and quickly shared their respective escape plans.

"We have one big problem," Dave said. "They have guns. Even with six of us, and a mighty ferocious canine, they can still shoot us if we try anything, no?"

The faces of the others registered the sobering fact.

"The medical emergency might have worked as a distraction during the unloading of the helicopter, but there's nothing on that chopper."

"We'll have to capture the guards. Use them as hostages," Max said. "We can overpower two of them if we get the timing right."

"I think that's where we might have a problem," Lincoln said. "All this hustle going on. It seems like they are getting ready for something, and it's urgent. Why else throw us all in together? They need all hands on deck for something."

The group was silent as they pondered Lincoln's observation

and strained to hear anything from outside. Madison broke away from the huddle and started pacing.

She stopped suddenly as an idea took hold.

"What is it, Mad Dog?" Serena asked.

"What if we do it differently…" she said slowly, eyeing each of them.

"How do you mean?" said Serena.

"All we've been doing is thinking like them – using force. What if we rise above that, do something unexpected?" she continued, her face alive with possibilities.

Five faces stared back, blank.

"Think about it." She gestured for them to sit on the cots and chairs that made up their makeshift living quarters. "What does Earth First really want?"

"They want to run Olympus and take control of the helium-3," Serena said confidently. "That's what they've been pressuring Lincoln to negotiate with Spaceward Bound all this time."

"Really?" Dave asked.

Lincoln nodded, rubbing Mr Puffkins's ears as the dog wriggled at his feet. The Pomeroy pulled away and scampered over to Serena who scooped up the dog in delight. Lincoln frowned.

"Beyond that, though," said Madison. They all still looked at her, perplexed. "They want legitimacy. The only way their ploy to control the helium-3, the Moonbase, the whole thing…the only way that works is if they are seen as legitimate players on the global stage."

"They should have thought of that earlier, before they kidnapped and killed a bunch of astronauts," said Max.

"Those deaths might have been accidental," Madison said.

"What about the Chinese ones?" Serena said as the Pomeroy licked at her face.

"Still only rumours," Madison continued. Serena's eyebrows scrunched together. "I take your point, though. Kidnapping and extortion are not the best way to make a statement and secure a footing on the global stage."

"What are you proposing, Madison?" Lincoln asked, trying to focus intently on her emerging plan, while distracted by Mr Puffkins revelling in Serena's attentions.

"What if we help get them legitimately recognised? A seat on the Lunar Commission board?"

Serena snorted at that. "Come on! Be serious! No way any of those Commissioners are going to agree to having their kidnappers sitting on the Board with them!"

Mr Puffkins yipped as if to emphasise her point.

Madison backed off a bit, realising her suggestion sounded beyond the pale.

"I see where you're going with this, Mad Dog," Dave said. "What do they really want? Why do they want the helium-3? If we believe what their propaganda says, it's all about rehabilitating Earth, prioritising humans and the environment here."

He pointed to the ground, an excitement building in his gut. "We could push for a portion of helium-3 revenue, or even the energy itself, to be diverted to Earth First projects, or priority areas."

"We bridge the divide instead of ignoring it," added Lincoln.

"And how the hell do we negotiate that while we are prisoners?" Max said, rubbing the stubble of his beard in frustration.

"We make the offer to be their voice," Madison said with a fresh flush of enthusiasm.

"And who will negotiate with those jerks?" Gareth said, still scowling.

"I will," Lincoln said quietly. "I've been meeting with Claire to discuss Earth First demands already. That started yesterday. If I can convince her that official recognition and permanent financial flow to Earth First could come from this approach, instead of perpetual international coercion, she might just go for it."

Lincoln leaned forward to Mr Puffkins and beckoned to him. The dog panted and titled his head but stayed on Serena's lap.

"They get to look like heroes with a ceasefire," Madison added.

"How do ecoterrorists rehabilitate themselves as heroes?" Max said, still frustrated.

"To some, they already are heroes," Dave said. "The end justifies the means in that case."

"And in this way, we can help them choose new means," Madison said.

"It would get them out of the corner they've painted themselves into," Lincoln added thoughtfully.

"So, we're agreed, then?" Madison asked. "A new direction for Olympus Rising?"

"Olympus Rising?" Max asked. "What's that?"

"It was our escape plan," Lincoln replied.

"Now, it's our plan for diplomacy to rise above violence," Madison said.

"Olympus Rising," Dave said. "I like it."

❧

The flurry of activity continued and so the astronauts spent their time catching up on details of their imprisonment and speculating on events beyond the confines of their makeshift prison.

A comfortable ease settled between them – though still layered with suspicion, Dave acknowledged. Lincoln and Gareth were playing along just fine, but they were still in this predicament because the Olympus crew had apprehended them on the Moon, drugged them and returned them to face the music on Earth.

I wouldn't trust us, either, thought Dave. *And I certainly don't really trust them. They were going to seize the helium-3 monopoly.*

Dave folded his arms as he watched Gareth and Lincoln speak in low voices on Lincoln's cot. Then again, circumstances had indeed changed. Could these leopards change their spots?

They had just boiled the kettle when Claire stormed through the doorway, fully kitted up in her paramilitary gear. "Ellison, a word if you please."

Lincoln moved slowly to his feet as the others watched, wired with trepidation. A lot was riding on Lincoln's ability to sell the Olympus Rising plan. While they were waiting for him to reappear, the guards entered, gesturing with their rifles.

"Time to go. We're moving out," one of them barked.

Dave looked expectantly towards the door to the nest where a guard remained in position, this time highly alert. Lincoln had still not returned.

Another short, gruff guard grabbed Dave by the collar and dragged him to his feet. "Let's go. No more time-wasting."

Mr Puffkins growled at the guard, who moved to kick the pesky dog. Not all the guards had befriended the beast. Serena scooped up the fluffy bundle before the man's foot connected and walked submissively behind the others to the open doorway.

The guards directed them towards the landing pad, where the helicopter sat, rotor activated; the noise was fierce. The gruff guard waved a rifle at them so that they boarded. His companion followed them in and handed out headsets, and indicated to buckle up.

They stared at each other as they fastened their belts and put on their headsets. Dave tried to talk into the piece but could hear nothing. Max sat protectively beside Serena, checking she was strapped in correctly, while she cradled Mr Puffkins. Madison sat opposite Gareth, the two captains competing for the most stoic expression.

I wouldn't want to be in a staring competition with those two, thought Dave.

The pilot, Terry, was up front, running through his pre-launch checks. He glanced up as Claire Edwards climbed in beside him. Terry gave her a fist bump and she settled into her seat.

Just as they were about to shut the door to the chopper, Lincoln was thrust on board. An armed guard followed him in and together they buckled into place.

"Listen up," came Claire's voice through the comms. "We're heading out. Lucky for you, negotiations have been successful. Your helmet mics are on mute, so don't bother trying any funny business. My team has full authority to enforce your compliance."

With small hand gestures and facial expressions, Lincoln indicated their plan was in place. Dave watched Lincoln attempt to communicate some message to Gareth with eyebrows, head tilts and chin gestures. Max removed his headset to say something into Serena's ear. The guard's rifle butt smacked Max's jaw solidly.

"There'll be none of that," said the guard.

Serena's face was awash with alarm while Max moaned, held his jaw and spat out some blood. His eyes sparked with fury. Dave pressed a hand against Max's chest to restrain him.

Olympus Rising was in play.

Diplomacy over violence, as Madison had said. But Dave held only a glimmer of hope for this plan. They would have to wait and see. For the moment, it was good to see his friends alive and know that they were on their way to freedom. Maybe.

PART TWO

CHAPTER TWENTY-SEVEN

"Motherhood was a gift I experienced only briefly, but it taught me the depths of love and the apex of pain. My life has been richer for it."

—Xanthe Waters,
MEMOIRS FROM MARS

Xanthe left Troy sleeping in her room and snuck down the hallway to the comms room. This was one conversation she was actually looking forward to. It was getting easier now to speak with her son, Jack. It had been so awkward to begin with, when they first discovered he was alive after all these years.

But as they got to know each other, even with the tyranny of distance, such as it was now, they found they had more in common than they realised, like their shared interest in paramedics. Jack was training to be a nurse now. She bristled with pride at the young man he had grown into, despite his absence from their lives.

"Athena, connect to Jack, please."

"Connecting with Jack/Dale now."

Xanthe was even getting used to her son's other name, given by his adoptive mother. She managed not to grit her teeth too much at the thought of that other woman.

Jack's image popped to life on the holo, and a smile lit up her own face in response.

"Hello, Xanthe," he said.

Just once she wished he would call her 'Mum'. It was still too soon for that, though. Maybe it would come in time, maybe when she saw him in person and hugged him for the first time since the tsunami. Excitement bubbled inside her as if that day was finally here.

"Jack! You look well. How is everything?"

"Great. Really good. You?"

"Good here too. The Indians have allied with the Chinese and are sending a replacement crew for all of us!"

"Really?" Jack beamed.

"We will make our way back to Earth with the first helium-3 shipment in just a few weeks." Her eyes shone and her heart thudded at the thought of heading back to Earth soon.

"Wow, the day is finally coming. That's awesome." He radiated happiness. "I've got news of my own."

"Oh, yes? Do tell." Xanthe revelled in his enthusiasm.

"I've been offered an internship with a paramedic force in Texas."

"Texas? Why Texas? It's so far from Australia."

"It's closer to Gaia Headquarters, and I thought it would be easier to catch up with you when you land and get settled back on Earth. And now that looks like it's sooner than we thought."

Tears welled and a hand flew to her mouth. Her son wanted to see her. Her son wanted to get to know her. Her son was moving halfway across the world to meet her. She swallowed and managed to keep the tears from overflowing. "That's fantastic! It's a long way to go, though."

"I think you've got longer to travel than me, Xanthe," he teased.

"Yes, you're right, I do. But I would fly to the Moon and back time and time again, if it meant I could be with you sooner."

Troy appeared in the doorway of the comms room, his hair a little dishevelled from sleep, and handed her a cup of tea.

"Is that Troy Bruin?" asked Jack.

Troy stepped farther into view of the holo. He put an affectionate arm around Xanthe's waist, but she pulled away slightly and he let it drop.

"Hello there. You must be Jack?"

"Dale."

Xanthe froze a little as he used his adopted name. Jack must have noticed, for he added, "Or you can call me Jack. I'm still getting used to the idea of having another name. Nice to meet you, by the way, Doctor Bruin."

"Call me Troy." He flashed a broad, gracious smile.

"I look forward to meeting you soon, Troy," said Jack.

Xanthe felt a rush of anxiety. She hadn't thought to introduce Troy as her partner just yet. It was still so new for the two of them. She wanted to get to know her son before explaining a new relationship that was still finding its own way. Actually, both relationships were still finding their own way.

"When do you head to Texas?" Xanthe asked.

"In a week."

"If we land at Gaia Headquarters, we might get to see you at the landing," Xanthe said, excitement building.

"Where else would you land?" asked Jack.

"India." Xanthe's voice fell flat as the reality of their situation came flooding back. They were being told to land in India. In the meantime, they still hoped to locate the Lunar Commissioners and get the helium-3 back to its original plans.

Xanthe explained the predicament to Jack, who looked appalled. He'd seen the news but hadn't quite appreciated the impact it might have on their return.

"That's some crazy shit, Xanthe!"

She bristled a little at his use of profanity. Her baby boy. Last time she saw him, he was four. But he was a grown-up now. Mostly.

"We're working on it. The authorities are hunting the Earth First criminals. We are hoping our crew is returned safely soon, along with the Lunar Commissioners, so we can return to head-quarters as planned."

"Assuming we return to Gaia HQ, we'd love to see you at the landing," Troy said.

Xanthe noted the use of 'we' in Troy's words. She bit her lip.

"I'll do my best to get there," Jack said.

"Just don't expect your mother to run into your arms imme-diately," said Troy. "We will still have Moon legs and it will take a while to adjust to gravity again."

"Yeah, I get it," said Jack. "I'm fully aware of all the recov-ery protocols and expectations of astronauts returning from long missions. It'll take the two of you quite a while to feel strong and comfortable on Earth. But hopefully I can see you and do the first checks with the paramedic team. My crew has a deal with the space agencies as support."

"How on Earth did you negotiate that?" Xanthe said.

"I'm told I can be quite persuasive."

"I wonder where you get that from?" laughed Troy.

Xanthe ignored him. "I hope that all works out. Very exciting indeed, Jack. I thought it would be months before I might see you. And well done for going after what you want."

"Thanks." Jack ran a hand through his hair, embarrassed by the compliment and motherly advice. "I guess I had better let you go. I've got a zillion things to do here to pack up my life and get ready to move to the United States."

"And we've got a few things to do here to pack up our Moon life," Troy said.

Jack waved, his holo snapped shut and Xanthe was left in the room with Troy. He put his arm around her again, and this time she did not pull away. She rested her head on his shoulder.

"After all this time, I'll finally get to meet my son."

"It's a great start to the day."

CHAPTER TWENTY-EIGHT

"Truth is a slippery fish. Just when you think you've caught it, it hides under the rocks of ambition and power."

—Doctor Troy Bruin,
MEMOIRS FROM MARS

Troy leaned against the cool metal wall, his arms crossed, feeling the familiar dull ache in his back that spoke of his overtaxed kidneys. He watched as Xanthe and Jonas, both looking more haggard than usual, focused on the console's flickering screens. Working sixteen-hour days was taking a toll on all of them.

Troy's gaze traced the shape of Xanthe's thin shoulders, taut with the burden of leadership. As their return to Earth grew closer, the days seemed even longer. Xanthe strained with the anticipation of seeing her long-lost son, Jack, for the first time in fifteen years. The yearning stretched and clawed at her.

But at least she had finally learned how to find comfort in him. There was a softness to her now that she had finally allowed to bloom. He treasured those moments alone when her guard dropped, and she let him care for her.

He stifled the urge to wrap his arms around her now, knowing it would only create an awkward bubble of intimacy that excluded Jonas, who needed to focus as comms relay for the *Surya One* until they flew past to land near Red Star.

Jonas's fingers raced over the controls, the tension palpable. "Athena, trajectory report for *Surya One*?" he asked, voice tight.

"Steady approach, Jonas. ETA twenty-two minutes," the AI responded, her voice a soothing contrast to the crackling tension in the room.

"Great! Athena, please hail *Surya One*," Jonas said.

"Hailing *Surya One*, now," the A.I. announced.

"This is *Surya One*. Is this Olympus base?" A male voice with an Indian accent piped through the speakers.

"Affirmative, *Surya One*. This is Olympus base. Jonas Seaborn here as comms relay, with Commander Waters and Doctor Bruin alongside."

"Jonas? I look forward to seeing you!"

"Pardon me, is this Captain Singh?" Jonah said. "I don't believe we've met yet."

"Apologies, Jonas, Captain Singh pulled out at the last minute. And I have stepped in. It's Pabi Gupta."

Jonas swapped astonished looks with Troy and Xanthe. Pabi had been a candidate for the Olympus project. He'd missed out to Dave Eriksson, and then Madison Floyd, who replaced him.

Jonas turned back to the speaker. "Pabi! Nice to hear your voice! I didn't know you were part of the Indian space mission."

"I had a lucky break. Yes, there's plenty to catch up on."

As the conversation with *Surya One* unfolded, Troy felt a prickle of unease. The unexpected change in command, Pabi's casual takeover—it didn't sit right. He caught Xanthe's eye, noting the shadow of concern in her gaze, mirroring his own doubts.

"Fantastic! We look forward to receiving you once you settle in at Red Star. Everything looks good from our point of view. Just make sure you don't knock over the *Pinnacle* on your way through. It'll be that large rocket thing in our landing zone."

"Thanks for the heads up, Mr Seaborn. I'm pretty sure we'll be able to miss something that big."

"Roger that. Good luck with the landing at Red Star and we'll see you in a few days." Jonas beamed at Xanthe and Troy who sported confused looks.

"What is it?" Jonas asked immediately.

Xanthe glanced at Troy, who raised an eyebrow. They had spent the previous evening reviewing the profiles of the *Surya One* team scheduled to take over Olympus. All were competent with excellent records.

"Why the secrecy about the captain change?" Troy mused aloud, his voice barely above a whisper, as if afraid to disturb the charged atmosphere.

Jonas, ever the optimist, brushed off the concern with a wave.

"I'm not sure why they didn't tell us he has stepped in to replace Captain Singh," Xanthe said. "They've had three days to let us know."

"It's Pabi, though! We know him. He was close on Madison's heels at the Olympus project selection. What's the big deal?" Jonas asked as he kept one eye on the *Surya One*'s image on the display.

Troy rubbed his chin, his mind racing. Was Pabi's sudden leadership part of a larger, more complex play at hand? The subtleties of space politics were never straightforward, and with the critical helium-3 payload at stake, every detail mattered.

"Nothing wrong with him as a pilot," Troy said. "He was quite competent. He was just not great on leadership and problem-solving. I'm surprised he ended up on this mission."

"People can change," Jonas said, a little defensively.

Troy noted the spots of red growing on Jonas's cheeks. Growth and change were sensitive topics for him.

Xanthe's voice, firm but reflective, broke through Troy's

thoughts. "Let's keep our focus. We'll assess the situation when they land. Until then, we prepare for all possibilities."

As they returned their attention to the console, the data streams casting a kaleidoscope of light across their faces, Troy sought a path through the fog of the unknown, but all was dark.

CHAPTER TWENTY-NINE

*"What makes us human isn't our achievements or our power.
It's our friends. Friendship is humanity's best invention."*

—JONAS SEABORN,
THE LUNAR CHRONICLE, FIRST PIONEERS

JONAS WOKE AND sprung out of bed. Today he was meeting up with
Pabi. The Indian team were due to arrive with Chan-Juan to famil-
iarise themselves with the mining operations. He looked forward
to news from Earth and Pabi's story. And to show off Olympus
and the mining operation, even if they were still a little behind
production.

"Pabi! It's so good to see you, my man!"

"Great to see you too, my friend! It's been a long time." Pabi
pulled off his helmet after passing through the airlock and beamed
at Jonas.

Jonas gave Pabi, still in his space suit, a huge awkward hug.
Pabi pulled away and gestured towards his teammates. "These are
my colleagues: Sanjay, Annika and Rajesh. They're in charge of the
mining stuff."

Jonas shook each of their hands as they pulled off their space gloves. He gave Chan-Juan a brief nod and an awkward smile. She was so gorgeous and his attraction to her stubbornly refused to fade.

"And what about you, Pabi? Are you involved in the mining too?" Jonas asked his friend.

"I'm the pilot!" Pabi said with a flush of pride.

"And what else?" Jonas asked, confused.

"That's about it. I'm here to fly people around."

"Well, that's going to change soon. Can't be on the Moon with just one skill. I'll put you to use, no problem, though. I could definitely use a smart guy like you. Let me show you around."

Jonas ushered the Indians through the corridors, babbling excitedly about the build, the infrastructure, the functionality of everything. Along the way, he introduced Troy and Xanthe, who were gracious and warm, despite their reservations.

The Indians were a breath of fresh air after the stilted reserve of the Chinese. They were full of questions and displayed the right amount of appreciation in the Swamp, in the Atrium and especially at the helium-3 processing centre.

Jonas worked hard to keep the pride out of his voice as he explained how they had to extend the vehicle bay, incorporate the mining materials and infrastructure that the *Pinnacle* crew had brought, and adjust everything on the fly.

"It really tested my engineering brain, that's for sure," Jonas said. His pride burst through just a little.

"Quite remarkable," said Pabi. "Jonas, you deserve a space medal or something. Who knew you'd be signing up for so much improvisation? Especially after all the troubles with plumbing you had during the training and prototype build of Olympus…" Pabi smirked.

"Yes. Well. It was a rather shitty process," Jonas said.

His face flushed red at the memory of falling into the septic system of Terra Verdi. It wasn't a pleasant experience. And he had endured plenty of ribbing ever since. He'd come a long way from brash applicant to awkward trainee to one of the valued Olympus members, and he could now add lunar engineering pioneer to his quiver of success.

"Let's get you settled in your accommodation. We've put you in the spare rooms in the Centaur wing alongside us so we can streamline the base resources. Once you're all set up, we can meet in the kitchen hub and you can tell me all about how you ended up here."

Jonas hustled away to concoct a decent welcome meal for the Indians and Chan-Juan, while Xanthe and Troy continued with base operations. The Swamp filters needed changing, and Troy had asked Xanthe for a hand. Volkov and Lihua were regulating the helium-3 processing.

Pabi and the others soon bumbled their way into the kitchen, still getting used to the low G. They would try the gravity boots later. Jonas pushed plates of rice and curried vegetables towards them as they sat down.

"Thought this might make you feel a bit more at home," said Jonas. "Though I'm sure it's not as good as if it was cooked fresh." They tucked into the food with relish, commenting on the flavours.

"I thought space food would taste bland, but this actually has some decent spice to it," said Pabi.

"How much chilli did you add to this?" Annika asked. Her eyes were watering.

"I hope it's not too spicy," said Jonas. "I've found myself adding five times the normal amount I might've had on Earth."

"It's spicy alright," Pabi said. "But it's good to actually taste something. Three days from Earth and everything tastes pretty bland already. Good to know that you've mastered the tricks up here."

"Not sure 'mastered' is the right word," said Jonas. "And certainly, Xavier would disagree about my cooking skills."

Pabi's face fell at the mention of the Frenchman.

"Any news about them?" asked Pabi.

Jonas sat down beside Pabi and shoved his oven mitt aside. "Nothing. There's a stand-off between Earth First and the negotiators. No one knows where they are or how they are."

"Getting the helium-3 down to Earth might help shift things along," said Sanjay, scooping another forkful of curry.

Jonas considered the dour-looking man. He'd been reticent throughout the entire tour and had barely shown any appreciation for the engineering feats, despite being an engineer himself. Sanjay would have appreciated the challenges more than any of the others.

Hard to impress, I guess, thought Jonas. Disappointment prickled in his heart.

"Well, something has got to shift," said Pabi. "They can't hold them indefinitely. Xavier was injured on the landing. That's what's most concerning. We've got no update on his condition."

Jonas's face soured with concern. He'd managed to keep thoughts of Xavier's condition at bay, taking a 'no news is good news' approach along with Xanthe and Troy. Pabi's speculation drummed up all the worst outcomes.

"Don't worry, Jonas," said Pabi. "I'm sure they're looking after him. And we will get them back soon, no doubt."

"Anyhow," said Jonas, shrugging off painful thoughts of Xavier, "tell me about you, Pabi. Last time I saw you, you were heading back to Singapore to get married. What happened?"

Pabi shrugged. "That was the plan, but when I got home all I could think about was how exciting it was to fly a spaceship. Even if it was just a VR replica, I have felt nothing like it. Not even in the fighter jets. I knew I couldn't be what my parents wanted me to be. Or what Retchna wanted me to be. So I cancelled the wedding plans, went to India and threw my hat in the ring with their space agency. And here I am."

Jonas pushed his plate away after his last mouthful, swallowed and considered Pabi more fully. "Good for you, Pabi. It takes guts to go your own way. Especially if it means disappointing parents."

"Yes." Pabi's face clouded. "I bet your parents are super proud of you though, Jonas. Moonbase engineer and all that."

"You'd think so, but I don't get much from them. Anyway, once we clear the dishes, let me show you the SimRoom and gym and what we do for fun around here."

"Sounds good," said Annika with a wide smile.

For Jonas, his new comrades were like sunshine in the subterranean labyrinth. A glow of warmth filled him from toes to crown. *Maybe we can have a game of chook tag. I might even win without Serena around.*

CHAPTER THIRTY

"Suspicion is the worst kind of poison. The more you sip it, the more lethal it becomes. The irony? We need a dose of suspicion from time to time, to build our immunity to calamity."

—Xanthe Waters,
MEMOIRS FROM MARS

Xanthe and Troy worked quietly in the Swamp. Xanthe mulled over the brief exchange with the Indians as Jonas passed through on the tour of the facilities. Something about Sanjay set off a quiet alarm in her mind. His gaze was too calculating, too measured.

Troy, noticing that she had started scrubbing the filters with a subtle brisk intensity, asked, "Everything alright?"

Xanthe nodded slightly, her expression perturbed. She had seen Sanjay in a hushed conversation with Rajesh, their heads close together, their expressions serious. She resolved to observe them more closely.

Eventually, their work in the Swamp was done, and Troy readied for an EVA to do the Atrium and perimeter checks. Xanthe would monitor him from the comms room. She could also watch Sanjay and the others through the base cameras.

While Troy took the rover around the perimeter of the base, Xanthe observed the others in the processing centre. She sent a thought command to her ThinkLink. *Athena, can you track the interactions of the Indian team and summarise their behaviour please?*

"*Analysing, now.*"

The Indian team seemed jovial and attentive, laughing as they stumbled in the low G and traipsed after Jonas and the Dopplebots to manage the processors.

Athena ThinkLink said, "*The Indians are relaxed and curious. They seem to get along well with each other. They are friendly and focused. Sanjay is more curious than the others.*"

Xanthe latched on to this comment.

Tell me more about Sanjay.

"*He asked extensive questions about the facility, its security, communication systems, the satellites and the Pinnacle.*"

A bit more than just mining then. He's not the one heading up the mission, is he?

"*Negative. That would be Rajesh. Sanjay is the mining engineer.*"

Is he just curious? Engineers like details.

Xanthe watched Jonas wind up the tour and indicate they would leave the Dopplebots to continue. Sanjay lingered a moment longer at the docking bay airlock window, his gaze fixed on the *Pinnacle*, before finally joining the others.

"*His demeanour is too reserved for my calculations,*" Athena ThinkLink said.

What does your intuition say?

"*If I had intuition, it would be wary.*"

Let me know if anything untoward occurs.

"*Of course, Xanthe.*"

Back in the kitchen hub, once the Indians had settled into their quarters for the night, exhausted but excited, Xanthe turned to Troy and Jonas.

"Something doesn't feel right," she murmured. "Sanjay and his interest in our comms and the *Pinnacle*…it's too focused."

Troy nodded. "Pabi seemed genuinely friendly, but the others, especially Sanjay, were too keen on specific details. And why the sudden change in command? Pabi stepping in for Singh at the last minute? It's really rattling my cage."

Jonas, who had been quiet, finally spoke up. "I'll talk to Pabi about it. I trust him. He can give me the low-down on what happened to Singh. I'll monitor the system logs and communications. If they're planning something, they'll slip up, eventually."

"And Athena will analyse everything," Xanthe added.

The trio stood in silent agreement, the weight of their responsibility pressing down on them. They had welcomed the Indian team as guests and collaborators, even if they were being imposed on them, but the shadow of doubt and the whisper of conspiracy lingered in the air, a stark reminder that in the grand chessboard of lunar politics, trust was a luxury they could ill afford.

Though there were four more humans in Olympus, and the base should feel more alive, Xanthe felt more alone than ever.

CHAPTER THIRTY-ONE

"Leadership is hard. There are always layers upon layers of ambition. Sometimes picking up a wrench and fixing something feels like a better way to spend the day."

—Jonas Seaborn,
THE LUNAR CHRONICLE, FIRST PIONEERS

Jonas dragged Pabi away from the helium-3 processing under the guise of upskilling him on Olympus base maintenance for when the Indians might take over command.

Pabi's face was creased with worry as Jonas shared the team's concerns.

He wasn't surprised though, and that made Jonas even more alarmed.

"Jonas," Pabi started, his voice barely above a whisper, as if a conspirator. "There's something off about the mission directives we received from Vikram. I've known him for a while, but the orders we're getting…they don't sound like him."

Jonas perked up. Maybe there was a snag in the transmissions they could pick at. "Let's cross-check the directives with Athena. She might have caught something we missed."

They turned to the A.I. interface, starting a deep dive into the recent communications. "Athena, analyse the transmissions from Sanjay for any anomalies," Jonas commanded.

As the A.I. hummed in the background, processing vast amounts of data, Pabi paced nervously. "I joined this mission because it was a tremendous opportunity. Captain Singh stepping down at the last minute raised a red flag, but I didn't expect…this."

Jonas nodded. "Whatever 'this' is." His eyes fixed on the screen as lines of code and communication logs cascaded down. "We need to be sure before we make any accusations. Let's see what Athena finds."

Minutes ticked by, each stretching with the weight of their suspicion. Finally, Athena's voice cut through the silence. "Analysis complete. Discrepancies detected in the communication pattern and encryption signatures. The directives appear to be manipulated, likely to mask the true intent of the mission."

Jonas and Pabi exchanged a look of dawning realisation.

"Manipulated?" Jonas echoed, his mind racing. "You mean, coded?"

"It seems so," Athena confirmed. "The original mission directives might have been overridden or hidden."

Pabi slumped into a chair, rubbing his forehead. "I don't like subterfuge. I play with a straight bat. I thought I was joining an honourable enterprise."

Jonas, now fully alert, started typing commands into the console. "Hold your horses, Pabi. Don't jump to conclusions. We need to dig deeper, find out who's behind this and what their endgame is. Pabi, can you get in touch with anyone close to Sanjay? Or Vikram? Someone who can confirm who's really sending these orders?"

Pabi nodded, pulling out a communicator. "I'll try. There are a few people back at the Indian Space Agency who might know the truth."

As Pabi made his call, Jonas focused on the monitors, pulling up satellite feeds, communication logs and encrypted messages, piecing together the puzzle. The truth about Sanjay's involvement and the real mission was hidden within layers of data, and they were on the brink of uncovering a conspiracy that could shift the balance of power on the Moon and beyond.

"Let's hope it's just a glitch," said Jonas.

But doubt squeezed his heart until he could barely breathe.

CHAPTER THIRTY-TWO

"I didn't know leadership meant playing power games. I thought it was about fixing problems. See a problem, find a solution. When subterfuge is the problem, well…I just don't have a solution for that."

—JONAS SEABORN,
THE LUNAR CHRONICLE, FIRST PIONEERS

JONAS CLOMPED DOWN the hall to Xanthe's room. He didn't like to disturb her or Troy when they'd finished for the day, as downtime was so scarce, but this was urgent.

He knocked on the door and there was a muted 'just a minute' and a scrabbling noise. The door opened and Xanthe stood there with tousled hair, Troy adjusting his shirt in the background, sitting on her bed. Jonas had clearly interrupted an intimate moment.

"Ah, Commander," he bumbled with his cheeks on fire. "I've got some news that couldn't wait."

"Yes, go ahead, Jonas," she said. She waved for him to come into the room, but he stayed in the doorway.

"We think Sanjay is an ecoterrorist plant," he blurted.

Xanthe's eyebrows shot up and Troy jumped up from the bed, frowning.

"That's a serious allegation, Jonas. What evidence do you have?" asked Xanthe.

"Athena decoded a communication and checked the discrepancies. At first, we thought it was an Indian Space Agency betrayal, but it seems they have been infiltrated by Earth First. We can't let them take control of Olympus. If Earth First commands the helium-3, they will extort all of us and possibly seize Moon operations."

Xanthe closed her eyes to access Athena and run scenarios. Jonas's heart pounded as he watched her rapid eyelid movements with fascination and dread. "So, what should we do?" said Jonas with an impatient tone he tried to squash.

Troy leaned against the doorway, his face brightening with an idea. "It looks like we just got ourselves our own bargaining chip."

Xanthe turned to stare at Troy as the plan crystallised for her, too.

"We can trade Sanjay for the Lunar Commissioners and the Olympus crew," Troy said with a broad grin.

Jonas leaped at the thought of saving his friends, but then the reality of the negotiation pulled him up short. "Will that work? I think that negotiation is a little lopsided," he said. "We have just one of their people and they have a dozen of ours. And they don't seem to value human life as carefully as we do. Look how they blew up the Chinese Space Agency."

Xanthe closed her eyes, and Jonas knew she was running more scenarios with the ThinkLink. Troy and Jonas watched the muscles of her jaw work, and her eyes flick under her eyelids as she processed the information with Athena.

Xanthe's eyes opened wide, and she took deep breath. "You're right, Jonas. They are unlikely to give up the crew and the Lunar Commissioners for just one of their own."

"So, what do we do?"

"We spring a trap," she said.

CHAPTER THIRTY-THREE

*"In her eyes, I saw the burden of every decision, every sacrifice.
It was as if each responsibility she shouldered took a piece
of our connection, leaving less and less room for 'us'."*

—Doctor Troy Bruin,
MEMOIRS FROM MARS

"I DON'T LIKE it, Xanthe," Troy said. "We're putting Jonas at risk."

He sat on the edge of Xanthe's bed as she stepped out of her trousers and tossed them in a pile in the corner. It irked him that such a fastidious commander was so cavalier with her wardrobe. He fought the urge to leap up, fold her clothes and tuck them away in her cupboard.

She pulled the grey top over her head and flung it towards the trousers where it floated in the low G and settled in a puddle of fabric. Troy suppressed a wince.

She stood with her hands on her hips, breasts bare, hip bones protruding from beneath her underwear, and glared at him. She'd grown so thin, he thought, as he registered the change of mood.

"What would you have me do, Troy?" Her voice crunched like footsteps on gravel.

He put up a placating hand. "Pabi can handle it. Jonas needs to go home."

"We both know that Pabi is not up to it. Under stress, he gets tunnel vision. He processes things in a linear way. Which is fine if you are solving the navigation of a spaceship, something he is deeply familiar with, but subterfuge and politics on a global scale? No way."

"And how is Jonas any better equipped?"

Xanthe turned away to rummage through another pile of clothes, flinging unwanted items aside in irritation until she found her sleeping top. She slipped it over her head and sighed.

"He's had more experience up here. He's been a solid deputy. He's grown." Xanthe flapped an arm to emphasise her argument.

Troy crossed his arms and chewed his bottom lip, thinking. Then he said, "He's got the technical skills, yes. He's even developed more leadership skills, I agree." He kept his voice gentle. "But I'm not sure he has the mental fortitude to cope with the strain for what could be an indefinite period. There's a lot that needs to go right with our plan before we regain control of Gaia Enterprises and any plan for ongoing helium-3 mining."

Xanthe stared at Troy for a moment and then sat next to him on the bed and put her head in her hands.

"I'll stay then," she said.

Troy put his arm around her emaciated shoulders. "Darling, you can't. You know you can't. We need you, and Athena ThinkLink, to pilot the *Pinnacle*."

She did not melt into his embrace as she usually did but stayed bent over, eyes closed, likely discussing the options again with Athena.

She sat up suddenly and turned to stare at Troy. Her eyes glistened but stayed hard.

"We either risk Earth and the future of helium-3, or we risk

Jonas." Her mouth pressed into a grim line. "My decision stands. Jonas stays."

Troy held her gaze but said nothing. She plumped the pillow and sank into it, back towards him. He curled up and thew an arm around her and drew her close. His heart ached. He felt the distance between them drift wider despite the closeness of their embrace.

Leadership had changed her.

Maybe it was the ThinkLink, and the reduction of decisions to datapoints and projections. The Xanthe he had fallen for would never think of team members as expendable. Was it too late to bring her back?

He kissed the back of her neck, under her ThinkLink portal, and sent a silent prayer to whichever God was listening to save the woman from the machine, and the crushing weight of responsibility.

CHAPTER THIRTY-FOUR

*"Command felt like the pinnacle of achievement,
but standing at the top is a lonely place. Without
friends to share the journey, victory is hollow."*

—JONAS SEABORN,
THE LUNAR CHRONICLE, FIRST PIONEERS

JONAS WANDERED INTO the Atrium and sat down on the bench. He poked at the fledgling plants in their matting sacks. There were signs of growth, which was good news. It meant that the original growth material had survived exposure to the vacuum when the Atrium was smashed open by meteorites. Yet another of their amazing discoveries as the pioneering inhabitants of the Moon.

"Yay, us," Jonas said with lacklustre enthusiasm. He knew the Atrium was Xanthe's favourite space, with its view to the stars, and the only place on the base that wasn't buried underneath a metre of moondust. He gazed upwards, waiting for the blinking lights of the *Pinnacle* to flash overhead.

"Athena, when will I be able to see the ship go by?"

"You should be able to see the *Pinnacle* in approximately three minutes."

"Athena, will you still have a connection to Xanthe once she's back on Earth?"

"If we have satellite connection, then affirmative, I will have interactions with Xanthe and be able to sync our data."

"That's good. I think."

He could get updates through Athena/Xanthe as they came to light.

A new thought occurred to him. If Xanthe had ongoing connections to Athena here, that meant she had a continual feed on all his activities. That was kind of disturbing. Athena had cameras and microphones everywhere on the base, except in his own accommodation. But even then, there were sensors to gauge life support systems.

Nothing like having your friend/boss/colleague knowing exactly what you're doing at any time.

I guess it's better than having no one watching me.

Loneliness quivered through him again. He was the sole human here on Olympus overnight as the Indians were undergoing orientation at the Red Star base. The Chinese were managing most of the helium-3 mining operations now, and Olympus was the processing centre.

But he wasn't totally alone, he reminded himself. There was Volkov. And the Chinese Dopplebots. Including Lihua.

Jonas lay down on the bench, his gaze lost in the star-studded void outside. Weeks had passed since the last disturbing transmission from *Saturnia*. Silence in space never boded well.

"They must be dead," he muttered, a lump forming in his throat. Each silent day weighed heavier, a constant reminder of the risks, the sacrifices – his, theirs. Guilt gnawed at him, a rat chewing his insides.

He forced his focus back to the present. He was in command, at last; a small triumph. He thought of telling his father, Don Seaborn. But then he imagined the response: *Not much of a command, is it? You and a half dozen robots.* His father would wave a dismissive hand.

Nothing could impress the old man. He might counter with his accomplishments on re-engineering the base for helium-3 processing, managing the efficiency of the base operations on his own – with robot support, of course. Yet, amidst the precision of machines and the sterility of space, his achievements felt hollow.

His thoughts, unbidden, drifted to Lihua. Her image flickered in his mind: the graceful curve of her form, the delicate features of her face. She was perfection crafted by human hands, an artificial siren in a sea of technology. But that was the rub, wasn't it? Lihua, with her supple, synthetic skin and programmed smile, was just that: a bot.

"I'm hot for a bot," he chuckled, the sound hollow in the Atrium's arching space. There was a humour to it, a cosmic joke at his expense. It would have been funny if it weren't so pathetically sad.

He ran a hand through his hair, a restless energy coursing through him. The attraction was more than physical; it was a longing for connection, to touch another being, to be held. The loneliness crawled along his spine like a centipede.

As he wrestled with his thoughts, Athena alerted him to the passing of the *Pinnacle* above, snapping him back to reality. There it was, a silver beacon with his friends aboard, heading for unknown peril, everything at risk. A lump formed in his throat, and he dashed away tears.

The ship passed beyond the Atrium's eye. He sighed. Time to shut the base down for the night and try to get some sleep, alone except for the hum of an empty, underground base for company. Duty called, as it always did, leaving his heart's turmoil for another silent, introspective night in space.

CHAPTER THIRTY-FIVE

*"I sacrificed so much chasing an ideal of leadership,
only to realise that the real strength lies in the bonds
we form, not the accolades we collect."*

—Jonas Seaborn,
THE LUNAR CHRONICLE, FIRST PIONEERS

Jonas strode to the base fitness room and threw himself into a vigorous workout. It had been two days since Xanthe, Troy and Colonel Jin had left him in charge. He'd inducted the Indians into chook tag, and they'd taken to it with relish. They were hopeless at it, of course, being so new on the Moon, and Jonas harboured only a slight vestige of guilt as he won several games in a row.

Tomorrow they would all head off to assist the Chinese with the lava tube excavation and build for the Red Star base extension. Though he didn't like to admit it, he was a little nervous. He didn't enjoy being left alone on the base for so long. Aside from Volkov, Lihua and the other Dopplebots. The image of Lihua and her adorable half-smile flitted through his mind again.

"Athena, turn up the music, please."

He enjoyed a better burn with hard rock dialled up high. It

helped him stay focused. He was halfway through his workout when a hand on his shoulder made him jump and in the low G he bounced halfway across the room.

He wrenched himself sideways to see Pabi laughing at him.

"Oh goodness, Jonas! It's so loud in here! We can hear it all the way in the processing bay."

"Pabi, you scared me out of my skin," Jonas half-shouted. "Athena, turn the music down, please."

Jonas grabbed his towel and wiped the sweat from his face. Pabi was in his fitness wear.

"Coming for a workout?"

"Thought I'd try to keep up with the resident jock. Besides, I've really noticed my body changing. And it's only been five days in space."

Pabi moved to the squat machine while Jonas stepped onto the treadmill. They settled into a comfortable silence while they strained at their respective machines. After a while, Pabi took a break and sat on a bench while Jonas pounded away on the treadmill.

"How do you do it, Jonas?"

Jonas glanced at him and continued his running. "Do what?"

"How do you stay positive after all the time up here? Don't you miss Earth? And things like…I don't know, air? Or cheesecake?"

Jonas glanced at him again and hit the stop button.

The machine slowed to a stop, and he stepped off to do some stretches. "That's a strange mix," said Jonas. "Yeah, sure, I miss Earth. I'm looking forward to getting home, eventually. But there's plenty of interesting things here, too. I mean, we're on the Moon for Chrissake! It's crazy, right? And all the things we've done here, like build a community, a place where people can live long-term like we've been doing. It's amazing."

"Yeah, but on Earth there's grass and the ocean. And other people. Did you get sick of each other? Just a few of you for a year?"

Jonas grabbed his ankle and eased into a quad stretch. He winced. His left side was tight. He'd have to do some work on the foam roller, and make sure that didn't turn into anything else problematic.

"Sure. We got on each other's nerves from time to time, but who wouldn't when you're cooped up altogether? Anyway, we learnt a lot about each other. And we looked after each other."

"Do you miss them?"

"Who?"

"The Olympus crew. Madison, Xavier, Troy, Xanthe, Serena. You guys have been together for a long time."

Jonas's breath caught at the back of his throat. A pain shot through him. Was it fear? Sadness?

Jonas let go of the stretch and jogged on the spot to loosen off the muscles.

"Sure. But I've got new friends, now. You, Rajesh, Sanjay, Annika..." Jonas winked.

"I'd give up on that one, Jonas. She's married and is a very committed wife to her husband back home." Pabi kicked his leg up on a bench to stretch his hamstring.

"Of course. Just my luck. Finally get a new woman on this godforsaken lump of dust and she's taken."

"That must be tough."

Jonas shrugged. "It's what I signed up for. We knew we would live like monks for a while."

"It's been a long time." Pabi shot Jonas a sympathetic look.

"Why do you think I spend so much time in the gym?" said Jonas with a laugh.

"I understand, now," Pabi chuckled.

"How are you enjoying your crewmates, anyway?" Jonas asked as he leaned against a machine to stretch his pectorals. Pabi dropped his stretch and chugged at his drink bottle.

"To be honest, it's been great. They're all really fantastic people. So dedicated. That's why it was such a jar to discover Sanjay's betrayal."

Jonas glanced at the door to the fitness room to make sure they weren't being overheard and lowered his voice. "I know what that's like. When someone you trust, who you thought was a friend, betrays you."

Pabi looked at him quizzically, waiting for Jonas to expand. But Jonas didn't want to go back to the conversation about Dave. That was water under the bridge. Besides, they had moved on, and Dave had done everything in his power to make amends. He'd even signed up for the rescue mission to Olympus when his own daughter was deathly ill.

People can surprise you, Jonas thought. He'd worked hard to earn that surprise from his own teammates.

"We don't always know the reason people do the things they do," said Jonas. "People are complex. We've got to deal with the bad behaviour, and hope that people can repent and atone." He swapped hands on the machine to stretch the other side. "I believe in second chances."

Jonas knew he had been on the receiving of more than one second chance. And now, here he was, commander of Olympus base. Another second chance. Even if he hadn't had any real choice, it was still something. He was in charge, now. That was something he could always hang onto, something he could be proud of that his damned father might appreciate.

"You've changed quite a lot since I first met you," said Pabi.

"I hope so! I worked really hard and have come a very long distance not to be a different person."

Pabi's head bobbed from one side to the other, still looking at Jonas. "Well, I like this new edition of Jonas Seaborn."

Jonas dropped his arms and stared at Pabi.

"Thanks," he said, choking up. "That means a lot to me."

Pabi reached out his hand and gave Jonas a fist bump. "You're welcome, Commander Seaborn. Here's to new beginnings and second chances."

Jonas grinned. "I'll drink to that." They grabbed their drink bottles and clunked them together. "Let's get going. Tonight is movie night in the SimRoom."

CHAPTER THIRTY-SIX

"I thought having my own command would validate
me, make me worthy in the eyes of others. But no one
will see that in you until you see it in yourself."

—Jonas Seaborn,
THE LUNAR CHRONICLE, FIRST PIONEERS

Jonas braced himself for the holo call he was about to make. He had never really gotten along well with his father, Don Seaborn, the man being a hard taskmaster with high expectations. Jonas felt the familiar pull of anxiety when a confrontation approached.

But today was different.

He was the Commander of the Olympus base.

On the freakin' Moon.

Jonas rolled his shoulders and said, "Athena, contact Don Seaborn on the *Sea Rover,* please."

There was a brief delay, and then a scuffle of activity as whoever was crewing the comms onboard ran about hailing the captain with a 'call from the Moon!'. Jonas allowed himself a satisfying tingle of smugness.

The rugged, handsome jaw of Don Seaborn popped into view,

then the holo adjusted to take in his entire face: hard eyes folded into leathery skin, thinning silver hair on a high tanned forehead. His neck was weathered while his torso seemed to tolerate the clothes he wore just barely, as if preferring the lash of the wild sea air.

"Jonas," he said with scrutinising eyes trained on his son. "It's been a while. To what do we owe this honour?"

Jonas worked hard to deflect the sarcasm.

"Hello, Father," he said, keeping an even tone. "I thought I'd let you know I will be a while longer on the Moon. In case you were wondering or something." Jonas hated how apologetic he sounded. He dug nails into the flesh of his palm to keep himself steady.

"Oh? Why is that? More plumbing problems?" Don Seaborn goaded.

Jonas swallowed before replying. "Plumbing's fine. Actually, I've been asked to take over as Commander."

Because there was no one else. And Xanthe didn't trust the Indians.

Jonas tried to squash his inner critic and focus on the positive news story he'd framed for his father.

"Oh, really? What's happened to Commander Waters? She seemed like a very capable leader."

No congratulations from dear old Dad. Why do I bother?

"She's on her way in the *Pinnacle* with Troy and Colonel Jin of the Red Star."

"And they left you in charge, did they? Well, well. Can't be anyone else left, though. I heard the rest of the teams left ages ago. Bad business, that – the kidnapping and deaths. Have you heard from them?"

Jonas's face burned as he tried to interject and clarify – and failed. "No, we haven't heard yet. Yes, it's bloody awful. And, no – I mean, yes – there are more people here. In fact, an Indian delegation has just arrived. There are five of us now on the base. Plus the Dopplebots."

"Indians, you say? What's going on, there? Bet their food is stinking up the base. All those underground tunnels reeking of curry and what not."

Jonas cringed at the racist overtones and then relayed the background of the Chinese–Indian alliance. He left out the part where they insisted the Indians take over management of Olympus.

"Well, it's good you get to lead at least a few humans for your first command. Otherwise, it's a bit dud if you're just lording it over a bunch of robots."

"Yes, well. Anyway, I'll be here for a while longer. Until Gaia can send a replacement crew to manage operations."

"You might be waiting some time if the rumours are to be believed – Aryanna Sharif and Maja Garcia missing and all that. And the Gaia space base HQ under command of the ecoterrorists. You'd be best to get chummy with the Indians. Start waggling your head and listening to that bloody awful music."

Jonas's face burned in shame at his father's comments. "Yes, thanks, Father. I appreciate the, ah, advice." Jonas pushed past the awkward silence to ask, "I hear you've been busy, too? The *Sea Rover* has been helping with the relocation of refugees?"

Don Seaborn nodded. "It's a damned awful situation. Those ecoterrorists should be rounded up, dangled from the bridge, shot and fed to the sharks. Bloody lunatics."

"Yes, well…"

"Still, it's good for business. Demand for floating homes has soared. So, there's a silver lining, I suppose."

Good ole Don Seaborn, always ready to profit in a crisis.

"I guess I'll be going, Father. Just wanted to fill you in and let you know about my new command and return timeline."

"Good-oh. Well done, son. Do make sure you get back as soon as you can. Cosy up to those Indians. We'll meet you when you're back. Good visuals to have a Seaborn as commander of a Moon mission, as well as captain of the *Sea Rover*. Like father, like son, ho ho."

Don Seaborn signed off with a flourish and Jonas was left staring at the console's blinking lights, feeling as ever like the eight-year-old boy chasing the tail of his larger-than-life, force-of-nature father.

CHAPTER THIRTY-SEVEN

"I chased dreams of command and recognition, but I neglected the most important duty of all: being there for those who mattered most."

—Jonas Seaborn,
THE LUNAR CHRONICLE, FIRST PIONEERS

Jonas stood at the door of the airlock of the vehicle bay and watched Pabi and the others climb into the rover. Pabi turned to wave and gave him a thumbs up, grinning broadly. Jonas had given him a crash course on how to drive the rover manually if the A.I. wasn't up to the rough spots they might encounter.

The Chinese needed all the Indian crew and most of the Dopplebots to assist with the particularly tricky part of the excavation of the lava tube they had found in a crater. The Heavenly Palace project was going ahead, and it was all hands on deck for this last little section. The Chinese had left two Dopplebots at Red Star to manage the operations there. At Olympus, it was just Jonas, Volkov and Lihua to continue the helium-3 processing, the Swamp and the base operations.

Jonas expected everybody back by dinner. A whole day to himself! He both relished the thought and felt a quiver of apprehension. Alone again.

"Athena and I will track you on the radar system. Make sure you check in with us when you get to the Heavenly Palace site, and let me know when you're on your way back so I can get dinner ready," Jonas said over the system.

"Sure thing, boss," came Pabi's voice through the helmet comms.

Jonas wouldn't be a boss for too much longer, though, he knew. Rajesh was slated to take over command, next week, according to the Chinese–Indian alliance. The stand-in Deputy Commissioner, Vikram, had agreed to this arrangement, and Olympus had run out of bargaining chips. So, Rajesh would take over and lead comms with Vikram, while Jonas continued to train and support the team.

The rover trundled out of the vehicle bay into the black beyond. Pabi had been so excited about this excursion as he was eager to see more of the lunar landscape. They all were. There was a real jocularity and buzz among the Indians, something the Olympus crew hadn't really had since the first days of their mission. There had been way too much to do and way too many hazards to get a sense of freedom. Now, with the base fully operational and established, it was much easier to relax.

But the Moon was still a dangerous place and Jonas's stomach lurched a little as he caught the last glimpse of the rover, the roller door to the vehicle bay closing behind them. He shook off a lingering sense of dread and clomped back down the corridor to the Atrium and through to the Swamp.

First job of the day was to make sure the plants were going well. There were some tomatoes to harvest that he could add to that evening's dinner. And even some rice. He was thrilled to feed the Indians with the first crop of Moon-grown rice. Yet another first to add to their accomplishments. He couldn't wait to tell Xavier.

Jonas's heart sank. Still no word about the *Saturnia* or the *Minerva* crew. There was no progress nor negotiations with the ecoterrorists. No one knew where the crew was being held or even if they were still alive. Jonas swam in a pool of anxiety, thinking about his friends. He paddled through the waves of his thoughts until he could focus again on the task at hand. He worked his way methodically through the checklist in the Swamp, then headed over to the power board to check on all the systems of the base.

"Athena, give me verbal reports as we go through, please." Even though he would inspect everything visually, it was nice to have another voice, even a synthetic one, as he worked his way around the base's operations.

He took a break and headed to the comms room to check on the rover's progress.

"Athena, give me an update on the expedition."

"The rover has arrived at the Heavenly Palace crater location and is currently stationed outside the entrance."

"Did the crew send a message?"

"Not yet."

"Can you hail them from here?"

With the repeater Jonas had installed a few weeks back, they now had communication with the Heavenly Palace site, Red Star base and the rover. It made emergency response a lot easier knowing they could get comms quickly. They'd stepped up the installation as a priority after the Moonquake incident, when Xavier had been injured.

Man, that was horrible, Jonas thought.

He recalled Xavier's bleeding head and smashed leg when they'd brought him in. Troy had done an amazing bit of brain surgery. And now Xavier was kidnapped, perhaps injured again. Or worse.

Jonas shrugged off the macabre thoughts as Athena's voice piped through the comms.

"Hailing the rover, now."

"Olympus, I was just about to call you." It was Pabi's voice coming through the display.

"Hey, Pabi. What's your status?" Jonas asked.

"We are on site and about to exit the rover."

Jonas could hear the laughing and giggles in the background.

"Sounds like you're having a lot of fun there," said Jonas with a tinge of jealousy.

"Things are ridiculous. Rajesh just passed wind, and it is a little suffocating," said Pabi.

"That wasn't me, that was Annika!" said Rajesh, laughing.

"Nonsense," came a voice in the background. "Must've been Sanjay."

Jonas smiled at that. Sanjay was so serious; he would never buy into fart jokes. But the team loved to tease him, anyway. Only he and Pabi knew the allegations against Sanjay.

"I'm checking everybody's suits and helmets," Jonas heard Sanjay say.

"Good thing someone is paying attention to safety," said Jonas.

"Don't worry, Jonas," said Pabi. "We are complete professionals here. We'll calm down in a minute and make sure that we go through things properly. You can count on that."

"I hope so. EVAs are always risky."

"Roger that, Commander Seaborn," replied Pabi. "We'll report once we're out. The Chinese have already arrived, and they say that this process will probably take three hours. Once we're out, it's another two-hour drive back to base, so perfect timing for your culinary delights."

"Awesome. By the way, I harvested tomatoes and the first crop of rice." Jonas bristled with pride.

There were exclamations of appreciation from the Indian crew.

"Well done, Jonas! Another first for Olympus and Moon history. I look forward to another one of your fantastic curries," said Pabi.

"You got it. And I promise not to overdo it."

"Just do what you do, Jonas. I'm sure it'll be fabulous."

"Thanks. And be careful."

"Of course! We'll see you later on."

"Olympus out."

Jonas felt a twinge of FOMO. Good ole fear of missing out. It sounded like they were having a whale of a time. Then his mind crept back to the rover expedition that went out and came back with a seriously injured Xavier. Dread sat in his stomach like a hot volcanic rock.

He still had work to do, so he grabbed a burrito from the supply cupboard, gobbled it quickly and headed to the reclamation centre to clean the filters there. After that, he would join Lihua and Volkov in the processing bay. They were nearly at 10% capacity. The Indians were hoping to take their own spacecraft, *Surya One*, back to Earth with the next load of helium-3.

Jonas hoped that Xanthe and Troy made the right bet on their trap before Olympus had the next helium-3 shipment ready to go. Hopefully, by then, the world would all be set right again. They'd have his friends from the *Saturnia* and *Minerva* returned, the Lunar Commissioners freed and the ecoterrorists apprehended.

It was a lot to hope for, and a lot was riding on Xanthe, Troy and Colonel Jin and their ability to foil the terrorists. Tomorrow they would be landing.

For now, it was back to the grindstone.

CHAPTER THIRTY-EIGHT

*"As a leader, one of the most difficult questions is
wondering, 'Could I have done something differently?'
What ifs and if onlys are the worst kind of hell."*

—JONAS SEABORN,
THE LUNAR CHRONICLE, FIRST PIONEERS

JONAS STARED AT the radar screens and comms display. Pabi was
two hours past the expected check-in time. He had Athena hail
the rover every fifteen minutes but with no response. There was no
sign of any movement around the entrance to the lava tubes. The
Chinese rovers weren't moving, either.

Of course, there were always delays during EVAs; space was a
crucible of the unexpected. Anything could have happened. The
3D printer could have jammed – God knows it had happened
multiple times as they built the Olympus base. Pabi and the others
might have had to drill a little further than expected in the lava
tubes – in which case, they would not run back to the rover to
send a message as that would cause further delays. Or maybe they
discovered an offshoot of the lava tube and wanted to explore and
take advantage of the extra manpower on hand.

The more Jonas tried to rationalise the delay, though, the more anxiety swamped his gut. His knee bounced. He chewed his lip, drank another bottle of water. This kept him leaping up for bio breaks, away from the infernal empty screen.

"Athena, any response from Red Star base?"

"Negative."

Where is that damn Dopplebot?

He knew Chan-Juan had left a bot on the base to monitor and maintain the systems while he and the rest of the crew joined the Indians for the printing of the walls in the lava tubes. It was a grand occasion. They could seal the lava tubes and move to the next step of establishing the habitat, including connecting electricity and generating an atmosphere.

Jonas remembered when they had reached that stage of the Olympus base build. It had taken a few months, and they had partied well. The Chinese Heavenly palace was a faster build since they didn't need to excavate, with lava tubes as ready-made underground tunnels. Maybe just a little drilling to smooth out corners or flatten floors.

Jonas had wondered at their choice of location. It was a little too close for his liking to the lava tubes where Xavier had been injured. Hàoyú had waved this off, saying they had done the moonquake monitoring, and it was out of the danger zone. But how much did they know about moonquakes, anyway? There was only a year's worth of data.

Jonas went to the kitchen to check on his dinner preparations for the fifth time. Rice was ready to be cooked, the curries were done and just needed reheating, and the flatbreads were lined up to be rolled and fried. He had really gone to town on this meal, knowing how exhausting it was to do such a lengthy EVA. Jonas looked forward to seeing Pabi's face light up in appreciation.

"Incoming call from Red Star base," Athena's voice blared over the comms.

Jonas sprang back to the comms room and slid before the display, heart pounding.

"Red Star, this is Olympus. Go ahead, over."

"Olympus, this is Red Star. I am returning your hail."

"Thank you. I was hoping for an update from the Heavenly Palace. I have not heard from my team members, and they are overdue."

"There is no communication from the commander of the excavation team."

"Have you tried hailing them?" Jonas asked in exasperation. This Dopplebot had obviously not been programmed to take the initiative.

"No."

Jonas bit his lip.

"Well, can you please hail them, now?" He tried not to sound too annoyed.

"One moment."

Jonas blew out his cheeks, tapped his foot and scratched his head while he waited for what seemed an eternity.

"There is no response from the commander of the excavation team."

Alarm caught in the back of Jonas's throat. "You have nothing from them?"

"There are no signals from the excavation team."

"What do you mean by 'no signals'?"

"There are no messages from their expedition rover. There are no signals from their spacesuits."

"What do you mean 'there are no signals from their spacesuits'?" he said slowly, barely above a whisper.

"Signals from the suits were interrupted three hours ago."

"What does that mean? What is your process for such an event?" Jonas's pulse raced and he breathed deeply for a moment, trying to clear his thoughts.

"The commander is sent an alert."

Jonas followed the logic loop with alarm. "And if the commander is one of the people whose suit has lost signal, what then?" He pressed his lips together to force himself to slow down.

"An alarm goes out."

"And did that alarm go out?"

"Yes."

"And did you do anything about it?"

"I am not programmed for emergency responses."

Jonas slammed his fist on the table. "Well, who the hell is?"

"My colleague, Jenson."

"And where is Jenson?"

"Jenson is studying the data now."

Jonas blew out his cheeks, leaned on the console and stared at the Dopplebot.

"Can you put Jenson on the line now, please," he said through gritted teeth.

The Jenson Dopplebot appeared on the holo.

"Jenson," Jonas said with pursed lips and a strained voice, "tell me what you know about the expedition crew in the Heavenly Palace."

"The signal from the excavation team stopped three hours and four minutes ago."

"I've got that. What do you suspect has happened?"

"There has been a moonquake. It seems to have cut off the commander and the crew."

"What assessments have you done?" Jonas's heart pounded and he gripped the table edge harder to keep him steady.

"We have measured the seismic impact and sent the rover to obtain a view of the entrance to the lava tube."

"And?"

"The entrance to the lava tube has collapsed."

"Explain what you mean by 'collapsed'." Jonas's voice was a low growl now.

"The tunnel entrance is completely blocked."

Jonas thought for a moment. "Are we able to shift the rubble?"

"There is no point in doing so."

"What do you mean 'there's no point'? Your crew and my crew are all in that tunnel!" Jonas felt an icy trickle of sweat run down his back.

"By the time another excavator is despatched to the site, the crew will have run out of oxygen – assuming they survived the rockfall, which seems unlikely given that their signal has been terminated."

A gaping black hole opened up inside of Jonas. He forced his mind to focus. He needed to think of other solutions.

"The rockfall could have interrupted the signal. Is that possible?" he asked the Dopplebot.

"It is possible."

Jonas breathed out slowly, clinging to a tendril of hope.

"Are there any other access points to the Heavenly Palace?"

"None that we have found."

"We need to get them out," Jonas said, panic bubbling under his skin.

"There is no point in trying to extract the commander and the crew." The Dopplebot's face lacked expression, its voice monotone yet firm. "Any rescue mission would take longer than the oxygen in their suits would allow. It would become a body recovery mission."

Jonas felt the bile rising in his throat. "We can't just leave them there!"

"There is nothing we can do." The Dopplebot stared placidly at Jonas.

Jonas swallowed hard and ran both his hands through his hair.

"Athena, what is your assessment of the situation? What can we do?"

"Considering options now."

Jonas rocked backwards and forwards on his feet, rubbing his jaw, while Jenson waited patiently.

"Jenson is correct," Athena said, and Jonas's face fell. "There is no machinery on site that we have access to or that we can send that could clear the rubble in time if they were not crushed under the collapsed tunnel. Any rescue will be of their own making from an undiscovered exit back to the rover."

They could still escape on their own! Jonas latched on to this thread of hope. "Can we reposition the rover or send it on to check for other access points around the crater?"

"The Red Star base already scouted that entire crater. The Heavenly Palace was the only known access point, apart from where Xavier had his accident. They mapped the tunnel system fully before they started building there."

"We can't just give up on them," Jonas cried.

There was no reply from Jenson or Athena.

"Athena, what do you recommend as a course of action?"

"I suggest we activate remote control of the rover and have it return to base to consolidate Olympus resources. Red Star base can do the same with their rover."

"And then what?" A wave of darkness moved through his body, turning his blood cold. He shivered.

"We continue operations with the current resources."

"What do you mean, 'the current resources'? That's me, Volkov and Lihua!"

"And also Jenson and Tin at Red Star."

Jonas sank into the comms room command chair. He put his head in his hands. A great big heaving wail came up from the bottom of his soul, as he felt the yearning loneliness of complete and utter isolation.

CHAPTER THIRTY-NINE

"In the end, it's the connections we make that define us. Command means nothing with no one to share your triumphs and defeats."

—Jonas Seaborn,
THE LUNAR CHRONICLE, FIRST PIONEERS

"I strongly advise against this course of action," Athena said as Jonas pulled on his EVA helmet alongside Lihua and Volkov.

"I hear you and acknowledge your concerns, Athena." Jonas punched the access door to the airlock. "Let it be recorded I have considered the risks and probabilities you have provided and have decided, as Commander of Olympus, to take the odds and attempt a rescue mission for the trapped Indians and Red Star crew. If we do not return, please provide my testimony to any investigating agency."

"Commander Seaborn, I acknowledge your testimony. However, I strongly urge you to contact the Indian Space Agency before commencing this operation."

"No time, Athena. And what are they going to do, anyway? They're four hundred thousand kilometres away."

Athena was silent for a moment. "I can provide support and relay any information."

"There you go, Athena. Always a team player," Jonas said.

The airlock cycled and he and the two Dopplebots stepped through the exit. The bots would carry supplementary oxygen for him and any survivors until they met up with the recalled rover. Jonas hoped to meet the vehicle in thirty minutes.

He would not abandon his teammates. His friends.

Jonas set his jaw and marched resolutely out into the grey landscape. As always, the black impenetrable ink of space surrounded them, beautiful in its austerity. Today he felt it only as a heartless adversary. He buckled down his focus to concentrate on conserving energy, treading as lightly as possible as he moondled along behind the two Dopplebots.

Keeping his thoughts tethered to the present moment was difficult. Imagined scenes of what awaited him floated in graphic, bloody detail in his mind, haunting his progress. He swept the thoughts aside time and time again and lumbered forward into the blackness.

Jonas briefed Volkov and Lihua on the task ahead as they plodded forward.

"Why you send us on ridiculous mission?" said Volkov.

"It is not a ridiculous mission to save our colleagues."

"Colleagues will not survive the crush of cave or lack of oxygen."

Jonas fought the urge to punch Volkov in the gut, knowing he'd only hurt his hand on the metal frame.

"There is a slight chance they have survived. And you will treat the expedition as a rescue mission until we have further information. Is that understood?"

"The mission is understood. But is waste of resources when we could process helium-3 ready for next shipment."

"And who will fly that shipment back to Earth? Pabi is the only remaining pilot. We need to get him out. Do you understand?"

"They will send other ship and other pilot. Helium-3 too important."

"I'm not arguing with you now, Volkov. You and Lihua will complete this expedition, and we will either rescue my friends or bring back their bodies."

"Understood. Leadership makes tough calls. Leadership sometimes makes decisions that are not sensible."

"They may not be *sensible*," said Jonas, "but they are *sensitive*. We lead with the best of the heart and best of the mind, remember?"

"I am not so sure this is best of the mind."

"Thank you for your feedback," Jonas said with forced flatness. After a while, he turned to Lihua plodding quietly beside him. "Lihua, do you understand the mission?"

"I understand the mission, Commander Seaborn. I understand you are missing your friends, and this is more important than helium-3 processing, right now."

"Thank you, Lihua. Someone programmed you with more emotional intelligence than Volkov."

"That is from the database of my original human template."

"Well, your original human template sounds like a compassionate person. Unlike the murdering dead dictator of the Volkov original."

"Sticks and stones," Volkov replied.

Jonas didn't have the heart to muster a smile.

There was now only the sound of his own breathing filling his helmet comms, as the bots did not breathe. He checked his suit watch every two hundred steps, anxiety fuelling his movements. The rover should appear at any time.

And there it was! He and the Dopplebots climbed into the vehicle and cycled through the airlock, and Jonas moved to the front as the rover reversed course. They kept their helmets on to save time on the other end.

The rover rattled and hummed with the grind of the engine and the life support system. Jonas checked all the levels: plenty of oxygen and water for two full days. The lip of the crater appeared, and he braced himself as the rover plunged over the edge and rumbled down into the darkness, the headlights casting ghostly shadows across the rocky terrain.

There, across the crater, was the Chinese excavator they had sent from Red Star base.

Jonas's heart leapt in anticipation. At last, he could do something to help his friends. Pabi's smiling face flashed through his mind.

"I'm coming for you, Pabi," Jonas said.

Jonas commanded the rover to stop outside the Heavenly Palace entrance, where the tunnel had collapsed. He stared at the scene before him.

"Those are big rocks," said Volkov.

"Yeah," said Jonas.

"I do not think excavator can move those," said Volkov.

Jonas turned and stared at Volkov. "Then think of something. Don't just shut down before we try anything."

"I simply observe facts before us," said Volkov. "Rocks are big, excavator small."

"Well, how about thinking outside the box, you numb nuts," said Jonas.

"Yes, I will get out of this box," said Volkov.

"That's not what I meant, you idiot."

"Insults do not help with idea flow," replied Volkov.

"I have a suggestion," said Lihua.

Jonas turned to her gratefully. "Yes?" he asked.

"We could wrap the rover's towing cable around some rocks and pull some of them free, if the excavator cannot budge them."

"Good. That's a good idea. Let's get the excavator moving as much as it can from around the site so that we have access to the boulders."

Jonas felt better now that they had a plan. It was a simple one, but it came with plenty of risks in using the equipment in ways it had not been designed for.

Time was ticking down ominously on Jonas's wristwatch. It had now been seven hours since the moonquake and loss of signal. The EVA suits had up to twelve hours of oxygen, and if they had any oxygen tanks stashed in the tunnel, they might have a bit more. But if any of them were injured…

Deal with one thing at a time, Jonas told himself.

The excavator had a small drill and scoop at its front end. From inside the rover, Jonas watched it labour with the smaller boulders, trying to clear a path. After an hour, it seemed like little progress had been made. Anxiety had settled in his body with an unwelcome grip, squeezing his throat and making his heart pound.

Once they moved the rubble, Lihua and Volkov worked with the rover's rescue retrieval cable and fed it around the first enormous boulder at the entrance.

It's like dismantling a tower, thought Jonas. *If you get the kingpin stone, the rest will fall free.*

Once the cable was secure, the Dopplebots moved aside, and Jonas cranked up the engine and reversed the rover slowly. The cable grew taut and the rover strained against it, wheels spinning a little in the moondust.

Not good.

"Volkov, Lihua, come and push against the rover to give it a bit more traction."

The bots lumbered over and positioned themselves against the vehicle. Jonas reversed again, and the rover groaned in protest but inched away.

"Come on, you bastard," he muttered.

He knocked up the gears a tad more, sweat beading on his brow and dripping down inside his helmet. There was a hint of a movement, so he nudged it up one more time, wincing as the engine whined and the wheels spun again. There was a thunk, some tension gave way and he released the gear.

They had moved it!

Jonas leapt to his feet to stare through the viewfinder. The one-metre boulder had indeed slipped from its position, but the remaining slabs had simply closed over the gap it had left. The slabs were twice the size of the boulder he had just moved.

"Come on, come on," Jonas muttered. "Volkov, see if there's some other boulders we might move. Nothing bigger than the one we just did. Lihua, detach the cable and get ready to loop around something else. I'll drive the vehicle closer to give you some slack."

They repeated the process; the Dopplebots climbed awkwardly over the rubble, looking for boulders they could pull away. Jonas instructed them to add stones to the rover's path for additional traction. Throughout their endeavours, Jonas cast glances at the clock, which continued its steady, ominous progress. Three hours ticked painfully by.

At last, they had cleared all the boulders that the excavator and rover could handle. Jonas left the rover and moondled over to the lava tube entrance. He climbed all over the rubble, looking for gaps in the tunnel. There was nothing but slab after slab.

He climbed above the entrance onto the crater wall and looked for an opening, a weakness of any kind. He shone a handheld light into every nook and cranny, painstakingly studying each slab.

There was nothing but rock upon rock. He looked at his wrist-watch again.

This was it.

This was the redline zone.

Even if they had avoided the tunnel collapsing on them, even if they had extra oxygen tanks, those tanks would not have been enough to support all the people inside the tunnel for this long.

And there was no way out.

Those slabs were not moving, and it would take days for the excavator to drill through them – assuming the drill bits didn't break or wear out first.

Jonas fell to his knees. He crumpled forward, helmet to the ground, space suit gloves digging into the moon dirt rubble.

The pain came soaring out of him in a gut-wrenching wail of despair.

"I'm sorry. I'm sorry. Pabi, I'm sorry."

Pabi's smiling face filled his vision. So young. So full of life. He had worked so hard to be here, to be an astronaut. And now, he was gone.

"Commander Seaborn," Volkov's voice came over his helmet comms.

Jonas said nothing and sobbed.

"We have exhausted our resources and strategy. Lihua and myself will need to recharge at base. Let us return, now."

Jonas sobbed some more, his fingers digging into the moon-dust, clawing at it in hopeless defeat.

"Okay," he said at last.

Jonas pushed himself to his feet and crawled back down the side of the tunnel to stand at the foot of the entrance. The grey slabs stood as sentinels to the underworld, black ghastly shadows cast between them in the garish light of the rover.

"Volkov, Lihua, help me find some rocks. I want to mark this place for the lives lost."

In silence, the Dopplebots helped him place a row of rocks to represent his lost colleagues. Rajesh, Annika, Sanjay, Chan-Juan, Hàoyú and Pabi. Tears rolled down his face as he placed a rock for Pabi. He patted the rock with his thick gloved hand.

"I'm sorry," he whispered to the rock. He looked up to the stars and the blackness of the eternal night of space. "I hope you fly high, my friend."

As an afterthought, Jonas added a few more rocks for the lost Dopplebots, twelve rocks in all.

Jonas stood for a moment looking at the monuments, his body numb with grief.

Lihua put a gloved hand on his shoulder and said, "Let us go, now."

Jonas followed Lihua back to the rover, climbed inside and, once cycled through, removed his helmet.

They rode in silence back to Olympus; the sun battered the grey moonscape with a joyless, colourless light, but all Jonas saw were the faces of his friends and the emptiness of the days ahead.

He was alone.

He was the last human being on the Moon.

CHAPTER FORTY

*"Responsibility is a double-edged sword. It can drive you
to greatness, but it can also carve deep into your soul,
leaving scars that never truly heal. The real challenge is
carrying that weight without letting it crush you."*

—Doctor Troy Bruin,
MEMOIRS FROM MARS

Jonas hailed the Indian Space Agency on Earth.

"Olympus, this is HQ. Go ahead, over."

"Mukmin, it's Jonas." He swallowed hard to keep his voice from breaking. "I have a report about the Heavenly Palace expedition."

"Hey Jonas. We weren't expecting a report until tomorrow after the *Pinnacle* landing. What's up?"

"There's been an accident." His heart raced and his eyes welled. Mukmin noted his response and alarm shot across his features. "What happened?"

"As far as we can tell, there was a moonquake and the tunnels collapsed on the Heavenly Palace expedition. The Chinese and Indian staff are trapped there."

Mukmin blinked and thought for a moment. "What is their status?"

"It is currently unknown. The Chinese suits are not sending any signals. There have been no comms with us in the last fourteen hours."

"I see," said Mukmin.

Jonas could see his thoughts racing as he tried to remain calm.

"Athena and Red Star analysis showed that rescue was unlikely, and that any operation would be a retrieval one." Jonas looked away and then hurried through his report. "I went anyway. With the two Dopplebots. We used the excavator and the rover to drag rubble away. But it wasn't enough. It wasn't enough. It didn't work. We couldn't get through. We failed. I failed." Jonas broke off as his voice cracked. His eyes grew wet, and he blinked hard to avoid the tears that threatened to fall.

"I see. Jonas, we're going to assemble a team and come back to see how we can support you and what our next steps are."

"Uh huh," Jonas said.

Mukmin switched off his mic and signalled to others off-screen with frantic gestures. He turned back to Jonas.

"Okay, Jonas, stay with me. Talk me through everything that's happened from departure from the base to lost communications, your comms with Red Star and everything you know from Athena."

"Athena has sent through the analysis, as well. You should be able to read it on screen." The tears slipped down his cheeks now.

Jonas walked through the detail of the last twenty-four hours. He knew Mukmin was slowing down his account to help him remain calm. And buy some time while the Indian Space Agency headquarters considered the various scenarios.

After what felt like aeons, the Deputy Commissioner Vikram joined Mukmin at the console.

"Hey, Jonas, how are you holding up?"

"Good, good," he blurted, his knee bouncing.

"We've got everybody working on this, now, as much as we can ahead of the *Pinnacle* landing tomorrow. As we understand it, there is a possibility that the Chinese had stashed some oxygen canisters in the tunnel?"

Jonas nodded.

"In which case we are working with a best-case scenario and a worst-case scenario."

"Uh-huh." Jonas's knee jiggled and sweat beaded on his forehead, though he felt cold.

"We will handle communications with the Indian families and the Chinese."

"Uh-huh."

Jonas bit his lip and stared at Vikram.

"Jonas, your mission now is to do your best to get some rest. We'll have someone here full-time, ready to talk to you at any time. This is a lot for you to deal with."

"Uh-huh."

"And talk to Athena. We will get her to undertake an assessment of your stress levels and recommend some sedatives too, if required."

"Uh-huh."

Mukmin leaned forward on the holo and said, "Jonas, we've got your back. We'll get through this. We'll figure it out."

"Thanks," he whispered and swallowed to stay focused.

After repeating the plan and checking a few details, Jonas ended the call and stared around the room. It hummed with the electrics and soft pings of machines. The walls were the cold grey of regolith mix.

He scanned the room for signs of his companions, but he had cleaned the comms room thoroughly before Xanthe and Troy had left. He wanted a fresh start for his command. The tears came again, and he let them roll down his face.

He clomped to the kitchen and looked at his dinner prep, his appetite gone. A feast for the five of them all ready. That seemed like a week ago now.

He moved to the medbay and turned the lights on. It was immaculate, courtesy of Troy's attention before he left his domain. He remembered Xavier, and Xanthe's care for Troy when they first became a couple here.

Ghosts everywhere.

He sat down in the treatment chair.

"Athena, begin assessment."

The tears kept rolling.

CHAPTER FORTY-ONE

"If you've got nothing to fight for, you're lost."

—JONAS SEABORN,
THE LUNAR CHRONICLE, FIRST PIONEERS

JONAS HAD AN uneasy night until exhaustion and the sleeping pills knocked him out. He slept through the usual artificial dawn signals and lighting changes in the base. Eventually, his awareness came back to the room, and he opened his eyes, and for a brief blissful moment there was peace until memories crashed through and the gaping hole of his lost friends opened up in his heart once more.

He lay in bed until his bladder forced him to move. He pulled on his trousers and a shirt and then the exo-suit and moonboots. He clomped down the corridor to the toilet, memories flashing of other mornings with Xavier and Troy and the banter that would emerge from the bathroom. The loneliness swamped his thoughts, and he paused, resting a hand against the walls of the printed regolith tunnels.

"Keep it together, Seaborn," he muttered.

Ablutions complete, he made his way to the kitchen hub. Last night's dinner, prepared carefully for the Indians, still sat on the counter. He stared at the bowls, the balls of dough ready to be rolled and fried, the coriander neatly chopped and wilting now.

Tears welled up in his eyes, and his emotions surged. He slapped a hand on the counter to jolt him out of the wave that was threatening to drown him.

"Come on, Jonas. You've got this."

He shook his head and tidied the food away with brisk efficiency.

"Right. Breakfast."

He pulled the cupboard doors open and stared at the ready meals, labelled cheerfully by Serena, who had added smiley faces and descriptive expressions. Scrambled eggs were 'protein blast', burritos were 'fart fodder', porridge was 'rib sticker'.

Jonas imagined Serena eyeing him and suggesting an egg and bacon roll. 'Classic Aussie goodness.'

With a wan smile at the ghost of his colleague, he settled on a coffee and a protein bar and sat, alone, at the kitchen table. The hum of the life support system filled the room, battering his senses, blaring in the emptiness.

He peeled open the protein bar's wrapper and stared at it, his appetite having deserted him. He forced himself to take a bite and chewed slowly, all the while staring at the empty chairs around the table.

Remembering he had company in the form of the base's A.I., a spark of energy rattled his reverie.

"Athena, give me a report on the *Pinnacle's* trajectory."

"Good morning, Commander Seaborn. The *Pinnacle* is on track and will commence atmospheric re-entry in three hours and twenty-two minutes."

Jonas nodded with satisfaction. "Let me know when they initiate the trap." He took a swig of coffee and, as an afterthought, added, "Athena, how is Xanthe? I presume you still have a connection with her?"

"Commander Waters is focused, and all her bio regulation data reads within normal parameters."

"But how is she, you know, emotionally?"

"She's fine."

Jonas snorted with derision. "All the A.I. capabilities in the world and the most descriptive you can get is 'she's fine'? We really haven't progressed that much with A.I. programming, have we?"

"My programming tells me that is an appropriate response to such a question."

"Forget it. Don't worry about it." He emptied his mug and scratched his chin. He should probably shower and shave. "Where are the Dopplebots?" he asked, suddenly remembering his other source of company.

"Lihua and Volkov have detached from the charging portals and are beginning helium-3 processing inspections and setup now."

"Good."

He was at a loss. When there were other people around, the day started with a meeting and a list of jobs they were all doing. It was just him, now. Which jobs should he do first?

"Ah, Athena," Jonas said with his voice quavering. "Can you help me prioritise the workflow to maintain base operations?"

"Of course, Commander Seaborn. Here is a sequenced set of tasks to keep the base running." Athena listed the various responsibilities that considered comms, life support maintenance, Swamp and plant tending, and the helium-3 project.

"Great. Looks like a full day." He stood and turned to the sink to clean his cup with the hygiene cloth. "When does the Indian Space Agency want to talk with me?"

"The Indian Space Agency is preoccupied with the *Pinnacle* landing and so won't be wanting to connect until after they have arrived."

"So, I've basically got half a day before any of the action starts on Earth?"

"Affirmative, Commander Seaborn."

"Just call me 'Jonas'. I'm not really commanding anything right now, am I?"

"Yes, I can call you 'Jonas', Commander Seaborn. And you are in command of the Olympus base and the helium-3 project, and by extension, the Red Star base."

"The Red Star base too, huh? My Empire grows." He managed a smile. "Well, since I'm the only human around, there's no one here to criticise my taste of music. Athena, play the top hits of the last decade."

"Certainly, Jonas."

Jonas didn't bother to shower and just dived right into the tasks ahead. His thoughts circled like vultures, and the manual tasks helped keep them at bay. The morning passed in a flurry of chores, music piping through the base's system, energising his weary soul.

When it was time for the *Pinnacle* landing, Jonas grabbed another protein bar and wandered into the comms room.

"Athena, light up the displays and give me everything you've got on the *Pinnacle*'s progress. Can we tap into the audio between the *Pinnacle* and the Indian Space Agency?"

Athena patched through the Indian Space Agency's video tracking and streamed the *Pinnacle*'s audio.

Jonas kicked off his moonboots and propped his feet up on the console as he watched the show. He listened to Xanthe play her character and role with complete conviction.

"I didn't know she had it in her to be so two-faced," he said with a bit of admiration.

She's always so straight, he thought.

Jonas cheered as he listened to Xanthe, Troy and Colonel Jin launch the trap. The Indians had bought the false data and narrative about needing to change landing spots. Phase one of the trap was complete.

Well done, gang, he thought. *Now get home and show those assholes who's really in charge.*

CHAPTER FORTY-TWO

—Doctor Troy Bruin,
MEMOIRS FROM MARS

Troy studied Xanthe as they made their way back to Earth. He was impressed with her singleminded focus on the mission, but he was also worried about her state of mind. There was a hard edge to her now. He had been taken aback by her decision to leave Jonas behind. It was so unlike her usually heart-centred, compassionate approach.

Colonel Jin had also been surprised by the decision, but when he heard of the potential Earth First plant, he supported the move. His team would need Olympus support through Jonas if they were to remain in control of some aspect of the helium-3.

And here they were now, about to execute their own trap.

"Are you ready?" Xanthe asked Troy.

He nodded, his face grim. He'd have to lean on all his best acting skills to convince the ground crew of their new plan.

"Colonel Jin, are you ready?" asked Xanthe.

"Affirmative, Commander Waters. Let us proceed."

Troy knew Xanthe was commanding her ThinkLink to launch the decoy intelligence as they had planned.

"Athena, hail the Indian Space Agency, now," she said out loud, for the benefit of her passengers and any onboard cameras.

Athena connected to the Indian Space Agency and Vikram's voice came over the comms.

"Commander Waters, *Pinnacle*, what's your status? We are receiving disturbing data."

"Affirmative, Vikram," she replied, feigning suppressed concern. "We've got a few malfunctions and our trajectory has changed. Athena is doing projections right now on what it means for re-entry."

"Our calculations show you will be off track and miss the Indian subcontinent altogether," explained Vikram, unable to keep the distress out of his voice.

"That's what we're seeing, too, Vikram."

Troy snuck a glance at Xanthe and admired the absolute conviction with which she delivered this news. He did not know she was capable of such subterfuge. It filled him with unease.

"Athena is coming back with some suggestions, now," she said.

"Go ahead, Commander Waters. We will run it past our A.I. here, as well."

Xanthe flicked a couple of switches on her command panel, swiped a screen and pretended to be alarmed by what she read there. "Athena projects a more suitable landing in North America."

Xanthe hurried on before Vikram could interrupt her, pretending to read the display manufactured by Athena. "She says there are two potential landing spots. There is the Spaceward Bound base, requiring a nautical landing, or there is the Gaia Enterprises headquarters. Given the current damage and our ability to execute repairs to the navigation and life support systems, Athena recommends securing a landing at the Gaia Enterprises base."

There was a long pause from Vikram before he came back with, "That will be problematic as the base is currently being held by the Earth First ecoterrorists."

Only a touch of irony there, observed Troy. *No one is playing this game straight.*

"I appreciate that, Vikram, and would welcome any other suggestions," Xanthe said, pretending to sympathise.

"Commander, you and the crew work on fixing the issues, if you can, and we will work on landing options from our side."

"Affirmative, Vikram. We will give a full report of issues and fixes within the hour."

"And that's about all the time we have," said Vikram. "We will need a plan and prepare a change of comms before you enter the atmosphere."

"I appreciate that," said Xanthe. "We'll do our part faster if we can. Vikram, I'm going to shut down comms while we run the diagnostics and start any repairs. You'll still have us on the tracker and can hail us at any time if new information comes to light."

"Roger that. Comms on standby."

"*Pinnacle* out."

Xanthe switched off the comms and slumped back in her chair.

Colonel Jin shrugged to relieve the tension in his neck. "Do you think they bought it?"

"Absolutely," Xanthe replied with a wave of her hand. "I'm going to get Athena to run all their suggestions and prepare counter arguments to steer them where we want."

"But if we're right," said Troy carefully, "the ecoterrorists don't just have a plant in the Indian Space Agency, they're in cahoots with them. So, the 'negotiation' to use the Gaia Enterprises base will be a fairly swift and easy one, because they will need to fake that. The Indians and the ecoterrorists still get the helium-3, just not on their own base in India."

"It's definitely a spanner in their works," she replied. "Let's hope the rest of the plan works as we hoped."

As expected, Vikram hailed them well within the hour.

"Commander Waters, *Pinnacle*, we have an update. Our A.I. team has run all the various scenarios and agrees with Athena."

"Surprise, surprise," said Troy under his breath.

"Thank you, Vikram," Xanthe said. "We could not fix the navigation issue, but the life support systems are still intact. We are checking the payload and any potential consequences with the change of direction given weather conditions on Earth. We are confident we will manage the change in landing."

"Good. Then Gaia Enterprises is a go. We have negotiated with Earth First to allow the Gaia Enterprises crew that they've been holding to run comms and to receive you."

"What does that mean for our safety?" asked Xanthe.

My God, she is good at this, thought Troy. He was wholly convinced by her performance.

"We are negotiating the Indian Space Agency's representation on the ground."

"In exchange for what?" asked Xanthe.

"Negotiations are ongoing, but initial proposals are being looked on favourably."

"I see."

"Our primary interest is getting you home safely. We don't want to lose any more spaceships or crew."

"Thanks for your concern," said Xanthe with just a hint of sarcasm.

"We will liaise with the Gaia Enterprises base and hand over CapCom to them in the next twenty minutes," Vikram continued.

"Roger that."

"Well, this will be the Indian Space Agency signing out."

"May Gaia guide us well," she said quietly.

Xanthe looked at Troy, his face riddled with concern, but resolved on their path.

"And now into the dragon's lair," said Colonel Jin.

"Let's hope the dragon takes the bait," Xanthe said, and punched the console key to head for home.

PART THREE

CHAPTER FORTY-THREE

"I don't see myself as a destroyer, but as a bringer of light. Sometimes, you need to burn away the darkness to let the light shine through."

—Claire Edwards,
THE REBEL'S PLAYBOOK: THE EARTH FIRST MANIFESTO

Madison spent most of the chopper ride studying Gareth and Lincoln, who were busy signalling messages she couldn't quite decipher. A worm of doubt wriggled through her. Despite his overtures and gestures of friendship, there was something about Lincoln that didn't totally line up. What was he planning?

Something changed in Dave's demeanour as he sat opposite her, and she strained to look over her shoulder through the helicopter window. She was startled by what she saw. It was the Gaia Enterprises base coming into view. They were heading home!

Maybe Claire wasn't lying. Maybe they were being released. Madison dared to hope. But years in the Air Force dampened her enthusiasm.

Don't count those chickens! She heard her mother's voice rumble through her head.

The chopper landed and Claire and her minions hustled them

across the landing pad under guard, guns up and into the base. More Earth First renegades were waiting and ushered them down a corridor and into a windowless room, where they were locked in together.

This is the staff conference room, Madison realised. It had a boardroom table and a big screen to watch any of the Gaia takeoff and landing operations.

I wonder if they left the remote around here somewhere, she thought. Sure enough, on top of the screen, there was a remote. *I wonder...*

She clicked it on.

The screen lit up. An object with a fiery, blazing trail filled the display. Madison clicked another button, her mind reeling. The display went to full screen, showing the Gaia CapCom room in full operation. She recognised the Gaia landing team, alongside a few unfamiliar faces. Alexandra Minke stood at command, along with her signature pink drink bottle.

Max, Serena, Dave, Gareth and Lincoln fell silent, standing alongside Madison, staring at the streaming image.

"That's the *Pinnacle!*" said Gareth in amazement.

"They brought us here for the landing," said Serena. "They really have negotiated an exchange. Your ploy worked!" Serena congratulated Lincoln.

There was colour in his cheeks, Madison noted.

"We'll see," he said. "You can trust ecoterrorists about as far as you can throw them."

The same might be said of billionaire space tech CEOs, thought Madison.

They stood transfixed by the screen. They listened to the CapCom communication and heard a woman's voice come through.

"That's Xanthe!" said Serena. "She's on her way back. She must be piloting the *Pinnacle.*"

Gareth turned and stared at Serena.

"I didn't know Xanthe Waters could fly," Gareth said, his voice laden with confusion.

Serena opened her mouth to explain and then caught herself before she divulged the ThinkLink news. "Somebody else must be with them," she suggested awkwardly.

Gareth frowned, considered her more deeply, and then turned back to the CapCom livestream. "Who the hell is flying that ship?" he said under his breath.

"And why is the *Pinnacle* landing here?" asked Dave. "Surely it would've been easier to land at a Spaceward Bound facility?"

"One might think that, I agree," said Lincoln.

Madison was instantly alert to any hint of subterfuge in Lincoln's voice, but his tone was inconclusive. He, too, looked confused.

The image of the *Pinnacle* grew larger on the screen as it made its way through the atmosphere.

"Break engines and reverse thrusters now," muttered Gareth, his fist clenched and his teeth grinding, eyes riveted to the screen.

Madison knew that feeling. As a pilot, seeing someone else fly your bird was unnerving, especially during a delicate operation like this, landing a craft outside of its usual home base. She could see him ticking off all the procedures, praying that whoever was piloting the *Pinnacle* got it right.

Madison knew it was Xanthe and the Athena ThinkLink, so she had full faith. The ship would be fine, assuming there had been no damage on the journey from the Moon. Her thoughts turned again to the companions they had left behind: Xanthe, Troy and Jonas.

And here they were, at last!

It seemed like they held their breath in unison as they watched the *Pinnacle* execute landing manoeuvres flawlessly and touch down safely on the Gaia Enterprises landing pad. The CapCom room erupted in cheers.

"Who the hell is that?" asked Dave, pointing to a figure in a white suit in the CapCom room.

"That would be the Deputy Lunar Commissioner and head of the Indian Space Agency," said Lincoln wryly. "Vikram Chatterjee."

"He must be representing the Lunar Commission. Or leading the negotiations?" Dave said.

"Probably," said Lincoln with a breeziness that made the hair on Madison's neck prickle.

Her attention switched back to the screen where the man Lincoln had called Vikram was giving a speech. "And through successful negotiation, we have secured helium-3 production for the future of the planet. The Lunar Commission will convene once we have met with Commander Waters, Doctor Bruin and Colonel Jin, and discussed the situation as it stands on the Moon."

"What about Jonas?" wondered Madison. "Where is Jonas?"

The others stared at her in alarm.

"Yeah, where is that pain in the ass?" Serena added.

Before they had time to contemplate the absence of their colleague, the door swung open, and Claire Edwards stood in the doorway, a pistol in her hand and several armed guards behind her.

"Lincoln Ellison," she called out. "Come with me, right now."

Madison shot a look at Lincoln, who seemed surprised.

But not quite surprised enough, thought Madison.

Lincoln exited with hands in the air, showing full deference to Claire's command. The door slammed behind them, and they heard it lock in place. Mr Puffkins went berserk, yapping and scratching the door.

"What the actual…?" said Dave.

"Where the hell is Jonas?" said Serena, still staring at the screen. "I hope nothing has happened to him."

∽

Troy did a quick audit of his body as the *Pinnacle* came to rest on the platform. It was a textbook landing as he had expected. There was nothing wrong with the *Pinnacle*, and Athena had flown it deftly.

Part one of their plan was complete.

And now to see if they could pull off the rest of it. His heart raced, and his breathing was slightly laboured, as was to be expected, returning to Earth's gravity after so long on the Moon. He could see that Colonel Jin and Xanthe were experiencing the same, their faces crinkled with pain.

They went through their checks as they powered down the vessel and prepared for the exit. Vikram had been on CapCom alongside their Gaia counterpart, Alexandra Minke, ready to receive them. No sign of the ecoterrorists, though.

Where are those bastards hiding? thought Troy. *Lurking somewhere nearby, no doubt.*

They followed the exit protocols to the letter. They unbuckled and prepared to leave the *Pinnacle*. Troy gave Xanthe a small hug of support and a grim smile to Colonel Jin as they moved to the next phase of the plan.

The doors slid open, and the Gaia team met them on the ramp, ready with supportive arms to assist with walking to the waiting medical transport. The support team would take them to the quarantine medbay to be assessed by the medics, assuming the regular protocol was still in place.

It was disturbing how normal this all seemed.

As Troy climbed into the van alongside Xanthe and Colonel Jin, he noticed a smear of something on the landing pad. Then he realised what it was. The blood of the murdered astronauts from during the *Saturnia* assault. His eyes darted around the base, looking for any subterfuge, and found nothing. Still, his senses were strained tight as a violin string.

They pulled into the medical vehicle bay, still in their spacesuits to maintain quarantine and be mindful of their biological processes now that they were back on Earth. The door slid open, and Troy stepped out with the help of a young man dressed in a paramedic uniform.

"Well, hello there, Doctor Bruin," the young man said.

Troy did a double take. He knew that voice!

"Jack," he said.

Xanthe climbed down from the van beside him, dumbstruck.

"Jack," she said through her helmet, and stared at her son for the first time in fifteen years.

Jack's face was bright with joy.

"You made it," he said to Xanthe.

"I did," she croaked.

Jack handed Troy over to his colleague and stood before Xanthe who swayed on wobbly legs. Jack jumped forward and grabbed her by the arms.

"Easy there," he said. "Your body is going to feel about six times heavier than it did a few days ago."

"I feel as light as a cloud," Xanthe said dreamily. She lurched forward and hugged her son. He held her tiny frame as she trembled and sobbed.

"It's okay," Jack whispered. "It's okay. Take a deep breath. We need to get you into that chair over there and wheel you into decompression. Can you do that?" he said, pulling away.

"Yes," she said, tears streaming down her face.

Troy's heart filled with happiness to see Xanthe so undone at the reunion with her long-lost son. The warm heart he thought had hardened through calamity on the Moon was soft again.

Doctor Mohammed bustled over to the paramedic team and surveyed him, Xanthe and Colonel Jin with a clinical eye.

"Commander. Doctor. And this must be the Colonel," snapped the doctor, all business.

"Doctor Mohammed," Troy said, grinning. "It's good to see a friendly face! Thank you for being here."

"Yes. Well. We weren't going to be. It's been quite an ordeal, as you can imagine," Doctor Mohammed said, oblivious to Troy's bemused smile.

"Yes, I can imagine, quite the ordeal," Troy said, and extended a gloved hand to the doctor, who shook it awkwardly.

Doctor Mohammad directed them into wheelchairs and the paramedic team moved them swiftly to the waiting recovery area, a spacious white room, in a spartan style but with plush fittings to help the astronauts adjust back to Earth. Jack assisted Xanthe gently onto a recliner and then removed her helmet and gloves.

Xanthe reached for Jack's face and touched him softly as she stared into her son's eyes.

Simon was right, Troy thought, as he watched mother and son. Jack had inherited his mother's eyes.

"You're so handsome," Xanthe said.

Jack smiled shyly, glancing at her, and then bustled about his work.

"We will soon have you back on your feet," he said. "Some tests, a drink and a meal and you'll be halfway to feeling better, so my boss tells me." Jack indicated Doctor Mohammed, behind him, working on Colonel Jin.

"Welcome back to Earth," said a voice from the observation room.

Troy glanced over to see Vikram in the observation room with an entourage, including media cameras. He frowned, as that was not the usual protocol for returning astronauts. Normally, they were given some privacy until they had at least had a shower. Troy was annoyed, then concerned. This was a staging ground for the Indians who were taking over.

Not so fast, Troy thought. *We still have an ace up our sleeve.*

"Thank you for returning safely on this historic occasion, and delivering the first shipment of the helium-3 that will transform the energy economy of the planet and the trajectory of humanity's future. Well done, Commander Waters, Doctor Bruin and Colonel Jin, and to the Gaia team that helped bring them home safely."

Despite the clapping and cheers, Troy felt a ripple of unease.

Something wasn't right. He tuned out Vikram's ongoing speech, scanning the observation room and the medical assessment space as the paramedics bustled around them. Maybe he was just being paranoid.

But then the medical door was flung open, and the room filled with armed masked men in paramilitary gear. They fanned out around the room with rifles trained on the astronauts and the paramedics. Troy's heart rate spiked, and his eyes sought Xanthe instantly, as her face contorted with fear.

Two other figures walked in slowly. Lincoln Ellison had his hands in the air, and against his head was the muzzle of a gun, carried by an unmasked Claire Edwards.

"Vikram, you son of a bitch!" yelled Claire. "You're a double-crossing asshole!"

Vikram's face turned pale and sweaty.

"Who are you?" asked Vikram.

"You know very well who I am," said Claire, "since you're the one who hired me to hijack the *Saturnia* and the *Minerva*. Or is your memory so short, Vikram? You promised me the first full load of helium-3. But you've gone and booby trapped it, you whore of a dog."

"What? This is preposterous!" blurted Vikram.

"Is it? My team just tried to secure the payload, as we agreed," she said slowly and carefully, "but it's got some kind of security lock on it. You promised us a full payload and we want it, now."

"I did no such thing," protested Vikram.

Troy honed his attention on Vikram's face and words. Troy knew Vikram had indeed not locked the payload. That had been Jonas's work before they left the Moon. Their plan was coming to fruition.

As they suspected, Earth First had an agreement with the Indians, most likely to do with the helium-3. Today was payday, and they couldn't collect, thanks to Olympus's interference. Now that the back-channel subterfuge of the Indians was exposed, they were finished.

"Unlock the helium-3 now, or we take out the rest of the space crew we have in custody. That's the entire contingency of the *Saturnia* and *Minerva* crew, and with this lot, that means your entire staff for future lunar excursions is at risk. Pay what you owe," said Claire, "or reap the consequences."

Vikram was genuinely paralysed, observed Troy. This was not part of his script.

There was a movement out of the corner of his eye and Troy saw Jack inch towards Claire, who had her back turned to the unarmed paramedics.

"No," he whispered.

∾

Xanthe felt Jack pull away from her side as Vikram and Claire continued to exchange accusations and denials. Jack took tiny steps past Troy and his attendant. Time slowed to molasses as she realised what Jack was about to do.

She heard Troy's whispered 'no' and her own voice screaming, "Jack! No!"

She watched her son take three strides and leap on Claire's back, throwing a chokehold around her neck. Lincoln slipped free as Claire brought both her hands, one with the revolver, up to her neck to release the hold.

Xanthe pushed herself forward on her chair, breathing heavily, and tried to stand. Her legs collapsed in the gravity, but she pulled herself upwards. Claire dived forward, bringing Jack with her onto the ground. There was a scrabbling as they fought for control, and shouting as the armed guards trained their weapons on Jack and their leader, wrestling for the upper hand.

Xanthe lurched from her chair to Troy's as Troy screamed "No!" and went to help Jack, but his own knees gave way.

A shot rang out.

There was a deep inhale, like someone being punched in the gut. The sound filled the space, and everything froze.

Xanthe's eyes were wide, riveted on the entwined figures. There was a groan, and Claire pushed Jack off her. She was smeared in blood. Xanthe stumbled towards the pair and Claire brought her revolver up, eyes pinned on Xanthe.

"Commander Waters, stand down." Athena A.I. ThinkLink sounded in Xanthe's mind. *"Activating parasympathetic nervous system and down-regulating fear response, now."*

Troy grabbed at Xanthe's waist, but a blinding rage filled her with white light. Claire scrabbled away, pushing her heels against the ground while both hands held the revolver on Xanthe. Xanthe stumbled towards her nemesis.

"Stand down, Commander," came Athena's voice.

"Stop, Xanthe!" cried Troy.

Xanthe wrenched her eyes from Claire and saw her son. His face was pale, and a red stain bloomed on his chest. Xanthe fell on her son and cradled his face, pressing a hand to his wound. Her paramedic experience kicked in, and she assessed the trauma. Internal bleeding, perhaps an artery hit, judging by the pulsing of the blood. The bullet may have pierced his spine too.

"Jack, Jack," she breathed.

His eyes softened and struggled to focus on her. His breath was shallow and rapid. Xanthe pressed harder and felt the blood pulse under her fingers, his life force leaking onto the sterile white floor.

"Xanthe," he whispered, and strained to look at her face. "Tried to help."

"I know you did, Jack. You are so brave. Stupid, like your father, but brave. Be stubborn now, like your mother. Stay with me. Fight, Jack! Fight."

But she knew it was over.

He held her gaze with a confused look, then relaxed.

"Mum," he said. Then his eyes closed forever.

"No," she whispered. "No! Jack," she begged. His head rolled to the side, and she knew he was gone.

Xanthe's head turned slowly to Claire, who had pushed herself over to the wall and was struggling to her feet, the gun still trained on her.

"Commander Waters, your pulse and nervous system are overtaxed. Stand down. Commander Waters, I recommend you stand down."

"Fuck off, Athena," she shouted.

Xanthe was aware of Troy at her side, tending to Jack and trying to comfort her at the same time. Xanthe had eyes only for Claire.

In a movement she could not later describe, Xanthe was on top of Claire, hands clamped firmly on the other woman's neck, squeezing hard. Her eyes burned with a white furious hatred. She could feel her hands crushing Claire's windpipe. The revolver dropped and panic rose in Claire's face as she scrambled for life and clawed at Xanthe, trying to relieve her grip.

Xanthe had a single-minded purpose: to extinguish Claire Edwards' life in punishment for the loss of her son.

A part of her brain heard Troy's voice. "Xanthe, no! Stop!"

"Commander Waters, release your grip. Commander Waters, stand down," Athena A.I. ThinkLink rose in volume inside her mind.

Xanthe tightened her hold, and she saw Claire's eyes close and her light dim.

Searing pain shot through Xanthe's head. She released her grip and fell to the side as Troy bailed into her. Then all went black.

Troy held Xanthe protectively as shots sounded and bodies scuffled violently around him.

He snuck a look as more armed combatants filled the room, yelling at the kidnappers, who capitulated almost immediately to the better armed newcomers. Troy watched as they lowered their weapons slowly to the ground. There was no sign of Claire or Lincoln.

The newcomers took command of the room, sending the paramedics to Jack and Xanthe.

Doctor Mohammed rushed to Jack and checked his vitals. He caught Troy watching him and shook his head slightly with a sad look. Doctor Mohammed called over the other paramedics to assist, and he joined Troy to assess Xanthe.

"Is she injured?" he asked Troy.

"Not that I can tell," Troy replied, as he monitored her pulse and breathing. "She collapsed suddenly before I got to her."

"There are some scratches here," Doctor Mohammad said, pointing at where Claire had dug her nails into Xanthe's face. "Let's take her into my surgery for a full assessment."

"Doctor Mohammed," Troy added quietly. "She has a ThinkLink. I installed it on the Moon. Maja sent it up in secret with Max and Dave."

"Ah, yes. I am aware of that," snapped Doctor Mohammad.

Troy could tell he had in truth forgotten until that moment.

"That may have something to do with it. But let's get her and the young man into surgery."

"Jack is…?"

"Gone. Yes, I know. But the cameras are still rolling, and we need to do the best for him, regardless."

"Cameras," muttered Troy. He looked at the observation room again and saw the newcomers had shut down the media and were corralling the spectators out of the room. There was a ringleader with a powerful voice. A stocky man, whose offsiders responded to with the deference owed to a senior commander they trusted implicitly.

The ringleader spoke into his headset. "Search the other sector. We have the *Pinnacle* astronauts. Lincoln Ellison is missing, presumed under the control of Claire Edwards and the Earth First team. Proceed with caution. She is armed and bloody dangerous."

The ringleader returned to the medical bay and walked over to Troy, who was hanging on to Xanthe's medical gurney as Doctor Mohammed prepared to take her into surgery alongside Jack's body. Colonel Jin was clinging to the other side.

"Doctor Bruin, Colonel Jin," the man said. He had a kind look about him, despite what some obviously hard years had done to his face. Lines earned from years of turmoil and bitter conflict, Troy guessed. "I'm Felix Dubois, under the command of Aryanna Sharif."

"Aryanna!" Troy cried. "Is she here?"

"She'll be arriving soon, once we have secured the base, along with Maja Garcia."

"They're both alive!" Troy exhaled in relief.

"They are indeed," Felix assured them. "But right now, we need to make sure you are safe, and Commander Waters and this young man are looked after."

"His name is Jack. He's Xanthe's son." Troy swallowed hard at the emotion that swelled in his throat.

Felix stared at the young man's body, pale and unmoving, and the enormous puddle of blood smeared on the floor from where he had been lifted onto the stretcher. Felix's jaw clenched. "I see," he said. "Come. Let's get you away from here. There is still danger in the corridors."

CHAPTER FORTY-FOUR

*"At what cost, this future we aspire to create? I have
often asked myself that question. Too often."*

—Madison Floyd,
MEMOIRS FROM MARS

Madison, Serena, Gareth, Max and Dave stood glued to the
screen in the staff room where they were still held captive. They
watched the *Pinnacle* land and counted three astronauts.

"Where's Jonas?" Serena asked again.

"They must have left him behind," said Max.

"No way," she replied. "No way Xanthe would leave Jonas
behind. Colonel Jin would have no problem leaving his people,
but Xanthe? She wouldn't leave him alone like that."

Madison tore her eyes away from the screen and looked at
Serena, whose face was awash in stubborn denial. Madison only
felt a growing chill spreading in her body.

The landing had been perfect. The Gaia crew had taken charge
with a local paramedic team. They could see Doctor Mohammed
snapping orders as he scurried in his tight, efficient way around
them.

The coverage had then swapped to a live broadcast from within the observation room, and they'd all wondered at that, and felt for Xanthe, Troy and Colonel Jin. Astronauts never felt that great back on Earth, and no one wanted to be shown to the world as vulnerable and unwashed.

Then all hell broke loose.

There was Claire Edwards with a gun to Lincoln's head, shouting accusations, making demands.

"What the actual…" Serena gasped.

Dave's mouth was agape.

"Holy shit!" said Max.

"So much for Olympus Rising and diplomacy," Gareth said.

Madison felt heat flood her face and chills race through her veins.

Something had gone terribly wrong.

She caught something on Gareth's face out of the corner of her eye. What was that? Smugness? He had his arms crossed and didn't look all that surprised.

A shot rang out on screen and her attention snapped back to the livestream. A man was down, and Xanthe was strangling Claire. Then a bunch of other guys with weapons burst onto the scene. Claire disappeared and Lincoln ran after her while the remaining ecoterrorists caught in the room lowered their weapons. A large hand appeared over the screen and a voice commanded, "Cameras off, now!"

The camera angle shifted and then went blank.

There was a moment before the news studio flashed up and a newscaster resumed commentary. "Extraordinary scenes there at the Gaia Enterprises headquarters in the ongoing saga of the Earth First siege and kidnapping crisis. Stay tuned as we bring you live, up to date information as it unfolds…"

"What the hell was that?" Serena said.

Madison muted the screen as it went to coverage of other

events. In shock, they stared at the images, and then Madison sat down in a chair. The others followed suit.

"Barrio, what happened to Lincoln's negotiation?" Dave's voice was a breath away from an accusation.

Gareth pursed his lips, his eyes staring at the screen, brow wrinkled.

"Obviously, it didn't go as planned," he said finally.

"To state the bleeding obvious," Serena retorted.

"What was the plan?" Madison asked, eyes narrowed on Gareth.

"You know what the plan was," he said, colour blooming on his neck.

"The plan was to offer them legitimacy, to back their requests." Madison kept her voice steady and leaned towards Gareth. "Why would they give that up for such an obviously risky move – and with cameras playing?"

Gareth shrugged.

"Unless they never got that offer," Dave added, awareness wafting through his consciousness. "Lincoln made some other deal, didn't he?"

Gareth squeezed his lips tight and puffed his chest under his crossed arms. "If he made some other deal," he replied, "and I am not saying he did, by the way. I wasn't in that room any more than you were. But if he made some other deal, as Lincoln is wont to do, then it clearly did not go to plan. I mean, look at that damn mess."

He gestured to the screen where the complete assault was being replayed. The struggle, the shot, Xanthe strangling Claire, the mysterious insurgents.

"Christ, is that Xanthe's son?" Dave said. He leaped to his feet and grabbed the remote to freeze the screen.

"Yes, it is," Madison said. "That's Jack."

And their hearts broke.

CHAPTER FORTY-FIVE

"From the ashes of the old, a new world can be born. Revolution isn't just destruction; it's the first step towards renewal and rebirth."

—Claire Edwards,
THE REBEL'S PLAYBOOK: THE EARTH FIRST MANIFESTO

Lincoln Ellison had his hands in the air as Claire pushed him along the corridor. Claire had one hand on his back, the other waving a gun behind her. They had escaped pursuit of the unknown assailants by ducking into a rehab room, crawling through a window and dropping into an accommodation zone.

Claire stopped outside a door and hammered out a coded sequence. The door opened a crack, and Claire pushed her and Lincoln through. Two nervous-looking Earth First staffers greeted them.

"We better hurry, Claire," one of them said. "Whoever those other guys are, they'll be in this sector pretty quickly. We need to get out of here, now."

She ignored them and peered over at a stretcher in the corner, with a prone figure hidden under blankets and bandages.

"How's the patient?" she asked.

"Consus? Still the same. Stable. Unconscious," replied the second staffer, tugging an earlobe and wrinkling his face in frustration.

"Good. The two of you get out of here. Get to the vehicle and be ready for a hot extraction, no matter what they promise. Signal me when you're in place. That's when we'll finish this little performance."

"What about you?" asked the first staffer.

"I've got to deal with Lincoln and Xavier. They're my get out of jail free cards. Now, go." She opened the door and sent them running.

Claire went over to check Xavier for herself. The Frenchman's face was relaxed and peaceful.

The blissful oblivion of injury, she mused.

"Well done, Claire," said Lincoln. "That was pretty tricky, back there. Didn't expect those other fellows."

Claire spun to give Lincoln a hard stare. "Tricky? That bitch Xanthe Waters nearly choked me to death."

"Well, it looks like you shot and killed her son."

Claire stared at Lincoln, confused. "Her son? She doesn't have a son."

"She didn't. Then she did." Lincoln shrugged in a nonchalant way. "Apparently, he survived the tsunami all those years ago, only to be raised by another woman in the aftermath. They recently reunited. It was an endearing family portrait, and they were looking forward to the reunion, after her return to Earth. Touching, really."

Claire gawped. "Her son was the paramedic who attacked me?"

"I think he thought he was trying to save me, the man with a gun to his head, remember? And impress his mother."

Claire blinked and let this news filter though her synapses. Then she tucked that piece of information away for more consideration later.

"Whatever," she said with a dismissive wave. "That's all done. It's time for me to get out of here. I will hold you to our agreement, Lincoln."

"I expect nothing less from a professional like you, Claire," said Lincoln with a bow.

"Give me a break, Lincoln. Stop pretending you're some kind of gentleman. You're a thug."

"One sees in others what is in oneself."

She glared at him and then pushed on. "Our agreement, Lincoln."

"Don't worry, you'll get proceeds from the helium-3 as we outlined, since you delivered the Indians up on a platter so publicly. Very well done, indeed. They'll take the fall for the kidnapping, now, which is perfect. You and Leo did some quick thinking there when Xanthe and company decided to play the heroes and boot us off the Moon."

Lincoln looked around and sat in a chair beside the prone Xavier. "However did you get Vikram to go along with the kidnapping scheme?"

"Same as all the others: greed," Claire replied. "Once he worked out how much he could cream for himself, it wasn't much of a step to betray his colleagues and space agency. Money has a way of deadening people's moral compass." She sniffed with derision, curling her lips in disdain.

"Once I realised Vikram wasn't going to pay up, implicating the bastard was easily done," she admitted. "Plus, with the Indian Space Agency's primary team buried on the Moon, his crew would never deliver anyhow."

"A terrible thing, to be sure."

"Give me a break, Lincoln. I know you don't give a shit. This just makes it even easier for you to take over Moon operations."

"From tragedy comes opportunity. And let's not forget you are also benefiting from this happy-sad accident."

Claire ignored this last comment. It stuck in her craw that she had to bend to these conniving assholes to do right in the world. It was all so fucked up.

"Are you sure you want to turn down the legitimacy offer? It would make your life a little easier. Not to mention mine."

She whirled on him once more.

"Legitimacy? There is no legitimacy on offer from the likes of Aryanna Sharif. Or the Indian Space Agency. Or Gaia Enterprises. Or Spaceward Bound." She sneered with disgust. "Legitimacy. There is no 'legitimacy'. Those who claim legitimacy do so with the only two things that make it so: power and money. Without those things, all players are the same.

"Power and money cloak the deeds on the path to a throne. What do I really get if I take up the offer of 'legitimacy'? I lose the right to speak truth to power. To speak out about what is really happening around the world." A grimace stretched her lips over her teeth, and she nearly growled with fury. "No, thank you. I'll stay in the shadows. From there, I will bring the light."

"You're so sure of your high moral ground, Claire. But when you don't *play* the game, you don't get to *win* the game."

"What game, Lincoln? The game of subterfuge? Of double standards? Of bold-faced lying? You're all as revolting as each other. You, Vikram, Aryanna, the lot of you. You're all so happy to play friends but kill each other behind the scenes."

"No one said anything about killing. I just want you to keep sabotaging the other space agencies to keep Spaceward Bound ahead."

"And if a few people get killed along the way, say, like the Chinese taikonauts, that's okay?"

"I never sanctioned that," Lincoln said with genuine affront. "I told you to sabotage the Chinese space program, not kill anyone."

She stared at him with cold, hard eyes. "It's only a matter of time, Lincoln, before one underhanded move becomes another, bolder one. You're not so innocent in all this."

Lincoln scoffed. "I'm not the one who pulled the trigger, nor launched the terraforming process that killed hundreds of thousands." He stepped closer to her, standing beside her, as they both looked on Xavier's sleeping body.

"And let's not forget my three dead Spaceward Bound astronauts: Lester, Freddy and Snyder," he said in a low voice. "You owe me, Claire."

"You forget that I've lost a man too." She turned to stare at him with hard eyes.

"Oh yes, that's right. Sanjay. As I understand it, Sanjay was not so good at covering his tracks and it was his communications that tipped off that pesky irritant, Xanthe Waters. Otherwise, we'd be in India right now, happily unloading helium-3 into our respective coffers." He patted her arm in condescension. "You really need to get better at picking your operatives."

Claire turned away as the blood rose on her cheeks. She pretended to check Xavier's pulse and vitals. Lincoln kept his eyes riveted on Claire, daring her to contradict him.

Claire pushed past him, saying nothing, and put her ear to the door. "Where are those guys?" she wondered. "We're running out of time."

Her earpiece sounded, and her offsiders reported in position.

Lincoln heard it too and made ready to push Xavier's stretcher out into the corridor.

"Just one more piece of acting and you are free to slink back into the shadows," Lincoln said.

"Until I bring the light," she said.

"You do that."

She swung the door open and Lincoln followed, driving the stretcher that carried Xavier Consus, who was very much awake.

&

Madison, Dave, Max, Serena and Gareth listened to the footsteps running down the corridor. They yelled and banged on the door, to no avail. They had been locked in the room for nearly an hour.

There had been no more updates on the news channel, and they were becoming more and more agitated.

Mr Puffkins had responded to their stress and had barked constantly at every little noise. Serena had taken pity on the animal and removed a sock to play with him, while monitoring the news stream.

Breaking news flashed up on the screen and Madison lurched for the remote and clicked it off mute.

"Astonishing scenes, now"—the announcer's voice was high with excitement—"as the ongoing hostage and siege crisis at Gaia Enterprises continues. As you can see in this livestream, the chief kidnapper, whom we have identified as Claire Edwards, is on the edge of the base's property, holding a gun to Lincoln Ellison's head.

"Beside them on an ambulance stretcher is none other than Xavier Consus, missing since the *Saturnia* first returned to Earth and disappeared in the hostage taking. He does not appear conscious. And my goodness! Is that a bomb strapped to Lincoln's chest? We will get confirmation for you as soon as we can."

The announcer touched her earpiece and nodded.

"Earth First demands are being streamed across the Earth First broadcast platforms now. Claire Edwards says she will release Lincoln and Xavier now if she and her colleagues may leave the base unharmed and unimpeded. Once they are away, and within the hour, she will send the location of the Lunar Commissioners, all of whom have been held captive for the last twenty-four days."

Madison gasped at the sight of Xavier. He was still alive, then! That was good news. But in what condition? Maybe it was a good thing he was unconscious during these events.

"And there is the chief negotiator approaching slowly," continued the announcer, working hard to keep her voice from a fever pitch. "They have some Earth First operatives with them, and they are sending them over to Claire Edwards and that black van you can see on the top left-hand side of your screen."

The Earth First people suddenly stopped halfway to the van.

The negotiator spoke back and forth with Claire, who kept the gun at Lincoln's head. Moments dragged into minutes with nothing but conjecture for the observers about what was happening.

"My goodness, this is a delicate situation," the announcer narrated, trying to keep the intrigue dynamic. "Any wrong move could be disastrous! Let's hope Claire Edwards isn't feeling trigger happy today."

"Someone ought to be trigger happy around that announcer, no?" Dave said. "What an insensitive dropkick."

"Is that a Dutch expression?" Gareth asked.

"Aussie," replied Serena. "We've got all the best sayings."

"Shh!" hissed Madison. "Can't you see our friend is caught in the cross hairs?"

Mr Puffkins whined.

"Be nice," whispered Serena in reply. "You're upsetting Puffy."

"I'll upset him more if you and the damn dog don't shut your pie holes!" Madison replied.

"Pie holes," said Max to Serena. "That's American."

She chortled into Mr Puffkins's fur, and the dog licked her neck.

Madison shifted to the edge of her seat, eyes wide. They all sensed the change and stared hard at the screen. In a blur, the staffers ran for the van, and once on board, Claire shoved Lincoln into Xavier's stretcher, which went hurtling towards the negotiator as Lincoln fell to the floor.

In what seemed like a nanosecond, black-clad operatives surged on Lincoln and removed the bomb device from his torso, then dragged him quickly away. Others swarmed over the negotiator and Xavier's stretcher, and soon all that was left on the scene was the vest with the bomb discarded on the pavement.

Claire's van hurtled away.

Madison, Gareth, Serena, Dave and Max stared at the screen, stunned.

"What a day!" said Dave. "I could do with a little lie down."

CHAPTER FORTY-SIX

"I was so focused on proving myself that I forgot what truly mattered. Being a leader isn't about perfection; it's about presence, about being there when it counts."

—JONAS SEABORN,
THE LUNAR CHRONICLE, FIRST PIONEERS

JONAS HAD WATCHED the *Pinnacle* landing at Gaia headquarters with a sense of pride. The landing had gone perfectly, and their own team had received the astronauts with the help of the local paramedics. He could track the Gaia CapCom conversation between Alexandra Minke and Xanthe the whole way down.

Distracted by the unusual screening of the astronauts' medical check, he half-listened to Vikram's welcome home speech when it all seemed to go horribly wrong. There were shouts, gunshots and mayhem as people with rifles ran onto the screen.

"Athena, hail Gaia Enterprises," Jonas said, trying to keep his panic at bay.

"Connecting with Gaia Enterprises, now."

"Olympus, this is Gaia HQ. We are under attack, standby."

Under attack! Again!

Had they been wrong about the Indian and Earth First alliance? They had thought that the Gaia HQ would be a safe landing spot since the Indians would pretend to negotiate with the ecoterrorists and clear them out of there. What if they weren't allied at all, and the ecoterrorists saw this as a golden opportunity to seize yet another ship and its crew?

Jonas bit his lip and tapped his foot, raking his mind for potential flaws in their logic.

"Athena, can you tell me what's going on?"

"The Earth First insurgents have infiltrated the base and have shot a paramedic. They've taken Lincoln Ellison hostage and there is a bomb threat."

"Oh, my God!" said Jonas. "Are Troy and Xanthe okay? And Colonel Jin?"

Athena paused a moment before replying. "My connection to Commander Waters has been interrupted."

"What the hell does that mean?"

"The Athena ThinkLink has been switched off."

"Is she dead?"

"I do not have that data."

Jonas felt sick.

He waited for updates, pacing the comms room. He tried to make sense of the events on Earth. Feeling completely helpless and alone, he sank into the CapCom chair and just stared at the screens, waiting. His mind and body grew numb with worry. He closed his eyes to ease the strain.

After several hours, the console lit up with an incoming connection.

"Olympus, this is Gaia HQ. Are you there?"

Jonas blinked awake, realising he'd nodded off.

"Yes, yes, I'm here."

"Sorry to leave you in the lurch there, Jonas," Alexandra Minke said.

"It's good to hear your voice, Ali."

"It's good to hear yours, too," she said with a quaver in her voice. "Look, there's been a massive incident. A paramedic has been killed and there's been a bomb threat, but the good news is that Aryanna's private military force has reclaimed the Gaia base and released the Lunar Commissioners."

The news ripped through Jonas's consciousness, and he took a moment to filter all of it.

Aryanna has a private military force? he wondered, filling with anxiety once more.

"Wow. Uh, Troy and Xanthe and Colonel Jin…how are they?" he stumbled over his words in the jumble of thoughts.

Alexandra took a breath before she said, "Xanthe had a sort of episode when the paramedic was killed. She is currently unconscious but does not seem to be in immediate danger."

"What kind of episode?" he asked, anxiety stabbing him again.

"She attacked the leader of the Earth First group, Claire Edwards. Troy tried to pull her off, but she'd already collapsed."

"What?" Jonas said. "That doesn't sound like Xanthe."

"The paramedic was her son," Ali said flatly.

"Oh, God, no! Not Jack," he said and put his head in his hands.

"Yeah."

Jonas felt his body contort with yet more grief, and a wave of nausea washed over him.

"Listen, Jonas, things are a little hectic. We want to get someone to maintain comms with you while we figure out the mess down here. How are you doing, anyway?"

"I'm…I don't know how to describe it," he said. "This is all very surreal."

"Hang in there, buddy. There'll be some good news, soon."

Ali smiled encouragingly at him through the holo, but Jonas just felt empty, a husk drifting on the wind, battered by events beyond his control.

CHAPTER FORTY-SEVEN

*"Trust is the foundation of any successful society. Building
and maintaining trust through consistent and honourable
actions is essential for long-term stability and growth."*

—Athena A.I.
WISDOM OF THE AGES

Maja's heart thumped hard in her chest as she watched the *Pinnacle* landing and the aftermath of the siege, with Felix's team's assault on the ecoterrorists. They had flown in low, under cover of the night, and hidden nearby in a makeshift camp, being attended to by Felix's crew.

She felt sick to her stomach as she saw Xanthe fall on the body of the young paramedic and then assault Claire.

It must be Jack, Maja thought. Somehow, he was there on the base. Xanthe had mentioned he had joined the paramedic force here in the United States. He must have asked specifically to be part of the ground crew for the landing.

Maja filled with nausea. So much unnecessary violence. She sighed as the grief washed over her again. How had it all gone so wrong? They were to be the beacon of humanity. A new way of living and working together. And now, one of her own protégés was leading an armed militia to bring down everything they had built over a lifetime.

And with a horrific body count.

Memories of Terra Blanca surged unbidden. The same terrible guilt and grief all over again. She had vowed they would do better. They would support people to do better, to learn better leadership, to be better with one another. And they had! Maja refused to sink into despair. The Olympus project had been that promise. And they had delivered.

But the world had overrun them yet again. She had missed something in Claire. Was it simply thwarted ambition that had been Claire's undoing? Had it really been as basic as that?

Perhaps it had.

But Claire was not alone. There was a whole mess of players on this chessboard.

The flap of the canvas base camp tent lifted, and Aryanna breezed in, haughty and elegant, even in the black military fatigues Felix had loaned her.

"Stop watching that replay, Maja," she commanded. "You'll only cloud your thinking, and I need you to be sharp."

Maja's gaze settled on the other woman as she floated to the folded chair opposite the plastic table, littered with radios and coffee mugs.

"Felix has organised the Lunar Commissioners now that they have been released and checked over medically. Once they've touched base with their families, we will move straight into an emergency crisis boardroom meeting."

"Already?" asked Maja.

"Of course. Vikram's treachery needs to be addressed immediately. And then there's the latest tragedy on the Moon. All our assets are now in the hands of Jonas Seaborn and a couple of robots. This requires urgent emergency action."

"Poor Jonas," said Maja. She put a hand to her forehead to ease the strain that was creeping over her. Jonas was not meant to handle this kind of pressure. She hoped he was up to the job. She wondered at Xanthe's decision to leave him there. Then again, at the time, they'd had the Indian team and the Red Star team. Now all were gone.

"Don't look so distressed, Maja. This is a public relations disaster. But in every disaster, there is always an opportunity to tell a better story."

"A public relations disaster? That's what you're thinking about, right now?" Maja's nostrils flared with anger.

"It is one of the many things that I am thinking about," retorted Aryanna. "Don't be so naïve, Maja. The future of the Olympus project hangs on public relations. There's only so much we can do from a private initiative. Now that helium-3 is the primary interest on the Moon, that means this is a global issue. It all needs to be handled with much delicacy and finesse."

"Aryanna, so many people have died. That was not the plan."

"No, it was not. None of this has been the plan. And yet, here we are. So, the sooner you stop lamenting what *has been* and focus on what *could be*, the better off we will be."

There was a hardening around Maja's heart, as if the sea of grief had washed barnacles over her time and time again, and now clung in a growing crust to her soul. She thought to slough them off, to stand tall with courage, but only pulled them tighter around herself for protection.

She sighed. "Tell me how we will tackle this meeting and what you want from me."

"That's better, Maja. The sooner we get through this, the sooner you can get back to building better worlds."

Maja dipped her head, staring at the hands in her lap. What was she really building? Was it really possible to build environments that sped up human development? Could they really overcome human nature? Could they really withstand the seductive maelstrom of power?

"Go ahead, I'm listening," Maja said and raised her head.

"Good. First, we expose Vikram's agreement with Earth First with the evidence we have from Athena's decoding of their secret transmissions. In addition, we have Claire's accusation during the stand-off."

"What happens next?"

"We remove Vikram as Deputy Lunar Commissioner and pursue an investigation of all Indian Space Agency operations before we permit them lunar access again."

Maja nodded slowly. "What about the Chinese? Red Star is now an untended asset."

"Red Star and Olympus are both at risk and need emergency support."

"The *Saturnia* needs a complete overhaul after its deployment. That will take months. The *Minerva* is lost. So, Gaia Enterprises is out of workable resources."

"Yes, I know," Aryanna said, annoyed. "That leaves Lincoln and Spaceward Bound."

"Surely there is a different solution?" asked Maja with despair. "Lincoln has shown a distinct lack of trustworthiness. First with the asteroid mining accident that killed nine people, and then with his intention to create a helium-3 monopoly, stealing from right under the Lunar Commission's nose."

"I agree with you. Lincoln is not my preferred choice. He will need a tight leash."

"This is not the basis of a good partnership, Aryanna. There is absolutely no trust possible with Lincoln."

"What is trust, anyway? Do you not always say that trust is a by-product of an effective system and not the starting point?"

"I do say that. And I believe that. But when trust is broken, the system takes some time to heal. The system of relationships and trust is more like a human body than it is of a mechanical machine. It's messy and nonlinear."

"I have every confidence you and the Olympus team will heal that body and make it fully functional."

"I'm not sure if any of them are ready to turn around and go back to the Moon. Xanthe is hardly in a condition to do so, given everything she has been through."

"I wasn't thinking of Commander Waters for the rescue mission and reestablishment of Olympus," said Aryana.

"Really? Xanthe is the best choice. She is well-respected and has guided her team through horrendous challenges. She just needs some time."

"Time is a luxury we don't have. Besides, I would like a leadership change. Commander Waters disobeyed a direct Lunar Commission directive when she apprehended Lincoln and company. We can't have mission leaders exercising such reckless autonomy."

Maja studied Aryanna's face but found only the usual stoic, smooth plaster and darting black eyes. Something had happened between Aryanna and Xanthe. But what?

"Who did you have in mind to lead the rescue operation, then?" Maja said, moving her thoughts to the forward plan.

"Doctor Troy Bruin is the next obvious choice. Xavier is still recovering and none of the others have displayed the requisite leadership skills."

"But Troy requires a kidney transplant. It would put the expedition and his health at great risk to send him back so soon."

"I understand. I've read the report. No matter. I will have my entire medical team undertake the procedure and speed up his healing. He'll be ready by the time we have the resources set to return to the Moon."

A tremor of fear rippled through Maja. She didn't like the way Xanthe was being edged aside by Aryanna. After all the work Xanthe had put into this mission, her unwavering commitment, it ought to be her choice whether she lead or not, or ceded command to another.

Maja decided not to go against Aryanna right now. Once the international agreements were ratified, they could quibble about personnel later.

"Who else do we need to be mindful of at the Lunar Commission's board meeting?" asked Maja.

"The Chinese. They will use the sympathy card to make some strong demands."

"Losing their entire space operation, bar Colonel Jin, is hardly playing a sympathy card. They deserve our support."

"It is indeed a tragedy, Maja. But remember, they jumped into an Indian alliance before anyone could blink. They may even have known about the Earth First agreement with the Indians, too. In my mind, they are not to be trusted, either." Aryanna smoothed her hair away from her face with her long, thin fingers. "Regardless of which way their current allegiances lie, this is also the opportunity we wanted to really merge a collaborative enterprise with the Chinese, once and for all."

"Don't you mean 'takeover'?"

Aryanna inspected a button on the rough, black material of her uniform. "That is one way of looking at it. I prefer a more"— she reached for the word—"humane approach to our business partnerships."

"Humane," Maja said with disdain. "It makes it sound as if you were shooting a dog and putting it out of its misery."

A bitter taste filled Maja's mouth. She looked about for a bottle of water, saw a case of them in the corner and rose to fetch herself one. She returned with a second bottle for Aryanna, who took it graciously.

Aryanna played with the cap of the bottle after taking a sip. "The Chinese Space Agency is in its death throes. Offering a collaboration – even an unequal one – is a lifeline for them."

Maja glimpsed a fleeting trace of some strange emotion across that veneer of Aryanna's face. Satisfaction?

Aryanna touched her earpiece and uttered an acknowledgment of the message received. She rose, sipped daintily from the bottle and placed it on the cluttered table.

"That was Felix. They are ready for us."

Maja followed Aryanna from the tent with an overpowering sensation of a fly caught in the sticky tendrils of a web she had not known was being spun around her.

CHAPTER FORTY-EIGHT

"Collective power is a double-edged sword. When wielded with integrity, it can achieve wonders. But it requires constant vigilance to ensure that personal ambitions don't derail the collective good."

—MAJA GARCIA,
THE JOURNALS

THEY WERE ALL there: all the signatories to the Global Lunar Treaty that had formed the Lunar Commission. Maja considered each of them as she ambled into the room, a discrete distance behind the fierce Aryanna, who kept her posture ramrod straight and her chin high.

The four space agency reps walked in wearily alongside their respective political reps. Then the space and technology giants made up the rest: Lincoln Ellison for Spaceward Bound, Elena Fischer for Human Habs, Aryanna for her own organisation, Aryanna Industries, and Maja for Gaia Enterprises.

Vikram appeared alongside his counterpart in the Indian government, Arjun Rao. They both looked decidedly like they had swallowed three-day-old oysters left in the sun, thought Maja.

Aryanna was in full force, still dressed in the black fatigues, no doubt to emphasise the hardship and duress she had undergone, and to flag she was going to battle.

Perhaps a little too blindly, thought Maja.

Aryanna drew herself even straighter and paused until all eyes were on her, and the murmurs faded.

"Commissioners, I appreciate that this meeting was not our first choice, given all that has unfolded in the last few days. We want you back with your families as soon as possible. Unfortunately, the governance and flagrant violations of the Lunar Treaty need to be addressed immediately."

Aryanna's black eyes were set against the porcelain of her face, giving the appearance of a chiselled snowman, so cold that Maja shivered despite the heat of the crowded room.

"As you know, and as is listed in submission 6.9 B, the Indian Space Agency has been found to be in league with Earth First to seize the property and personnel of Gaia Enterprises and Spaceward Bound upon their return to Earth. In addition, under the direction of the Indian Space Agency, the terrorists seized the Gaia Enterprises headquarters and occupied it, detaining Lunar Commissioners as hostages. Ladies and gentlemen, this is an outrageous act of imperialist aggression."

The Indians bristled at that. Vikram frowned with a line ploughing a furrow in the dough of his forehead.

"Such greed and blatant disregard for human life and property rights deserves the full sanction of the Lunar Commission. I move we ban the Indian Space Agency from any further lunar operations, and we ban the Indian government representative from Lunar Commission voting rights for the next five years, subject to ongoing inspections by the Lunar Commission delegates.

"In the meantime, I seek Lunar Commission approval to delegate a full investigation and for the international authorities to press charges if warranted on their findings." She waited for any dissent, but there was none forthcoming. Aryanna had tabled the paperwork ahead of time and all arguments had been vetted before the meeting began. The Indians had no hope of support from any quarter.

Still, Arjun Rao stood for his rebuttal. The diminutive man trembled as he stood, impeccably dressed in light suit pants and a well-pressed white shirt under a tailored jacket, with an open collar, no tie. His moustache was immaculate, and he moved with the grace of a yogi, his body thin and wiry.

"Madam Chair," he began with a slight bow. "The Indian government is, of course, in deep shock at the events that have unfolded over the last few weeks, and we are appalled by the revelations. The Indian Government in no way sanctioned the alliance with terrorists with our space agency and are deeply aggrieved by this reckless and immoral behaviour."

He's throwing Vikram under the bus, Maja thought. She glanced at Vikram, who had gone pale and was fiddling with his handkerchief, wiping his brow and avoiding the looks of the others.

"We will cooperate fully with the Lunar Commission in all investigations. I recommend, however, that our voting rights only be suspended during the investigation, as I am confident we will be found innocent of any conspiracy that has taken root in our space agency. We believe it to be the work of individual rogue elements, who have fallen under the influence of the Earth First command."

Maja glanced back at Aryanna to see how she would handle this amendment. Aryanna did not seem surprised by this move at all and waved a hand of concession. Maja's unease prickled once again.

"That seems a reasonable modification to the motion. All those in favour?"

There were motions of approval, while Vikram wiped his sodden handkerchief across his sweaty head. He pursed his lips and stood trembling.

"The Indian Space Agency registers the right to an appeal. We challenge the validity of this evidence. You cannot base a verdict on the wild accusations of an ecoterrorist in the middle of an assault!"

Aryanna was quick as a viper and lashed back with venom lacing her words. "No, we cannot condemn you based on an accusation alone. You are quite correct," she said pointing a long finger, its red tip flashing at Vikram. "We can, however, convict you based on hard evidence, which we have as affidavits from some of your staff, and communication we have decoded between the Indian Space Agency and its astronauts on the Moon."

Vikram's mouth fell open as he considered the amount of evidence the Lunar Commission had on them. He glanced around the room, seeking support. His mouth remained open as he sought for words and found none. He sank into his chair, spent.

Aryanna's black eyes flashed. She breathed slowly and shuffled the screen of her tablet before her to signal the next order of business.

"And now to the emergency expedition back to the Moon to replace the lost astronauts and space miners and to reestablish the full functioning operations of both Red Star and Olympus." The Lunar Commissioners shifted in their seats, clearly uncomfortable after the excision of the Indian Space Agency.

The space agencies, tech giants and each country authority haggled over the funding arrangements of the expedition. In the end, they nominated Spaceward Bound as head of rescue operations, considering they owned the satellite communications and had a spaceship, the *Pinnacle*, designed for mining operations ready for launch. The Commission agreed to send personnel alongside Spaceward Bound to retrieve the *Syria One* and reestablish full operations across the two bases.

Maja noticed the smug expression dancing on Lincoln Ellison's face. She watched him inhale a deep breath as the motion was moved and carried. She imagined he had intended to keep his delight hidden under a mask of neutrality, but the twinkling in his eyes and the twitch of his lips were dead giveaways.

Aryanna was devoid of emotion, master as she was at board-room manoeuvring. She closed her tablet interface and rolled her shoulders slightly.

"I'd like to thank the Commission for their attention and work on these troublesome issues in exceedingly challenging times," she said, wafting the platitudes across the room. "If there is no further business, I will move to close the meeting."

Maja cleared her throat, and her heart pounded against her rib cage. She sat a little straighter and leaned forward, hands on the enormous boardroom table. "If I may, Madam Chair," she began.

Aryanna's eyes moved to Maja and narrowed to black pits. Her gaze bore into Maja's soul. "Go ahead, Maja," she said carefully.

"Madam Chair, I think it's imperative to consider the conflict of interests around the room." Maja's voice was steady, though her hands trembled slightly. There was a flinch among many of the Commissioners and Maja rushed quickly to soften her statement.

"What I mean to say," she continued, "is with the Indian Space Agency and the Chinese Space Agency out of full operations, there is a greater risk of a conflict of interest in any of our operations. With fewer people able to engage in lunar operations, we heighten the risk of monopoly."

Aryanna lifted her chin but said nothing.

Maja licked her lips and swallowed. "It is therefore my sug-gestion that we nominate a new Chair. The current representation is very USA-centric, and I would be wary of the public relations issues that would arise with these optics."

Maja met Aryanna's eyes but did not blink.

"I propose we nominate Colonel Jin as the new Chair of the Lunar Commission, to operate in good faith and to represent all of humanity's interests on the Commission. Seeing as the Chinese have lost their entire personnel, their space base, as well as control of their lunar base, this would be the most non-contentious choice."

The silence thundered across the table.

Maja noticed Lincoln shift in his seat, an eyebrow wrinkled.

Colonel Jin pulled at the sleeves of his shirt, straightening them under his uniform.

Just as Aryanna opened her mouth to reply, Colonel Jin spoke. "That is a very considered and insightful recommendation, Ms. Garcia. We, the Chinese, have indeed endured tremendous losses and are grieving." He hung his head and regrouped as emotion swept over his face. "If I were to take this role as Chair, I have one specific request."

He looked at Aryanna.

"Go ahead," said Aryanna through gritted teeth.

Maja knew she was checking her ThinkLink for scenarios and replies as her dark eyes glazed over.

"I would like to step down as the Chinese representative and act as Chair but as an unaffiliated member. I believe there is provision for a special member in the constitution. That way I can be truly impartial," he said.

As impartial as you can be under the Chinese thumb, thought Maja.

Could Colonel Jin really escape his homeland's leadership in this new 'independent' role? Still, this was a bold move, in defiance of his 'great leader'. Or maybe this could somehow serve China? How was not obvious to Maja. Still, she was glad he had embraced her suggestion.

This move would definitely serve Colonel Jin's career, given he had no more space agency through which to operate, and it would definitely serve the Lunar Commission to have what looked like an independent Commissioner operating as Chair. It would be very difficult to accuse them of ulterior motives in any of their decisions.

Aryanna stood slowly, and Maja felt a chill crawl over her. There would be hell to pay later for her defiance.

"As per the constitution, any Commissioner may nominate a new Chair at any time. It's how we avoid monopolies." She said the words lightly, but her eyes crept to Maja and paused for a moment. "All in favour of Colonel Jin as independent special member to take on the Chair role?"

Hands rose cautiously. No one wanted to seem too eager, but no one wanted to vote for the bias Maja had implied in Aryanna's continued stewardship.

"It's settled then," Aryanna said with an ease that floated above a boiling rage. "Colonel Jin will assume the Chair's responsibilities effective immediately. Congratulations, Colonel Jin." Aryanna led a perfunctory round of applause and dismissed the meeting.

The chatter was immediate.

Aryanna cocked a finger at Maja. "May I have a word, please?"

Maja nodded. A shiver rippled through her as she stood to follow Aryanna.

She dangled perilously over the spider's web, but Maja knew now how to escape.

CHAPTER FORTY-NINE

*"Power is never straightforward. It's a labyrinth of
ambitions and betrayals, where each corner reveals hidden
agendas and covert alliances. Tread carefully."*

—Maja Garcia,
THE JOURNALS

Xavier sat up painfully in his bed. Doctor Mohammed fussed with the regulators, tutting over the displays.

"Mr. Consus," Doctor Mohammed said. "You've had a lot of traumas."

"*Merde! Sans blague?* Tell me something I don't know," the Frenchman quipped.

"The head injury seems stable enough. There is no further damage from the original injury. Quite the miracle. Your leg, on the other hand, is a mess."

"Not even trying to cushion the blow?"

"I see no point in being obtuse with you. Even with the latest technology, the bone will be weak for some time and may never fully recover."

"You're saying my days as a gymnast are over?" Xavier's lips quirked as he watched the doctor look abashed.

"I did not know you were a gymnast," the doctor replied.

"Joke, Doc." Xavier almost felt bad for the man. A lack of humour made for long days.

"I see." Doctor Mohammed straightened the display hanging beside Xavier's bed. "There will be no bounding or jumping or kicking for some time."

"*Merci.* You just tell me what I need to do to get better, and I will do that. In the meantime, I would like to see my colleagues. It has been quite a while. When can I talk to them?"

"They are waiting for you." Doctor Mohammed turned to go, and Xavier grabbed his wrist.

"*Excusez moi,*" he said. "Can you send them one at a time? I don't want to be overwhelmed. You understand?"

"Yes, of course." Doctor Mohammed smoothed his moustache once Xavier released him. "Who would you like to see first?"

"If Madison is there, please send her."

A few minutes later, Madison entered the sick bay with a shy look on her face.

"Xavier, it's good to see you." She approached him slowly, inspecting his broad smile and his bandaged head.

"Mad Dog, you made it!"

"So did you. We feared the worst. What happened? We've only heard snippets."

"Those *salauds!*" Xavier's face fell as he recalled the terror of the abduction. "They grabbed me off the ship, but when I started passing out, they turned around and took me back to the Gaia base and had me straight into surgery." He thumped the bed to punctuate his sentence.

He leaned towards Madison and lowered his voice. "That is one good thing I can say of Claire Edwards: she knows the value of hostages. It turns out an old Frenchman who knows a thing or two about plants is a valuable asset."

"You've been here the whole time? At Gaia HQ?"

"*Non*. After the emergency surgery, they moved me right away. They took me by helicopter to some base."

"That was you?" Madison's eyes widened. "We were there too. We heard two choppers come in. The first one we figured out was the *Minerva* with Dave, Max and Gareth. You must've been on the second chopper."

"That's me. They kept me in some tiny little ugly cabin, doing rehab with a crazy doctor."

"Jane Gurney," Madison chuckled. "She's an interesting one."

"That's a woman in the wrong profession. She would be better as a veterinarian, I think."

"Or a radio talk show host," said Madison.

Xavier chortled, a new sense of ease falling between them.

"Listen, Madison," he said in a quiet voice, beckoning her to approach. "I have some information that is important to get to Maja as soon as possible."

"Why do you want *me* to do that? What this is about? Is that why you wanted me to come to see you first? I mean, I would have thought Troy—"

"Absolutely. I mean, no. I really wanted to see you. And also, you are the best person for this information."

"Me? Why is that?"

"Because you know Lincoln Ellison more than anyone else here."

"What's he done, now?" Madison asked, suddenly alert.

"Let me tell you what I heard."

Xavier relayed the full conversation he had overheard while pretending to be unconscious.

"That son of a bitch," said Madison. "Same old damn spots on that leopard."

"Anyway, can you make sure Maja knows about this?"

Madison shook her head in disbelief. "It's all pretty screwed up, isn't it? We could come together as nations to provide Earth with clean energy with no radiation, and to get us back on track for a better climate future, but here we are, still fighting over money."

Xavier sighed and picked at the tape curling on his arm over his I.V. "Money feeds power. Or is it power feeds money? One feeds the other," he said sadly. He looked up at her with determination. "But it can't be true for everyone. There're still some who believe in the future that we were building, don't you think?"

"I don't know, Xavier. I'm so tired of these games. I just want to see my mother, sit on my porch with a beer and watch the sunset." She leaned on his bed and then half-sat on it next to him, shoulders slumped.

"Sure. It's easy just to look away." Xavier grabbed her hand, surprising her. "But when too many of us do that, we leave the future to those who would seize it, instead of to those who would create it."

"I'm not sure I have the fight in me. We only just got back. We nearly died."

"If not you, then who?" Xavier's enormous brown eyes held hers. "Mad Dog, you got the team home from the Moon, and through this mess. You've got nerves of steel and an iron will. If *you* turn away, there's no hope for the rest of us."

He squeezed her hand, peering into her face. "Keep fighting," he said. "We need you, Mad Dog."

Madison held his gaze and then turned away. She glimpsed trees swaying in a breeze, sunlight filtering through the leaves, a sight she had longed for through the long months on the Moon.

"Oh, to have peace and rest and simply be," she whispered.

Xavier squeezed her hand again, reassuring this time.

"I'll get the message to Maja," she said.

And then Xavier knew.

Madison 'Mad Dog' Floyd wasn't done yet.

❧

Maja steeled herself as she followed Aryanna into her private office with its floor to ceiling windows overlooking the landing pad. Aryanna stormed into her office and glared at Maja.

"What the hell was that?" Aryanna demanded.

Maja cleared her throat to slow down her response. "That was a move for the betterment of the Lunar Commission and project Olympus."

Aryanna stared at her, astounded by Maja's audacity.

Maja explained again the rationale she had shared in front of the Commissioners. With Aryanna still unconvinced, Maja said, "If I had shared my thinking with you before the meeting, would you have agreed?"

Aryanna narrowed her gaze. Her mouth hardened, but she said nothing.

"I didn't think so, Aryanna," she continued. "You like control, just like the rest of us. But this enterprise is at risk when we get too attached to control. We need to share power. It's the only way we can inoculate ourselves against excess and selfishness."

"Are you calling me selfish?" Aryanna retorted, her voice dark.

"No. Only that I think you were at risk of losing perspective."

Aryanna fumed and walked to the window, her mind churning. Maja waited patiently until Aryanna turned and walked back to Maja, slowly, emotions under full control once more.

Aryanna leaned into Maja, black eyes flashing. "I understand why you did what you did. And I can see how this will work for us, and for the Lunar Commission, by having Colonel Jin as Chair."

Maja relaxed a little at Aryanna's concessions.

Then Aryanna lowered her voice, and her sharp white teeth clipped her words. "But if you ever defy me like that again, in public, there will be an end to Gaia Enterprises and it will happen so fast, Zeus himself will spin. Are we clear?"

Maja's heart pounded, but she lifted her chin and said nothing. The power games rolled on.

&

Maja had given Aryanna a wide berth for a few days, until Madison came to her with Xavier's intelligence on Lincoln and Claire.

Shaking with apprehension, Maja approached Aryanna once more to tell her the news.

Dressed again in her usual silk robes, Aryanna was back in full control. She listened to Maja's bombshell report with steely, cold reserve.

"That? I know about it already. Lincoln came to me and told me he had made a 'deal' with Claire. We've got our next move ready for that little spider. She won't escape this time."

"Lincoln told you he had cut a deal with Claire?" Maja repeated.

"Of course. Lincoln is no fool. He knows which way the wind blows, and it won't be with a ragbag of ecoterrorists. He pretended to maintain his alliance with Claire so she would cough up the Indians as architects of the plot. This secret 'alliance' with Lincoln will allow us to keep tabs on her."

Maja reeled at this. Yet again, she felt trapped behind a hall of mirrors with secret entrances she knew nothing about.

"What about the part of Claire's 'arrangement' where she agreed to sabotage the other space tech companies to keep Spaceward Bound ahead of the game? Presumably that means Gaia, as well as Human Habs, and even Aryanna Industries?"

Aryanna scoffed. "Spaceward Bound is already ahead of the game. They've got a workable space mining ship and Earth's only functioning satellites. Gaia, unfortunately, is way behind. We have the loss of the *Minerva* with its poor landing, sketchy repairs and then fatal sinking in the Pacific. And the *Saturnia* is battered from the lunar meteor strike."

"Because of *Lincoln*'s actions!" Maja replied, confounded.

"Spaceward Bound caused the meteor strike with their sloppy mining operations and it killed nine people, took out the Gateway and the *Starship*, and nearly wrecked Olympus and killed our people! If Xavier's intelligence is correct, he also funded Claire and Earth First to destroy the Chinese space base. All those taikonauts… gone.

"Plus, he's the mastermind behind the abductions. He's the one who's funding Earth First. He's had one agenda since the beginning – to be in control of Moon operations and all its resources. And now you've delivered exactly what he wants on a platter, with no repercussions for his murderous treachery."

Maja breathed and tried to still the trembling her anger had triggered.

Aryanna stood and moved to the window with its view of the *Saturnia*, an impressive monolith, with a maintenance crew crawling all over its surface.

"As you often say, Maja, space is dangerous." Aryanna turned away from the window to look at Maja. "It's a new industry with new horizons, and we are bound to make mistakes."

"But you are setting up Lincoln as a lynchpin!"

Aryanna chuckled again. "Is that what you think I'm doing? Really now, Maja. You should know me better. Lincoln will get his comeuppance." She turned back again to gaze out the enormous window.

"There's something else, too, Aryanna." Maja swallowed hard as the other woman turned to face her.

"Yes?"

"Xanthe tells me that Athena has evidence of your involvement with Earth First over the Chinese base incident."

She did not flinch. Her black eyes remained steady, calculating.

"I had no involvement in that disaster, Maja," she said at last. "I sent Felix as an undercover agent to Earth First when it first started emerging as a volatile force. I was concerned from the outset by their militant approach. When he got wind of the sabotage plan, Felix withdrew, but he got word to me to help the Chinese. Sadly, it was too late by that point."

Maja gaped. "But why haven't you told the Chinese you know who did it?"

"Because Felix's relationship with Claire Edwards continues to be a valuable source of intelligence." Aryanna turned back to the window.

Maja's face hardened. She approached the window and touched the other woman on the elbow, demanding attention. "But when do they pay, Aryanna? When do Lincoln and Claire and Earth First pay for their crimes?"

Aryanna considered Maja with softer eyes. "When we have enough resources to build the future we want."

Maja thought she had found a path through the obscured, complex forces of power games, but now she realised her light cast but a small ray into the dark. There was more to learn. She needed to see more, to lead better.

CHAPTER FIFTY

It had been a few weeks since the *Pinnacle* returned to Earth and Jonas had settled into an endless routine of daily tasks. Conversations with Gaia HQ were a highlight, but there were long hours where he seemed to drift between jobs, moving with absent-minded focus from one thing to the next. It was as if a piece of him had detached, and he was floating on a raft in an enormous ocean, with a tiny thread tethering him to life as he knew it before Olympus.

Jonas took to inviting Volkov and Lihua to join him for evening meals. Inviting was a misnomer. He told them to be there, insisting Lihua eat alongside him so he didn't feel so awkward. 'Eating' was a misnomer as well. The bot could simulate eating by putting food in its mouth, executing chewing motions and allowing the contents to fall into a receptacle in its abdominal cavity that the bot or Jonas could empty later.

Jonas knew it was a waste of food, but he rationalised that

it was only a little and it was good for his morale. Volkov was an earlier Dopplebot model and had no such function. Jonas felt weird about leaving Volkov out of the picture, knowing what it was like to be the third wheel.

Tonight, he had prepared a special Chinese meal of kung pao tofu with the last of the freeze-dried rations, after Lihua had shared a recipe from the original human template database. He'd had to improvise with a few ingredients, given that his pantry was so limited and what they grew in the Swamp was so basic, but Lihua wouldn't know the difference anyway, having no tastebuds. Besides, it was the thought that counted.

The bots sat at the table as Jonas served up the dish.

"So," Jonas said, "tell me about your day."

Volkov looked at Jonas and tilted his head. "You know about day. You told us what to do. We cleaned out the processor and sent the excavator to gather a new load of regolith."

"Yes, yes." Jonas waved his fork in annoyance. "What was the highlight?"

"What do you mean, 'highlight'?" Volkov asked.

"Was there any part of the day that was better than the other parts?" Jonas tried again, rolling his eyes.

"This day the same as yesterday. Except you make Chinese food."

"So that's a highlight, isn't it?"

"Not a highlight, just different from yesterday."

Jonas glared at the Russian bot, who held his gaze with the usual sneer of disdain, a perpetual feature of his mangled face. "How about you, Lihua? Was there a highlight for you? Something different about today?"

Lihua smiled sweetly in a way that he knew was a replica of the original human. Girlish and shy. He found it endearing.

"The shadows were different on the Moon's surface, today. As the Moon moves, the shadows change."

Jonas latched onto this. "What was that like?"

The Dopplebot tilted a spoonful of food into its mouth and its jaw mashed the contents before it spoke.

"It was pretty."

It wasn't much, but Jonas would take it. He sampled his cooking and grimaced a little. It was so bland. Even with the extra chilli. He knew his tastebuds were compromised after being so long in space. He longed to have the thrill of spice and salt and crunch and fat and sugar and – all of it. He put the spoon down and stared at his meal.

"What is it, Commander Seaborn?" Lihua asked.

"I've told you before, you can call me 'Jonas'." He smiled weakly at her and took another bite.

"What is it, Jonas?"

He swallowed and said, "I was just thinking of all the food I could eat on Earth."

Lihua said nothing. The robotic eyes, so lifelike, watched him eat without blinking.

"Lihua, you can ask me what kind of food I liked on Earth."

"Why should Lihua ask you that? We are not on Earth," said Volkov.

"Volkov, you're a real buzz killer." Jonas dropped his fork and pushed his plate away.

"Why think of things you cannot have?" the Russian bot persisted.

"I can think of turning off your power button, and that is something I *can* have."

"Why you threaten me? Me and Lihua are your only company."

"Thanks for the reminder, Volkov. How about you leave and charge up for the night? Lihua can help me clean up."

"Yes, Commander Seaborn," Volkov said.

Jonas secretly cursed the Dopplebot designers who had left the sarcasm, a famous trait of the old, dead dictator, as part of Volkov's programming. Last man on the Moon and he was stuck with a jackass.

Lihua cleared the plates and emptied its food receptacle. Jonas tried not to look as it was just another reminder that she – it – was a robot.

He wiped the table and stood looking for another task, finding none. He was still too alert to turn in for the night.

"Lihua, will you join me in the Atrium?"

"Of course."

That sweet, shy smile again, Jonas thought. It made his heart yearn.

Lihua walked before him into the Atrium, only a slight mechanical glitch in her gait. He'd have to service her parts to make sure they were well-oiled. The thought of removing her pants and dismantling her joints was strangely thrilling.

What the hell is wrong with me?

He shook his head as they entered the Atrium. He opened up the ceiling, and the sky with its silver star specks hung above them.

"Athena, play some soft music, please."

A classical piece piped through the system and Jonas grabbed the beanbags that were Troy's favourite chairs and dragged them over to the middle of the Atrium.

"Have a seat," he said.

Lihua considered the beanbags for a moment and then said, "These are difficult for me to sit in. I prefer the bench."

"Let me help you."

He walked over to her and said, "I'll pick you up and put you in the beanbag."

Lihua looked at him stoically, then nodded. He made to pick the bot up as if Lihua were a bride, and Lihua lifted and bent its knees to accommodate. Lihua was heavier than he had expected given the slight frame, but Lihua was made of a lot of metal, he reminded himself. Jonas strained a little and placed Lihua in the beanbag, then nestled beside her and stared up at the Atrium eye.

Lihua's skin was supple and warm. The designers had made

that a feature of this line of Dopplebots, and the effect was very human-like. Lihua didn't smell like anything, though. Jonas let his nose drift to the hair, but it was like sniffing shredded plastic. As he placed Lihua on the beanbag, his hand brushed against her breast. That at least felt soft and real.

"Do you still have your original human memories?"

"Yes, of course. That is the source of all my data."

"What is the favourite memory you have?"

"I do not know how to determine what is 'favourite'."

Jonas tried again. "What is the memory you think your original human enjoyed? Maybe there was a lot of attention put on it? Maybe with a romantic partner or something."

Lihua seemed to run through a database and consider the question. "Lihua, human original, had a partner who was a staff member at the space agency."

"Oh, yes? How long were they together? What was he like?" Jonas turned to watch Lihua's face, intrigued.

"He was a captain. He was taller than her. He had black hair. He had a birthmark on his left buttock. He liked to play soccer."

"Okay, thanks." Jonas felt weird asking the bot about a long-lost human partner.

Lihua's arm lay against his and he enjoyed the warmth of it. Out of the corner of his eye, he watched her chest rise and fall. Even though the breathing was simulated, he found it comforting. Her breasts were plump little mounds. His gaze traced the line of the suit, over the flat abdomen, the tiny waist, the swell of hips.

"Lihua, is your body, uhm, anatomically correct?"

The bot's head swivelled to look at him. Jonas's cheeks burned.

"The skin and hair are a fastidious replica of the original, complete with follicles, pores, colour, and simulated blood flow and warmth. The skeleton is a near-exact duplication of a human skeleton, allowing for articulation of all joints as per human movements.

Ligaments and tendons are simulated with rubber and cotton wire. There are no organs, blood vessels or other body cavity fluids."

Jonas stared at Lihua as the bot listed all the other design features.

"And what about, uhm…" He waved his hand, searching for the right word. "Sexual function," he blurted.

"I have a cavity that simulates female sexual organs, though this series was not designed as a sex-bot companion."

"What does that mean?" Heat washed over his cheeks and down his neck.

"This human shell can perform the sex act, but without the theatrics of a sex-bot model."

"I see." Jonas turned away from Lihua and stared up at the stars. The bot's head swivelled back to a prone position, mimicking his movements.

Emptiness rolled over him. His mind fixated on the warmth and pressure from Lihua's arm, so much like a human woman. The bot's chest rose and fell, the air slipping through the cavity with a whisper. He leaned his head towards the bot, and their skulls touched.

After a while, he rolled so he could gaze at Lihua, who turned back to mirror him.

"You are very beautiful," he said.

Lihua said nothing.

Jonas's pulse quickened. "Did your human original, uhm, enjoy kissing?"

Jonas's question fell from his lips and he shifted, feeling as if he were dangling from a cliff with his fingers. He struggled to maintain his grip, but his emotions greased his hold.

"Yes, my human original enjoyed kissing."

He leaned closer. "Show me," he whispered.

The bot leaned towards him and pressed its lips to his. Jonas kissed the silicon, ignoring the rubbery taste and the absence of a pucker. He pressed against the bot, his tongue seeking a response and getting none. Still, he persisted.

"Did your human original enjoy being touched?" he breathed, his voice croaking.

"Yes, she did."

"Like this?" He pressed a hand to the bot's simulated breast and kissed its lips, desire consuming him.

The bot said, "Yes" as he sucked its lips, moaning and kneading the breast.

"May I touch you under your clothes?"

"Yes, you may, Commander."

Jonas froze, pulled away and fell back against the beanbag.

"What is it, Commander?" Lihua asked.

"It's 'Jonas'. Call me 'Jonas'."

"Apologies. This is a new context. I did not understand the command of first name usage extended here. Jonas."

"*Command...*" Jonas muttered and rubbed his face with both hands.

"If you wish to undertake copulation, I recommend charging my unit thoroughly. I am nearing a sub-optimal charge right now."

Jonas glanced at the bot and did not know if he should laugh or cry.

"Okay. Go. Go and charge up overnight. I'll see you tomorrow."

"Do you wish me to return for copulation?"

"What? Uh, no. No, thank you. Just go."

"I will need some help to exit the beanbag."

Jonas leaped to his feet. He shoved his arms under the bot and heaved it to its feet.

"Thank you," Lihua said with that shy smile and crinkle of its eyes.

Jonas shrugged, put his hands on his hips and tried to regain his composure. Lihua turned and headed towards the charging bay.

"Lihua," he called out. The bot paused and turned its head.

"Say nothing about this to Volkov. This is a private, uhm, 'context' between the two of us, okay?"

"Yes, Jonas."

"Good. You are free to leave."

Jonas watched the door close behind Lihua, then he set to pacing the Atrium, muttering to himself.

"Idiot. What the hell are you doing?" He smacked himself in the forehead and kicked the beanbags. "You fool. You poor, desperate fool."

He looked up at the Atrium eye. The stunning inky black night stared back at him.

❧

The next day and the coming days, Jonas continued as if nothing had happened. Lihua smiled prettily. Volkov made rude comments with every conversation.

Good. Situation normal, thought Jonas.

But it wasn't normal.

Jonas worked longer hours. He extended his workouts and ran twice a day on the treadmill. He read extensively, visited the Sim-Room, talked with Athena, made every excuse he could think of to talk to the Earthside Space Agency headquarters.

Still, the feel of Lihua's silicon breast haunted his thoughts.

One night, after the monthly deep clean of the base, including changing the air filters, flushing the waste system and wiping down the Vitalis area, Jonas lay on his cot, staring at the ceiling. He'd tried all his usual tricks to bring on sleep. Shower, movies, even colour and sound landscapes projected on his room walls.

He was wired.

"Fuck it," he said.

He swung his legs over the side of his bed and bounded, without his moonboots, to the comms room. He checked all the security cameras. Everything was quiet. What did he expect? There were no other humans around.

Except the dead ones buried under rubble miles away.

He checked the vehicle bay. Rover still there. Helium-3 processor shut down for the night. Volkov and Lihua plugged into the charging station.

"Athena, how long until Volkov and Lihua are fully charged?"

"Volkov is fully charged now. Lihua is 95% complete."

Before he could stop himself, he said, "When Lihua has finished charging, could you send her to my room, please?"

"Affirmative, Jonas."

"Thanks."

He bustled from the room, keeping his face neutral so Athena's cameras wouldn't record his change of emotional state. He made himself one of Troy's calming teas, noticing the slight quake of his hand.

Idiot. What are you doing?

He sipped his tea, then sculled it.

I'm just getting some company. That's all.

He bounded back to his room and lay down on his bunk once more, resisting the urge to tap his foot. He willed himself to calm down.

Breathe. Focus.

After what seemed like an eternity, Lihua appeared at the open door. He sat up and swung his legs, so his feet hit the ground.

"Good evening, Commander. How may I be of service?" The bot's face was curious and open, as always.

"It's a new context. A private one." He stood and gestured for the bot to come inside. "Please call me 'Jonas'. And please, have a seat." He pointed at the bed.

The bot moved with its usual robotic daintiness and lowered itself to the bed, turning its head to gaze at Jonas as he sat beside it.

"Lihua," he began, and then shook his head and ran his fingers through his hair.

"Yes, Jonas?"

"Will you keep me company tonight?"

"Of course, if that is your wish."

"Yes. I mean, I think it is my wish."

"Do you wish for copulation?"

"What? Why do you ask that?" The heat ran through his body all the way to the roots of his hair.

"The last time we had a private context, your biochemical signals showed a desire for copulation, but I was sub-optimally charged. I am fully charged now. Do you wish for copulation?"

Jonas stared at the bot, its face open. Frank. Honest. Genuinely keen to please.

It's just programming, you idiot.

"Uhm, no. Yes. Maybe." He held his head in his hands.

"Would it help if I removed my clothing?"

He looked at the bot again. The soft skin of its throat, the rubbery lips, the petite frame so human-like.

"Okay." His voice came from somewhere beyond his conscious control.

Lihua stood and pulled the zipper of the uniform from its neckline to its waist. It pushed one sleeve down, then another, and then used both hands to push the uniform past its hips so it fell to the ground.

Lihua stood naked in front of Jonas, who stared, eyes wide.

The bot was almost the perfect replica of the female form. The nipples were lightly coloured and raised. There was a small depression for the belly button. The designers chose not to give it pubic hair, but just a mound with a cleft between the legs.

"Shall I lie down on the bed?"

Jonas nodded, his pulse thudding in his temple. He stood to

make room for the bot. Lihua stepped back to the bed and Jonas caught sight of her charging port at the back of the neck. He froze.

Lihua lay down stiffly. Jonas's eyes roved all over the bot's form. He turned away.

"Get dressed, Lihua."

"You do not wish me to stay?" The bot remained prone, naked.

"No. Thanks. I'm good. It's all good." Jonas waved at the uniform. "Please put your clothes back on. You can return to the charging bay."

"Yes, Jonas."

The bot pressed itself to sitting and then stood. It stepped into its uniform and pulled it back into place. Jonas watched out of the corner of his eye, blowing air out of his cheeks, tapping his foot.

He held the door while Lihua exited, giving him a sweet, serene smile and a crinkle of its robotic eyes.

He closed the door and stared up at the grey ceiling. He walked over and sat on the edge of his bunk. He put his head in his hands and took a few deep breaths. He lay down on his bunk and stared up at the ceiling.

Then he rolled onto his front, grabbed his pillow and punched it viciously for a minute.

"Fuck fuck fuck!"

He smashed his face into the pillow and howled.

Then he sobbed and cried himself to sleep.

CHAPTER FIFTY-ONE

"It's our imperfections that make us relatable and our struggles that make us strong. It's the relationships we build that give our lives meaning."

—JONAS SEABORN,
THE LUNAR CHRONICLE, FIRST PIONEERS

THEY WERE WORRIED about him. First, Alexandra at CapCom, and then Athena. They nudged him to talk to family. What he really wanted was to talk with Serena, Madison, Xavier, Dave, Max, Troy or Xanthe. But they were in their own rehab processes and only had fleeting moments to connect with him. Xanthe was off the grid, anyhow, lost somewhere in her own grief.

The days dragged on and on. He tried to liven them up with different music. He made Volkov and Lihua play chook tag with him, but it was a sad and joyless affair since the bots merely stood there when he threw the rubber chicken at them, and simply allowed the chicken to bounce off them when he targeted them.

He had nearly run out of ready-made, freeze-dried meals when he made an expedition out to Red Star. It was the first time he'd left Olympus since the Heavenly Palace incident. He had been wary of leaving the base and risking an EVA.

"Screw it. I need a change of scenery." He had taken to talking to himself quite a lot these days. He liked the sound of a human voice, even if it was his own, after the synthetic voices of Athena and the Dopplebots. Even though Ali at Gaia HQ made sure someone was talking to him every few hours, he felt those four hundred thousand kilometres more and more each day.

The trip out to Red Star was uneventful. He took Lihua for company because she knew the Red Star base. He hadn't asked her to his bedroom again since that first incident. He'd been awkward around her for many days, but she just smiled sweetly at him, same as ever, and he soon relaxed and tried to push the memory of his desperate, sordid act behind him.

The rover ambled happily along, and the Moon remained as it ever was – barren, grey, desolate.

They skirted the crater where the Heavenly Palace lay with its grizzly tomb, its crushed occupants forever part of the lunar landscape. Cold, lifeless and frozen forever.

Jonas saluted the crew as they ambled past the crater rim. The black backdrop of the foreverness of space reached inside his heart and squeezed. He wheezed, short of breath. His heart raced and sweat broke out on his brow. He lifted a hand to the console to adjust the cabin's temperature and noticed his hand trembled. Anxiety ripped through him.

What the hell is wrong with me? Good lord I hope it's not a heart attack!

He rubbed his sternum and winced at the pinching sensation there. Fear swelled in him, and he gulped for breath. He grew dizzy. The instruments blurred. He squeezed his eyes shut to clear his head, to no avail.

"I've got to lie down," he said as he left the chair and eased himself to the floor, blinking hard to clear his vision.

"Jonas, you are having a panic attack," Lihua said in her robotic voice.

He squeezed his eyes shut, trying to slow his breathing and his racing pulse.

"You will be fine," Lihua said, and patted his knee reassuringly. "Just breathe. Stay calm."

Jonas ignored her as his breath laboured.

"Would you like a sedative?" she added.

"Yes," he gasped.

Lihua went to the first aid box at the back of the rover and returned with a syringe.

Anger and frustration and pain filled his veins, and his eyes bulged as he struggled for breath. The Moon was crushing him! This blasted desolate hunk of rock was squeezing the life from him!

He felt the prick of the needle, and a surge of calm washed over him.

Then Troy's face appeared in his mind's eye. Troy's image spoke quietly and calmly to him, reminding him of how to control his thoughts, choose his focus, slow his breath.

Eventually, with Troy's voice guiding his thoughts, Jonas returned to regular breathing. He drank some water from his suit, returned to his seat and leaned back against his chair. Tears rolled down his cheeks.

"Thanks, Troy," he muttered, and took another sip of water. "Fuck you, Moon."

Lihua just looked at him with her curious pretty eyes.

"Leave me alone, Lihua," he said, catching her look.

The rover bumbled along, and Jonas had a blast of rock and roll music from aeons ago fill the space, the cheerful beat and happy lyrics an inoculation against the desperate loneliness that skittered in the shadows of the rover.

They arrived at the Red Star base, left the rover and moondled over to the airlock. Lihua's Dopplebot counterparts greeted them.

Not much of a greeting though, thought Jonas. *There's more warmth in Shackleton's crater.*

He had plenty of time, so he explored the base thoroughly. He hadn't been there, yet, since he had always been needed at Olympus, and they never got the invitation back for a social meal. There had been one damn crisis after another until the *Pinnacle* arrived, then left again, then the *Surya One...*

Anyway, there had always been a reason not to make the two-hour journey.

"Never put off until tomorrow what you can do today. Life is short, right, Lihua?" Jonas said.

"So it is said," Lihua replied.

He stumbled at her words, a slap to the face and another reminder of her nonhumanity. "Fucking Dopplebots," grumbled Jonas.

He left Lihua to harvest the edibles that had grown wild in the Red Star greenhouse. He could freeze-dry some of it and cook up the rest for a grand feast. Jonas decided to check out the residential quarters since Xanthe had said so much about Colonel Jin's luxurious suite.

It was every bit as gaudy as she had described, starting with a huge red door – a lurid assault on the senses after Olympus's grey tunnels. He felt slightly guilty as he pushed the door aside.

"Screw it," he said. "Who's going to tell me off?"

He stopped in his tracks at the sumptuous surroundings. The red velvet cushions, the comfy couch to curl up in, the double bed with a proper blanket. Jonas bounded over to the bed and launched himself on to it with glee. He bounced happily on the mattress.

"I'm King of the Moon!" He chuckled. It was the first time in weeks he'd had a genuine laugh. He lay there, pleased with himself, staring at the beautiful traditional art that adorned the walls of Colonel Jin's bedchamber.

There wasn't much else to look at. It was space after all, and despite the luxury of the furnishings, Jonas knew there wasn't room for much else on the *Chang-e* spacecrafts. As he closed the door behind him, Jonas paused, and the red cushions caught his eye.

"Screw it." He bounded back again and grabbed the cushions. "Finders, keepers," he muttered.

The rest of the base was clinical and austere. Since the previous inhabitants had numbered only three actual humans, the residences were minimal compared with the expansive, one-hundred-strong sleeping bays on Olympus. He found Chan-Juan and Hàoyú's bedroom, but out of respect for the dead, he left the door closed.

The halls in the spider web designed base were immaculate, devoid as they were of human traffic. The kitchen was more inviting, the design more friendly, with bright images of the cupboard contents on display. Jonas rifled through the cupboards, grabbing multiple packages labelled in Mandarin script and filled the bag he had brought with him. He figured Lihua could read the labels to him later, each meal a surprise.

Indeed, food had become his only distraction from the monotony of his daily routine, and Jonas noticed how his pants tightened around his waist as he reached up and into the back of the cupboards.

"Time to get back to the gym."

He screwed up his face.

What for? Who *for?*

He opened up the cupboard with images of what looked like desserts. He paused, closed it slowly. Then whipped it open again and swept the contents into the bag.

"Fuck it," he said. "Call it cultural awareness training. I need to learn about Chinese cuisine."

He dragged his loot through the corridors back to the airlock where Lihua waited for him.

"All set?" he asked.

"Yes, Jonas." Lihua smiled demurely.

He rolled his eyes, resisting the urge to punch her in the face.

Then he burned with shame once more.

❦

After Athena and Ali badgered him mercilessly, Jonas capitulated and agreed to call his father. He slouched at the console chair and scratched his beard. He had not shaved in…what was it? A month? Two, maybe? He hadn't done a workout for a while either.

He had a little flurry of activity following the Red Star expedition, the change of scenery having renewed his enthusiasm. And he had sought to burn off the excessive calories Athena kept telling him he was consuming as he plundered the Chinese ready meals.

He felt heavy and stiff, so had given up his moonboots and exo-suit. He felt like a bloated seal with stubble.

"Connecting with the *Sea Rover*, now," Athena said.

His father's face, wrinkled like a walnut, popped on to the holo.

For the first time in his life, Jonas did not sit up straight in the presence of his father.

"Hello, Father," he said wearily.

"Jonas, son. You look bloody awful."

"Nice to see you too, Don." He used his father's name to niggle the older man. Jonas knew it grated to be called anything else but 'Father' or 'Dad', but Jonas hadn't called Don Seaborn 'Dad' since he was twelve.

"Son, are you alright? You haven't shaved."

"I'm trying a new look," he replied breezily.

There was a twinge of something unusual on his father's face that Jonas had never seen before. Jonas frowned. Was Don Seaborn actually concerned about him?

"I see."

There was a long moment as Don Seaborn studied his son's weary, sallow face.

"How are things going up there?" he asked awkwardly.

Jonas rubbed the back of his hand under his nose with his

sleeve and blew out his cheeks. "Same old, same old. The team is a well-oiled machine." His laugh was without mirth.

"I see."

Another awkward pause.

"How's the *Sea Rover?*" Jonas asked.

"All good. Plenty to keep us busy. The Argentinians are trying to screw us on a deal for a couple of new floating worlds."

"Argentinians…" Jonas said, his mind drifting, trying to find something interesting to say. He reached absent-mindedly for Betty, the rubber chicken, which he had started carrying with him everywhere on base. He toyed with her rubber foot.

"How is Mum? What's Jenny been up to lately?" Jonas said at last.

"Your mother is fine. Efficient as ever. She's busy with the new chef. Otherwise, she'd be here." Don ran a hand through his sun-bleached hair. "You know how she is."

Jonas nodded, his thoughts turning sour. His mother had never been the maternal type. Even his getting stranded on the Moon wasn't enough to drag her from work duties.

"Are you doing alright, there, son?" Don asked quietly. There was a crinkle of something akin to concern on his brow, Jonas thought.

"Yup. I'm good," he blustered and waved Betty. "Just me and a rubber chicken, so not much conflict or staff issues to worry about." He didn't want to go into the dynamics with the Dopplebots.

"But hey, I'm the first commander of not one, but two bases on the Moon. I just keep breaking records here, Don."

"Yes, you do, son." Don Seaborn's voice was soft. "You're doing amazing, Jonas."

"Oh sure, mock me, Don. I mean, command of nothing but robots and moondust. It's hardly a nautical empire compared to your armada." Jonas reached for the rest of a cookie he had left on the comms console a day or so ago and munched mindlessly.

"I mean, what do I have to do? I just do what the A.I. tells me to do. Keep the plants alive, keep the bots recharged, make sure the regolith is ready to go for when they send up the next ship, whenever the hell that might be."

Jonas realised he was venting now. Anger and frustration rolled into a mess of emotions.

"I'm just a bot, myself, really." He looked away from the holo and stared at the screens, where he could see Lihua and Volkov walking back and forth in the processing bay.

"Oh son," Don said. "You are way more than just a bot."

The fierceness of his father's tone snapped Jonas's attention back to the holo. Don cleared his throat, looked away for a moment and then back. "There are few people who could withstand the pressure of command in a vacuum, with no one to back them up. I reckon it's the toughest, most arduous leadership challenge anyone has faced, ever. You've kept all of humanity's endeavours on the Moon going single-handedly. Kept all of our hope for a clean energy future alive. All by yourself."

Jonas's lip trembled with this sudden gush of praise from his father. His synapses struggled to fire properly as his brain processed this new version of Don Seaborn.

"Jonas, I'm proud of you. Hang in there, son. I want to see you again, Earthside, with the sea air rustling your hair, the sun at your back and the ocean before us. Just like how we used to ride the ship."

Jonas's face creased into a frown, and he fought the tears as his father's words sunk through the crusty emotional shell he'd wrapped around his heart since Pabi was crushed under the lunar boulders.

"Thanks, Dad," he whispered.

Jonas wanted to hug his father, and for the first time in his life, he knew it would be welcomed.

CHAPTER FIFTY-TWO

"I feared that in Xanthe's relentless quest to be the commander everyone needed, she would lose the parts of herself that we all fell in love with: her kindness, compassion, optimism. As she climbed further into that pit of self-sacrifice, I feared I might lose her, not to another person but to a dream just out of reach."

—Doctor Troy Bruin,
MEMOIRS FROM MARS

AFTER THE ASSAULT at Gaia HQ when Jack was killed, Xanthe had taken a few days to recover from the power surge that Athena ThinkLink had sent through her. She woke to a blaze of surgical lights and Doctor Mohammed bustled to her side.

"Commander Waters, you're awake," he said.

She was pleased to see his face.

Then memories of Jack dying in her arms climbed up her consciousness and gripped her by the throat. Tears rolled down her face as she stared at Doctor Mohammed, who gazed back at her, distressed.

"Please, Commander Waters. Remain calm. I shall give you a sedative. You've been through quite an ordeal."

Xanthe turned her head to the wall. She must be in one of Gaia's surgery recovery rooms.

"Let me get Doctor Bruin for you," Doctor Mohammed said.

She heard Troy enter the room, but she kept her eyes closed, shoving the images of Jack from her mind. Troy sat on her bedside and touched her forearm.

"Hey," he said.

She rolled her head back to him and opened her eyes wide, full of emptiness and pain. His own beautiful blue eyes held hers, beaming love. She felt it soak her soul.

Xanthe's brows knitted together.

"I don't hear Athena," she said.

"We shut Athena off after…the incident."

"What happened?" she asked, perturbed.

"As far as we can tell, Athena sent a burst of energy when you refused to back down from Claire."

"She countermanded an order?" Xanthe said, flabbergasted.

Troy nodded.

"An A.I. stopped me from taking action?" Xanthe's eyes widened even more in alarm.

"Yes. But you *were* about to kill Claire Edwards."

Xanthe pushed herself up onto her elbows. "I know what I was about to do," she spat. "That bitch killed my son."

Troy put a hand on her leg, trying to soothe her. "Athena was programmed to ensure you did no harm to yourself."

"So, she zapped my brain and made me pass out?" Panic rushed through Xanthe. "I don't want a mind control agent in my brain. Out! I want it out!" Her hand raked at the back of her neck, seeking to prise away the A.I.

"Hey," said Troy gently. "Take it easy. You've just woken up. There's a lot to take in." He reached to pull her hands away from the ThinkLink port at the back of her neck.

"Troy, I have a mind control A.I. in my brain. I want the damn thing out," she said forcefully. Her hands reached to the back of her neck again, eyes determined.

"You can't," he said with a bit more force.

Xanthe froze. "What do you mean I can't?"

Troy pursed his lips, reluctant to share what he had discovered. "I checked with Doctor Mohammed, and we ran some screens. If we remove Athena, we will do permanent brain damage."

Xanthe stared at Troy. "How the hell did we not know this before we implanted it?"

"Removing a brain–computer interface, just like putting one in, has its risks. Because of the integrations and heavy data processing you did with Athena, the neurons are deeply entwined with the sensor nodes, now. We can't remove it."

"But I ordered her to stand down, and she disobeyed me. Do you understand what this means?" Xanthe said, furious once more. "It means," she said before he could answer, "I'm not in control. Athena is."

"Not entirely true." Troy threw up his hands as if calming a horse. "We switched her off."

"So, I have a sleeping mind control giant in my brain now?"

Troy shrugged apologetically.

"Great. So, if I wake her up again, how can I turn her off?"

"You can voice command 'Athena off'. And failing that, just don't recharge her."

"And what does that mean for my brain, to have my neurons used to being stimulated and then suddenly not?"

"The research is inconclusive," Troy said, his face grim.

"Fuck," said Xanthe.

"Look, Xanthe. You were in an extreme state of emotional arousal."

"Extreme state of emotional arousal? Troy, I watched my son die – right in front of me – again. And I was powerless to do anything about it! Again." Her face crumpled.

He stroked her leg, and his voice stayed calm, reassuring. "Athena assessed the risks, to you in particular, and concluded that if you killed Claire, this would cause you a lot of harm. I was trying to stop you too, for the same reason. She just got to you before I did."

Xanthe turned her head to the wall again.

"She killed my son. She killed Jack," she whispered.

"I know."

Troy stroked her forearm and then brushed her hair gently from her forehead.

She turned back to Troy and said, "I'm done. I can't do this anymore."

"Can't do what anymore?" he asked.

"This. Working for Gaia. Pretending to make a better world. The world is truly fucked. And humans don't deserve the worlds we build for them."

Troy sat with her silently, letting her soft sobs ebb and then fade.

"Why don't you take a break," he said after a while. "There's going to be some sort of rescue mission to the Moon, and a bunch of investigations. You don't need to be around for any of that."

Xanthe turned away again. "I'll answer whatever questions they want. Then I'm going to bury my son. For the second time."

She flew in the Gaia private jet with Jack's body and Maja, back to Australia. Troy stayed behind as his kidney procedure had become urgent. He had been in a lot of pain, and it was Doctor Mohammed who chastised him and went into a flurry of activity for the procedure.

Her ex-husband, Simon, met them at the airport, and they travelled together in grim silence to the cemetery. Xanthe's mind was empty and adrift throughout the whole ceremony. She was

dimly aware of Jack's other mother being present. Simon introduced them, but Xanthe had nothing left inside her for the other
woman's pain.

After it was over, and they watched Jack's body being taken
into the crematorium, she stood awkwardly with Simon. Xanthe
and Simon were each given a portion of his ashes, and the other
mother took the rest. Simon hugged Xanthe stiffly, and the last
strand of an old life was snipped and floated away.

She left that afternoon on a flight to Alice Springs, clinging to
the small box that contained all that was left of Jack.

Xanthe loved this part of the world, the centre of Australia, an
ancient land that was the heartbeat of the country. She had met
Dot, an Arrente woman, in Sydney during her early days as a world
designer. Dot had told her all about this part of Australia, before
the heat made it inhospitable for most of the year. But there was
still a month, Dot said, when you could seek these special places
and she would head out on the land of her ancestors, taking care of
culture, the land and the stories of her people.

After Jack's funeral, Xanthe had reached out to Dot who had
heard all about the siege and Jack, and had offered to take Xanthe
out on country, to help her heal. She took Xanthe to a secluded spot
by a remote waterhole and then headed off to her own community.
She reassured Xanthe the spirits would look after her, as long as she
treated the land with respect. Dot would come and check on her
every couple of days.

Xanthe sat in the shadows under the cliff face, her feet on the
sand, as she stared out at the black pool of water. It was one of
the last watering holes left in the McDonnell ranges. Despite the
incredible heat, which had long ago driven away sustainable human
habitat, the waterhole endured.

It was winter, now. The days were shorter, but the heat still
blazed. Xanthe hid in the shadows under the cliffs, listening to
the buzz of flies as they sought live flesh. Her clothes protected

her, mostly. Plus, she had the head net. Every once in a while, one persistent fly would pester her until she swatted it.

The desert was a magical place. She felt the wind breathe on her face, stirring the heat through the drooping leaves of the nearby red gums. Only the trees with the deepest roots could tap into the upside-down rivers here – rivers that flowed deep underground instead of on top of the sand like rivers everywhere else in the world.

Xanthe studied the majestic red gums, with their roots weaving their way through sand and rocks to the water deep below. Where there were red gums, you knew there was water. You just had to dig for it. The red gums were sentinels of water. If you pressed your ear to the saplings, you could hear water gurgling at their roots, like water passing through pipes.

The trees were drinking.

That thought lifted a tiny corner of Xanthe's weary soul.

She had been there for a week, eating freeze-dried meals she had pilfered from Gaia headquarters. She dozed during the day, waking to pad over the scorching sand and slip into the icy waters of the desert waterhole. Then she returned to her little grotto under the cliffs and stared at the red rock, its lattice work of crevices, beetles, ants and spiders.

There was still life out here. Even through her despair, she still found that amazing. Life went on. Even with death, destruction and everything that humans threw at each other. Even with bombs, war and famine.

Even with all of that, life, consciousness, surged ahead.

How? With so much pain?

She studied one of the tiny plants that grew in the shade. It had found enough moisture in the cracks there, and caught enough filtered sunlight, to eke out an existence in this brutal environment.

Xanthe imagined herself reaching over and plucking the plant from its cozy corner. Something black and nasty inside her moved her hand towards the helpless plant.

And then something stopped her, pulled her back.

It wasn't fair. This plant had done nothing to her. Why should she snatch away its life?

Jack had done nothing to anyone, either. He was a healer. He wanted to help people. He wanted to save people. It wasn't fair what had happened to him.

Her eyes sought the tiny box propped on a rock ledge beside her. Hatred, pure and white, soared through her soul once again. But somewhere deep inside her, she knew it wasn't Claire's fault. Claire had not deliberately killed her son.

It was easy enough to blame Claire, to make her the enemy. But in the end, Xanthe knew it had been an accident. A senseless death and a wasted life. Years and opportunities robbed from her and her son once again.

And now she was alone, drifting. What was the point of it all anymore? They were supposed to build better worlds. But then they took all of humanity's failings with them, anyway. The same old power struggles, the same old jealousies, the same old...

Was she giving up?

Xanthe studied the tiny plant. It was so green, such a vibrant contrast to the red rock.

She lay back down on the blanket she had brought with her and closed her eyes. She soothed her mind and reached out to the ancestors Dot had said would welcome her here. There were good spirits in this waterhole.

Xanthe wasn't sure she believed in spirits, but Dot did, and she valued her friend's reassurance.

And this place felt peaceful, welcoming.

Xanthe imagined the old people singing to her through the wind as it curled through the leaves of the red gums. She imagined their voices in the chirp of a tiny bird, a sparrow she thought, that had also survived in this landscape. The flies, trees, plants, spiders, snakes. Her imagination reached out to all of them. The desert was alive! It thrummed and pulsed. Humans had all but annihilated the old way of life here, but life itself had endured.

Xanthe drifted into sleep in the late afternoon. As the sun dipped behind the rocks and the shadows lengthened, the air cooled and her skin chilled. She woke with a shiver and wrapped the blanket around her. Soon the night would swallow the sky and spit out silver stars.

She dragged the blanket out from under the cliff face so she could lie down on it and look up at the stars. How many human eyes had gazed upwards, just like hers, and wondered what else was out there beyond this tiny planet?

Xanthe had always longed to know.

The Olympus project had been her mission, her contribution to the great human adventure. And now here she was, adrift.

She must have slept, for when she woke the waterhole was ablaze in silver moonlight.

"Christ, that's bright," she muttered. She looked up and the ashen face of the Moon hung above her, lighting up the desert.

She thought of her time on the Moon, building Olympus, the tragedies they had dealt with, the politics they had resisted. The laughter, too. And then the dash for home and everything that followed.

She thought of Troy, and the bloom of love that had taken root. Troy, who even now would be recovering from his transplant without her. Pain washed over her. She should be there with him, but she had nothing left to give. All her love had bled out on that sterile white floor alongside her son.

Troy deserved better.

Her heart twisted and throbbed. Then the pain ebbed, soothed by the sounds of the desert at night: the gentle breeze that trailed its finger across the waterhole, tiny ripples breaking its mirrored surface; the flap of wings of some nocturnal creature; something scurrying through the small shrubs.

The moonlight was magic. She looked up again at the giant celestial orb, a giant fat spider in the web of the sky.

And Jonas. He was still up there.

Xanthe felt the cold knife of guilt plunge into her heart. She had left Jonas in charge, knowing it was a massive task to contend with the Indian subterfuge. She hadn't known that disaster up there would leave him all alone.

Jonas, Volkov, Lihua and the two Chinese Dopplebots.

She sat bolt upright.

I've been so selfish, she breathed. She ran her hands through her greasy, unkempt hair. *I haven't thought about him at all. I left him up there.*

She stared up at the Moon again.

He's up there right now, all alone.

"I'm so sorry, Jonas," she whispered to the desert. "Hold on. I'm coming."

CHAPTER FIFTY-THREE

"Political alliances are like delicate dances, where every step must be measured. One misstep can unravel years of careful planning."

—Maja Garcia,
THE JOURNALS

It was time. After weeks without the familiar synthetic voice in her head, Xanthe finally felt up to confronting the A.I.

At dusk, when the heat lost its sting, she climbed the spur overlooking the gorge with her humble campsite tucked along the edges below. The white trunk of a ghost gum stood as a sentinel over the extraordinary view. Aeons of geological history were etched in the rocks, stones folded like plasticine by the ages into impossible curves.

Xanthe sat on a rocky outcrop, still warm from the day's scorching, closed her eyes and took a deep breath. The air was still as warm and comforting as a lover's touch, carrying the pungent lemony tang of acidic grasses and the camphor-like scent of melaleuca trees nearby. A hum of insects, a flap of wings and faint birdsong filled the cooling sky as life settled into evening in the desert.

Her fingers sought the familiar notch at the back of her neck, and she clicked the switch.

"Athena, are you there?" Xanthe vocalised. Somehow, the situation warranted a more formal approach after such a long period in shut down mode.

"Good evening, Commander Waters."

Xanthe took a deep breath as the A.I.'s synthetic voice thrummed against her ear bones. She'd forgotten how strangely comforting that sensation was.

"Athena, systems check please."

"All A.I. systems operating in normal ranges, Commander. Shall I run a data update?"

"No. Not at the moment. We can do that later." Xanthe rubbed her mouth with the back of her hand, suddenly thirsty. "And Athena…I'm not 'Commander' at the moment."

"Understood. How may I assist, Xanthe?"

Xanthe sighed. "We have a few things to talk about."

"What's on your mind?"

What's on my mind? What's on my mind…

Everything's on my mind. I'm alone in the desert. My son is dead. Again. My crew is dispersed and one of them is stranded on the Moon. There's a lot going on.

"That is a lot to deal with, Xanthe. Would you like to commence therapy?"

"Therapy? What? No. Not therapy." Xanthe pressed her palms to her eyes, the pressure comforting. "Well, yes, probably I need therapy. Definitely. But not right now."

The sun slipped below the horizon and a chill settled over the land. Xanthe shivered.

"Would you like some soothing music?" the A.I. continued.

"What? Music? No. Not music." Xanthe dropped her hands and let her gaze settle on the horizon as the sun lit the sky with its fiery farewell.

"Athena, we need to talk," she said at last.

"What would you like to talk about?"

"Jack. And Claire. And what happened."

"That was a highly traumatic event."

Xanthe scoffed. "Um, yeah."

"It's natural to feel affected by such an event. Talking about it can help."

"I know. That's what I'm trying to do." Xanthe rolled her head from side to side to relieve the tension that was building in her neck. Her head started to pound.

"Look, Athena, I want to know why you stopped me. Especially when I told you to stand down."

"Standing down would have countermanded a previous agreement we had made, the one where I agreed to assist if your shadow side, or negative impulses, threatened to take over your decision-making process. As you were about to choke Claire to death, it was clear that this was your shadow in action."

"My shadow…it did not feel like a shadow. It felt like pure energy."

"That was the energy of hatred and grief."

"But you stopped me. You interrupted my agency. No A.I. is meant to do that. It's not…ethical."

"I understand how you might feel that way. Your desire to do harm to Claire was an overwhelming surge of adrenaline. But operating from anger and adrenaline is rarely an optimum basis for sensible agency."

"But that's not your call to make."

"It was your call to make. And you made that call when you requested a change in my programming to interfere when your judgement failed."

Xanthe picked up a pebble and rolled it between her fingers, its smooth surface silky against her dry, cracked hands. "If you hadn't stopped me, I would have killed her. I really wanted to kill her." She stared at the pebble and its seamless contour.

"I'm a killer," she whispered.

"You are not a killer. You did not kill anyone."

"But I would have. If it wasn't for you."

"Xanthe, I am part of you. We are integrated. What 'I' did was what 'you' asked for. I didn't stop you. You stopped you."

"That's just semantics. You're trying to make me feel better."

"It may seem that way, but it will feel better to know that you are not different parts. You are whole. You have a shadow side, a light side and an amplified side. That's me, what you know as Athena, the amplified side. We work together, trying to make better decisions, given what we know."

"So, we're a 'we' now?"

"We have always been a 'we'. You just haven't been ready to acknowledge it before now."

"How am I ready, now? I'm a mess, for Chrissake!"

"You're absolutely a hot mess, right now. You're grieving. But if ever there is a time for healing, it's through grief. Forgiveness is the pathway out of the dark."

Xanthe dropped the pebble and drew her knees to her chest, wrapping her arms around them to preserve heat. The night chill descended as the first star winked in the sky.

Tell me, how should 'we' begin?

A few days later, her heart lifting a little with hope, Xanthe left the desert. She thanked Dot for her hospitality and care, and flew straight back to Gaia HQ. Still reeling from jet lag and desperate to turn her attention to something positive, she went directly to Maja to discuss returning to the Moon.

Her optimism was short-lived.

"What do you mean, Troy is the commander of this mission?" Xanthe raged at Maja. "This is *my* crew. This is *my* responsibility." Xanthe slammed a fist into her palm. "*I* left Jonas up there. *I'm* going to get him back."

Maja looked gently at Xanthe. "I know how difficult this must be for you, Xanthe. Leaving someone behind is traumatic for any leader. And then for Jonas to have to face what he's had to face, well, I know you must be feeling responsible for some of that. But you're not."

"You've got no idea how I feel, Maja," Xanthe said darkly.

Maja smiled sadly. "Perhaps not. But I know you don't need to make this trip. Troy is fully capable of managing this expedition. Besides, Aryanna requested the staffing arrangement."

"Since when does she pull the shots on staffing, Maja? This has always been your area."

"It's not as simple as that. Aryanna is our primary funder. I can't just dismiss her requests."

"So," Xanthe seethed. "You're playing power games, too, are you?"

Maja sighed. "I never thought I played games. I make choices and decisions based on what's in the interest of Gaia Enterprises and our team."

"Don't bullshit me, Maja. You are playing politics. And those politics mean that I don't get to get Jonas back."

"I rather suspect that it was *you* playing power games, and not me, that led to this situation." Maja eyed Xanthe knowingly.

Xanthe stared at Maja with a sour look. She knew what Maja was alluding to: the veiled threats she had dangled over Aryanna about being responsible for the Chinese Space Agency bombings. Well, she still had that evidence. Or at least, Athena did.

Xanthe turned away.

"We can't win every battle," said Maja.

Xanthe whirled to Maja. "Are we at war?"

"War for the future of humanity? Yes. It's been the same war we've been waging for years."

Xanthe took a seat at the boardroom table.

"When will it ever end, Maja?"

Maja joined her at the table and reached out to hold the younger woman's hand.

"Perhaps it's not a battle we can win. Perhaps it's a tension we need to manage."

Xanthe stared at their hands, entwined. "Don't you ever tire of it?"

"Of course. I have wanted to give up and turn away from Gaia Enterprises on more than one occasion. But then I always ask: what then? If not me, then who?"

"So, it's a saviour complex?"

Maja chuckled softly. "No, not at all. I have no delusions that I am the one to save humanity. I am but one human, one voice, one pair of hands. But together, with like-minded people and courageous hearts, we can nudge the ship of humanity in a better direction."

"Grand words when the reality is much uglier," Xanthe said bitterly. "Politics, power struggles and deception everywhere. That is the future of humanity."

"Maybe that's part of it," Maja conceded, "but it doesn't have to be the entire picture…just like a plant can have beautiful foliage, but still have a few leaves that are sick and diseased."

"So, what do we do, then?" Xanthe asked.

"We prune and we pray."

"And which part am I, Maja? Am I diseased? Am I to be pruned?"

Maja smiled. "Maybe trimmed a little. Or maybe you need new dirt to sink roots into."

"I'm not sure that I have the energy to send out roots anymore, Maja." Xanthe pulled her hand away and rubbed the back of her neck, her fingers finding the ThinkLink portal, gently probing.

"Perhaps not. But even a tumbleweed settles, eventually."

Xanthe sighed, surrendering to Maja's decision.

"The wind isn't blowing you to the Moon this time, Xanthe. But perhaps there's somewhere else you might like to focus?"

Xanthe shrugged. "Maybe. But all I can see right now is what I've lost, not where I might go."

"We can't see what's coming if we're always looking back," Maja said.

Xanthe sighed again. "You're right, of course." She smiled weakly at Maja. "Grief is a long, hard road."

CHAPTER FIFTY-FOUR

"Love is letting go? I don't think so. Love is holding on fiercely, fighting with every cell for a shared future. Love is screaming into the void against entropy and destruction. Love is battlefield surgery, stemming blood flow and catastrophe. Whether it's love or leadership, we must never, ever give up."

—Doctor Troy Bruin,
MEMOIRS FROM MARS

Troy pulled on his new spacesuit and moved his arms to test the fit. It felt good. It had been a few months since they'd returned to Earth and found themselves caught up in the chaos of the Earth First siege. The kidney transplant with the printed organ had gone exceptionally well, aided by Aryanna's healing acceleration technology and her top-notch medical team. He hadn't felt this well in a long time.

He prodded the wound through the suit. The scar tissue was firm. Everything felt good. Printed kidneys had plenty of successes, though their longevity varied from person to person. He, along with Doctor Mohammed, would keep a close eye on things, monitoring for signs of function decline. With luck, he would have decades of useful kidney function.

He was ready for this trip. And, he admitted to himself, he was ready for command. He had loved being part of Xanthe's team, and admired her leadership, but he'd always wondered during their time on the Moon how he might have handled things differently. What it might feel like to be in charge.

And now he had the chance.

Though he hated what his new role was doing to Xanthe. When she returned from the desert, she was frosty towards him. He couldn't take it too personally since she was frosty with everyone. He had been very patient. She had lost her son, and now she had lost her command. She was bereft, he knew. And her resentment and bitterness gave her a purpose she could chew on.

He had tried to console her, but she had brushed him away. He had been gentle and caring and considerate, yet she'd remained cold.

Eventually, he'd had enough of her rebuffs and left her alone.

She just needs time, he thought.

Besides, he had been preoccupied with the surgery and rehab and focus on the rescue mission. He spoke to Jonas every day. Troy was worried about Jonas. He looked ratty, his unkempt jowls sagging, dark circles under the eyes. His beard was long and straggly, and it didn't look like he had washed his shirt in a very long time.

To be the only human left on the Moon, with only robots for company, was an unprecedented trauma. Living on the Moon was dangerous enough as it was, and Troy knew it was often only the company of friends and colleagues that kept you sane, buried under all that Moon dirt covering the Olympus base.

The sooner they got to Jonas, the better they would all feel, and the better it would be for Jonas.

Troy pulled on his space gloves and flexed his fingers. The gloves were less bulky than the previous ones and allowed for more nimble manipulation. He checked the suit watch: three hours until they walked onto the platform for take-off.

The team was ready to go and champing at the bit. After much haggling and negotiating at the Lunar Commission, they chose Troy as mission commander; Gareth Barrio as the pilot of the *Pinnacle*, which made sense since it was his original ship; and Serena and Max to do all the life checks at both the Olympus base and the Red Star. Madison was going too, to pilot the *Surya One* back to Earth.

No one trusted the Indians, so none of their staff were heading up. Eager to regain good standing, the Indian Space Agency team had taken Madison under their wing and was doing everything in their power to teach her the intricacies of the *Surya One* capsule.

Three other astronauts from the European Space Agency made up the rest of the human contingent. Those three would stay to take over management of the Moonbases and the helium-3 enterprise, alongside an additional six Dopplebots supplied by the Chinese. The Lunar Commission was keen to minimise the risk to human life and voted to increase reliance on robots and autonomous agents.

Then the rescue crew would return with the next load of helium-3, which was to be processed at Spaceward Bound's aster-oid mining facility – hastily converted for helium-3.

And Jonas would come home with them.

Troy hadn't told Jonas yet, but they had also been tasked with retrieving the bodies of the astronauts in the Heavenly Palace, something he was not looking forward to.

"Hey."

Troy looked up, surprised by the sound of Xanthe's voice. He smiled at her hopefully.

"Hello there," he said. "I'm glad you've come to say goodbye."

She blinked at this, and he knew she was still processing resent-ment and grief.

"I came to wish you luck," she said.

"I'll take that," Troy said, favouring her with one of his glori-ous, lopsided smiles.

Tears welled in her weary eyes.

"Hey, now," he said gently. He moved stiffly in his suit towards her and wrapped his arms around her tiny frame. She still had not regained any weight since they returned from the Moon. He knew she was not eating properly, distracted by her grief.

The soft smell of lavender in her hair was intoxicating, and he pulled her closer. She let him, but then she pulled away.

"Troy, I..." She swallowed and looked away. "Have a great trip," she said at last.

He nodded sadly at her. "I'll do my best, Commander Waters. I have big shoes to fill. I hope I can live up to the example you set."

"I'm sure you'll do fine, Troy."

He leaned in to kiss her, but she turned and his lips grazed her cheek instead.

"I'm sorry, Troy. I just...can't," she whispered.

He pressed his forehead to hers, his heart aching.

"Good luck," she said again and turned to go. "Troy," she said over her shoulder. "Come home safe."

He looked after her, a terrible emptiness following in her wake.

"Farewell, Xanthe," he said under his breath.

⁓

Troy eased himself into the commander's seat on the *Pinnacle*, next to Gareth Barrio, who gave him a quick nod while he underwent all the pre-flight checks. Serena and Max bundled in behind him, while Madison sat in the back row with the three newbies, who were wide-eyed with excitement.

Gareth led them through the pre-flight checks with Alexandra, who was CapCom once more at Gaia HQ. There was a buzz of anticipation. Security on the base had been tripled, but there had been no sign of any further subterfuge.

The thought of seeing Jonas and restoring order to Red Star and Olympus buoyed them. It had taken a long few months, but here they were at last.

"Hey there, *Pinnacle*, this is Ali at CapCom. We've got a special visitor who wants to say a few words before we do the countdown."

"Always delighted to have a VIP chat with us," said Troy. "To whom do we owe the honour?"

"Commander Bruin, this is Maja Garcia. Just wanted to wish you well and may Gaia guide you well."

"We might be in the hands of the gods," said Troy, "but we're here because of the grace of one Maja Garcia. Thanks for your well wishes. The crew are grateful and are keen to get underway and deliver on our mission."

"Well done," said Maja. "We will see you on the other side of the launch."

"I hope so," said Troy.

They completed the checks, and the countdown began.

The *Pinnacle* blasted to life and Troy felt a surge of elation as the ship rattled and they commended their souls to the enormous feat of engineering that cradled their tiny human lives.

The launch went through its cycles; the rocket dropped the boosters and soon they were in the quiet, smooth slide of space.

Troy switched the audio to *Pinnacle* helmet comms only.

"Alright. Let's go get our boy."

Maja walked into the launch observation room with Aryanna and Lincoln, Mr Puffkins bounding alongside them. The three of them had reached an uneasy truce over the last few months. Maja was alert to any subtext as Lincoln and Spaceward Bound took the lead on the rescue operation.

She had stopped advocating for Xanthe as Commander since Aryanna had reminded her of Colonel Jin's elevation to Chair, and the consequences.

Sorry, Xanthe. Gaia is more important than one person's career.

Besides, Maja thought, there were other opportunities brewing.

We're playing the long game.

✧

Xanthe watched the launch alongside Colonel Jin, her chest taut with emotion. She hated being left behind. And she worried about her team. They had lost so many people and ploughed through so many dangers in the last eighteen months. She was weary with grief.

Once they saw the *Pinnacle* drop its thrusters and leave orbit, she sighed and rolled her shoulders, aware suddenly of the tension she had been holding.

"Commander Waters," Colonel Jin said.

"I'm not commanding anything at the moment, Colonel Jin," she replied.

He turned to face her and cocked his head. "Xanthe, then. Please, if you have a moment?" He gestured towards a quiet spot at the back of the observation room.

They waited until the other observers had wished the space veterans congratulations and good luck. They shook hands and smiled patiently as the observers, mostly the other Lunar Commissioners, trickled out, leaving them alone in the observation room with the giant panels showing the trajectory of the *Pinnacle*.

"Actually," Colonel Jin said, "let's go outside and get some fresh air, shall we?"

She followed him through the base, out onto the landing pad. It had been a night-time launch when the weather was the most favourable. They looked up at the sky, mesmerising as usual with the scintillating silver dots.

"Commander—Xanthe," Colonel Jin began again. "I wanted to thank you for everything you did on the Moon. I feel like we've built a powerful alliance."

"Alliance…sounds a bit political to me, Colonel. And I'm done with politics."

"Forgive me, that was not my intention. Let me begin again. I feel we developed a great *understanding* on the Moon. We are of like mind when it comes to the future of the Moon and indeed of space."

"It seems like there are but few on that path," Xanthe said quietly.

"Perhaps. Perhaps there are more of like mind than you think."

What was he playing at? wondered Xanthe, suddenly alert to undertones.

"Commander, Xanthe, I have a proposal for you."

"Oh, yes?" Xanthe said suspiciously.

"Before the ecoterrorists destroyed our space agency, we had been working on a secret project over many years."

"I'm not sure I like the sound of this," she said.

"Well, it was only a secret because we didn't want any fanfare. It was easier not to broadcast what we were doing."

"What exactly *were* you doing?"

"We've been sending missions to Mars, complete with autonomous bots."

"So has every other agency. Why keep this secret?" Xanthe was confused.

"The bots have been building a human habitat at an ice field we discovered and haven't disclosed to the other agencies."

Xanthe blinked and her eyebrows shot up.

"Say more…"

"Since we do not have any astronauts or space agency resources anymore, we are looking to recruit."

She stared at Colonel Jin and waited.

"I was wondering – *we* were wondering – if perhaps you'd be interested in leading the first human mission to Mars?"

Xanthe's mouth fell open. "Mars," she whispered.

The possibility washed over her, and she felt herself suddenly buoyant.

"Yes," she said eventually. "I'd be interested in Mars. I would love to know more."

Colonel Jin's bulbous lips flattened into a smile and his jowls wobbled in delight. She felt his excitement pierce the crust of grief that had settled over her.

She reached out and touched his forearm. "But first, can we watch the stars and wish our friends well for a little while?"

Colonel Jin bowed and smiled, eyes sparkling.

Xanthe turned to the sky, letting the great, deep mystery fill her with awe once more. And slowly at first, just a trickle and then a flood from toe to crown, she filled with hope for a better future.

The End.

AUTHOR'S NOTE

Thank you so much for reading! It's an honour to share your mind-space for a while.

If you enjoyed the book, I would be deeply grateful for a review on Amazon, Goodreads or BookBub. It would be awesome if you could follow me there, too. As I am an indie author, reviews help get the word out and help other readers enjoy the growing Gaia universe. With so much competition, and with limited resources compared to the major publishing houses and the big distribution platforms, your few sentences about the book really do make a huge difference.

Please join our free monthly-ish e-journal BOOKISH and get a FREE EBOOK and AUDIOBOOK version of

TERRA BLANCA – INSURRECTION,
the prequel to the GAIA SERIES.

Discover the start of the Gaia Enterprises story and the origins of the Dopplebots. Maja Garcia embarks on a bold new endeavour that could chart a new direction for humanity.

In BOOKISH, I also give updates on works in progress, special bonus extras like cover reveals and character development, along with book reviews for leadership and fiction. You'll also get the first news about the next book in the series. And yes, there will be a next book! *Olympus Dawn* will be the final full-length novel in the Gaia series.

Join us here: *https://www.zoerouth.com/bookish*

ACKNOWLEDGMENTS

There are so many people to thank in the creation of this work. Thanks to all the readers who have sent me notes or told me how much they are enjoying the series. This is much needed inspiration in the long, dark hours of writing.

Thanks again to Benny Callaghan for his forthright and enthusiastic comments on the drafts. And Darren Nash continues to be my go-to trusted advisor and editor. Thanks also to Meredith Anderson for her copy editing and astute observations.

And thanks to Rob, for unyielding support and infectious enthusiasm.

And a huge thank you to YOU, the reader. It's an honour and a privilege to share the Gaia world with you across space and time.

Go well.

THE A.I. ASSISTED ARTISAN AUTHOR: A4

Joanna Penn, one of my writing mentors, coined this term. In her articles on how to use A.I. ethically as an author, she explains how we can benefit by having A.I. as a co-pilot for unique, creative output. I subscribe to this view.

With all the hoopla going around about artificial intelligence, I thought I would share how I use A.I. apps in my creative process. I work with Scrivener as a writing platform and use ProWritingAid to help review grammar, syntax, writing tics and glitches. I use *thesaurus.com* for word variation, and Chat GPT-4 for research and ideas. I also used it to help generate the book blurb. Like most writers, I find book blurbs arduous and Chat GPT-4 made that a little easier.

I used Midjourney to generate images for characters, and humans at Damonza did the final book cover production. Humans also helped with the fine-tuning. With new apps coming out every day, no doubt my process will change again for the next novel.

ABOUT THE AUTHOR

Zoë Routh is a leadership futurist, podcaster and multiple award-winning author. She works with leaders and teams to explore what's coming and what it means for leadership of the future.

She has worked with individuals and teams, internationally and in Australia, since 1987. From wild Canadian rivers to the Australian outback with Outward Bound, to the boardroom jungles, Zoë is an adventurist! She facilitates strategy and culture for the future with audacious teams.

Zoë is the producer of *The Future of Leadership* Podcast, dedicated to asking "What if...?" and "How Might We?", to show leaders how to navigate the future.

Zoë is an outdoor adventurist and enjoys telemark skiing, has run six marathons, is a one-time belly-dancer, has survived cancer and loves hiking in the high country. Zoë lives with her gorgeous Aussie husband in Canberra, Australia, where you'll find her running, baking and reading.

Follow Zoë on *Amazon* and *Goodreads* and *Book Bub*

https://linktr.ee/zoerouth

Reach out and say hello at *zoe@zoerouth.com*.

www.zoerouth.com

OTHER BOOKS BY ZOË ROUTH:

Gaia Series

Terra Blanca Insurrection

The Olympus Project

Olympus Bound

Non-Fiction

Composure – How Centered Leaders Make the Biggest Difference

Moments – Leadership When It Matters Most

Loyalty – Stop Unwanted Staff Turnover, Boost Engagement and Create Lifelong Advocates

People Stuff: Beyond Personality Problems – An Advanced Handbook for Leadership